DIRE WOLF MATES

Volume Two

C.D. GORRI

Dire Wolf Mates
Volume Two
by C.D. Gorri

Includes:
Kickin' Sass
Love That Sass
Kiss My Sass

Edited by BookNookNuts

To my family,
For being my inspiration, my loudest cheerleaders, and my home.
Del mare alla stella,
C.D. Gorri

Before you begin sign up for my newsletter here:
SUBSCRIBE HERE

VOLUME TWO

DIRE WOLF MATES

The Dire Wolves are parking their bikes for good on the outskirts of Blue Valley. But can these sexy prehistoric Shifters find their mates and plant roots of their own?

Includes:

Kickin' Sass

Summer fun meets eternal love in this sass kickin' fated mates romance!

Love That Sass

Can a fun loving bad boy Dire Wolf find redemption with a curvy human?

Pinch of Sass

Can a Dire Wolf with *the sight* find his future with a wanted female?

KICKIN' SASS

DIRE WOLF MATES

BLURB

DIRE WOLF MATES

Summer fun meets eternal love in this sass kickin' fated mates romance!

Phoenix Tala is taking a break from his new home on the border of Blue Valley where his Pack and MC have recently settled down.

With his Dire Wolf feeling out of sorts, he takes a road trip to clear his beast's mind. But the Fates have more in store for him than an easy ride.

Tracey Donner is tired of her upper-crust parents' disapproval. After a shopping trip gets nasty, she takes off for the one place she felt happy as a child. Maccon City, New Jersey. She is ready for some serious changes in her life. But until then, a girl could have a little fun, couldn't she?

Of course, she never expected to run into that fun face first.

Literally.

A spontaneous moonlight skinny dip turns into something else when she swims into a midnight bather with more muscles than she knew was possible for one man to have.

Willing to dive into a vacation fling with the bad boy biker, Tracey is all about the moment, but Phoenix has forever on his mind.

Can he convince the luscious female to be his mate?

PROLOGUE

DIRE WOLF MATES

The smell of fire filled her nostrils and young Tracey gasped as the air grew thick with it. She hid under the bed, scared of what was happening. Mother had called her naughty again and Tracey was so ashamed.

She had embarrassed her mother in front of her friends again, but she didn't mean to. The fancy women were all dressed up and sitting outside on the enormous stone patio beneath the bright yellow awning Father had ordered specifically for Mother's tea parties.

Tracey had only wanted to join in the fun. She put on her best Spring dress, but she'd only just come home from boarding school, and it was from last year. It was too tight and squeezed the chubby parts of her belly and arms, but she had to look just right.

Mother would never approve of her wearing her school clothes to a party. So, she squeezed herself inside of the uncomfortable outfit and slathered some of her mother's blush and lipstick on her face.

She looked grown up now, for sure. Maybe Mother would finally smile at her the way other children's parents smiled at them when they were proud or happy. Tracey knew if she could just make her mother proud, she would like her more.

"What are you doing, you naughty girl?!" Mother had screeched when she spied Tracey standing proudly in the doorway in her too tight dress and borrowed heels.

"I wanted to surprise you—"

"Go to your room right now, Tracey Donner. Wash your face and burn that dress. I have never been so embarrassed," she'd snapped, pulling Tracey by the elbow into the hallway.

Burn the dress?

But it was the only one she had. Tracey's lip quivered, and she shook. Her mother's brilliant blue eyes flashed like lightning, and tendrils of fear snaked up her spine.

"I never should have let your father talk me into allowing you to come back here," Mother snarled.

"I'm sorry," she whispered.

"Yes, Tracey, that is what you are. Sorry and pathetic. That is all you will ever be."

Tracey did not understand the reason for her mother's cruelty, but that night, something new had happened. That night, Tracey stopped trying to win her mother's affection and approval. That night, she became angry for the first time in her young life.

But while she was coming to grips with her anger, an accident happened. A small fire broke out during her mother's tea party and that beautiful yellow awning father had ordered special burned to ashes.

Smoke wafted into the house, up the stairs, and to Tracey's room, making it difficult to breathe. She waited there for what seemed like hours after the sirens had come and gone, nevertheless, no one came looking for her.

She heard Mother and Father talking downstairs. Her parents rarely argued, but they seemed in the middle of a big one now. They were discussing her school and her time home, and misery the likes of which she'd never known filled her. Mother wanted her gone, but Father seemed against it—and still, she waited.

No one came to check on her, and she'd yet to move from her

hiding spot. Her stomach was rumbling by the time the sound of unfamiliar footsteps climbing the stairs reached her ears. This was it. The moment some driver her parents hired came to take her back to the boarding school she hated.

Tracey stifled her scream with a hand over her mouth. But the simple sneaker-clad feet stopped in front of her bed. A woman kneeled down, her wide smile easing some of the hurt Tracey was feeling.

"*Hola, linda,*" she spoke softly.

"Hi," was Tracey's shy response.

"My name is Rosa, and your parents just hired me to take care of you. Would that be alright?"

Tracey's tiny heart pounded inside her chest.

"You're coming to school with me?" she asked curiously.

"No, I am too big for school. You will take the bus with the other kids, but I will be here when you get back. We are going to be great friends, *si*?"

Tracey nodded. For the first time in her life, she had a friend.

CHAPTER ONE

DIRE WOLF MATES

The department store reeked of expensive perfume samples and cosmetics. Between that and the heat outside, it was positively stifling.

Still, the overpowering fragrances should have stopped bothering Tracey now that she'd moved on, but they were still making their way through her olfactory senses. Her allergies were the very devil. Easily influenced by minor changes in her environment—*and these were not minor.*

For Pete's sake, they must have used a thousand civets to make one stinking bottle!

Tracey had tried to dodge the pushy women trying to sell the bottle of high end French perfume at $350 an ounce, but she got her with two generous squirts. It was all Tracey could do not to sneeze all over her.

Luckily, there was a tissue box nearby. Her mother was not at all amused. Really, she should have been better prepared, but who knew you needed tactical defense lessons before visiting a mall?

Oh well.

She'd smiled apologetically, grabbed a second tissue, and followed her mother, whose patented glare was boring holes into Tracey's head. She was there for one reason only, and that was to assist her mother with whatever she needed. Apparently, checking out the newest summer arrivals in the shoe department was a necessity.

After forty-eight minutes and thirty-three seconds of browsing and watching her mother try on one pair of painful looking heels after another, Tracey was more than ready to call it a day. Shopping was sheer torture with the woman. Why had she ever agreed to go?

Because you still want Mommy's approval.

Pathetic? Probably. But Tracey had always wanted to be closer to her mother. If she could just figure out what it was exactly the woman didn't like, maybe she could fix it and they would both be happier.

"Tracey? Are you listening to me? Hand me the other pair. These must be irregularly sized," Daniella Donner—first lady of the upper crust community of Rumson, New Jersey, and Tracey's mother, made a tsking noise as she removed the ridiculously expensive sandal from her freshly pedicured foot.

"Sorry, I was just thinking," Tracey murmured and moved to grab the next box from the ever-growing pile of uber high-heeled, strappy, pointed toe, rhinestone studded, and grossly uncomfortable footwear.

It was a shame, really. There were plenty of trendy shoes out there —orthopedics, recommended by her podiatrist—that would definitely be a better choice for her mother. But Tracey kept her lips zipped, knowing she would never even consider it.

No matter how tight the older woman tried to hold on to her youth, some things were inarguable. Such as the fact her mother's foot had grown a size and a half over the years, starting immediately after she'd become pregnant with Tracey some thirty years ago.

Not that she'd admit it. To hear her tell it, Tracey might as well be an alien. She looked nothing like either of her beautiful parents.

Not only was she what her mother called *unpleasantly plump,* but her coloring was all wrong. Comfortable in her size sixteen Levi's, Tracey might have too many curves for her petite stature, but she was fine with that. It was the fact she stood a whopping five feet three inches tall compared to her elegantly thin five foot eight inch tall mother, and her six foot tall father, that was so dang disappointing. But hardly her fault.

As if that was not bad enough, Tracey also lacked the trademark crystal clear, sapphire blue eyes of both her parents, Daniella and Daniel Donner—*the Donners* of Rumson. Though, admittedly, her father's eyes were a few shades darker than his wife's.

Good thing or she'd have suspected something seriously wrong.

Ew.

Still, both her parents were very attractive people. Positively dazzling, in fact, and thoroughly admired by their friends and coworkers alike. The dynamic duo was like neighborhood royalty. As was their due, Tracey supposed. After all, the Donners were a power couple.

They had worked hard to get where they were, and they ruled the Gold Coast of Lower Fairfield County. Her mother sat on the board of several organizations supposedly dedicated to charity, but Tracey knew it was never about the actual charity.

The men and women involved in those things did it more to suck up to one another and to forge connections to further the careers of spouses and loved ones. Most of the very wealthy couples in that affluent neighborhood worked in or out of Manhattan, and sometimes Boston. Her father used to have offices in both cities, as well as connections in London, Paris, Berlin, and Rome. Alas, that was years ago.

When you were as rich as the Donners, you simply retired early and lived off your interests. Tracey often wondered why her parents didn't travel more, but she knew her mother would never leave Connecticut. Daniella Donner had worked too hard to be at the top of the in crowd. A crowd that had always made her daughter feel like an outcast.

The Gold Coast had its own brand of snobbery, and Tracey had never fit in with her mother's hoity toity friends. She preferred art and literature to wine tasting and jewels.

Tracey's idea of a good time involved sifting through flea markets and exploring old churches. Things like that often horrified her staid parents.

"Tracey!" Her mother's shrill voice interrupted her train of thought, and she jumped, dropping the shoe box she'd been holding.

"I swear, child. You never have any idea what's going on."

"Sorry," she apologized, her eyes darting to the shoe salesperson who'd just returned with the next round of sandals—all of which were probably in the wrong size.

The fact they were not alone didn't seem to stop her mother. She hissed, narrowing her eyes like some feral cat, and Tracey braced herself for what was coming.

"Maybe if you paid a little more attention, you'd be able to lose some of that extra weight you gained this past winter. Maybe then Felix wouldn't have left you sitting in that restaurant to eat alone. How could you? I can't even imagine! Making a spectacle of yourself like that. You could have just left without eating, Tracey," she snapped the last bit with just enough venom that Tracey's stomach clenched.

"Left me? For your information, I asked him to leave, Mother. It was our first outing together, and since I had already ordered, he left, and I stayed. What is so wrong with that?" Tracey asked, swallowing her gasp at the very real hurt that hit her harder than usual at her mother's cruel words.

Typically, she could ignore her mother's harsh commentary. But after her last relationship had ended in disaster, she was feeling vulnerable. And honestly, it was her mother's fault.

She'd started a relationship with Felix online without ever really seeing him. Those little avatars everyone used on social media were fun, but Tracey had never thought about it as hiding who she was until the man she thought she knew threw it in her face.

"You know, you have a pretty face. But you're a lot fatter than I expected.

Since your mother and my mother are club friends, I thought you would be fit. But now I see why you have an avatar as your profile picture."

Felix's hurtful comment was like a slap in the face. Not only had she ended the date immediately after he'd said those hateful words, but she blocked his ass on every social media account.

Jerkface.

CHAPTER TWO

DIRE WOLF MATES

Of course, Tracey could always count on her mother to pick at scabs. She heaved a sigh as her mother's pinched face grew even tighter.

"Well, you say tomato," her mother hissed, wincing as she used a shoehorn to squeeze into a tight pair of Manolo Blahnik mules.

"What does that even mean, Mother?"

"Dieting was never your strength, but you can turn that around with some work, Tracey. Then maybe you can catch a husband."

"Gosh, you make a man sound like a disease," Tracey whispered her reply.

"Your father is trying to persuade the governor to give the proposed expansion of the highway to his friend with that development company. What is his name? Oh, yes, Jeb Collins. He has a son named Trevor. If your father succeeds, there will be plenty of mingling with their family."

"So what, Mother?"

"So, he might make a match for you. And you can do your part by losing a few pounds. You know, bathing suit season is here—Gertie! You're here!"

Her mother greeted her rail thin best friend with air kisses and pats on the shoulder.

"Darling! Oh! Those are cute," Gertie said, eyeing a pair of silver wedges her mom had discarded.

She did not acknowledge Tracey, which was par for the course. Not that she minded. She disliked most of her mother's friends.

"Jeb Collins is eighty, and any son of his is probably fifty or older."

"He's fifty-three, Tracey, but what would you have me do? You'll be thirty soon—"

"Oh my god, Mom," she growled, frustrated. "I am thirty! I don't know that man. And what are you saying, you would what, sell me to him?"

"Hardly, dear," her mother replied, her pinched face looking even angrier than usual. "He would be doing *us* the favor, not the other way around."

Gertrude snorted into her elbow at the cruel jibe, and Tracey's humiliation doubled.

"That's not funny," Tracey responded with as much dignity as possible.

"It was not meant to be," her mother responded.

Tracey's whole body tensed with hurt and disgust for her parent.

"What happened to you, Mom? Why are you like this? You were never kind and loving like the other kids' parents when I was in school. In fact, I don't think you even like me."

"What are you talking about? Get a grip, Tracey."

"Get a grip? All you do is make snide comments about my appearance and rude remarks about me being single."

"Am I wrong? Look at you. You are at least forty pounds overweight. You don't care at all about our image. And as for the other, I am trying to help you."

"I happen to like how I look, Mom. And the last time I listened to you about a man, he cut me up with his cruel remarks about my weight. I don't need a man like that—"

"What are you talking about? Without a man, what will you be?"

"How about happy, Mom? I don't need a man to complete my identity," she said, ignoring her mother's cruel laughter.

Gertie said something waspish, and she and Daniella cackled at whatever thinly veiled insult she'd just thrown at Tracey. But something was happening to her she'd never felt before. Her body was buzzing, her head pounding, and for the first time, she understood she would never be happy until she freed herself.

"Where are you going?" her mother asked as she gathered her purse and the bottle of water she'd been carrying.

"I'm leaving, Mom. You know, I happen to like myself just the way I am."

"Oh please," the older woman snorted.

"You know, I am very sorry for you that you never took the time to get to know me because now it's just too late. Goodbye, Mother."

"Tracey, you are being ridiculous. Get back here!"

But it really was too late. Tracey had already decided. She was closing the door on years of hurt and disappointment, gathering her last bits of hope and courage and holding them tight to her chest. Tracey turned one last time to take in her mother's posh appearance and cold expression.

"You're supposed to love and accept me no matter what. I am your daughter. That's what mothers do. How can you sit there and make fun of me?"

"Don't be so sensitive. Come now. We can find you a one piece to wear to the club. Maybe Jeb will be there. Here," she said and turned to find the saleswoman who'd been helping them since they entered the expensive department store.

"Janie, please find Tracey something suitable for this weekend's clam bake."

Clam bake was a bougie term for the extravagantly catered affair her mother was throwing to celebrate her father's one year retirement anniversary. They had an image to uphold, after all.

Tracey got nauseous just thinking about it. Her mother hadn't heard a single word she'd said.

"Of course, Mrs. Donner—"

"No need, Janie. I am not staying."

"Tracey, do not embarrass me in public—"

"You did that all by yourself, Mother. Goodbye Gertrude, Janie," she said, nodding at each red-faced woman. "Oh, and Mother, I won't be home for your clam bake this weekend. I have other plans. Tell my father congratulations for me."

Her heart thundered like a thousand runaway horses running down a hillside. The sound echoed in her ears. She couldn't believe she was doing this. But it was past time, she supposed.

Tracey pulled her cell phone out of the big boho bag she'd fashioned herself out of 100% organic cotton fabric colored with vegetable dyes. The patchwork pattern formed an image of her favorite animal, a large wolf baying at a yellow moon with twinkling stars she'd made out of glass beads.

The result was a sturdy, fun, and bright bag that was perfect for summer. Tracey opened an app and ordered an Uber to meet her at the small café on the corner of the department store.

Unfortunately, in her thirty years on the planet, she'd never learned to drive. An oversight she was determined to correct that summer. Might as well, since she wouldn't be spending it at home. Closing her eyes, she dialed Rosa, the Donner's longtime housekeeper, next.

The woman had practically raised Tracey. If anyone was going to miss her, it would be the feisty little woman who had taught her sewing and embroidery. She also taught Tracey how to wash her clothes and how to cook at least a dozen different varieties of homemade empanadas.

Rosa was her rock. She was the one who comforted Tracey whenever life got hard, or her parents had upset her—which was often.

"Donner residence," she answered the phone.

"Rosa? It's me. I was just calling to let you know I won't be home for dinner."

"Okay, *linda*. Anything else?" Rosa asked, calling her the same endearment, meaning pretty, as she had ever since Tracey was a child.

Rosa was probably the only person who showed her any real affection. Ever cheerful and ready with a hug or compliment. God, she loved that woman. Tracey's heart pounded. She couldn't just leave without giving her an explanation.

"Actually Rosa, I won't be coming home till, *well*, I don't really know when. I'm, um, making a change," she said, her voice trembling.

"Are you okay? What happened, my Tracey?"

"I'm okay. I mean, I'm thirty years old. Mean words shouldn't have the power to hurt me anymore."

"Words do have power, *linda*. But I agree, it's time you take your power back."

Tracey sniffed and cleared her throat. Leave it to Rosa to give her strength when her own faltered. She smiled, her vision blurring with unshed tears.

"You're right. I'll be fine. Don't worry."

"Of course, I worry about you, silly. Who else would if not me? Now, tell me where you are going, so I don't worry too much."

"Um, I am going to the beach," she said on impulse.

"The beach? Well, good. But be careful. The beach is full of men looking to take advantage of a pretty and innocent girl like you. Wait a second, *mija*, don't listen to me. If a sexy man comes along, you have my permission to say yes," Rosa told her.

"Rosa!"

"What? Look, if someone does approach you, who knows? He could be just what you need. Like someone from those books you love to read."

"Rosa, have you been looking through my tablet again?" Tracey teased.

"You know I love those sexy stories. You could meet a mystery man, an oil sheik in disguise, looking for a princess to call his own, ooh yes! Or a pirate coming to whisk you away on his ship to ravage your body. *Si, linda*, you need some of that in your life."

"Oh my God! Rosa! You are banned. Stop reading all my smutty romance novels without supervision, young lady," Tracey mock scolded.

Her cheeks were burning from embarrassment, which was silly because no one could hear her conversation. Besides, at least she was laughing now.

"Smut is fun, Tracey. Besides, it happens. I was just reading the one where the male escort decides he wants a woman to keep him in a fine condo and Armani suits, but then he falls in love with her and does his best to win her heart and trust after his lies come out. Anyway, never mind. Listen to me carrying on now," Rosa said and sighed wistfully.

"I'm going to miss you, Rosa."

"I will always be with you, *linda*. Whatever happens, you can do this. It is past time you ran away from this cold home, my Tracey."

"I know. You are right," Tracey answered, smiling through her tears. "I love you, Rosa."

She did, truly and deeply. Rosa Marquez was the only real mother she had ever known.

"I love you too, my Tracey. It will all be okay. Now, you text me on this fancy phone you got me for Christmas when you get to where you are going. You hear me? And if you decide not to come back, send me an address and I will make sure your things arrive safe and sound."

Relief and nervousness warred within Tracey as she nodded her head, ever the obedient child. She'd always been so eager to please Rosa, and why wouldn't she be? The woman had done nothing but reward her hard work with affection and honesty in ways her own parents had failed to do.

"Yes, Rosa. I will. Let me go before I change my mind."

"Don't do that now, *linda*. You are so close to finding yourself. May flights of angels protect and guide you, my Tracey."

"You too, Rosa. Bye."

Tracey clicked end call and walked to the corner as the Uber she'd ordered pulled into a vacant space. The man looked normal, and the car was spotless.

This was it. The moment of her great getaway.

"You Tracey Donner?" The older man asked.

"That's me."

"Where you headed?"

"Maccon City," she said, surprising herself with the certainty she heard in her voice.

"That's three hours away," the man said, eyebrows raised. "Your reservation said you were going ten minutes away—"

"I'll give you five hundred dollars cash," she said, cutting him off.

"Yeah? Well, okay then," he readily agreed.

Tracey nodded and stepped inside the car before she could chicken out. She had always been a homebody. Went to the nearest college and even finished her degree online. Her parents were not abusive.

Not exactly. They were a little cruel, but that was because they just did not understand her. She could never live up to their impossible standards. It was time she admitted the truth, even if only to herself. Tracey was tired of trying.

Her childhood had been a series of disappointments for both her parents and for herself. When she was twelve, she had wanted to go to this sleep-away summer camp for art, instead they sent her to a weight loss camp for obese children.

Yes, Tracey had been pudgy even then. And when she'd returned from camp after spending a miserable six weeks there, she had actually gained three pounds.

Total. Failure.

It took her a long time to love herself after that. And the one thing she could always say whenever her mother harped on her weight was at least she was healthy, even if her mom thought she was unattractive. Tracey's yearly physicals and blood tests always came back with proof she was eating healthy, if a little more than her mother thought was okay, and she was exercising regularly.

She was just a big girl, for fuck's sake. The world was not going to end because Tracey Donner wasn't a size zero—*someone should tell that to her mother.*

But fat camp was not the end of her long list of ways she'd disappointed her folks. When she'd graduated from high school, she'd refused to attend Boston College, or her mother's alma mater, Smith College, and opted for art school.

Her parents were so angry, they'd refused to pay. Luckily, a great-uncle on her father's side that she had never met had bequeathed her his entire estate when he had passed away years before. She was not rich, per se—especially not after paying her tuition. But Tracey had her own money, and it was past time she used it to live her own life.

"Time to find my place in the world," she whispered.

"What was that?" the driver asked.

"Nothing," she answered.

Biting her lip, she watched the scenery fade as she embarked on this, her first journey as an adult. Tracey had never been reckless or foolish. But there was a first time for everything. Maybe that was why she'd asked to go to the one place she remembered she was truly happy growing up.

Maccon City, New Jersey.

Rosa had taken her there for the weekend when she was thirteen and her parents had been away on vacation. How she'd loved that buzzing ocean side town!

Something was missing in Tracey Donner's life. She'd allowed her mother to bully and boss her around. She'd let her father's disapproval weigh her down. She had neglected her own wants and needs for way too long.

Time to start living for myself.

CHAPTER THREE

DIRE WOLF MATES

Go. Go. GO!

Phoenix Tala jumped on his Screamin' Eagle V-Rod and hightailed it out of the *Serious Moonlight* parking lot. His inner Dire Wolf was chomping at the bit.

He'd always been able to sense and hear his animal inside his mind's eye. The relationship between every Shifter and his beast was different, but Phoenix would have it no other way. Two minds, one body—and no one knew him better than the enormous buff colored monster snarling and scratching inside of him.

His animal was desperate to get on the road. About a year had passed since the Dire Wolf MC—that was what they called his Pack, so the normals around them did not grow suspicious—had settled down on the outskirts of Blue Valley, New Jersey.

It was the longest Phoenix had ever spent in one place. A full year of the same scenery and crowds. The same boring routine.

Okay, that was not exactly fair. He was proud of them and the success they had with their roadhouse and bar, *Serious Moonlight*. They'd opened their doors with plans to cater to both normals and the surprisingly large supernatural community on the East Coast, and they'd done it.

The place was great. So was the old homestead that came with the property. They'd managed to renovate the almost dilapidated building, turning it into a bonafide Pack house in the neighboring lot. And that was not all they did. They converted the old barn into a multi-vehicle garage.

The Pack could work on their bikes in a safe and convenient location. Cole was their expert mechanic, but the rest of them muddled along just fine. In fact, Phoenix had just replaced his scratched-up old seat with a cushioned Tallboy, extra wide and deep, with a high back for a passenger.

Not that he had anyone to ride double with him, but whatever. The second he saw the black leather seat, he knew it was for him. Tinkering with his bike and working on the computer setup for their business kept him busy for the first few months.

He'd watched as new customers became regulars and faces grew familiar. It was an odd experience for him, and at his age, that did not happen very often.

Dire Wolves aged more slowly than most Shifters, with almost twice the lifespan. He might look thirty, but he was twice that. But Phoenix had never felt his age more than these past months as he watched his Alpha, and two of his Pack mates, get mated.

Sure, he was happy for them. Life was good for the Dire Wolf MC. But something was missing from his life. He'd felt it keenly over the last few weeks.

It was the call to the road. That same feeling every member of the larger, and mainly nomadic, Dire Wolf Pack had felt and was best described as an irresistible urge—an almost magnetic pull to get on the road. Like destiny was breathing down his neck until he couldn't stand it another minute.

He'd tried to resist. Really, he did. But it was impossible. The Wolf was growling constantly. The urge to Change into his fur two times a day was taking its toll.

"Derrick, I gotta run, man. Please, I need some time on the road."

"How long?"

"I dunno. A few weeks at least."

That was the sum of his conversation with his Alpha the night before. Inside, he'd been begging the big man to understand. Hurt thrummed through their Pack bond, but bigger than that was compassion. Derrick was a good, strong Alpha.

He would never poison their bonds by ordering Phoenix to stay. The Alpha had narrowed his eyes at his Wolf, measuring the seriousness of Phoenix's request. Then, he'd stepped around the polished bar and grabbed him in a fierce, backbreaking hug, more befitting a Bear. But Dire Wolves weren't like any other canid species, supernatural or otherwise. They were the oldest, biggest, baddest, and most powerful canid Shifters in the entire world.

Their natural dominance was tempered by their desire for solitude. Derrick Rand was a good Alpha, and Phoenix would follow the man anywhere. But it was time he moved on. Well, for a little while, anyway. This was his Pack, his MC, and he would never leave for good.

Yeah, he'd come home alright. Could be a month, could be a year, but he would return. All he knew was he had to settle the wildness he felt growing inside and he couldn't do that there.

"Do what you need to, brother. We'll be here for you. All you have to do is call."

Phoenix packed his saddlebags and left before the sun came up the next day, having kept his goodbyes brief. Lord knew he couldn't handle any tearful platitudes from their Alpha fem. Lucy was expecting a cub in a couple of months, and that meant the woman was even more emotional than normal.

"You go find whatever it is you're looking for, Phoenix Tala, then haul your furry butt back home before this baby is born!"

"I promise, Lucy, I'll call you whenever I land somewhere, okay?"

"You better."

Getting back on the open road was like seeing an old friend after a long absence. With his supernaturally enhanced lifespan, sometimes days bled into the other. But it really felt like a long time since he and the prehistoric beast he shared his soul with had gone exploring.

He revved his engine, loving the power between his thighs as he ate up the miles fast and furiously. Phoenix missed this. But missing the open road wasn't the real reason he'd felt so uneasy lately.

There was something else out there calling to him. Something he was looking for. He just had to find it.

Not it. Her.

His Wolf growled the words inside his head, and Phoenix had to agree, the creature was right. That was the real missing link. Phoenix's Dire Wolf was on a mission to find his fated mate.

Fuck.

He wasn't a mystic like Thor, or a ladies' man like Weylin. He had good points, though. Phoenix had a healthy respect for the opposite sex and for the Fates who predetermined mated pairs—as was one of their purposes and their right.

A lot of folks were mistaken, and thought the Fates took away free will. But Phoenix had been around long enough to know that was not true. Sure, the Fates could bring folks together, but will and commitment, bone deep affection, compromise, and plain old fashioned hard work—well, those were the things what kept mates together.

He'd been watching Derrick and Lucy, Sheila and Leo, and Ariella and Brock for weeks—the six of them seemed happy as a couple of pigs in mud.

Each was just wild for the other. Who knew love could be so damn fun? But watching them, Phoenix learned it really could be. He was happy for Derrick, Sheila, Brock, and their respective mates. The Fates had done a really good job finding mates for three of his favorite people in the world.

He just hadn't realized the cause of his unrest until right then. It was time for Phoenix and the Fates to get together and get him settled.

Well, shit.

Now, what did he do? Put out an ad? Troll the bars? How the fuck was a rugged, rough-looking Dire Wolf like him gonna find a woman willing to settle down? Especially when he had nothing to offer a female.

What could he really give to a woman? Phoenix was not bad off, but he was not really wealthy either. The Pack had money, but he'd never put much stock in material things. He had a bedroom in the Pack house, his motorcycle, and a pretty sweet computer set up—but that was it.

Shit.

That was what happened when a man spent more time designing landscapes and avatar add-ons for online roleplaying games like *Wolf-Moon*—as was his side job for *Graves Enterprises*—than with building up his stock portfolio and buying property or whatever the fuck people who wanted to have families did. What kind of woman would look at him and see a prize?

Fuck. Fuck. Fuck.

This was not like him. His Wolf snarled inside his chest, angry at him for selling them short. Maybe he was. After all, Phoenix wasn't a total loss. He was physically fit, had muscles chicks seemed to dig, and his face was okay, too.

His dick worked. That was a plus. And he knew his way around a female's body. Yeah, his communication skills could use some work, but he was a guy. That was sort of their mo, right?

It wasn't that he was bad with women, he just never connected with them. He was not a stumbling virgin or anything. Dire Wolves, like most Shifters, were highly physical beings. Honestly, it had been a good, long while since he'd scratched that particular itch. But sex was like riding a bike. You didn't forget how to work the pedals just because it had been a while.

Now that he'd thought about it, he realized why the women who'd come on to him recently had been unappealing. His Wolf wanted his mate's touch. No other would do. But how should he approach this unique problem? He needed time and space to think this through.

There was only one place that would offer the kind of atmosphere Phoenix needed to think. One environment that could help him plan and perhaps solve his little *mate-trimonial* dilemma.

Beach.

Grinning like the predator he was, Phoenix gunned his engine and sped towards the best damn shore town he'd ever visited in all his years.

Maccon City.

The Jersey shore town was home to the infamous Macconwood Pack—a cool bunch of Werewolves he'd had the pleasure of meeting a time or two.

Yesssss.

His Wolf sped him on, urging him to drive faster. Maccon City was perfect. He could just sit on the beach in the soft summer sand and contemplate his future, devise a plan to find and woo his mate. His chest vibrated with his beast's assenting growl.

Grrr.

For the first time in months, Phoenix felt energized and excited. Like he was headed for the ride of his life. He could almost taste the saltwater on the air despite the miles he had to go.

With a cocky grin and a rumble in his throat, he sped down the hot asphalt with one thought in his brain—and it was set on repeat.

Mate.

Mate.

MATE.

CHAPTER FOUR

DIRE WOLF MATES

"What do you mean, you're full? You can't be," Tracey moaned.

She tried frowning hard at the young man behind the desk, but the guy looked like he honestly regretted telling her the news.

"I am very sorry, miss. But we are all booked."

Tracey closed her eyes and tried one of those deep breathing exercises she'd learned from the childhood psychologist her mother insisted she see.

Crap, she was bad at this. She exhaled quickly, almost passing out from lack of oxygen.

"Um, are you okay? What are you trying to do?"

"What? Yeah. Um, can you check again? I just need a minute," she mumbled, shaking her hands and pacing the small office.

"Of course," the young man replied with a sympathetic nod.

Crap. Oh damn. Ass. Shit. Fuck.

Ugh.

Tracey sucked at cursing, and at running away, too, apparently. What the heck was she doing here, anyway?

Doubts filled her mind as she stood in the small lobby of the Oasis Beachside Resort. It was newly renovated, charming really. She liked it better than all the glitzy hotels her family made them stay at when they'd gone away together, which was rarely.

Oasis was the last stop on the strip that ran along the beach, with private homes beside it, and a pathway to the pine barrens beside that. She hadn't been expecting this at all. In truth, she'd been pretty much unprepared for everything she'd encountered thus far.

It was already evening, and of course she couldn't find a room. It was August, for Pete's sake. Everyone was down the shore, trying to slow the last few days of summer. Tracey should have figured they would be crowded. Places like this depended on tourism to keep the economy going all year long.

Naturally, they were booked. Maccon City was a tourist favorite, especially with all the festivals, concerts, boardwalk craft fairs, and other events that took place every single weekend all summer long to keep the crowds happy. It made perfect sense.

She'd been one of them. A happy-go-lucky tourist from the second her Uber driver dropped her off. Unfortunately, she'd been so worked up over finally taking her independence back, she hadn't bothered to find a hotel. Not once on the whole drive down from Fairfield had she even considered looking for a place to stay.

Instead, she exited the car, wishing her driver safe travels back. Then she went shopping for some clothes and toiletries, even treated herself to an iced tea and fresh-baked lemon-blueberry scone.

Walking along the shop-lined streets was peaceful, relaxing even. She'd found the cutest little bead store and had talked with the owner for a full twenty-minutes about her purse and this idea she'd been toying with for her designs using glass beads and different texturized fabrics.

Sigh.

It had felt wonderful not to be looked down on for her craft. Her mother positively hated the fact that Tracey would rather make her own bag than buy an expensive designer one.

Double sigh.

Why hadn't she called for reservations first? Tracey was in such a rush to get away from her life, and her harpy of a mother, she hadn't been thinking clearly at all. Maccon City had always been a sanctuary in her mind, but the reality was she'd been neglectful.

Going home was the last thing she wanted, but what else could she do? Sleeping on the beach was illegal in New Jersey, not to mention totally unappealing.

"I am so sorry, miss. We are still booked. Have you tried the Seaside Escape?" the polite younger man asked.

"Yes, I went there first. This is the last place on the strip in the entire town, actually."

Could she really have messed this up so badly? This place was the last stop on the list of hotels she found on her phone for the whole of Maccon City.

She looked down at her smart phone's lit screen, but no matter how hard she stared, the words *no vacancy* refused to go away beneath every hotel name.

Crapola.

"Folks are here from all over the country this weekend, you know, for the festival. I'm Marco, by the way," he said.

Marco was nice enough, and a manager too, according to the little pin he wore on his shirt. He smiled and pointed to the framed poster displaying sailboats and smiling tourists under a banner with *Maccon City Annual Boat Show* splashed across the top.

Apparently, it was a big deal. The festival lasted the whole weekend and there was even a food truck festival, fireworks display, and a discount bracelet day on the pier for the rides to celebrate it.

Double crapola.

Tracey huffed a sigh and closed her eyes for a moment. She just couldn't believe it. Of all the stinking luck. The sound of the lobby door opening was distant, but she registered the fact that she was not alone with the friendly manager any longer.

She huffed a sigh and moved over to allow the newcomer access to the man. This was so like her. Tracey cringed at what her mother would say. Something about how irresponsible she was, for sure. And for the hell of it, the woman would throw in something having to do with her weight, because obviously that was why anything bad happened to her.

Stop it.

She shook her head, slightly admonishing herself for the unkind thoughts. It was better to simply avoid thinking about her parents at all than to harp on the negative. It was not her mom's fault she hadn't even bothered to call for a reservation the whole drive from the North Shore. She was fine owning it, but it sucked.

Huffing out a frustrated sigh, she wondered what she should do next. Maybe just take in the scenery, then she could try the next shore town for a vacancy. It wasn't what she wanted, but it was a plan.

At least Marco, along with every other guy she'd spied during her search for a room, was good to look at. Maccon City was positively crawling with hotties.

The Oasis hotel manager was too young for her, but she could appreciate his beauty all the same. Someone cleared their throat, and she turned her head to the right just as she took a sip from her now warm bottle of water. That was a mistake.

Tracey damn near spit all over herself as she took in the enormous male standing there. If young Marco was cute, then the outrageously tall blond with piercing green eyes, and more muscles than she knew the human body could have, was positively stunning—in a totally drop dead gorgeous, way out of Tracey's league, kind of way.

"Hi," she said, once she'd swallowed, eyes wide.

The man frowned at her, like not a sad frown but a look of intense thought and concentration. It was actually kind of scary, so she turned to Marco.

"You don't mind if I sit here while I call some other hotels and look for a car?" she asked.

"Of course not," Marco replied easily, though his gaze was fixed on the stranger.

The strange yet beautiful man seemed to have a tickle or something in his throat. She sat down as far from him as she could get. He was making all kinds of weird grumbling noises, and she sincerely hoped he wasn't sick. That was the last thing she needed. To catch a virus or bug. But it would be just her luck.

Deciding to mind her own beeswax, Tracey started scrolling nearby towns. She wasn't having much luck, though. More grumbling, and some whispers sounded to her left, but she ignored the two attractive men.

Maybe Rosa was right. Maybe this place was full of hotties, looking for a rich chick to sidle up to.

Maybe I should take out an ad and try to find one. It would read, chubby heiress looking for fuckboy to give her multiple Os and cuddles. Will pay for rent and food.

Great, Tracey. Just great.

She was losing her freaking mind. There were no male escorts searching for someone like her in Maccon City. And if there were any, surely, they were busy. Besides, she wasn't the type of woman who could pay for pleasure.

Then again, desperate times.

She laughed out loud, ignoring the stares of the two men in the lobby. Hell, she was entitled to her little freak out. Everyone thought she was nutty, why not them?

No explanations were forthcoming or necessary.

Tracey was in semi-panic mode. True, this train of thought was not helping, but she was on a roll now. Was it too late to turn back?

Yes. Probably. Definitely. Dang it.

Was she sweating? Why was it so hot? She sucked in a breath and exhaled slowly to try to calm her growing hysteria. Was the air condition not working?

One flick of her gaze to the vent in the ceiling told her air was coming through, but boy, was she hot! Her skin was on fire. Maybe that growly hot guy really was sick. Maybe he gave her some kind of cold or flu!

Yeah, Tracey, and you got sick ten seconds after meeting him. What is wrong with you?

She breathed again, aware of eyes on her. But Tracey was used to being regarded as a freak. She stared down at her phone. Maybe she could find a room to rent in someone's house if she couldn't find a vacancy at a hotel.

That was a new idea, and a much better one than paying for a night of companionship. Her cheeks were burning, but she played it off like she wasn't having some sort of psychotic break in the tiny lobby of the Oasis hotel. She searched frantically for rental properties, hardly aware she was being addressed.

"Um, miss. Miss?"

"What? Oh! Sorry," she mumbled, dropping her phone in her haste to face Marco.

"Sorry, miss—"

"Tracey. My name is Tracey," she replied, bending down to grab her phone. "Hey, do you know if anyone has a room to rent? I'm sorry for just sitting here, and taking up your space—"

"Please, make yourself comfortable, Tracey," a deep, unfamiliar voice said.

Wowza.

She almost dropped her cell phone again at the sound of her name spoken in an impossibly sexy voice. Ripples of shocking awareness spiked through her as Tracey looked up into a pair of sparkling green eyes.

Like Columbian emeralds, she thought. More aqua than green. So much more intricate than any other pair of eyes she had ever seen. Complicated, in fact.

The color was so unique it was almost indescribable. The artist in her was floored by the way they seemed to change before her own eyes. Aquamarine, then gold, then bright bottle green, and back to sea foam green.

Beautiful.

"I studied a book on eye color once, when I was researching my own boring muddy jade color, my parents are both blue-eyed. Anyway, the book had thousands of pictures of different colored eyes, but I don't recall coming across anything like yours."

"Pardon?" the stranger said, cocking his head to the side.

"Your eyes. They're, *um*, unusual. Pretty," she said, clearing her throat.

"Thank you, Tracey. No one's ever called me pretty before," the handsome man replied.

He looked amused, not angry, with his eyes tracing her face and his head still tilted to the side. He reminded her of a stray dog she fed by the house when she was younger.

"I guess not. Sorry," she murmured.

The poor animal kept coming back, and he would wait, head cocked to the side just like this, to see if Tracey would hurt him or not. Of course, she never did. Just gave him bits of her food. Her mother had found out and called animal control to take him away.

"Don't apologize. I like it," he said, but she was too stuck in her head to answer right away.

That was not a happy memory. She'd been trying to figure out why she'd not been blessed like her parents with crystal blue eyes, but she pushed away any sadness the memory evoked as she tried to find her voice to answer the strangely beautiful man.

It was like a whole universe existed in his gaze. The green was positively glowing with inky swirls of blue swimming in the depths. His face was tense, but she could sense his patience and innate goodness.

"You do?"

"I do."

"Oh," she said, dumbly.

It must be his aura, getting her all mixed up. He was a dominant personality, and she was a mouse. But despite his innate power, he was being patient and gentle. Kind, even. She didn't know what to make of him.

"I think you're pretty too, Tracey," he said.

"Oh, you don't have to—I mean, thank you," she mumbled, telling herself it was alright to accept a compliment.

"Just lovely," he said.

His voice was even better than his face, which was almost too good to be true. He had a face artists would kill to sketch. Tracey was more of a craft person, but even her fingers were itching for a pencil.

"Thanks," she whispered.

The sound was more sigh than statement. Not at all like her. Tracey didn't fawn over men, no matter how sexy they were.

"I believe Marco has found you a vacancy in the hotel."

"Oh? Really! You did?" She shook her head, breaking eye contact and turned to Marco, who was watching the byplay with more than a little interest.

"Uh, yeah. Last minute cancellation," the younger man said and nodded.

"Perfect!"

The stranger left the lobby and though she didn't want him to go, she hardly had cause to ask him to stay. With any luck, she'd see him around the place.

"Credit card?" she asked and handed Marco her Visa.

"Thank you. Let's get you entered here," he said.

Tracey felt both elated and anxious. She had no idea why, but she felt as if everything was finally working out. It was like Maccon City had called to her, and yeah, it was bumpy at first, but she'd come to the right place.

"Can I get you anything else?"

"No, I think I'm going to be just fine," Tracey told the hotel manager, accepting her key with a wide grin.

And for the first time in her life, she meant it.

You're free to be happy, Tracey.

CHAPTER FIVE

DIRE WOLF MATES

"She's here," Phoenix growled into his cell phone.

"Who?" Thor, his Pack mate, asked.

"It's her, bro."

"Phoenix, I have no idea what the fuck you are talking about," growled the baldheaded Wolf in reply.

Fuck. He was right. Phoenix should probably start at the beginning.

"Where are you, bro? You left with like no fucking warning."

"I'm at the *Oasis* in Maccon City."

"By the Macconwood Pack?"

"Yeah man, look, I fucking found my mate. She's human."

"Human?" Thor asked, and Phoenix's Wolf growled in response to the perceived judgement.

His animal side did not always have patience for his Pack mates, even if the man knew better. Thor was not being judgmental. Other Shifter species chose humans as their mates all the time. But that was not the case with Dire Wolves.

"Yeah, human and fucking perfect," he grunted.

"Alright, man. So, have you talked to her?"

Such a simple question and so loaded. Phoenix had a hard time controlling his instincts when he first spied her talking to the young Macconwood Wolf, who happened to be the manager at the hotel.

"Not really," he grumbled.

"Why the fuck not?"

"Because. I don't know!"

Phoenix muffled another curse as Thor remained silent on the line. He could count on the Pack Enforcer to have his back, but Thor was more than that. The Wolf was touched by the Gods, gifted—a Seer. Rare even among their kind, he needed the man's insight to let him know if he was on the right track.

"I need a minute," Phoenix growled, his Wolf pushing hard.

As he expected, Thor remained silent. He was good Pack, a good man—the very best.

Phoenix wrestled with his Wolf. He replayed recent events in his head. The sudden road trip and the unease his Dire Wolf had been feeling just lately—all of it had led him here, to Maccon City.

He'd stayed at the Oasis before, knew it was run by the Beta of the Island Stripe Pride and his Wolf Shifter mate. They served many supernaturals there, able to provide safety and secrecy their kind needed.

"Bro, I hate to cut this short, but I gotta go on an errand for Derrick. Say what you need to say."

Thor's voice brought him back to the present, and Phoenix closed his eyes and tried to focus his scattered mind. He saw her in his mind's eye. His beautiful mate. He really had found her.

She was so damn beautiful. His Tracey—such a simple name for such a complex person. He could sense she had more layers to her than met the eye, and he couldn't wait to reveal them all.

Mine.

"I met a woman here. My fated mate, Thor. She is the one," he told the other man confidently.

Once he said it aloud, he felt as if the entire world shifted two degrees. He felt lightheaded, dizzy, but once it settled, Phoenix knew this was right.

The tiny human female was his destiny. His Dire Wolf tossed his head back and howled into the metaphysical plane where he dwelled, alerting the entire MC through their pack bonds that he'd found his one and only.

"Wow. I felt that shit, bro. I am really happy for you. Did she accept you right away?"

"That was the reason I called. I haven't told her—"

"Fuck. Phoenix, bro. That part is complicated, but it is vital to your journey."

"I know. Got any advice?"

"I don't know from personal experience, but from what I've seen, you just gotta be honest. Don't be quiet about your feelings, yeah? Stay safe, bro."

"Thanks, man. You, too."

Be honest.

Seemed simple enough. And yet, not so simple. Phoenix was positive Tracey was human. She wouldn't know anything about Shifters and fated mates. How the hell was he going to break it to her?

It wasn't like he could just walk up to her and reveal the truth about the supernatural world and have her jump into his sometimes furry arms. Fuck. How was he ever going to convince her to give him a chance?

Phoenix ended the call and went back to his room. He needed to devise a plan, like now. From the displeasure he'd seen on that pup manager's face when he'd all but insisted the female be given a room on the unofficial Shifter only rooftop of the resort, Phoenix figured he had less than a day to get the curvy goddess up to speed.

The young Wolf, Marco, had only given in after Phoenix had allowed his own beast to shine through his gaze. His Dire Wolf was more dominant than the younger male, but Phoenix knew without being told he was going to be dealing with someone from the Macconwood Pack Wolf Guard, or maybe even the Alpha himself, eventually.

Shit.

Derrick was going to be pissed. Phoenix would just have to explain what the situation was when they came knocking on his door, as they undoubtedly would.

He ran a hand through his hair and tried to regain his composure. It wasn't like he could just rush out there and jump on the woman. No matter what his Wolf thought.

Sniff, bite, hello mate.

Yeah. Right. Not happening.

He rolled his eyes at his silly animal's ideas on wooing the female. Listening for any sign of her, he decided it was stupid to stay in his room. But he couldn't pretend to sit by the pool in his present getup. Phoenix tore off his jeans and boots, opting for a bathing suit, tank top, and a pair of Crocs bearing the *Serious Moonlight* logo before heading out to the rooftop infinity pool.

Say whatever you want about the rubber footwear, they were the most comfortable things he'd ever felt on his size fourteens. And yes, he'd groveled apologetically at Sheila's feet after the woman had gifted each of their Pack a pair of the things, along with the tank top he had on and other swag items bearing the roadhouse's name.

"Oh, wow. This is gorgeous!" Tracey's voice floated over to him, and he turned, eyes landing on her immediately.

She was standing in the doorway of her room, right next to his, and *oohing* and *aahing* over everything appreciatively. Odd, she had no luggage, only one large, rather pretty bag on her shoulder.

Marco was saying something to her that caused her to smile amid the rambunctious pups and cubs running and jumping into the pool. He supposed it was going to be difficult to hide what they were from her. But with any luck, he wouldn't have to for long.

Thor's words replayed in his head, and Phoenix trembled with anticipation—or was that fear? Fuck, if he knew.

Be honest.

His stomach clenched, muscles bunched and at the ready. He frowned, realizing his Wolf did not like how close Marco, the young and handsome hotel manager, stood next to her. In fact, he was considering rearranging the smaller man's face before he caught himself stepping towards the pair of them,

Shit. He needed to get a grip on himself. The young Wolf was only showing her how to use the key card. Once she was inside, Marco turned and walked back to Phoenix.

Here it comes, he thought with a grin.

"I've placed Miss Donner in the room next to yours, as you requested. I'm sure you are aware we don't usually allow normals up here, Mr. Tala."

"I am aware. Thank you for accommodating my request."

"Protocol dictates I inform my Pack."

"I understand, and have you?"

"Yes."

"Very good. When you talk to them again, as I know you will, make sure you tell them the human woman is my fated mate, and I have every intention of informing her by the end of the weekend."

Marco held his gaze a beat longer than he expected, and Phoenix grinned at the younger man's tenacity. Good for him.

"That would probably be wise. Good luck, Mr. Tala."

"Thanks. I might need it," Phoenix replied, jaw dropping when his soon-to-be woman came back outside with her hair hanging down her back in soft waves.

She was wearing a black bathing suit and a sheer sarong that molded to her ample curves and made his inner beast stand up and take notice.

Holy fuck.

The woman was a knockout. His heart pounded in his chest, the sound of his blood pumping through his veins was louder than the crash of waves against the sandy shore.

Thump thump. Thump thump. THUMP THUMP.

CHAPTER SIX

Phoenix growled deep in his throat. Tracey slipped past him, and a burst of her natural fragrance invaded his nostrils. Her scent was heavenly. Like freshly laundered cotton and blossoming fields of daisies.

Natural. Unique. Untainted.

He sucked in air greedily, but she was already gone. Whatever of her scent that lingered nearby, it wasn't enough. The beast went into hunter mode, and Phoenix took the stairs two at a time. Where had she gone? How long had he stood there, immobile, and frozen in place?

Fuck.

Summer afternoons were notoriously long on the East Coast. The sun was still shining brightly in the sky, but the beach was nearly empty. Afternoon crowds were headed to the pier for more of the local festivities, carnival rides, and boardwalk snacks.

Phoenix scanned the horizon. Cars drove past, playing loud music with eardrum breaking bass making his Wolf snarl. Families and couples milled about, searching for food and fun. A flock of seagulls called and dipped down from the air, plucking French fries from a forgotten container tossed carelessly on top of a trash can.

He jogged across the street from the hotel to the beach, snarling at a car that took the corner too fast and screeched to a halt in front of him. The older driver honked the horn and looked ready to curse, but seemed to change his mind when he met Phoenix's angry glare.

Grrrr.

Typically, he did a better job at hiding his Wolf. But the animal was right pissed with him. Angry at his human side for losing their mate.

It wasn't a good idea for him to be outside when he was less than a hundred percent in control. But he couldn't run back to his hotel room now. Not until he found her.

Warm sand greeted his bare feet as he reached the shore, and Phoenix squinted against the glaring rays of the sun. This semi-private strip of beach belonged to the hotel and was marked off by ropes and a stand for lounge chair and umbrella rentals. There was also a row of a dozen potted palm trees and a small tiki hut selling fresh fruit and drinks.

The area had cleared out since this morning. All the families with young children and couples looking for entertainment had already left to prepare for the evening's delights. Boardwalk fries with malt vinegar, carousel rides, and carnival games, he could only imagine. Would Tracey enjoy a visit to the boardwalk? Would she enjoy rides or sharing cotton candy? He couldn't wait to find out.

Suddenly, he stilled. Phoenix closed his eyes, allowing his preternatural senses to push forward as he filtered through the lingering smells of suntan oil, picnic lunches, salty air, and beach traffic. There. He opened his eyes, head whipping around to find his tantalizing Tracey standing near the surf.

There she is.

His Wolf growled softly, the beast pressed him to move. But Phoenix stood his ground, just watching her. Relief filled him at the mere sight of the delicious woman.

She was completely safe and sound, walking with her sandals held high and a smile on her pretty face as the waves tickled her feet with their foam and teasing little laps. He admired her from afar. Just breathing in the same air she did seemed to settle his beast.

Damn, she was beautiful. She had a steady confidence that called to him. Like she was utterly and completely happy in her own skin, and fuck, wasn't that attractive?

Phoenix drank in the sight of her greedily. She had curves for miles, and a smile that lit up the world. Outlined in the orange gold glow of the afternoon sun, Tracey Donner was a vision.

Everything else seemed to fade away as he stared. The entire world could have been swallowed up by a black hole, and Phoenix would have been totally unaware of it.

There was no noise. No seagulls or tourists. Even the ocean fell silent. All he could see, hear, breathe, was her.

Just her.

Mine.

She sat on the sand for a long while, just looking out at the sea. He felt like a voyeur, but fuck, if he could have moved, he would have. Phoenix was glued to the spot. Caught between wanting more and simply wanting to observe. Every nuance of expression, every sigh and gasp at the beauty surrounding her, were all stored away in the deepest recess of his mind.

She giggled when the water touched her bare toes. Scowled when a seagull dove too close to her face. Sighed when an elderly couple walked by holding hands like teenage lovebirds. Tracey was a romantic.

Good to know.

Time passed quickly, and the sun had already started to dip in the sky. Maybe he was a coward for not approaching her, but Phoenix did not regret the hours he spent taking her in at a distance. She stood up, dusting sand from her bottom, and walked farther down.

He followed her stealthily as she trekked along the surf to an even more deserted part of the Oasis' private beach. Bordering a sectioned off plot of sand that was sheltered from the public eye by high dunes and a sign that read *private property,* Tracey paused.

Phoenix wondered who owned the stretch of beach that forbade his mate entry, but he took a deep breath and got his answers. The private section carried the same Tiger and Wolf scents as the hotel. It must belong to the owners of the Oasis, just like the mansion a few dozen yards away.

He crouched behind another row of potted palm trees, watching as Tracey glanced behind her before crossing into the private section of beach. He grinned in surprise. The little female was a rule breaker. He hadn't expected that.

Rebel rebel.

He knew the family was not home. His Wolf could sense it. Tracey was safe for now. He was curious to see how far she would go. So, Phoenix waited with bated breath, crawling on his belly past the dunes so he could get to her if she need help. He stayed out of sight, hiding his large frame behind some tall beach grass, just to see what she would do.

Holy fuck.

Phoenix never expected the cute as fuck little human to strip to her skin in public. He almost swallowed his tongue as she pushed her bathing suit down her body, revealing acres of creamy skin and ample curves.

Did he call her cute? Fuck that. She was gorgeous. Long, blonde hair fell down her back in waves reflecting sunlight like spun silver and gold thread, a myriad of colors, all of them breathtaking and precious. He was dying to run his fingers through those seductive, long locks.

Her hair hung past her shoulders, all the way down, teasing the dimples over her round, peach of an ass. Phoenix drooled. Like he actually fucking drooled.

Gulp.

CHAPTER SEVEN

DIRE WOLF MATES

Wiping his mouth on the back of his hand, he tried to swallow his growl, but there was no containing his beast. He wanted her more than he wanted anything else in his entire life.

The briny ocean breeze was no competition for the fresh, warm scent that floated off her skin to his eager and sensitive nostrils. Like sugar cookies and warm vanilla. Sweet, delicious, and oh, so tempting.

Fuck.

He was going to lose the tremulous hold he had on his restraint. Already, his cock was stone hard, damn near punching a hole through his swim shorts. He hissed a breath as he adjusted himself. Somehow, afternoon had faded to evening, and the ocean glittered before them, inviting, but deadly. Everyone knew not to swim at this hour.

At least, he thought they did. Before he could yell a warning, Tracey dove into the waves, and he couldn't help himself. He had to join her. To protect her, sure, but also to be near her.

Phoenix took off his shirt and kicked off his sandals before diving into the water a good hundred feet away and out of her line of vision. The Jersey shore beach was calmer in August, and he was dazzled by the play of water clinging to her ripe breasts as she turned and floated on top of the waves.

She looked like a sea nymph or goddess, just gliding on the water with a soft, serene smile spread across her beautiful face. All he wanted to do was kiss her. His Dire Wolf urged him to go on. Hurry and claim her before someone else did, but he reined in his beast.

Hell. He couldn't just jump on the woman. In fact, he was pretty sure that was illegal. Plus, he did not want to frighten or overwhelm her. The sun dipped down lower, and the cool Atlantic grew dark. His senses were on alert, aware of the dangers that lurked.

Once more, he was reminded of the fact they shouldn't be in the sea at this time of night. It was feeding time for beasts and other things. Subtle movement beneath the waves alerted him to the presence of a natural predator.

Fuck.

Tracey floated on, blissfully unaware of the danger, but Phoenix was already on the move. He pushed his body through the water, growling menacingly at the shark. The apex predator made no noise, but from his position beneath the darkening tide, Tracey must have resembled something tasty.

Too bad for the shark, the little vixen was spoken for. Phoenix lunged, bopping the bull shark on the nose, and the animal, sensing a hunter more vicious than he, swam away without further incident.

Watching to make certain the shark was not coming back, Phoenix forgot to pay attention to where he was. Tracey, the seductive siren, was still floating on her back, unaware of him—that was, until she swam right into his body.

Ooops.

Electrical charges charged through his blood at the inadvertent contact and whatever attraction he'd felt since first laying eyes on her amplified innumerably. Her strangled scream and consequential splashing had him swallowing a mouthful of salt water before he knew what happened.

"What the hell? Oh damn! I'm sorry, I thought I was alone!" Tracey gasped as he coughed and spit water.

"S'fine," he growled, hoping it played off as a result of swallowing saltwater. "You are alone. Just me, and a hungry shark."

"Shark?" She screeched again, making him hunch at the sheer decibel of her voice.

Tracey splashed backwards, looking around, and he immediately felt guilty for scaring her.

"No worries. He's gone now. I didn't mean to scare you," he said, trying his best not to stare at her pretty tip-tilted breasts.

"Well, you say shark, of course I'm gonna be scared. Say, is this some line you use to trick swimmers into being grateful to you? Hello? My eyes are up here," she snapped.

To his utter sadness, Tracey covered her luscious pink nipples with one arm as she moved into more shallow waters, and Phoenix had to bite back his growl.

What was wrong with him? He was acting like a dog with a new bone. She deserved better from him than to ogle her lady bits without permission.

He was downright fucking ashamed of himself and couldn't even help the growl that rumbled through him. Her shocked eyes met his, and he turned it into a cough. This was not like him. Phoenix had better control of himself than that.

Sorta. Maybe.

"Uh, what?" he asked.

"Never mind. I have an overactive imagination."

"Ookay," he mumbled, following her, but not too close.

He was stunned. Phoenix did not know what to say, and that was a fucking first for him. Her reactions had him completely flummoxed. Most women would scream and holler if a man found them naked in the ocean, but she didn't. In fact, she hardly seemed aware of her nudity.

"I suppose that's what I get for trespassing and thinking I was alone. Is this your place?"

"No," he replied, shadowing her as she moved towards the shore.

"Then you're trespassing, too."

"Yeah, I guess I am."

Awareness suddenly flashed between them, and Phoenix could sense her growing embarrassment. But it was slightly less than the curiosity he saw sparkling in her eyes. The two emotions seemed to war inside her, and he hoped like fuck the latter won out.

In fact, greedy bastard that he was, Phoenix was positively rooting for it. Tracey tilted her head, eyeing him once, then flitting her gaze to her clothes still sitting in a pile on the shore.

"I suppose I should thank you for saving me from the shark," she teased, and he knew she didn't believe him.

That was fine. It wasn't exactly important to the rest of their story, far as he was concerned. She did not have to know the truth about her near miss. She had the fealty of a monster now. His Wolf was already bonding to her, and they'd barely spoken two sentences to one another.

Amazing.

"My pleasure," he answered, and meant it.

"So, are you a gentleman or not?"

"Depends on what you mean," he answered.

"Well, we're both in here and I am assuming we are both naked—"

"I have on trunks," he replied, grinning at the pink blush that crossed her cheeks.

"Oh, well, that's not fair."

"Here, I'll even things up," he said, pulling them off and tossing them onto the shore faster than any human should be able to move.

Ooops.

"Wow. That was crazy," she murmured, eyes wide. "Okay, well, now that we are both naked, I propose I exit the water first and you, *kind sir*, avert your eyes."

"Are you kidding? Why would I do that?" Phoenix asked, perplexed.

"Because I don't even know your name. I'm not about to jog out of here and flaunt my fun bags and all my jiggly bits in front of you," she said with a giggle.

"In that case, my name is Phoenix Tala, and you are Tracey, I believe? I'm staying at the Oasis. I think I saw you there today," he replied with a grin.

"Yep, Tracey Donner," she said, and laughed. "And true, we might be introduced now, but turn around anyway, Phoenix Tala."

"Yes, ma'am. My mama raised me to be a gentleman, so I'll give you ten seconds before I even attempt to sneak a peek," he told her, only half-kidding.

"Oh, a mama's boy? I like that."

"Ha! I'll tell her you said that," he murmured.

"That's weird. We're strangers."

"Not anymore. You know my name now."

"True, Phoenix," she replied, biting her lower lip. "Okay, turn around. No peeking."

"I'll turn around, but no promises," he replied honestly.

He was an honest Wolf and wouldn't steal a look. Probably. Maybe. Hell, he sure wanted to.

"You are such a tease. Okay, here I go," she called, already swimming to the shore.

Phoenix bit the inside of his cheek and counted to twenty before turning around. He caught the sweet curve of her ass disappearing into her swimsuit and the sight was temptation itself.

"My turn to get out, I guess," he said, catching her wide-eyed stare.

"I won't look," she told him.

"I don't mind if you do.

He lingered, paddling slowly through the cool water. The moment was intense, and his Dire Wolf stirred inside of him. The very air seemed charged with feeling. She had all his attention, man and beast watched her with covetous eyes.

She pulled her straps over her arms, turning to face him boldly, and Phoenix's smile grew even wider. She was a knockout, and not just because of her looks. Tracey was brave and confident, and that was even better than all the glitter in the world.

"Here I come, little one," he growled, giving her one last chance to keep her modesty. But she didn't avert her eyes. In fact, she lowered them, staring at that part of him that so obviously wanted her.

"Wow," she whispered, but his Wolf ears picked up the word just fine.

A small gasp escaped her lips and Phoenix had never been so glad of his physical appearance as he was at that moment. He moved languidly, standing tall and proud as rivulets of water snaked down his skin. He allowed her to look her fill before he picked up his shorts and tank from the sandy shore.

"Oh my God, I'm a peeping Tom!" Tracey squeaked, turning her head.

"Don't you mean Tomasina?"

"I don't know. I suppose," she mumbled, and her embarrassment made her even more adorable.

Phoenix chuckled as he slipped his tank top over his head and grabbed his Crocs from the sand. Her blush deepened from pink to red, and he'd never seen anything so damn cute.

"I should go," Tracey said, but she remained glued to the spot, as if she did not want to leave him just yet.

Good. That was good.

Phoenix did not want to go either. She was so sweet. Pretty and kind. Honest and brave. He wanted to know all her secrets. To learn everything he could about her. His Wolf growled and scratched, the animal wanted her too.

Fuck. No.

He didn't want her to leave. He wanted more time with her. He wanted everything. And he wanted it now. Patience never was his strong suit, but he needed to find some. She was a normal and would not understand his instinctual need for her. His certainty that she was it for him would likely look like some lame pickup line, and Phoenix did not want that at all.

"You wanna leave me, already? After all we've been through?"

"What?" she asked, a grin teasing the side of her mouth.

"I mean, I rescued you from a near shark attack and we went skinny dipping together. We're practically engaged."

"Oh my God! You did not just say that."

"It's true. What kind of woman plays with a man's emotions and then leaves him flat?

"Are you serious?"

"As a heart attack, Tracey Donner."

"Well, what can I do to repair your tainted view of me?" she teased.

"Well, I think you can start by letting me feed you."

"Feed me?"

"Yeah, Tracey. I wanna feed you. Come to dinner with me," he growled, eyes eating her up as she danced around, giving him an answer.

She was delightfully flustered, and he could tell she was wavering. Beautiful, smart, pretty little siren. He watched her come to a decision, marveling at her absolute cuteness, then braced himself.

"Okay, Phoenix Tala," she said, using his full name, and fuck, it sounded good falling from her lips.

Gonna sound even better when she screams it.

"Okay what? Is that okay yes or okay no?" he asked, anticipation making his chest pound even harder.

"Okay, I'll have dinner with you." Tracey said, gifting him with a megawatt smile just at the end.

And just like that, the female owned him. His Dire Wolf scratched at his skin, the beast wanting her more and more. There was something different about her, and not just because she was his mate. She had this inner glow, like magic. It was like her soul was all lit up from within and his Wolf could see it.

He wanted it for himself—*selfish creature.* But he more than wanted her, he needed her. Phoenix already coveted the lovely female. His beast did, too. He wanted to protect her, to possess her, to get her so used to him she couldn't possibly leave.

Fuck, he was losing it.

Grrrrr.

CHAPTER EIGHT

DIRE WOLF MATES

When Tracey left her new hotel room, the manager of the Oasis had suddenly found for her, her first thought was to go straight to the beach. So she did.

There was no one to tell her not to, after all. No one to remind her she was not beach body ready or to scold her choice of bathing suit. Years of Mother's constant criticisms were ingrained in her brain, but Tracey had been working hard to push them right out of her head.

She was her own person, and that might not be what Daniella Donner wanted in her daughter, but that was too bad for her uptight mother. Tracey was worthy of love and respect, and she deserved to be happy.

It was a hard lesson, learning happiness did not grow on trees. There would be no happy ever after within easy pickings for Tracey. But those were lessons she'd learned early. Tracey always knew she would have to endeavor to find her own happiness. Good thing she didn't mind a little hard work.

Giggling like a child as the cool Atlantic bathed her unpolished toes, she tried not to picture her mother. The woman who birthed her would be horrified her only child had failed to get a pedicure before stepping onto the beach. But Tracey didn't care.

In fact, she realized in the short time she'd been in Maccon City, a lot of her stress and anxiety were caused by the same thing. Fear of displeasing her parents. Blame them as she might want to, truth was, this was Tracey's fault. Her mother and father were not bad people, but she had failed to define her boundaries.

By not speaking up, she had allowed them to pick at her very soul. But no more. She needed time away from them so she could like herself again and get her feet on solid ground. It was a blessing that Tracey was financially independent.

Fact was, she did not require her parents' approval to be happy. She could live her life as she saw fit, pursue her craft, and just be happy. Tracey was just not anything like her parents, and that was okay.

She was fine with being different. It didn't make her bad or less than in any way at all. She'd made peace with that a long time ago, and yet she'd failed to convey her feelings to the two people who should have cared about her most of all. Maybe her unfortunate confrontation with her mother had been necessary.

It was just the push she needed to go out there and do the things she liked and wanted to do with her life. It was scary leaving home, but she was a big girl in more ways than one.

"You're gonna be alright, Tracey," she told herself in a low whisper.

Maccon City had one of the prettiest beaches she had ever seen, and it was no wonder so many tourists flocked to New Jersey to visit every year. Tracey sat and watched the waves for hours, spying a pod of bottlenose dolphins a few hundred feet out into the blue Atlantic. The constant breeze was soothing to her soul, as were the warm rays of the afternoon sun. Children laughed, lovers held hands, and the ambience was like a balm to her hurts. She had definitely come to the right place.

Beautiful. Peaceful. Magical.

After a while, she stood and walked along the shore until she saw a private property sign. Feeling a little reckless, she continued on, making sure no one was around. Something about the water was just so inviting, enticing even.

In a completely uncharacteristic move, Tracey stripped off her cover up and bathing suit, allowing the summer wind to caress her warm, naked flesh.

The act was like making a statement. A proclamation that Tracey was in the here and now. She was alive and in the world. She was her own person. Worthy of love and respect. A familiar refrain played itself over and over in her mind.

I am woman. Hear me roar.

Tracey grinned and took off at a run, diving between the beckoning waves of the still cool Atlantic. Smiling and bursting with pride at her sheer nerve, Tracey kicked her feet and used her arms and hands to slice through the water in a clumsy breaststroke. She flipped over, floating on her back and allowed the water to surround her. She couldn't hear anything but the sound of her own breathing and the rapid beat of her heart with her ears beneath the surface, and that was fine with her.

The Atlantic was doing a good job, lifting her up and washing away all her cares and worries. It felt so good, so invigorating. The salt water caressed her naked skin, and wow, she felt so free without a stitch of clothing on.

How many times had she been taught to hide her body as if it were something shameful? How many times had her parents set her up with gym memberships, personal trainers, dieticians, and fat camps?

Some of her worst memories centered on her parents' reactions to her weight and body shape. She'd tried it their way for years, and even when she had lost weight, she never kept it off. Her body just seemed to like chub. What could she say?

She ate healthy almost all the time. Choosing fish over steak, plenty of leafy greens, lean poultry, whole grain breads, and the like—but yes, she also occasionally indulged in mint chocolate chip ice cream, chocolate covered strawberries, and coffee with cream.

She exercised, sorta. Tracey loved to go for walks and got a few miles every day, either outside or on the treadmill. She was a real woman with real curves. Tracey had friends who were thin and naturally slender, and they were still not a hundred percent happy with their bodies. The way she saw it, every body was a work in progress. And regardless of what Mother said, every body was a beach body, too. Yes, she carried some extra pounds, but she refused to feel sad about it.

Lost in her thoughts, Tracey did not realize she wasn't alone until she collided with what felt like a wall floating in the ocean—*albeit a warm, muscular, living wall.*

"What the hell? Oh damn! I'm sorry, I thought I was alone," she shrieked.

Tracey was completely mortified. How had she not seen this gorgeous man getting into the water?

Crap.

This was a private beach. Was it his? She had never done anything as reckless as this, but Tracey couldn't seem to help herself. With the sun dipping low in the sky as afternoon mingled with evening, she'd been sort of inspired—*and then she'd been caught.*

Double crap.

Tracey should get out. She couldn't, though. Holy hell, she had almost forgotten she was totally and completely naked. All her girly bits were hanging out. Thank goodness the water was not crystal clear. New Jersey had clean beaches, but the algae and whatnot tended to be more opaque than the tropics.

I AM NAKED WITH A STRANGER. OMG. OMG. OMG.

"S'fine," the gorgeous stranger grumbled. He was super handsome, and his grin had her tummy doing somersaults as he flashed it her way. "You are mostly alone. Just me and a hungry shark."

"Shark?" Tracey screeched again, practically jumping on the man.

Thank goodness, she remembered herself before she did anything else humiliating. Nerves wracked her body, but one look in the man's crystalline gaze had her calming right down.

Holy cow. He is beautiful.

He really was the best looking man she had ever seen. Even better, he seemed to enjoy talking with her. Could she handle a little casual flirting? She wouldn't know if she didn't try.

Eeeeek!

After some minor discussion, she convinced the hunky man to turn around while she got out of the water. It took a second, but she pulled on her bathing suit and called out to him.

He'd stayed turned around the whole time—at least she thought he had. And for some reason, that disappointed her.

Good manners are nice. Dirty boys are nicer, though.

Unfortunately, Tracey did not offer him the same courtesy. He strode from the water naked as the day he was born, *and holy freaking hotness,* the man was glorious.

She was dumbstruck as the man stepped out of the darkening waters, looking like a sea god about to embark on his reign over the dry lands.

He can reign over me anytime with that body. OMG. Did I just think that? I am a total slut.

She shook her head and dropped her gaze as he pulled on his trunks. What kind of person was she? Ogling a stranger—*not a stranger, his name is Phoenix Tala*—like he was some prize stallion was not becoming of a person with morals.

She should be ashamed of herself. Would be, too, as soon as she got the image of his perfect body out of her head. Which would be like two weeks from never. The man was packing some serious heat between his thick, rugby player thighs.

A person had to work out to have legs like that. Was he a professional athlete? It would not surprise her at all with his muscular build. Unfortunately, she knew fuck all about sports. Holy cow! Tracey was even cursing in her thoughts now.

"I should go," she mumbled.

"You wanna leave me, already? After all we've been through?" Phoenix replied and gave her a panty, *er,* swimsuit melting grin.

She was shocked at the easy banter that followed, and found herself agreeing to have dinner with the man. Phoenix caught her hand in his and sent her pulse racing with the simple gesture. Had anyone ever wanted to hold hands with her like that? She could not remember a time. He made her so nervous she couldn't even walk in a straight line.

"Sorry, I'm clumsy," she said, almost tripping once they got to the sidewalk. She was embarrassed and tried to laugh it off, stepping away from the man. But Phoenix held strong.

"You're not clumsy, Tracey."

"No, seriously, I am. And I'm so sorry about all this, roping you into dinner—"

"I was the one who asked you," he reminded her gently, and she warmed to him a little more.

"Why are you so nervous now? After a little trespassing and skinny dipping, dinner should be no problem for a badass like you," Phoenix said.

"Me? I think you're getting a little ahead of yourself. I'm no badass. More like a short, chubby, stick in the mud, who still lives at home with her parents and never does anything for fun, or at least, I did up until a few hours ago," she admitted to her shock.

"Well, I don't know who you're talking about, but the Tracey I know—and yes, I consider myself an expert by now—is daring, courageous, beautiful as fuck, and has me completely captivated," Phoenix said, and damn, her stomach was doing somersaults at his praise.

Holy cow. The man's smile should be classified as a lethal weapon. Tracey tucked her damp hair behind her ear with her right hand, her left firmly encased in his. She licked her lips, cheeks were burning with embarrassment.

"Captivated, huh?" she asked.

"That's right. Now, I wanna get to know you, Tracey Donner."

"Why?"

"A hundred reasons, and yet, they all amount to the same thing."

"What's that?" she asked, wondering what kind of spell he was weaving around her to make her ask such questions aloud.

"I'll tell you," he said, clicking his tongue behind his teeth and looking slightly nervous for such a jaw-dropping gorgeous man. "After we eat, though. So, what do you like?"

"I like everything, obviously," she murmured.

"I don't know what you mean, why is it obvious?"

"Are you serious?"

"Yeah," he said, cocking his head to the side.

Holy crap, she could tell he was really serious. The man was not making a rude comment or joke about her weight, and she had no idea what to do with that information other than stand there in awe.

"Um, it's been pointed out to me before that I was overweight. So, when I said it was obvious, I eat everything, I guess I was being self-deprecating. Phoenix, I would like to apologize for that now—"

"You don't have a damn thing to apologize for, and anyone who ever made you feel less than is not worth a minute of your time, Tracey. Now, I like the way you look. Hell, I more than that, and if you need proof, well, I've been rocking a boner since I laid eyes on you. Now, I'm not telling you that to scare you," he continued, unrushed. "I have no intention of doing anything you don't want, you control the pace, I'm just throwing that out there, so there is no misunderstanding. I want you to know I find you incredibly hot."

"Wow. Well, first, thank you. That was quite the compliment," she said.

Tracey paused, casting a quick glance towards his swimsuit clad nether regions, and sure enough, the evidence of his admiration was right there, filling out his trunks with what had to be ten to eleven inches of long, hard man.

Yep, he's got a boner. And I gave it to him.

"But I wasn't apologizing for anyone else. I was apologizing because I should never have said anything like that. I'm turning a new leaf, Phoenix Tala, and you caught me right at the cusp."

"Really?"

"Yes, you see, I decided I like myself, curves, and quirks, and all. I won't be apologizing for myself anymore. And I am not looking for a man to save me or change me. Just thought you should know that up front."

It was the boldest statement Tracey had ever made, but she meant it. Sure, it was way too early for her to speak so plainly to the man, but maybe it would save her a little heartache to get it out in the open now. She stopped walking and looked into his face, expecting rejection and maybe even anger. Instead, Tracey was floored when she saw something closely resembling pride in his glittering green gaze.

"Good for you. Don't take anyone's shit, Tracey. Not ever. Least of all mine."

"You are the strangest man," she mused, and Phoenix tossed his head back and barked a loud laugh.

"Yeah," he murmured. "I get that sometimes. How about Mexican food?"

"I like Mexican," she replied as they fell into an easy rhythm side by side.

"So, what brings you to Maccon City?"

"Oh, well. That's a long, boring story," she replied, liking the feel of his warm hand around hers.

Rarely in life had Tracey ever felt small or dainty, but next to the behemoth of a man, she felt positively petite. The way he looked at her warmed her insides, and raw attraction flooded her system. It was pretty difficult to ignore the physical awareness blossoming between them. With his boner statement and all, it was a wonder she hadn't melted into a puddle of needy woman at his feet.

"I doubt any story about you could be boring," he returned.

"Why? You don't even know me," she stated, laughing a little at his bold reply.

Men didn't usually flirt with her. Especially not men who looked like him, so she couldn't be entirely sure that's what was happening.

"I'd like to get to know you, Tracey. Really, I would," he replied, taking care to look both ways before walking her across the street.

"Wow. So, you fake save me from a shark, get naked with me in the ocean, listen to part of my sob story, and you're still here, wanting more? I am not sure what you want from me, but you are wasting your time if you think I'm desperate enough to fall for a line like that," she said bluntly.

"It's no line," he growled, turning to face her. "I apologize if I offended you with my blunt talk earlier, but I meant everything I said. I want to spend time with you."

"You really do?"

"Yes."

"Okay, then. Let's get some Mexican food."

"Good," he said, and seemed to relax once more.

They started walking again, and she did her best to stay even with his long strides. Impossible really, since it took two of her shorter, less elegant steps to make one of his.

The man moved like a dancer. Or maybe a professional soccer player. All grace and understated power. No awkward stumbles or half steps for him. She couldn't imagine what it was like to be born with such innate dignity. He was really perhaps the most beautiful man she had ever seen.

Which begged the questions—what was he doing here? And why was he alone?

Sexy, puzzling man. I wonder what he's searching for.

With any luck, Tracey might find out.

CHAPTER NINE

Gathering her courage, Tracey looked up at Phoenix, admiring his profile. She'd never gotten butterflies in her stomach just looking at a man—*except for when she saw Harry Styles in concert but come on—that was Harry Styles.*

Love him as she might, Harry had nothing on Phoenix Tala. His face was just as gorgeous, and his body, god-like.

"So, why are *you* in Maccon City?"

That brought both golden eyebrows up, and Tracey grinned. It was about time he got frazzled. But even more than the little bit of satisfaction she got from surprising the man, she really was curious.

"Well, I was itching for a road trip. So, I told my Alph—*er*, I mean my boss, then I jumped on my bike and wound up here."

"Your bike? Wait—you have a motorcycle?" she asked, mouth gaping.

"Yeah. A Harley."

"OMG! Of course you do," she mumbled, rolling her eyes and shaking her head.

"What?" he asked.

"It just figures," she replied, and exhaled a laughing breath.

One of Tracey's most secret naughty girl fantasies involved a sexy stranger swooping in on a big badass motorcycle, wearing leather and denim. It was a hot dream. One that always made her motor run—*pun intended.*

Of course, skinny dipping with a sexy stranger was number two on her list of secret naughty girl fantasies. She'd thought she was one and done, but this hot boy had a Harley.

Swoon. Swoon. SWOON.

"Do you not like motorcycles?" Phoenix asked, looking down at her with concern in his glowing green gaze.

Sexy, sexy man.

His eyes were gorgeous. Sometimes they looked aquamarine wrapped in gold. Columbian emeralds, she mused. It must have been a trick of the light. But they were beautiful, stunning, like nothing else she'd ever seen.

"No."

"You don't?"

"No! Yes! I mean, I love motorcycles," she replied rapidly.

"I see." He grinned, beaming at her, and she thought he squeezed her hand a little longer that time.

"Well," she continued nervously. "I think I do. I've never actually been on a motorcycle before."

"I can rectify that. Just say when."

"Really?"

"Sure. Anytime you want. Hell, we can go right now."

Tracey stopped in her tracks. No man had ever offered to take her for a ride on his motorcycle before. Her mother would think it was undignified. Her father would consider it lowly.

But they weren't here right now. And even if they were, so what? Tracey was thirty, not thirteen. She did not need her parents' permission to do something wild—*like jumping on the back of a Harley with a complete stranger.*

"I'm sorry. Did I make you uncomfortable again?"

Phoenix frowned. He looked like he wanted to take back his invitation, but Tracey didn't want that. Her stomach was doing all kinds of somersaults, and she knew she was bound to make a fool of herself.

Bottom line, Tracey was finished living by other people's rules. Grabbing her courage, she shook her head at the gorgeous man.

"Okay, first, no, you did nothing wrong. I am actually surprisingly comfortable with you. Second, I would very much like to go for a ride on your Harley, but I have something to confess—"

"What?" he asked, looking completely enamored and making her tingle down to her toes.

"I'm starving. How about we have dinner first?"

"Sorry, I shouldn't have dallied," he murmured. "Let's get going."

He tugged on her hand gently, and Tracey felt like she was holding on to a live wire. Electricity zipped up and down her body, lighting her up like a neon sign from within. Pleasure hummed along her skin, like the breeze coming off the Atlantic. And all because of the almost impossible to believe knowledge that Tracey and Phoenix had this brand new, exciting, growing mutual attraction between them.

"You should know, I've never gone out with a guy I just met," she stated, hoping against hope her brutal honesty wasn't about to cost her the night.

"No?"

"Nope. In fact, I don't have much dating experience at all."

"Well, I guess you and I can practice together."

He was grinning again, and she felt her heart skip a beat. She figured a guy who looked like that didn't chase women very often and imagined she was one in a long line of women who he'd asked out.

Crap.

What was she doing? He was gorgeous, and she was just her. Phoenix had to know the effect he had on women. Far too good-looking not to be aware of it.

OMG.

What if Rosa was right? What if he was some man who only went after rich women? Like a real live gigolo, wooing the first single woman he saw, and wanting her to pay for his lifestyle. He was certainly hot enough to be a kept playboy on the prowl.

No freaking way.

She was being an idiot. Tracey didn't believe that about Phoenix for a minute. Then again, what did she really know about him? Anything was possible, she supposed. If he was a kept man, his ridiculous hotness alone would command a pretty penny for the pleasure of his company.

"I'm sorry, I know this might sound rude, but are you by any chance a playboy?"

"A what?" Phoenix burst out, stopping in his tracks.

"Well, a friend of mine read about handsome men who come to places like this, like a beach resort, to prey on lonely, wealthy women. They get them to fall in love, or lust, and, *well,* they just love off them, I guess you could say. I'm not judging, I swear, but anyway, this friend planted this seed, and I thought it important to find out first. And, oh my God, I sound crazy. I will totally understand if you think I am nuts and want to call off dinner."

Crap. She was a nut job. He was so walking out on her. Why couldn't she just keep her big mouth shut?

Damn. Damn. DAMN.

"Uh, okay. First, thanks for the compliment. I mean, I think there was sort of a compliment in there about me being handsome," he replied, and he sounded like he was smiling, but Tracey couldn't tell. IN fact, she could not see his face at all since she was covering her eyes with her hands.

"Tracey, I am not a playboy, gigolo, or prostitute of any kind. Scout's honor," he teased.

"Oh my God! You're a boy scout? Now, I am really mortified," she squealed.

Deep, rich sounds of masculine laughter accompanied by large hands on her shoulders had her peeking out from behind her hands. God, he smelled good. A delicious combination of whatever spicy masculine cologne he wore and the fresh sea air.

"Tracey, it's okay," he said.

"Really, it's okay that I basically called you a-a—"

"A hooker?" he asked, and she slapped her hands over her mouth to cover up her squeak.

"OMG! I am so humiliated."

"Why? You know, I haven't been taken by surprise in a very long time. I think you are funny, smart, and so fucking adorable," he said kindly.

"I think you mean crazy, ridiculous, and not a good prospect at all," she replied, shaking her head.

"Nope. I said what I meant, beautiful."

Double swoon.

CHAPTER TEN

Was there anything about this man that was unattractive? He was too good to be true.

"Phoenix Tala, are you some kind of angel walking on earth? I mean, you are just too good to be true."

"I'm no angel, Tracey."

"Well, you're not just a man either. You're too kind, too hot, and you even offered to take me for a ride on your bike after dinner."

"All my pleasure."

"How can you say that?"

"Easy. I get to be with you," he told her, and damn, her heart started pounding in earnest.

"This has been some day," she told him, exhaling as she tried to find her nerve.

Phoenix linked their hands again and pulled her through the sparse crowd. His shoulder brushed against hers, and tingles raced down her spine.

"How do you mean?" he asked once she was beside him again.

"For one thing, I ran away from home—yes, at my age, that is still possible. Then, I jumped in an Uber and traveled to Maccon City with no hotel reservations during peak season and almost wound up sleeping on the beach. Next, I went skinny dipping in the ocean with you, as it turned out. And now, here I am, insulting the sexiest man I ever saw and still getting him to take me to dinner."

"You've been busy, beautiful."

"Yeah, you can say that again. My whole life has gone upside down. Strangest. Day. Ever."

His glittering aquamarine eyes sparkled down at her, and she felt his attention down to her toes. He really seemed interested, and that, in itself, was amazing and awesome. Even more amazing, Tracey was enjoying herself. She'd embarrassed herself a dozen times or more, but he was still there, so maybe she was doing something right, after all.

"You know, if you want to talk about it, I'm here for you, beautiful."

"You really are too good to be true. Are you sure someone didn't hire you to be nice to me?" She wondered aloud, biting her lip when his eyebrows furrowed in confusion.

"What? Woman, I don't know who you've been hanging with, but it is a privilege to be anywhere near you, and if it takes forever and a day, I'm gonna make it my job to make sure you believe that," Phoenix stated, narrowing his eyebrows.

Tracey stared, wide eyed. No one talked like that. At least not to her. Her pulse was racing as long-forgotten parts of her woke up with interest. When was the last time a man's gaze had made her feel so feminine and desired?

Never. Never ever ever.

But standing on the semi crowded sidewalk with this man, well, Tracey felt every bit the siren he seemed to think she was. It was a good feeling—*a very good feeling.*

Tracey did not want it to end. Could she trust it, though? That was the real question.

"Come on, beautiful, let's get some food and beer, or wine, if you prefer. We can chat or just enjoy the silence. Whatever you like."

"Okay, just answer me one question. Why did you ask me to go out to dinner with you?"

"Tracey, you seem to be operating under some false belief that you aren't the most spectacular fucking thing I've ever seen. Let me clarify exactly how I feel about you right now."

He tugged on her hand, pulling her flush against his body. They were both still damp, smelling of sea salt and summer. Tracey's pulse raced, and even more amazing was the fact she could feel his own heartbeat pounding like a runaway train inside his chest. He dipped his head and brushed his lips against hers.

Holy crap.

The whisper of a kiss was so soft, so light, so full of promise—she felt it down to the soles of her bare feet. He brushed his mouth against hers, once, twice, and the third time, well, that really was the charm. He crushed his mouth to hers, one hand cupping her neck as he pushed past her semi-closed lips and delved inside her mouth with his long, hot tongue. Phoenix blew her mind with that kiss. She couldn't think or move. For several long seconds after he pulled away, Tracey remained breathing heavily. She still stood pressed against him, eyes half-closed, mouth throbbing from his passionate kiss.

"You believe me now?" he asked, his voice impossibly deep.

"Whoa."

"Yeah, whoa. If you hadn't agreed to come with me when I asked, I planned to ask you again tomorrow. And the day after that, and so on. I meant it, Tracey. I wanna get to know you," he said and brushed her hair back with his hands, dropping another soulful kiss onto her ready and waiting lips.

"Now, I know you're too good to be true," she whispered, and reached up on tiptoe to kiss him back quickly before she ran out of courage.

"Nope. Just honest. You got me wild for you, Tracey Donner," Phoenix growled against her mouth, deepening the kiss for a moment before pulling back.

She shook her head and tried to come up with something clever to say. There simply were not words for how she felt about this man.

"I think you are trying to seduce me," she blurted, half hopeful it was the truth.

His deep chuckle reached her ears, and Tracey blinked rapidly. Had she said that aloud?

Double crap.

The feel of his callused finger beneath her chin as he gently tilted her head upwards had her opening her eyes. Phoenix Tala was staring down at her from his incredible height, and damn, the man was potent this close.

Her whole body seemed to tremble and wait for him to do whatever it was he was about to do. She couldn't have made a bigger ass of herself if she'd tried, but he was still there. And God help her, Tracey wanted to know why.

"If it will help you to know what I am planning, beautiful, let me spell it out for you. First, I can hear your stomach growling, and I need to feed you—call it a biological imperative to see to your needs, if you like. Second, I plan to share that meal in your very delightful company. And third, I have every intention of seducing you, Tracey."

"What?"

"Come on, the restaurant is right here."

CHAPTER ELEVEN

DIRE WOLF MATES

Dinner. We are having dinner. Sure, I can do this. I can sit through dinner with my fated mate and pretend to be a normal for the night.

If he said it to himself enough times, maybe the urge to drag her to the floor and taste every inch of her would go away. His Wolf snarled, seeming to roll his eyes at him.

Yeah. Sure. Moron.

Phoenix waged war with his carnal desires as he guided the sexy female to an outdoor table inside an enclosed section of sidewalk just a few streets down from their hotel. The place claimed authentic Mexican cuisine, boasting fresh seafood and local ingredients.

Even better, they didn't have to waste time going back to change. Tracey had a pretty, soft-looking blouse she'd pulled out of her bag and threw on over her bathing suit. It went with the sarong she had wrapped around her waist. The whole ensemble was hell on his nerves, with little sheer strips revealing tantalizing glimpses of skin—*like it was playing peekaboo with him.*

Grrrr.

She looked gorgeous with her golden hair flowing in the breeze, and those creamy jade eyes of hers staring up at him all full of secrets and laughter. She was an enigma. A mysterious little beauty, and he could not wait to get to know her better. After their rocky start, and those tempting kisses that left him wanting more, having dinner should be a piece of cake.

Famous. Last. Words.

Phoenix's Dire Wolf was determined to claim the female tonight, and it was all he could do to talk the beast down. But it was all coming together so quickly. The delicious scent of her arousal told him she was interested, but she was a *normal.* A somewhat shy and sheltered normal at that. She would not understand what being fated mates to each other meant.

No. He had to slow it down. It was difficult, though. Being with her was just so easy. She might be shy about her appeal, but she was downright bawdy with her humor and stories. Phoenix loved it.

He'd never been big on conversation, trusting computers more easily than people. But Tracey was different. She was exciting and alluring. He hadn't broached the subject of relationships yet. He was enjoying himself too much for reality to set in.

"Can I take your order?" the server asked, and Tracey turned a brilliant smile at the man that had Phoenix wanting to claw the fucker's eyes out.

Easy.

He hardly caught what she'd ordered, but knew from the amount of time it took, it was not nearly enough.

"For you, sir?"

"Can you double what she asked for? Great. Then add twenty chipotle wings, well done. An order of your famous "trash can" nachos with habanero mango salsa. Fresh guacamole. Oh, and six *birria* ṭacos, please."

"Um, yes, sir. Anything to drink?" the server asked.

Phoenix really loved a good tequila when he was enjoying

Mexican cuisine. He looked at Tracey, catching her staring at him wide-eyed.

"Wanna split a pitcher of mango margaritas with me?"

"I shouldn't," she replied. "But that sounds wonderful."

"Excellent," the server replied and hurried off to put their order in.

A few minutes later, he came back with a frosty pitcher of mango margs, a couple of waters, and some appetizers. Phoenix grinned, and served Tracey before himself, laughing when she appeared stunned at the amount of food he'd ordered.

"Did you invite like six other people to dinner with us?"

"No, are you fat shaming me?" he teased.

"Hardly," Tracey replied, taking a guacamole filled tortilla chip right out of his hand and another from his dish.

"This is so good, but you need to try it this way," she told him, smiling vibrantly, and damn, if this woman didn't light up like a star when she was happy.

Phoenix loved watching her. She was full of surprises and hidden depth. She lifted a spoon, proceeding to do about the most amazing thing he had ever seen. While chewing the chip she'd stolen from him, she prepared another with just a smidge of guacamole and mango habanero salsa before leaning over and offering it to him.

"This is the perfect chip," she whispered, eyes wide, as if she only realized the intimacy of what she was doing.

Hell if he was going to let her balk now. Phoenix took the proffered bite, nibbling her fingertips gently and moaning appreciatively. She was right. Perfect bite, indeed.

That little offering of hers sealed it. This sexy normal was definitely his mate. Phoenix could not remember the last time he'd shared food with anyone. But here he was, in public, taking nibbles from her hand like a puppy with its new master.

Grrrr.

The Wolf didn't necessarily like the comparison, but that was too fucking bad. Even his beast recognized her as his. He could have crowed, he was so dang happy. For too long, Phoenix had thought he was broken. He figured he was too rough for a woman, a nomadic creature like him. Then Derrick made them put down roots, and he'd been at sea.

"Ooh, try this," Tracey interrupted his thoughts, snagging the chip he'd almost gotten all the way to his mouth and adding some shredded jalapenos and lime juice with some Mexican table cream on top.

Phoenix opened like a good boy, loving the fact that she was feeding him and talking animatedly. Last time Weylin tried to snag a chip from his plate, Phoenix had wrestled the bastard to the ground, and they'd bled all over the kitchen floor at the Pack house.

His inner beast was territorial about food. But his Wolf didn't seem to mind Tracey taking from his plate. Not at all.

"Everything tastes so good," she moaned around a mouth full of shrimp ceviche.

Fucking hell.

The woman was downright noisy when she ate. Moaning in delight over the tasty goodies. Brock's mate, Ariella, was notorious for her eating noises, but damn, Tracey could sure give the Lioness a run for her money.

"Here you go," the server returned, interrupting Phoenix's train of thought.

He swapped out empty plates, and food they were finished with for new, full dishes with their entrees. Phoenix had doubled her order and added more to it. As if the man knew how much Phoenix enjoyed sharing with her, the server had set it all up on platters, bringing two empty plates for them to share.

The next hour went by unrushed, and the more she relaxed, the happier his Wolf was. She was perfect. He frowned, worrying over her reaction to his secret. Would she run? Fuck, he didn't know if she could survive it. The more time he spent in her company, the more his Wolf bonded to her, and Tracey was quickly becoming hella important to his very survival.

Mine.

"I know you're this big, beefy guy, but I can't believe how much you eat," Tracey said, laughing as Phoenix put away his eighth taco.

"I'm dainty as fuck," he joked, offering her the last bite of his *birria* taco.

"I can't, I'm stuffed."

"Interesting word, beautiful," he growled, winking to ensure she caught the innuendo.

"OMG. You did not just say that to me," she replied, and snorted behind her hand. "OMG. I snorted! Real attractive."

"I sure think so. Here, let's order dessert next," he whispered, taking her hand in his as the server cleared the dishes.

A few minutes later, the man returned with a tower of dessert nachos doused in cinnamon sugar, drizzled with chocolate sauce and caramel, and topped with sliced berries and vanilla bean ice cream.

"You're trying to kill me," she moaned, eyes huge as she stared at the delicious confection.

"Never. You are one hundred percent safe with me, beautiful. Now, it's my turn to feed you," he murmured, taking a chip and adding a bit of this and that from the plate.

He growled softly as Tracey opened her mouth, allowing him to place the dessert in her mouth. She chewed and swallowed it down with a satisfying hum that made his dick hard in his shorts.

The fact she trusted him to feed her was deeply rewarding to both him and his Dire Wolf. The beast inside longed to chase the bite of dessert with a deep, soulful kiss, but he didn't think he could stop there. It would have to wait.

Patience is a virtue. Grrrr.

He wasn't known for his patience. But being there with her was almost enough to fulfill him. She was so open and positively bubbling with sweetness and hidden depths.

"Do you like art?" Tracey asked.

"I do," Phoenix replied with a warm smile. "Though I admit folk art is my favorite. I spent a couple of months in my youth just biking through South America. I visited ancient ruins, rainforests, cities, and quaint little villages where the local men and women wove the most amazing rugs and tapestries, ponchos, blankets, you name it. I keep one I got in Ecuador in my bedroll on my bike."

"Really? That is amazing," she replied, and he heard the truth in her voice.

Her eyes lit up as she spoke, and he wanted to keep that light there. He wanted to make her happy and excited, always. Wondered how she would glow for him once he got his hands on her. Would she be noisy like when she liked something she ate? Would she give him one of those heart-stopping smiles he coveted from her?

Oh, the things he was going to do to and for his sweet mate. What did she like? How would she taste? The questions were rolling through him like a freight train, and he had to fight for control as his baser instincts pushed to the forefront. He should have known better than to think he could take things slowly. The physical pull to his mate was undeniable.

Shit.

She was saying something, and he was gonna fuck himself up if he missed even a single word of it. Tracey was that special to him already. He never wanted to be absent for a moment of the time he spent with her.

"I'd love to go there," she said, and her eyes took on a wistful glow as she spoke. "I've always wanted to travel. I mean, I went away with my family, but it was always stuffy hotels and scheduled trips to museums and things like that with groups or nannies."

"I see. Well, was it all bad?"

She paused and seemed to consider the question. Curiosity piqued, Phoenix realized he was truly interested in her reply. He wanted to know more about her. No, he didn't like her sadness, but he wanted to know everything.

The good. The bad. All of it. All of her.

He would take it inside, make it part of him, and learn how to please and care for her based on her past. Already, he made plans inside his head to take her on a trip to see the folk art of countries like Columbia, Peru, and Ecuador. Hell, he'd take her anywhere she wanted.

I'd do anything for her. Anything at all.

Mine.

"Not all of it, no. It was nice sometimes. My parents aren't bad. We're just different. I mean, I did kinda run away from home to come here."

"You waited a little while to run away. How come?"

"Stupid. Scared. A combination of both maybe?"

Her soft derisive snort almost missed his sensitive ears, but he caught it and frowned as she sipped from her glass of water. They'd finished the pitcher of margaritas and switched to water halfway through the meal.

Other dates he'd been on with women usually ended with him having to do the ordering and choosing, but he liked this so much better. Tracey knew her own mind and her likes and dislikes. She ate and drank what she wanted with no pressure or leaving it up to him or anyone else.

She thought she was a coward, but he knew different. Tracey was a motherfucking superstar, kicking ass and taking names.

"I don't believe that for a second. Weren't you the badass stripping down to her skin on private property and jumping into shark-infested waters?"

"Ha! Yeah, right. Thank you for that though," she replied and giggled.

"Nothing that isn't true, beautiful."

"I'm sorry, I don't want to put a damper on our evening so, let's just say I have never really gotten along with my mother. Besides, I am thirty years old. I don't need permission to go to the beach if I want to."

"I don't suppose you do," he returned.

"This was nice," she said as he paid the bill at his insistence.

"It's only day one, Tracey. I plan on showing you a lot more nights like this," he promised.

She had no idea what she was in for, and Phoenix could not wait to show her.

CHAPTER TWELVE

DIRE WOLF MATES

Tracey woke up the next morning with her heart pounding a steady tattoo in her chest. Her dreams were feverish, dirty, erotic—all the above. And they featured one man. Phoenix Tala.

The gorgeous, *not a stranger anymore,* hottie had walked her to her door after dinner and dessert, which, ironically, happened to be next door to his own room at the *Oasis*.

Oh, she'd wanted more than the delicious kiss he'd given her, but Tracey was new to this sort of thing. Insecurities had threatened to send her packing, but the big, beautiful man shook his head and grabbed her chin, stealing one last, deep kiss before forcing himself away.

He liked her. She felt it to her bones. And dammit, she liked him too. It was way too soon for these feelings, but Tracey had never been good at playing games and waiting. Another thing her mother and her rich friends made fun of her for. But Tracey could not care less about them.

He kissed me.

Her skin buzzed with anticipation as she showered and dressed.

Phoenix had asked her to spend the day with him, and she couldn't wait to start.

"Oh my, who is it?" Tracey asked when someone knocked at the door.

She'd just pulled on a floral printed sundress and was still scrunching her hair when she pulled it open. There he was, looking tempting and hot with the sunshine lighting him up from behind.

"Good morning, beautiful." Phoenix smiled, handing her a to go cup of coffee from the posh place down the street.

"Thanks," she replied, taking it from him. "I really need this."

"I know. You said so last night," he replied with a sexy chuckle.

Last night was the best date Tracey ever had. It was the first time in memory that a man hadn't mentioned her weight or eating habits, and she had actually enjoyed herself. Thoroughly.

About damn time, girl.

"Ready? I have some plans for us today," he told her, and his grin was infectious.

"Well then, let's get started," she replied, taking his offered hand.

That was another something new. Phoenix couldn't seem to help it. It was like he enjoyed touching her, and wasn't that new? Even better, she liked it, too.

Last night he'd held her hand when they walked, and at dinner, he seemed to find excuses to brush her fingertips or touch her shoulder or leg while they ate. And not in a grabby pervy way, either. He made her feel special—*pretty, too.*

Tracey liked those feelings. A lot. The man was weaving some sort of spell around her, and as she closed her room door, her coffee in one hand, his hand in the other, she wondered if he knew it.

"Do you believe in magic?" she asked out of the blue.

"Yes," he replied instantly. "Why?"

"You'll think it's silly," she murmured, walking down the stairs to the street with him beside her.

"I won't. Promise," he said, nudging her shoulder and squeezing her fingers carefully.

He stopped walking, and she was forced to stop, too. Her eyes met his, reluctantly, jade green to glittering Columbian emeralds. Damn, he was beautiful. Like some hero from a book. She might as well get this over with. He would probably laugh it off, anyway.

Find your backbone, Tracey. You got this.

"Talk to me, beautiful," he whispered, and she relaxed.

He was the only man who'd repeatedly called her that, and her heart melted a little more with every utterance of the word. With Phoenix, Tracey felt beautiful. Even more so, she felt confident, and that was a good feeling. One everyone deserved to experience.

"It's just, I feel like this whole thing, you and me meeting in this place, is kismet," she whispered, eyes widening as heat seemed to fill her.

Phoenix moved closer, brushing her body with his as he let go of her hand and moved it to her neck. He'd already tossed his coffee cup into the trash can at the foot of the stairs. Both hands were on her now and as his head lowered and he nuzzled her lips with his own, Tracey gasped. Sizzling zaps of electricity raced up her spine, and she swayed on her feet, needing him to kiss her more firmly.

"Me too, Tracey. I feel it, too."

Then he kissed her, hard and deep, tasting of coffee and man. The combination was delicious, and she loved every second of it. Too soon, he ended the kiss, and they continued down the street with him holding her hand.

They grabbed some Jersey shore breakfast sandwiches—pork roll, fried egg, and cheese on a roll with salt, pepper, and ketchup. Delicious.

After they'd eaten, they headed for the beach. Phoenix had a cabana all booked for them, and she was glad she wore a bathing suit beneath her sundress.

They spent the afternoon swimming, and talking, sharing tidbits of information about each other. She learned his likes and dislikes, discussed movies, books, and random pop culture factoids.

He was so interesting, and he seemed eager to get to know her better. They were treading water, enjoying the low tide, and Tracey was so focused on his answer to her latest question, she didn't see the wave sneaking up on her. Phoenix's head shot up.

"Tracey, watch out!" he yelled.

Before she could blink, he swam half a dozen feet of water and pulled her beneath the rough wave, keeping her safe in his steel embrace. She clung to him as the wave passed over them, gasping for breath when he dragged her up.

"Are you, alright?" he asked, hands going over her worriedly.

She was sputtering for air, but nodding her head as she took in the scene around her. Other swimmers had been knocked sideways, and lifeguards were blowing whistles and helping bathers get their bearings. The Atlantic Ocean was infamous for sudden changes in roughness, and soon things had returned to calm.

"Let's get out a while, okay?" he suggested, and she nodded, still trying to find her air.

"Phoenix?"

"Yeah?" he asked, grabbing a huge beach towel and wrapping it around her shoulders as he helped her sit in one of their rented chairs.

"How did you do that?"

"How did I do what?" he replied, but he wouldn't meet her eyes, and was busying himself grabbing waters from the cooler.

"You practically blurred across the water to reach me."

"I'm just a fast swimmer, I guess."

But that was not entirely true. She hated he was not giving her a real answer, but she took the offered bottle, watching closely as relief crossed his face when she took a sip.

"I'll accept that answer for now, Phoenix Tala. But I know you are keeping something from me. Secrets are never fun and always discovered," she murmured.

"I promise I will tell you everything you want to know, it's just, let's just have today."

"What do you mean?"

"I mean, I don't want you running from me before you get to know me," he confessed, kneeling in front of her and rubbing her towel covered arms.

He looked haunted and unsure. It was the first time she'd seen the man look anything other than confident. It rattled her, but Tracey wasn't willing to end her time with him over some vague response to what was probably a trick of the mind.

"Hey, you're growling," she whispered, placing her hand on his chest.

Phoenix trembled under her touch. His aquamarine eyes were wide with some unspoken emotion, but before she could question it, he sat back, leaving her hand hovering in the air, and ran a hand over his face.

Trouble. The man was trouble.

If she was not careful, Tracey was going to lose her heart to this man with so many secrets. She could be patient if she wanted to be, and for some reason, she did. This all felt too right to dismiss. He felt right to her.

"You okay now?" he asked.

"Yes, much better. But I think I'm done with the beach for the day," she replied, and smiled.

"Alright. Come on, let's go change for the rest of our adventure day."

Phoenix stood up and pulled her up with him. He tossed some bills at the rental station, taking her hand as he led her off the sand.

She went with him easily, but her curiosity warred with her need for caution. It was a sour note on the otherwise perfectly delightful day. Tracey hated the distance between them after that wave incident. She should have zipped her lip, but she could not go back to being the scared girl taking whatever crumbs of affection the people in her life offered her.

If Phoenix wanted to be in her life. He was going to have to give her more. She deserved that.

CHAPTER THIRTEEN

DIRE WOLF MATES

Tracey hummed as she stripped off her swimsuit and stepped inside the shower. Two days had passed since she first swam into Phoenix's hot and naked body in the cool Atlantic waters. Two days of adventures and dates, steamy kisses, and endless conversations.

She'd had more fun in his company than she ever had with anyone else before. He took her swimming, bicycling, and hiking. They'd gone out for every meal, sometimes picnicking it on the beach. The man loved to eat, and he was always encouraging her to try things and steal bites from his plate. Last night, they'd gone to the pier and rode the amusement rides and played boardwalk games.

She felt like a teenager with her first crush. But it was more than that. Phoenix was quickly consuming her every waking thought. For the first time, her body stirred at the mere thought of a man.

She'd never been overly sexual. In fact, one of the few times she'd tried sex, her partner had called her cold and unfeeling. That remark had hurt Tracey for years. But maybe the fault wasn't with her because sure as the sun was shining right now, Tracey felt anything but cold with Phoenix.

No, they hadn't had sex yet, but she wanted to. Last night they were so close. They'd stayed up till dawn, making out like horny teenagers and talking like old friends.

Phoenix had walked her to the hotel room door last night and kissed her again, and again, and again, leaving her wanting before rushing off to his room right next door.

They hardly ever stayed just at the hotel, but this morning they'd shared breakfast, creamed chipped beef on enormous buttermilk waffles and fruit salad, on one of the poolside picnic tables on the lower level. After that, they swam and hung out, enjoying the amenities at the Oasis.

They spent the day swimming and playing in the pool like kids. Then they'd gone across the street to the beach. Tracey had never felt so uninhibited and free.

Her skin was soft bronze from her time in the sun, but he was even darker. For a blond, the man had tanned nicely, and his skin had a natural bronze glow, people paid good money to replicate, without that burned orange look so many sported. Tracey had never been so sun-kissed before.

They'd had lunch by the water and talked for what seemed like hours, but he didn't act bored with her. There was more to Phoenix Tala than met the eye.

"You work with computers?" she'd asked.

"Sometimes, yes. I have many interests, but I am also the partial owner of a roadhouse in Blue Valley."

"Really? What's it called?"

"Serious Moonlight."

"I heard of that! That is so cool. Who are your partners?"

"My Pa—my friends," he'd replied, strangely. "How about you?"

"Well, so far, I've done very little. I went to college, had a couple of jobs I didn't like."

"Doesn't sound little to me. What is it you want to do with your life, beautiful?"

No one had ever asked her that before, but the answer seemed to matter. So, she told him the truth.

"Truth is, I've always wanted to open my own store. I want to design bags. My parents would hate it, of course, but I've been making them for a few friends and myself over the years. I made this one," she'd confessed.

Tracey had picked up the large tote bag she'd designed and decorated with a mosaic of fabric tiles into the shape of a wolf howling at the moon. It was one of several pieces she'd made for herself, and a favorite of hers. She loved wolves. There was just something so wild and free about the beautiful creatures.

"That is beautiful. I didn't know you were an artist."

His eyes had zeroed in on the gold-outlined wolf she'd created out of different fabrics, and she'd felt her cheeks go warm at his praise.

Surprising, dangerous, sexy man.

Her time spent with Phoenix had been wonderful. Only one thing marred it—the secrets he kept from her. She'd felt it, that distance he worked so hard to keep hidden. It hurt her knowing she shared bits of her soul with him, but he wasn't willing to do the same.

Coupled with the way the sexy hottie kept halting their physical relationship, to her unending frustration, Tracey was losing her mind. Of course, in the light of day, she understood she should appreciate his restraint.

Sex wasn't easy for Tracey. She'd only been with two men, and both had been longtime boyfriends before she'd slept with them. But appreciation was the farthest thing from her mind.

Her entire body was screaming for her to jump the big, sexy man. She was so done with the light petting and deep kisses. Tonight, she was determined to shake him up. With a little luck and some seduction, she was hoping to make this vacation fling into something more. But wanting to be with him, was not the same thing as being able to handle a one night stand with the man.

If only I was a casual sex kinda girl.

Wasn't his fault she was falling for him, or was it? He was intelligent and funny, and genuinely interested in her as far as she could tell. He seemed so tender and attentive to her needs. Being with him felt right. It felt huge. He was important. And call her crazy, but Tracey believed he felt the same way.

Was she wrong about his feelings? Only one way to find out. Finding the courage to ask was going to take everything she had, but Tracey had to know if the man she was falling for wanted her too.

Tonight, Phoenix was going to take her for a ride on his Harley. Tracey was nervous and excited. She'd always fantasized about riding behind a big sexy ass man on a motorcycle and now was her chance. She was more than ready. She'd had enough of stuffy and stodgy in her life.

No, thank you.

Tracey wanted wild and free and fun. Phoenix was all that, and so much more. The man with the aquamarine eyes was surprisingly deep. She was curious about him, what made him tick, what he liked, what he saw in her.

She loved the way he watched her. Like she was something worth seeing. Oh, and the way he was always touching her made the butterflies in her stomach turn into turbo jets.

She'd made one phone call to Rosa in all that time. The woman seemed so happy to hear from her, but when she'd asked about her parents, it was more of the same. The Donners were angry she didn't make their party, and her mother expressed said anger by leaving their Fairfield mansion and charting a yacht for the remainder of the season.

Guess you really miss me, Mother.

She tried not to let the sting hurt her. Her parents had chosen their lives, and now it was time for their daughter to do the same. And Tracey Donner was determined to have a life of her choosing.

It was fast, for sure, only a few days since she'd first bumped into him, but Tracey was positive Phoenix was going to be part of her life. She felt things she'd never imagined with the man. The phone rang, and she landed belly first on the bed to grab it.

"Hello?" she said breathlessly.

"Hey, beautiful. Look, I am heading out to gas up the bike, but I'll be back in a few minutes. You almost ready?" Phoenix asked, and she could almost see his panty-melting grin through the line.

It gave her chills. Her heart seemed to want to beat out of its cavity whenever he came near her.

"Perfect. Yeah, I'll probably need about fifteen or twenty minutes," she guessed.

"You got 'em, beautiful. I'll come to your door to get you when I'm finished."

"Alright. See you soon," she replied, hanging up and gasping.

God, he was so romantic. Always walking her to and from her door. Those first worries she had about him being out of her league seemed to lessen every day. He made her feel cared for, protected, and desired.

That afternoon, a tall, skinny, bikini-clad woman had tossed a frisbee in the direction of the blanket she was sharing with Phoenix, and Tracey's stomach had clenched. The woman was clearly flirting, but he didn't even blink. He just caught the bit of plastic before it could collide with Tracey's face and tossed it back straightaway.

Sexy, hot man.

Tracey could never compete with the model skinny woman, but with him, there did not seem to be a competition. Sure, she was all curves and chub, while the other woman was lithe and lean, but Phoenix seemed to prefer her.

The way he looked at Tracey made her blood boil. Another reason she was being extra careful with her appearance tonight. She wanted to give him her very best efforts. He was more than worth it, and so was she.

Tracey left her hair down, the way he liked it, and she slipped on another sundress she'd bought at one of the boardwalk stores. It had purple flowers on it and hugged her curves just right. She applied dark mascara with smokey eyeliner to her jade eyes, bringing out the creamy green color, and she added a tinted cherry red lip gloss to her lips.

Tracey worried her lower lips as she slipped a pair of slinky boy shorts beneath her dress. The undergarment was barely there, but it held her in and would hide her butt while she rode on the back of his bike.

She finished the look with a pair of comfortable flats. She felt good about herself in this outfit. Young and pretty. Flirty, too.

Outfit complete, she waited impatiently for seven to roll around. She had a few minutes left until he got back and decided to wait by the rooftop pool.

It was so pretty up there, and the view of the ocean was incomparable. Tracey exited her room, grabbing her bag and key. She wasn't paying attention to where she was walking when she tripped over something hard and furry.

"Ooof," she grunted as her knees collided with the slip-proof floor tiles.

Before the familiar feeling of humiliation at her own clumsiness could rise, Tracey blinked at the object that had tripped her.

"Tracey! Are you okay?" she heard someone call her name, but it was too late.

"Excuse me, I—" Tracey faltered, eyes glued to the enormous striped beast in front of her, she scrambled back, covering her mouth with her hand.

"Oh my God! It's a *tttiiiigggerrr!*"

She screamed, right before she passed out.

CHAPTER FOURTEEN

DIRE WOLF MATES

"I'm sorry! I didn't mean to do it!"

Dean Jr. wailed as he clung to his mother's knees, naked as the day he was born. Phoenix patted the cub on his head, pacing as the doctors looked his mate over.

"I know, baby. It's okay. The nice lady will wake up real soon," Violet Romero, the cub's mother, cooed in a pleasing voice.

Unfortunately, the boy's father, Dean Romero, Neta of the Island Stripe Pride, was not as easily appeased. He growled at Phoenix with the force of his beast, irritating the fuck out of his inner Dire Wolf.

"A human? You brought a *human* here? What the *fudge*, man," he spat the non-curse word with as much ferocity as if he'd dropped the f-bomb in front of his son.

"I am sorry. I expected to have told her by now. NO disrespect intended, Mr. Romero. And, yes, Tracey is a normal, just as your Nari once was."

Phoenix tried reasoning with the man. After all, Violet was a human before she'd been claimed by the Tiger king.

"That is irrelevant. She could out us all, man. There are laws for a reason," Dean retorted.

"She is my mate, Neta. And I am not of your Pride. Please, do not try to use your Alpha voice on me. It just pisses my Wolf off."

Phoenix spoke in an even voice, trying hard to keep control of his beast. It happened now and again where a Shifter would try to challenge his prehistoric monster of a creature. Usually, the result was a gory mess of epic proportions. He really, really did not want to go there.

"Sorry. I am protective of my family, and the woman startled my cub," Dean hissed, running a hand over his face. "Look, I've heard of your kind. Dire Wolves are tough, secret creatures and my Tiger can feel your dominance. It is making me anxious. Truly, I have no quarrel with you. I have enough to keep me busy with my Pride and my family," he explained.

"I get that. NO worries. I am not here to challenge you. I was just trying to take it slow," Phoenix explained, cursing himself ten times the fool for the bad way he'd handled this whole thing.

His animal had chosen her the moment he saw her. The Fates had brought them together, yes, but it was his human side falling in love with the beautiful woman. More and more with every second that passed.

"So, she is yours?" The Tiger king asked.

Phoenix nodded. He applauded the man's efforts to rein in his own dominant as fuck cat. It was not easy, being a monster.

"Yes," he said, his voice full of his Dire Wolf as he gazed upon Tracey's still unconscious form, where he placed her on her bed.

The animal was not fucking happy. Not at all. His beast snarled and scratched inside of him, but he kept his skin. Phoenix refused to allow his Wolf to master him. After all, the child was not to blame, and Dean had a point. He should have explained things to her as soon as he knew she was his.

Fucking hell.

"Dean, take it easy. Our cub is fine, and she is his mate. Naturally, he is trying to take things slowly," Violet said to her husband. "I'm going to take Junior back to our room for a bath to get him settled down. Good luck, Phoenix. I hope for the best," she replied kindly.

She kissed her mate on the cheek and offered Phoenix a small smile. The cub turned his big eyes on him, and his Wolf relaxed, allowing him to smile for the child.

He had no quarrels with cubs. The boy was just doing what boys did. Besides, this rooftop was his playground. A Shifter-only floor at the hotel, where the rest of the human guests were off-limits.

"I am sorry, little one, if my mate scared you." Phoenix told the cub in a gentle voice.

"S'okay mister. But she's gonna be really mad at you. Daddy buys Mama flowers when he makes her mad. Maybe you should try that?"

"Thanks for the advice, sport. I will take it into consideration."

He grinned at the tyke and nodded. It was sound advice, after all.

"Okay, we will leave you to it," Dean said, smiling at his boy. "Oh, and uh, I'll intercede with Rafe Maccon. I will explain the situation since he's already been apprised by the guards here," Dean said, surprising Phoenix with his generosity.

"I appreciate it, Neta."

Phoenix bowed his head slightly in reverence to the man's position. His Dire Wolf would not allow him to submit to anyone but his own Alpha, but the beast was not interested in asserting his dominance at the moment.

No. He was far more concerned with how to approach the precarious situation he found himself in. The Pride doctor came out of the room, explaining she was fine, just in shock.

The moon was low in the sky and a thousand stars sparkled above them. It was beautiful, but nothing compared to his sweet mate. He watched as her chest rose and fell with every breath. The tempting little dress she wore revealed her petal soft skin and stirred him like no one else ever could.

Tracey moaned, creamy green eyes blinking slowly as she came to. A smile teased the corner of her bow of a mouth and Phoenix dropped a soft kiss there, unable to stop himself.

She was all things tempting and tasty. His own personal beauty. A sultry seductress who could bring him to his knees without even trying. And the incredible female did not even know it.

"Phoenix, what happened? How did I get back in my room?" Tracey asked, and sat up slowly.

He noticed the very moment she remembered. Fear and curiosity seemed to war within her. Eyes wide, she scrambled up and out of the bed.

"There was a tiger outside my room. I tripped over him. W-what? How? I think, uh, I'm losing my mind," she said and covered her eyes.

"Hey now, sweetheart, come here. Let me explain."

"Explain what? How I'm going crazy?" She shook her head, near hysterics.

He hated she was so upset. Knowing he was to blame didn't comfort him. But he was a man, a Dire Wolf, and he would do what he must in order to bring any degree of peace to his mate's mind. He took her hand and tugged her close, wrapping her in a tight embrace.

Her ready submission to his touch unnerved him. Fuck, she was so trusting and sweet. Generous with herself in ways he had never imagined possible.

"I'm so sorry, love. This is all my fault. I should have explained better."

"Explained? How can you explain my delusions?"

"Tracey, you are not delusional," he said, cupping her face gently in his hands.

"Phoenix?"

"What you saw was real, and it's all part of the secret I've been keeping from you."

"What? Are you part of some underground exotic pet ring or something?" she asked, confused.

"No, of course not. The cub you saw was a Tiger Shifter."

"A what?"

"A Shifter. Like a Werewolf, but different. This hotel is owned and operated by Shifters, and they specifically cater to families. This rooftop is supposed to be a haven for those families to be who they are naturally, without fear or consequence. When I told Marco to give you a room up here, it was because I knew the moment I saw you, you were mine."

"What are you talking about?"

Phoenix exhaled a breath and tried to find the right words. He was fucking this up.

"They were out of regular rooms, and I had to beg Marco to allow you to stay here. I told him I would tell you immediately what we were to each other, but I did not want you to run, Tracey. I waited. It was a mistake, and I am very sorry," he told her.

"You aren't making any sense, Phoenix."

"*I* am a *Shifter,* Tracey."

"What? You're a Tiger?"

"Huh? No. I'm a Wolf. A Dire Wolf, actually, and you are my fated mate. Supernaturals exist in the world, under the radar of the human world. We have since the beginning of time," he explained.

"Are you making fun of me?" she asked in a small voice, and he hated he made her doubt herself.

"Never," he told her earnestly. "Shifters and other supernaturals are very real. Part of our connection to the universe is an understanding with the Fates, who we believe have selected our mates before our births. You are my fated mate, Tracey Donner. I knew it the second I saw you."

"You're saying impossible things," she whispered, tears welling in her beautiful eyes.

Fuck. He looked at her for the first time tonight and was stunned. Tracey was a knockout anyway, but tonight she'd put more effort into her appearance. The smoky accents around her eyes made their color so much more intense. She was so beautiful, he could hardly breathe.

"No. Not impossible, beautiful," he told her, cupping his hand around her neck. Thank fuck, she did not flinch from him.

"I should have told you right away. But I wanted to wait until you got to know me better."

"Phoenix, I confess I thought you were too good to be true since day one," she began, and this time, she did pull away from him. "Now it makes sense. You're delusional, too!"

"No! No, I'm not delusional, and neither are you," he growled impatiently.

Shit.

"Great. Just great. You're the first guy I've considered sleeping with in like a year and you're batshit crazy. I think I liked it better when I thought you were a male prostitute," Tracey muttered and shook her head, wiping the stray tears that rolled down her cheeks.

"I never should have left Fairfield. My mother was right, I'm a mess. I have to go."

"Tracey! Wait! I will prove it to you."

"You know, I poured my heart out to you. How could you do this?"

"Do what? I am just trying to talk to you," he tried again, but her mixed emotions and reactions were wreaking havoc with him.

Her myriad of feelings was egging his Wolf on to a near fucking panic. And that was so not good. The beast was wild to calm her down, to do anything to make her feel better.

"You don't have to pull this kind of stunt to get me to leave you alone. Making fun of me is not okay," she replied, and her misery was so clear it gutted him.

"What are you talking about? I don't want you to leave me alone, Tracey. I can't live without you!" He roared.

Shit.

He was really losing it. Fear, unlike anything he ever felt, gripped him as she walked away. He could not let her go. Not until he got her to listen! That he caused her fear and pain was nauseating. Phoenix would never hurt her.

Fucking hell.

He would chew off his own paw before he did that. But it looked like he had without trying. He wanted to hunt down every single person in her life who made her doubt herself.

All of those ingrates who'd savaged her pride and esteem that she would believe herself unworthy of his affection or attentions. Those people did not deserve to know her. But what now? She thought he was playing games.

Fuck. Fuck. FUCK!

"Wait!"

"What? What is it you want? To make up some more crazy stories?" She turned and yelled back, causing his own eyes to widen and lips to quirk.

Holy shit.

His Wolf growled appreciatively when he saw what was really in her eyes. Tracey wasn't afraid of him. His mate was royally fucking pissed.

Joy spread through him like wildfire at the prospect of his sexy little mate being madder than fuck at him. Her pain would eat him alive, but her anger? Well, that he could deal with.

"Want to know what I want?" he growled, stalking her until her back was up against the railing overlooking the sand.

"Yes. What do you want?" she asked, eyes flashing in the moonlight and chest heaving.

Fuck.

His dick was being strangled by the jeans he had on. He'd dressed for a ride, and was walking languidly to get her, trying to give her time to finish dressing.

He'd heard her screaming and cursed himself for wasting time, daydreaming about the night to come and what he had planned for them, when her panic slammed into him. He'd climbed the stairs three at a time and found her on the floor and the cub in tears.

Fucking denim had no give, and he was ready to burst just from being near her. He backed her up till she was stuck between him and the guardrail.

Phoenix slammed his hands down on either side of her, noting her sharp intake of breath and the heady scent of her lust that filled his nostrils. It was better than any other scent or drug he could ever have imagined. She was fucking dynamite—and like it or not she was his.

"What I want is you, Tracey. Only you," he growled, making sure she saw his Dire Wolf shining out through his gaze before claiming her mouth in a kiss neither of them would ever forget.

Mine.

His Dire Wolf howled in that metaphysical plane where he dwelled, waiting for Phoenix to call him forward. The sound pierced his eardrums till he thought he would never hear another thing in reality.

"Wait a minute," she grunted, pushing against his chest.

Phoenix loosened his hold. It would always be her choice to give him access to her body or not. He would never force any woman, much less his mate. Her needs and desires were everything to him.

"You said I'm yours. Does that mean you're mine?" she asked, and he nodded.

"This isn't just some game to you?"

"No games, Tracey. My Wolf has already bonded to you. We pick one, one mate, and I knew the moment I saw you what you were to me."

Watching her closely, he waited for her to decide, satisfaction humming through him as her eyes lit up like fire. Holy fuck, her creamy jade eyes seemed circled with orange red flames, and he growled deep in his chest. She was breathtaking.

One minute, she was watching him with those hypnotizing eyes, the next, Tracey grabbed the collar of his t-shirt and tugged him back down to her welcoming mouth. Tracey moaned and wrapped her arms tight around his neck, giving as good as she got, and Phoenix knew it would be okay.

Mine.

Thank fuck.

CHAPTER FIFTEEN

DIRE WOLF MATES

What am I doing?

She moaned as Phoenix slipped his tongue past her lips and devoured her in a kiss so hot, it turned her knees to jelly.

Seems clear enough, Tracey. You are being kissed stupid by a man who claims to be part animal.

Tracey knew she should stop him, and she would. In just another minute. Tangling her tongue with Phoenix's beneath the light of an almost full moon with the August breeze wafting off the Atlantic to tease and tickle her senses was like the culmination of every fantasy she'd ever had.

Makes sense if you think about it. The man is inhumanly fast and strong. Growly, too.

Wonderful! She was starting to believe all the crazy! Heck, was this even happening at all? Maybe she was still unconscious?

That made much more sense to her than thinking this gorgeous, giant, sexy hunk of hotness was actually devouring her mouth like she was air, and he needed her to survive. Things like that simply didn't happen to her. And yet. Here she was.

Tracey moaned as his hands traveled from her face down her shoulders to her waist, then hips. He didn't seem to mind the softness of her frame, the extra packaging on her ass and thighs as he squeezed and fondled her with exquisite care. Her panties were damp, and her breasts swelled with need under his careful ministrations.

Phoenix felt so good pressed up against her. Untamed and dangerous. His body was so big and warm. His stance was a heady combination of protective and possessive. She'd never felt so small and cherished as she did in his arms.

"Want you so bad," he growled, nipping her chin gently with his teeth and running his tongue along her jaw and neck.

Fuck me. That feels good.

"Mine," he growled, and the roughly whispered possessive verbiage sent spikes of desire shooting through her veins.

"Get a room!"

Phoenix broke the kiss, turning to growl at whoever yelled the embarrassing yet accurate suggestion. She pushed against him, and he stepped back, turning to face her immediately.

"Shit. I got carried away. Are you alright?" Phoenix asked.

Tracey nodded, but the truth was, no. She wasn't alright. Not in the least. Her heart was beating like a drum. She'd seen things that night that had her head spinning. The least of which was not the fact that two seconds ago she was practically having sex in public!

"Tracey, please look at me."

"So, you're saying you are like the Tiger I saw—what did you call yourself—*a Shifter?*"

"Yes. Shifters are dual natured, we live with our animals as part of ourselves," he explained.

"Well, are you even human at all? How does this work? Can I see your Wolf?" she asked, trying to reconcile the world she knew with the one Phoenix had introduced her to.

He took her hand, and she accepted his readily. No matter what was about to happen, Tracey had to be honest, if only to herself. She liked him. More than that. She felt right with him.

It was as if Tracey was more herself with him than with any other person at any other time in her entire life. How was that for a revelation?

"Yes, let me explain. I am a man, but I am more. Shifters share their souls with another creature that exists on a separate plane while we wear our human skin."

"So, Shifters are part animal?"

"Yes, and no. Our animals are not the same kind you see in the zoo or that live in the wild. They are imbued with magic. A spirit animal, but not so much totem as real and physically manifestable."

"So, this is real. You are real. What were you saying about mates?"

"Yes. I am real. And so are my feelings for you. Mates are what you would call soulmates. A mate is the one person who completes both sides of a Shifter. Other supes have mates too, but I can only tell you how it is for me."

"And you are a Wolf."

"Yes, sort of. My animal is a prehistoric species of Wolf. A Dire Wolf. My beast is ancient, and he is sure you are ours."

"Holy shit."

"Yes. I guess you could say that." Phoenix grinned and squeezed her hand. "There are a lot of different things out there, love. More than I could tell you about or that either of us could imagine—"

"Should I be scared?"

"Of me? Never."

"Why?"

"One thing at a time, love," his voice dropped as he spoke.

"Wait, did you say Dire Wolf? Like in that show?"

"Sort of," he replied. "Dire Wolves are prehistoric versions of the animals that roam so few and far between in the world today. Why are you grinning?"

"It's just, you're so tall and golden. Like your hair and skin. I would've thought you were an eagle or something." She shrugged.

"You thought I was a bird?"

He feigned insult, and Tracey couldn't hold in her laugh. Good. That felt good.

"I'm sorry, I didn't mean it as an insult."

"And you're my Dire Wolf, right?" she asked with a grin, and he looked thoughtful for a moment.

"Wait one second," he replied and looked around as if to ensure they were alone before he unzipped and divested himself of his jeans.

Tracey's mouth went dry. With his clothes on, Phoenix Tala was the most devastatingly handsome man she'd ever seen. Without them, he was a golden god.

A look of concern passed across his handsome face, but something made him hold his tongue. He stepped back, and Tracey held his gaze. Then, suddenly, the most incredible thing happened.

She watched with rapt attention as his whole body hummed and glowed with pulsating power. A shimmery sheen of golden light surrounded him. She heard the crack and rip of what must have been tendons and bones shattering and re-knitting themselves, but it was too quick for her to be sure. Then poof, Phoenix was gone, replaced by an enormous buff-colored animal.

Tracey gasped and covered her mouth with her hands. The creature was huge, bigger than any Wolf she'd ever seen at the zoo. Even larger than the special bred Great Danes her father kept when she was just a little girl. Of course, she was never allowed to play with those animals. Never allowed to pet them.

Her fingers itched as she stared at the well-behaved Wolf, who was her Phoenix. The beast sat on his haunches, unmoving, completely unthreatening. Under that warm, golden-aquamarine stare, her heart resumed its natural pace.

Tracey felt safe in his presence. Even more so, she felt protected, and something else. Some other elusive emotion emanated from the stunning creature.

"Phoenix?" she whispered his name softly, and the Wolf stood up.

Reaching out with one hand tentatively, she closed her eyes, afraid for a split second she'd misjudged and would soon be missing an appendage. But instead of sharp teeth, she felt soft fur beneath her fingertips.

Phoenix's Wolf padded towards her slowly. A soft whine escaped his massive maw, and Tracey giggled. She gasped when his cold nose nuzzled her palm, then moved up her arm, stopping at her wrist then on to her shoulder, neck, and cheek.

"Okay. You are much better than any old eagle," Tracey relented as she ran her hands over his beautiful coat.

He was so big and powerful. She felt the muscles of his chest, and the warmth of his skin beneath the thick, cream colored fur.

Beautiful beast. Dangerous. Sexy. Mine.

Suddenly, her hands were skimming flesh. The Wolf had retreated, and Phoenix was there once more, standing in the cradle of her thighs wearing nothing at all. His body emanated heat, but still she shivered.

Not because she was cold, but because, for the first time in her life, Tracey felt desired. His lusty gaze fell on her lips, and she tensed, ready for him to stake his claim.

"Come on, beautiful. Let's go before I lose my mind," he growled.

"But where are we going?" she asked as he tugged on his jeans.

"I promised you a ride. And I don't want to rush you, Tracey," he murmured, stealing a kiss before he shrugged his shirt on.

Tracey licked her lips. Yes, she wanted to go for a ride on his Harley, but that was not all she wanted. Was it? The question was, was she ready to do this? To run off with a Wolf biker and to hell with her old life.

Hell. Fucking. Yeah.

CHAPTER SIXTEEN

DIRE WOLF MATES

"Are you okay?" Phoenix asked, his voice deep and husky.

"Uh huh," she replied, her voice a husky whisper in his ear.

"You sure?"

"Yes."

"Squeeze your legs tighter around my hips. Like that," he growled, unable to hide the Wolf.

"Okay," she whispered breathlessly in his ear.

"Is that alright?"

"Yes. It feels good."

"Good."

Next, Phoenix gunned the engine of the powerful machine between his legs. He and his Pack mates had added custom improvements to their bikes to support their massive weights, and the increased speeds they preferred. Not that he would speed with his mate riding behind him.

Her safety was tantamount to all else. His Wolf growled softly in his chest. The beast still preening that she'd approved of him. It had been touch and go for a moment back then. But she was brave, his mate. Strong and courageous.

Damn, she was sexy, calling to his beast with all the seductive force of a siren's song. Phoenix wanted nothing more than to sink into her wet heat, but he had other plans for wooing his mate first. And it started here and now, on his bike on a strip of sand behind the hotels and streets of Maccon City.

The docks and rocky shores of the intracoastal waterway were deserted at this time of night. Good thing. He was about to show his sweet Tracey how to ride.

"What if I fall off?"

She squeaked when he gunned the powerful engine and held his waist tighter. He did it again just to feel her squeeze him with her thighs. Okay, he was a jerk sometimes, but he never said he wasn't. This woman made him want things he'd never dreamed of.

He wanted her. All of her. The good, the bad, the beautiful, and the gritty. She was so damned important, did she even know it? If not, it was his job to show her.

"I got you. I won't let anything bad happen to you, beautiful. Not while I live and breathe."

"You swear?"

"I swear. You trust me?"

"Yes. I know it's dumb, but I trust you more than anyone, Phoenix."

That single admission meant more to Phoenix than a thousand promises anyone else had or could have ever made to him. Tracey Donner was the best damn woman he'd ever seen, and he knew in his heart, his soul, and his beast, that she was the only one for him.

"Hold on to me, beautiful."

She did, and satisfaction rumbled through him. Phoenix loosed a short howl, then he took off. Speeding along the tightly packed rocky sand, Phoenix revved the engine and headed for the surf. Grinning madly while Tracey squealed with glee, the tires made the surf spray up to wet the two of them, but it was worth it.

Hearing her exuberance, the sheer joy flowing through her as they raced up and down the small strip, was worth the wet boots and jeans and a hell of a lot more. Happiness coursed through his veins, as he rolled to a stop a few feet from where they'd dropped his bedroll and backpack with some things he'd brought with him.

Marco had assured him this place would be empty, but he used his Shifter senses, anyway. Needed to make certain they were alone. His Wolf would tolerate no intrusions.

He wanted his mate. Needed her now. Alone.

Mine.

"That was incredible," Tracey said, still grinning.

Her lips were still red from the gloss she wore earlier or from biting them, he wasn't sure. So soft and sweet, like cherries and sin. He was dying for a taste.

The mood changed with the next breeze, and the earlier playfulness they shared receded. The moon was bright, an inch closer to full, and he could feel it pulling the tide and calling to his beast.

But he was not running tonight. Oh no. Tonight was not for fur. It was for skin. His and hers. Theirs.

"Phoenix," she whispered his name on a soft exhale, sending shivers down his spine.

He felt like a boy again. Young and green and desperate for a stolen kiss or a secret moment with his favorite girl. No doubt about it, Tracey made everything new and sweet, and so damn sexy.

Shit.

If he was not careful, this would be over before it began. He was trembling with need, dick pulsating in his pants, eager to burst. She was so damn potent. Her inner beauty called to him like nothing ever had.

Phoenix was falling more each second. Even now, the Dire Wolf demanded he claim her with his bite. He struggled with the creature, trying hard to rein in his beast. He needed to be gentle. To treat her tenderly. But fuck, was it hard.

"Uh uh," she whispered, pulling her mouth away from his. "I want all of you, Phoenix. Don't you dare hold back on me now."

"Mine," he growled, and claimed her mouth once more.

He was clumsy and unpracticed in his attempts to peel her clothes off, but she helped him. Unshy and surprisingly in control as she slid the tight dress down her hips and silky thighs.

Standing proud and bare breasted, with a sexy pair of hip hugging boy shorts on, Tracey appeared before him like a warrior goddess. His mouth went dry, cock straining in his wet jeans, and Phoenix's growl rose uncontrollably in his chest.

"You said I was your mate," she began.

"Yessss," he replied, voice thick with his Wolf.

"What does that mean?"

"I want to claim you with my bite. The Wolf needs to."

"Claim me?"

"Yes, I want you to be mine. My woman. My mate. My partner. Forever, sweet Tracey. There are no take backs for me if we do this. I will be bound to you for eternity."

"Forever might be long enough," she whispered, pulling those sexy little shorts off and revealing her entire beautiful self to him.

"Fuck, woman, you are killing me."

"Will it hurt?" she asked as she took a small step towards him.

"I'll take care of you first, beautiful."

"Alright then," she said, waiting, but he was frozen. Was this real? Did she really want to be his?

"Well? Are you going to claim me or not?"

"Fuck yessssss," Phoenix snarled.

His chest was heaving as she approached him slowly and carefully. Her face was all seriousness and gravity. Tracey stopped with only a hair's breadth between them.

"I want you to claim me, Phoenix. Tonight, I want to become yours, and I want you to be mine."

"Then I will, Tracey, tonight under the moon and stars, with the Fates blessing, I'm gonna make love to you. I'll give you my mating bite. It will tie us together in a bond no human or supernatural can ever break. We will be together, Tracey, you and I, a family, until the sun burns out in the sky or maybe even longer."

Phoenix stopped talking and waited. It was the hardest thing he ever had to do. Everything inside him said don't wait, claim her, kiss her, make love to her until she was screaming, begging for his bite. But she deserved so much more than that, and he refused to manipulate her. Finally, she lifted those creamy jade eyes to his.

"I want that too. No more waiting."

"No more waiting," he agreed.

Then she touched him, and the leash he had on his control broke with an audible snap.

Mine.

CHAPTER SEVENTEEN

DIRE WOLF MATES

Tracey was no virgin, but the way Phoenix was staring at her brought a rosy blush to her skin deeper than any other time she'd ever been naked in front of a man.

Maybe it was because he was so very handsome. Or maybe it was because they were technically in public, though this section seemed to be completely deserted.

Nah. It's because of him.

She felt the truth of that sentiment down to her toes. Phoenix loomed over her for a moment, tearing his clothes off in a whirl of movement that any other time would have made her head spin. But she was too caught up in the acres of tight, bronzed skin and the rippling muscles revealed to her.

Holy moly.

Her sexy Dire Wolf mate was incredible. And yes, he was hers. Had said so himself. She wasn't sure when she'd stopped believing in magic. Sometime when she was too young to have had such doubts.

Between fat camps and her parents' social engagements, Tracey had lost that naïve trust in all things fantastical every child should have. But she had it back now. In spades. He had done that.

Phoenix had restored her faith in magic. That same magic filled the very air she breathed. She felt it dance along her nerve endings, especially when she was kissing Phoenix.

Oh my.

The man sure could kiss. Her sex throbbed with need as he teased her senses with his expert caresses and multi-talented lips and tongue. Those torturously slow touches continued until she was mindless, aching, and desperate, all but begging him to give her what she needed. And all she needed was him.

"Good, mate. Want you to burn for me," he growled into her ear, sending her spiraling into ecstasy with the slightest of touches.

Mate. The word had sounded foreign to her ears when he'd first whispered it to her. Now she felt its rightness. It was like her mind, heart, body, and soul knew the meaning and wholeheartedly accepted it, accepted him.

Yes. She wanted him to claim her. To make her his in every way. Hell, she was impatient, flexing her hips in a silent plea for him to tend her where she wanted him most. But the big, frustrating, but oh-so-sexy man would not be rushed.

His mouth closed over one throbbing breast, teeth tugging on her tight nipple, and Tracey moaned aloud. Moisture dripped down her thighs, her sex readying itself for his invasion. She could feel the hot, hard, and heavy press of his magnificently thick and long cock on her thigh.

Fuck. So good.

She could hardly wait to have him deep inside her. Knew without a doubt he would not leave her wanting. Phoenix would take care of her needs. Every single one of them.

Still, he was being damned obstinate about it. She panted as he moved to her other breast, sucking her nipple while his blunt fingers edged closer and closer to her aching pussy. Phoenix seemed satisfied to take his time, but Tracey was dying.

"Please," she whimpered as one thick digit traced her nether lips, only to pull away before he really touched her.

Her hands wound in his thick, blond locks, and she tried pushing him down her body, but he was immovable. Looking down, she was a smile teasing the corner of his lips.

Oh, so that's how it's gonna be.

Tracey growled a little like a Wolf herself, then pushed his shoulders, making him lift up so that she could reach between them. Once she held her prize, his eyes flashed to hers. The golden-aquamarine gaze of his beast glittered as she pumped his iron-hard shaft with her fist, tracing the pearl of precum that dripped from his slit.

"Tracey," he grunted.

"What?"

"Fuck, baby, you gotta stop that."

"Why?"

"Because I won't last a minute. Need you."

"Good. Then take me already, Wolf. Make me yours," she commanded.

With a deep, guttural growl, Phoenix pulled his hips out of her reach and slid down her body, draping her legs over his shoulders. Her sex quivered in anticipation. She'd never been good at this, but with Phoenix, she felt like a fucking goddess.

"Need to taste you," he grunted and without pause, closed his hot, wet mouth over her pussy in a searing kiss that tore a scream from her throat.

"Fuck, beautiful, you're delicious," he growled and drove his tongue into her again.

Licking her from her clit to her asshole and back again, Phoenix left no inch of her unexplored. A primal growl seemed to rise from his chest as he continued to devour her slick flesh.

She was completely undone. Her body wound tight, she grabbed his hair, holding on for dear life. Her man was pure magic, and he was eating her like she was ambrosia. Heat pulsed through her, and she felt the stirrings of something amazing about to happen.

Close. So close.

Finally, he pushed her over the edge, and Tracey came, gushing like an uncontrollable tide. Fierce, hot pleasure shot through her body, wave after wave of inexpressible feeling as her body flew into bliss. She was conscious of him, his beautiful mouth still lapping at her heat, but she was too raw to come down yet. She still needed.

As if he knew it—*like he could read her mind*—Phoenix reared up. His masculine growl filled the air as he spread her legs wide, baring her for his steady stare, his eyes filled with need and possession.

"S'beautiful, mate. Gonna make you come for me again. Want that? Want me to make this pussy mine?"

"Yes. Oh yes," she pleaded.

Phoenix palmed his thick cock, placing the mushroomed tip at her slick entrance. His long fingers grabbed her hips, and his gaze never left hers as he pushed himself inside.

One. Inch. At. A. Time.

And he did slowly—*so damned slow*—Tracey thought she would die before he filled her. Finally, his hips were flush against hers, and he stayed there for a beat, maybe two. Then the bastard withdrew.

"No!" She screamed, scratching at his shoulders.

"Easy, mate. I got what you need," he growled and lowered his hips again.

Over and over he drove into her, each time his cock stroked her inner walls just right, taking her to the brink of pleasure, but pulling out before she hit that pinnacle.

Fucking Wolf was a beast. Her tits bounced as he pumped harder, faster, and she envied him his teeth and claws. She wanted to claim him, to mark him sure as she wanted him to bite her flesh and declare her his to the whole damned world.

She'd never felt this wild drive to be possessed, but she wanted it now. Needed it.

"Phoenix," she moaned his name.

The fucker laughed. The deep, masculine sound was thick with his Wolf. He knew exactly what he was doing to her, and she was already plotting her revenge. Tracey was sure she could treat him to the same delicious torment.

Oh, the pleasure she would get in circling his broad-headed cock with her tongue. Licking the drop of precum she knew would seep from his slit. She would fondle his heavy balls, tease the sensitive skin there, while she lapped along the rim with the flat of her tongue.

Oh yeah.

She could do that. She would do that. Right after he made her come again.

"So hot. So sexy. Mine," he growled, and doubled his efforts.

Thrust, flex, withdraw, and repeat.

Fuck, Tracey couldn't think anymore. Both she and Phoenix were writhing against each other. His invasion deeper, heavier, faster, and harder as he pounded into her so damn good.

"So tight, love. You're squeezing me so good," he growled.

She wanted to speak, to say something about the magnificent stretching *oh so good burn* his cock was treating her to, but she was incapable at the moment. She needed more of that delicious friction, wanted more of him. Deeper, faster, harder. And just like that, he was moving again. No more playing. Phoenix's palms held her down gently by her wide hips and she retaliated by wrapping her legs tight around his waist.

In an out, in a dance old as time, he pumped, and she swiveled. Together, they moved in time until Tracey could hardly breathe. Just when she thought she couldn't go any higher, he pushed her to another level. She tasted the salt on his skin as she kissed everywhere she could reach.

Their moans and the sounds of skin slapping against skin filled her ears, drowning out even the ocean. And why shouldn't it? This was bigger, deeper, and more eternal than any sea.

Phoenix Tala was laying claim to her, and she, Tracey Donner, would be alone no more.

"Tracey," he growled, pumping his hips harder and deeper.

"Tracey."

He called her name again.

"Tracey!"

Once more and she was spiraling.

"Tracey. Mate," he snarled.

This time his mouth, full of fangs, flashed in her peripheral vision and her core heated, tightening around him, until she thought she'd burst into flames. Then, pain exploded in her shoulder, interrupting the burning pleasure pulsing in her very blood. The hurt lasted only a moment before her pleasure increased tenfold.

"Phoenix!" Tracey screamed his name, scratching at his shoulders.

Red hot flames consumed her, and she thought she saw them encircling their bodies, Phoenix's shocked gaze met hers as he released her flesh, roaring loudly as his movements turned jerky. She felt the force of his orgasm slamming into her. Warm hot jets of his cum filled her, sending another climax spurring through Tracey's body.

Eons later...or maybe just minutes...

Her body hummed with pleasure. Her heart was swollen with emotion. Shock at the beauty of the lights that still floated in the air, some kind of magical afterglow from their mating.

"Mate," Tracey sighed the word as she snuggled into the warm embrace of her mate and lover.

"You're magic, beautiful," he whispered.

Phoenix's big body curled around hers on the blanket he'd laid out for them, protecting them from the coarse sand. After he'd emptied himself inside of her, he'd pulled her on him, till she was practically using him as a mattress. A position she had no quarrel with.

Maybe a lifetime ago it would have bothered her, but she felt no shame or embarrassment. Tracey was all curves and thickness, but her mate seemed to love it. He could not stop touching her.

Now that he'd claimed her, she wondered if his desire would lessen. But she knew in an instant, their passion would only grow. It was like Tracey could see and hear inside his very heart.

"It's the matebond," he whispered, kissing her head and cupping her ass with his hand.

"Can we read each other's minds?" she wondered aloud.

"Not really, but maybe in time. It's more like we can feel each other's emotions."

Tracey breathed deep, and as incredible as it seemed, she dug within herself, amazed at the pulsing bond she felt between them.

"You love me," she said aloud in shock at the force of feeling that flowed into her from him.

"I love you," he replied, and she felt joy emanating from his admission.

Holy cow. Phoenix Tala loved her. He would protect her, would be her safe haven. And even more amazing, he liked her, too. She grinned and kissed his chest as happiness seemed to flow from him to her. It was unlike anything she'd ever felt. So pure and light, warm too.

Like magic. Like fate.

"It is fate. You are my destiny, Tracey, and I am yours."

The rightness of that sentiment poured through her along with all the feeling and thoughts he had in his mind. It was like a river of information, and Tracey wept at the beauty of it. She knew his heart, and it was time she trusted hers as well.

"I love you too," she confessed, leaning up to kiss his lips.

"Good. Come here," he growled and pressed his mouth to hers.

Heat pooled between her legs and Tracey moaned as he cupped her sex with his callused fingers.

"My turn," he growled.

CHAPTER EIGHTEEN

DIRE WOLF MATES

Phoenix's Dire Wolf growled contentedly once he had his woman back at the hotel, inside his bed. They'd dressed quickly when the rain had started, laughing as they went. He did not know what to make of the blast of gold fire that had encapsulated them when he claimed her, but fuck, it was amazing.

She was amazing. His beast insisted he get her warm and safe after their outdoor romps, and he had, first with a shower, then inside his bed. He was insatiable for the woman, and if she'd ever harbored any doubt about his attraction to her, Phoenix had laid that all to rest over the past few hours.

She stirred beside him, and his cock stood to attention again. Sexy woman did not know what she did to him with her little moans and groans. Her tanned skin glowed in the darkness of the room, and her delicious feminine scent, like sugar cookies and something else, was now mingled with the fur and spice of his Wolf.

He looked at the bite he'd given her on her shoulder, frowning at the hurt it had caused, even if only momentarily. Amazingly enough, she seemed to heal fast, which was astounding since he didn't think humans could heal that quickly.

Phoenix had sent a text to Derrick, explaining to his Alpha that he'd found his mate, and the man congratulated him. He could not wait for her to meet his Pack, but first, he wanted to take her on a trip. She'd planted the notion in his brain before they'd fallen asleep last night. And it was thoughts of ways to fulfill her desires that had woken him up.

"Will you take me to see the world, Phoenix? Just you and me and your bike?"

"Anything, my love. I would do anything for you."

And he would. That much was true. He'd already started planning, but first, they had to make one stop. She might not like it, but Phoenix believed in closure, and his sweet mate deserved some.

"Your thoughts are too loud," Tracey moaned, pressing her curvaceous backside against his cock as he spooned her from behind.

Phoenix hissed. Fuck, she was gorgeous.

"Mmm, you feel good, woman."

"Mmm, good. I want you to make me feel good, mate," she said, and fuck if he was not ready for the challenge.

Phoenix cupped her soft tits, squeezing them as he rocked his hips, sliding his cock between her slick folds. He kissed and nipped her neck and shoulders, loving the feel of her ripe ass cushioning his hips. He was a rutting beast for the woman. She called to his primal side, and there was nothing he would not do for her.

"Lift your ass up, beautiful. Like that," he growled, turning to kneel behind her as she lay down on her belly.

Tracey lifted her ass, spreading her legs for him and fuck, she was gorgeous. Her sex glistened, dripping with her arousal as he traced her crack with his thick fingertips, all the way till he reached her swollen nubbin.

"Need you," she moaned, pressing back and rubbing against his dick.

"Gonna make you crazy first," he growled.

Phoenix was so damned hot for her. He leaned forward and

plunged his tongue into her heated core, rubbing her clit with one hand, while he teased her forbidden hole with his other.

He felt her pussy quiver and tremble, and before she finished shouting his name, he covered her. Pushing deep inside her slick pussy as her orgasm started had Phoenix crossing his eyes with how good she felt.

Nothing else existed while he was buried in her sweet body. There were only the two of them. Tracey was everything good and beautiful and pure in this world, and he would do awful things to keep her safe, cherished, protected, and by his side.

"Love you, mate," he growled as ecstasy took hold.

He gritted his teeth, determined to keep her right there with him. But he didn't have to wait long. Her body was responsive, reacting to his as if she were made for him—and she was, he supposed.

"Phoenix!" she yelled his name, her walls tightening around him.

Her next release rocketed through to him, and fuck, he had no choice now. Hot jets of cum pulsed from his cock, filling her as he bucked into her mindlessly. He moved until he was empty, completely, and totally undone by what they had shared.

"You are part of me now, Tracey. The best part," he grunted, withdrawing so he could clean her and care for her.

Sweet, strong woman. My woman.

T*wo days later...*

Phoenix cleared his throat as he sat in the clinical greeting room in the Donner's home. He would've rather been sitting anywhere else in the world. Tracey had not been happy about this little detour, but he was determined she should get some closure for all her pain.

From what his mate had told him of her family, his justifiable anger on her behalf for the way she'd been treated by those who should've loved her most was not out of place. He understood her reasons for not wanting to visit the cold estate where she'd grown up.

But Tracey should have some of her own things before they embarked on their life together. She should be able to look the people she came from in the eye and let them know they did not break her. No other woman he'd ever known was as deserving of respect and love as this woman.

He would give her that. He would give her everything.

She'd tried calling her parents when they'd arrived at the posh manor, and she was waiting for them to video conference her back from the yacht where they were spending the rest of the season.

Meanwhile, she had some of her things to collect, and as for the rest, she had planned to have everything packed up and sent to the Pack house behind *Serious Moonlight*.

"Phoenix, this is Rosa."

His mate's face beamed as she returned to the sitting room with an older female in tow. The woman looked kind and genuinely happy to see Tracey if the fierce hug she gave her was any indication.

"Hello, Rosa. I'm Phoenix."

"Oh, my Tracey! He is a handsome one. Nice to meet you," she said, then turned back to his mate with unshed tears in her eyes.

"I am so glad to see you. Look at you! So carefree and happy. You look beautiful, *linda*," the woman cried.

Phoenix smiled, pleased to see someone who'd cared for his sweet mate while she'd been growing up in that cold and hostile home. Rosa released Tracey and his mate rushed to him. Her emotions were high, and her jade eyes sparkled with unshed tears.

"It is nice to meet you," he told the other woman and took her offered hand, bending down to kiss her cheek.

She had the same sugar cookie scent about her as Tracey and he paused a moment, wondering why that was.

"I see you," the woman whispered into his ear, a grin teasing the corner of her mouth.

Before he could question the odd statement, the laptop Tracey had set up on the coffee table beeped and soon Tracey's parents were there.

"Hello? Tracey? What is this about, young lady?"

Daniel Donner frowned into the camera, giving himself a double chin. Clearly, he was not a technology fan.

"Well, what is it? I see you came back with your tail between your legs after embarrassing us like that. Ha. See, I told you," Daniella Donner snapped.

She turned her heavily made-up face to her husband with a waspish expression that boiled Phoenix's blood. The couple looked nothing like his beautiful mate, and again, he could not reconcile their familial connection. Lucky for him, she was different from these cold, unfeeling people.

"See. She is back. Just like I knew she would be, Daniel."

"Wow," Tracey replied. "I was gone for days and that's how you talk to me. You don't even ask me how I am?" Tracey questioned, and his Dire Wolf growled.

She squeezed his hand, stilling his urge to close the laptop and disconnect from those two scowling faces.

"What is it you want, Tracey?" her father barked the question.

"Hi, Dad. Nice to see you, too," Tracey said to her father. "You know, Mom, I used to want to be like you when I was a child. Beautiful and poised, but now I know nothing I ever do will earn your favor."

"You could never be like me," his mate's mother returned nastily.

"Tracey, what your mother means is you simply don't have the constitution. Now, I suggest you come home and forget this whole mess—"

Phoenix could not believe his ears. These people were the worst. How horrible did someone have to be to treat their own child this way? His Wolf was pissed, but the beast understood she needed his support, not his anger. The animal stilled inside of him, waiting in case she needed him.

"Sir, Ma'am, I think you should both just quiet down and listen to your daughter—"

"Wait a second, who is that?" her mother screeched.

"Tracey! What is that strange man doing in my house?" her father demanded.

"Mom, Dad, this is Phoenix. He is with me," Tracey replied, and straightened her shoulders.

Phoenix moved to her side, offering her his strength and support lovingly and freely. He probably should have worn something other than worn denim and his leather cut, but they'd ridden up on his bike, and Phoenix believed in comfort above all. He'd even gotten her a pair of sexy as fuck jeans and a black leather vest fitted over a ripped up t-shirt with the *Serious Moonlight* logo on it.

"Mr. And Mrs. Donner," he growled, unable to keep the hostility out of his voice.

"Oh my God! Tracey! What are you wearing? You ran off with a biker?! This is just more embarrassment!" His mate's mother screeched.

"What does it matter if he rides a motorcycle, Mother? He makes me happy. I make him happy. And I didn't come back with my tail between my legs, I came back to tell you I am leaving home for good. I am going to be with Phoenix, and we are going to see the world," she told her parents, turning her head to flash him that thousand watt grin he loved.

His whole body responded to her happiness, vibrating with pride and need. He wanted to kiss her, hold her, tell her how brave she was to face these two horrible, uncaring people. It was obvious they were not the tender, doting parents she deserved, and the loss was theirs. Tracey was fucking wonderful. He would tell her that, too. As soon as they left this house, that felt colder than a cemetery to him and his beast.

"I forbid it," Daniel Donner yelled, wagging his pasty finger on the screen.

"The hell you do," Phoenix growled, the threat of someone forbidding his mate anything had the animal riled.

"You see how she really is? I told you, Daniel," Tracey's mother yelled, a look of poisonous triumph on her face.

"How can you ruin us this way?" her father asked.

"Dad, this is not about you. Try to understand."

"After everything I did for you. I tried to raise her correctly, Daniel, but look at the girl. She could never be the daughter we deserved," her waspish mother griped.

Phoenix could barely contain his growl. Tracey tried to reason, but her parents' vicious insults and demands would not be silenced. At least, not until Rosa stepped in.

"Enough!" Rosa said in a loud, clear voice that emanated with power.

"You will both stop this right now. Years I have watched you fail to rise to the honor of being her parents."

"Rosa, I don't think—" Tracey's father replied, but his sentence was cut off by Rosa's sharp hiss.

Good for Rosa.

Phoenix growled, in full agreement with the slight woman.

"Tell her the truth now."

Phoenix's jaw dropped as the older woman's façade faded away. No longer was she the Donner's housekeeper. Rosa was something else. Something that smelled distinctly like sugar cookies and Tracey. Her age lines receded, gray hair turned black, and those muddy brown eyes lightened to a creamy jade—much like his mate's.

"Rosa?" Tracey gasped, covering her mouth with both hands. Phoenix moved behind her, placing his large hands lightly on her shoulders.

"*Oh linda,* I am still your Rosa. Daniel and Daniella Donner, you were charged with raising this daughter of the *Doñas de fuera* until she could find her way. We had assumed you would treat her with love and dignity, but you have failed in this. Now, you owe her the truth," she announced.

"Rosa? What are you talking about?" Tracey asked, a hiccup in her voice told him how emotional she was feeling.

"Finally!" Daniella Donner screeched again. "I am not your mother. I never was. Your father here cheated on me! And you, you were the fruit of his misguided affair. To think I had to take you into my home and raise you. My husband's bastard! I never even wanted kids."

"What are you saying?" Tracey asked. She gasped again as tears fell from her eyes, and Phoenix squeezed her to him tightly.

"Tracey, it is true," Daniel said, and the insect cleared his throat. "I was young and foolish, and Thea was very beautiful—"

"Oh, please," Daniella hissed.

"Shut up, Daniella. Thea was beautiful and Rosa is right, we did a lousy job raising my daughter. Tracey, I am sorry if we failed you," the man said, and to Phoenix's preternatural hearing, he truly sounded remorseful.

"Tracey, there are things you need to know," Rosa said, turning to face his shivering mate.

"I can't," she said, shaking her head.

Phoenix wanted to pick her up and run out of there, but he knew something incredible was about to reveal itself. Tracey deserved to know her truth, and he would be right beside her to give support and anything else she might need.

"Hey, you got this, beautiful. I am staying right here with you, and I won't let anything harm you, I promise," he vowed.

"Okay. If you're with me, I can do this," she said, and her gaze flicked back to Rosa.

"You have found a good mate, Tracey," Rosa said approvingly. "Now, to begin, I suppose I should tell you that your father, Daniel, met my grandniece on a business trip. They had an affair, and she became pregnant. We of the *Doñas de fuera* have mixed our bloodlines with humans for thousands of years."

"But what does that mean?"

"Ah, I see. Well, the *Doñas de fuera* literal translation is *women of the outside*."

"Outside?" Tracey asked.

"Witches," Phoenix replied. he had heard tales of mysterious women but thought they had been driven from this world by that mad machine that was the Inquisition.

"I see your mate knows our history. And true, Torquemada's reign had almost destroyed us with the Inquisition, but we are a resistant breed. Not just Witch, *linda*. The *Doñas de fuera* have Fae blood," Rosa enlightened them.

"I'm a fairy?" Tracey blurted, and gods, he could not have loved her more.

"*Mmmm*, sort of. Your mother was just a quarter, making you a little less, but my dear, we are people of the arts. Your love of sewing and your creativity are blessings. I came to live with you to ensure you were being nurtured and treated well, just in case you developed powers of your own. I did all I could without directly interfering."

"Is that why you were always watching and waiting with cookies and tea? You were protecting me. Heck, you were always more mother to me than she ever was, Rosa."

"I tried my best to stay out of the most of it. This is not a kind world, *linda*, but you are a shining light amongst all the gloom. Your powers will be coming in faster now that you have met your mate. His Wolf will call to that wild side of you. Embrace it, my love. You will be better for it, I swear. I am so grateful I was here to see you find your feet. Your mother would have been proud—"

"What happened to her?"

"She passed away the night you were born. I am so sorry. I have a picture for you though, here," Rose said and removed a chain with a heart locket hanging from it from around her neck.

She handed it to Tracey, inside was the image of a woman with long blonde hair and the same green eyes staring back at her. On the other side of the image was a picture of a baby. It was Tracey.

"It is yours now," Rosa said.

Tracey gasped and handed the chain and locket to Phoenix, who fastened it around her neck while she bravely tried to stop crying.

"I always felt so out of place here. Now I know why," she whispered. "But I was so happy with you, Rosa."

"I have loved every minute I got to spend on this plane with you, but I have to return home to our realm. Like many Fae, the *Doñas de fuera* have retreated from this plane. But should you ever need me, just think of me and I will get the message," Rosa told her before hugging Tracey, then Phoenix.

"I am so proud of you, my Tracey. You and your mighty Dire Wolf mate will be blessed, I have foreseen it. He will be your champion now."

"I will. I swear it. I would do anything for her, Rosa. You have my word," Phoenix pledged.

"I know, Wolf. Like I said, I see you," she told him.

"Tracey?" her father called her name from the laptop, and his mate turned to face him after Rosa winked out of their plane of existence.

"I am not ready to discuss this with you. Not yet, and maybe not ever."

"I understand. All I can say is I am sorry," her father replied.

"I've left an address for my things to be forwarded. Rosa put it all in boxes already and a delivery company will be by in a few days. Goodbye."

Phoenix growled deep in his throat, closing the laptop before Tracey's stepmother's cruel words could reach his mate's ears. She was other, true, but her magic seemed to be tied to her love of art, and her innate beauty.

He couldn't wait to travel the path to finding out more about her supernatural nature at her side. His sweet Tracey. Beautiful mate. So full of surprises.

"You ready?" he asked.

"As I will ever be," she told him, closing the door on her past, ready to live in the now.

They left soon after, and he heaved a sigh of relief as Tracey snuggled up behind him on the massive Harley. He felt her wonder and curiosity, smiling to himself because he knew she would be fine. They had each other now.

"I love you. You know that, right?"

"You better," she returned and nipped his back with her blunt teeth.

"I do, mate. And I will prove it every damn day I get to live on this planet with you," he growled, and she beamed at him.

"I love you, too."

They sped off, eating up the miles, both their hearts beating in unison. Phoenix didn't think anything in the world could top the high of riding his Screamin' Eagle with his gorgeous mate clinging to his back.

It was pure fucking heaven.

EPILOGUE

DIRE WOLF MATES

Serious Moonlight was busy despite it being a Wednesday. He bypassed the roadhouse and parked his bike just outside the Pack House.

His Pack mates already knew they were coming, after a few days on the road, sightseeing, he wanted Tracey to meet everyone and have some downtime before he took her to visit South America, like she wanted. Gods, he loved that woman. Like nothing else in this world. She was everything to him.

He held open the door for her, greeted by a chorus of shouts as his Pack came forward one at a time. She squeaked when Derrick grabbed her for a hug, followed by a very pregnant Lucy.

"I am so happy to meet you," the Alpha fem said, lip trembling. She was so emotional these days.

"Thank you. I'm happy to meet you, too."

And so on, she went down the line, taking the claps to her shoulders, and quick hugs like a champ. Dire Wolves were touchy feely things, after all.

Tracey's hand gripped his, and he smiled down at his beautiful mate's pretty little head while she watched curiously as one of their biggest members lifted the sacred chest with his magicked ink and bamboo quills from their special spot on the shelf.

"Thor is favored by the gods. The old graybeard in our first MC called him that," Weylin explained.

"What does it mean?" she whispered.

"Well," Lucy interrupted, rubbing her protruding belly. "It means he's gonna close his eyes and get a vision of your future with this ol' puppy doggy right here, then he's gonna ink it on his back."

"Really?" Thor muttered from across the room. But the big man wasn't annoyed. Not really.

"A tattoo?" Tracey gasped.

"Yep. Don't worry. He does fine work," Sheila, the only female Dire Wolf in the Pack, inserted.

"'Sup, Phoenix?" Leo, her Lion mate, asked.

"Good to see you, bro. Tracey, that's Leo, he's Sheila's mate and a cop."

"You're a Dire Wolf, too?" she asked.

"What? No way. I am a far superior species of Shifter," he told her with a wink. "I am a Lion. Ooof!"

Sheila elbowed him right in the gut, rolling her eyes at the man.

"Superior, my ass," she muttered.

"I was just kidding," he wheezed, and Tracey snorted a laugh.

"OMG! She snorts. How fucking cute are you?" Lucy gushed, hugging her again.

"Okay, um, there, there," Tracey replied, uncertainty in her voice.

"I got this," Derrick said, and lifted his mate up, snuggling her on the couch to Phoenix's, and his mate's, relief.

Phoenix looked around at the lot of them, his Pack. There were four mated pairs with him and Tracey now. The rest were still searching. And with any luck, they would find their Fate soon enough.

Phoenix felt the ties that bound them warm and tighten. Yes, he was going to take Tracey on a road trip, but they would be back. After all, this was their Pack.

"This is home," Tracey whispered, looking up at him with stars in her creamy jade depths.

She understood his heart's desires even before he voiced them, and though he understood it was fast, too fast for *normals* but not for his mate who was something *other*—he loved her so much it hurt. A good kind of hurt. The kind that told him he was alive and one lucky sonofabitch.

"Kneel."

Thor's voice had that deep, monosyllabic tone that told everyone there he was in the middle of his vision. Phoenix's pulse raced. This was a defining moment in his history. An event he'd envisioned for a very long time.

Dire Wolves' lifespans were longer than normal Shifters, and as such, his mate's would increase and match his, drawing on their bond to give her longevity.

"Tonight, I gift you with your claiming tattoo. Wear it proudly, my Dire Wolf brother," Thor growled, eyes glowing in the dimly lit room.

Silence fell across the crowd. Phoenix heard nothing except the sound of Tracey's heartbeat and the soft flow of her tears as he turned away from Thor. His mate watched as the male etched their future into Phoenix's back.

Sheila, Ariella, and Lucy bracketed her on either side, the three had become quick friends, and he hoped Tracey would form a bond with them, as well. She was good like that. Open and kind, she deserved to have real friends, sisters of the heart.

How could they resist her? He certainly hadn't been able to. His mate was so brave, watching each slice Thor made across his skin.

"There's so much blood," she whispered.

"He isn't hurting him, sweetie," Sheila whispered.

"He's a tough old dog," Lucy seconded.

Phoenix found her with his eyes, and her tears stilled. So much courage and pride shone on her face. She straightened her back, offering him bravery in the face of one of their most sacred rituals.

The bamboo quills cut deep, deeper than any other tattoo needle would have during a typical inking. It had to be that way to really scar the skin, otherwise his supernatural abilities would heal him far too quickly. Combined with the magicked ink, the tattoo would last as long as he and their love did.

Eternity.

His Dire Wolf howled inside of him. The ceremony was rigorous and long. Hours later, Thor dropped the last quill onto the floor, next to the other dozen he'd used, and slumped over on his side. Derrick kneeled down, offering Phoenix a hand while Leo and Brock lifted the Enforcer and brought him to his room to recover.

"Congrats, bro," the Pack Alpha said.

"Thank you, Alpha. What is it?" Phoenix's eyes flashed to Tracey's, unable to wait.

His mate had stayed the entire time, waiting patiently while his claiming tattoo was etched onto his skin. He had others, of course, but they were small compared to the massive piece Thor had just given him, guided by the gods themselves.

Phoenix was aware of Tracey walking behind him. Derrick had already moved away, giving them space. The Alpha helped Lucy sit down on the couch. Phoenix had a moment of concern for Thor, but he knew he was in good hands. The Wolf was always exhausted after channeling the gods during one of these rituals. He sucked in a breath, waiting for Tracey's reaction as he felt her slide to her knees.

"Oh, Phoenix," she whispered, and the tremble in her voice rocked him to his soul.

"What? What is it, love?"

"It's beautiful."

The others moved to see the image too, but he didn't care what they thought. Only Tracey's feelings mattered.

As it should be, his Wolf pushed the thought at him, and he accepted it.

The beast was right. Her emotions were the only ones that meant anything to him.

"Tell me."

"It's your Wolf, baying at the full moon and a woman—"

"Not a woman, you," he corrected.

"Yes," she said, and he heard the smile in her voice. "*Me.* I'm standing beside you, a baby in my arms. We're shrouded in gold lights. There are spirals that look like roads on a map, a cross, a needle, the moon, the sun, and waves. It's like a roadmap of our life together. Ruins in the background, a skyscraper on the left, a field of daisies in the distance—but I've never seen these things or places before."

Phoenix turned and pulled her to him. His heart was so full, it damn near burst. Gods, he loved her so much. She was so beautiful, heart, mind, body, and soul.

"We'll go together, mate. We will see the world beside one another. We will make a family. We will be each other's home."

"And when you're done, y'all will come back here where you belong. You're Pack now, Tracey Donner," Lucy butted in, and Phoenix felt his mate's happiness surging through him as if it was his own.

"Enough, mate. Let's leave these two alone," Derrick growled and picked his woman up and out of the room.

"Maybe she doesn't want to be alone with him," Lucy answered her husband.

"Yeah, I do. Every night from now until the day I die," Tracey whispered as she tilted her head for a kiss.

"Forever," Phoenix growled, claiming her lips with all the love he had for her in his soul.

He'd left the Pack House less than a week ago, and he was back now with his mate in tow, even if only for a little while. But they would be back. Roaming was fun for a little while, but this was where they would grow their roots.

"Forever sounds good, but what is time anyway, when you have your mate?" Tracey asked, grinning. She'd learned fast that they could communicate through their *matebond*. That little gift was not true telepathy, but they could send feelings and emotions, sometimes messages too, all without opening their mouths.

"Some might experience forever in a night."

"Is that so? Wanna test that theory?" he asked, kissing her sweet mouth.

"Hell yeah," she asserted. "I felt that way with you that first hot night we met. Like I'd known you forever, Phoenix Tala."

"Me too, mate. Me too."

"I love you."

Phoenix exhaled, his entire body trembling with joy, need, and gratitude. He was one lucky Dire Wolf.

To have found his kick ass fated mate and to have earned her love was the greatest accomplishment of his life. He would cherish her.

Always.

"I love you too, Tracey Donner."

Then he lifted her up, carrying her to his old bedroom, and he showed her.

Again and again.

Bodies surging together, entwined in that ancient communion of flesh and souls, Phoenix and Tracey loved each other till the sun came up. They climbed higher with each coming together, exploding into the pure ecstatic bliss only true fated couples ever experienced. He was whole for the first time in his life. And she, well, she was everything to him.

After breakfast, they got on his bike and headed for the border. He'd promised to show her the world, and he was going to start right now. He was in no rush, after all, they had the rest of their lives.

"You ready, love?"

"I'm ready, mate."

Love really was an adventure, and theirs was just beginning.

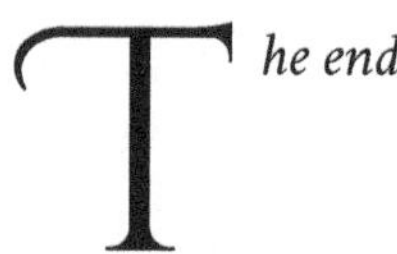

he end.

Liked this story? Want more Dire Wolf Mates?
Grab the next book, Love That Sass, at https://www.cdgorri.com.book/love-that-sass.
Or
Follow the whole series at https://www.cdgorri.com/seres/dire-wolf-mates.

Thank you and happy reading!

LOVE THAT SASS

DIRE WOLF MATES

BLURB

DIRE WOLF MATES

Can a fun loving bad boy Dire Wolf find redemption with a curvy human?

Weylin Scott is the original DWMC playboy. The stud muffin Wolf has always been the love 'em and leave 'em type. All his conquests know the drill. No harm, no foul, right?

But what happens when a human with a heart of gold catches the attention of the ramblin' redhead? His Alpha says she's off limits, but his Wolf can't stay away.

Will he endanger the Pack by revealing what he is too fast, too soon?

Gwendolyn Hoffer needs to come up with some quick cash to pay for her grandfather's care at a local assisted living facility. It's slim pickings on the job market, but applying at the new roadhouse seems the perfect solution.

Raised by the former deacon to be a good girl, she vowed to save herself for marriage. But how is Gwen supposed to stick to her virtuous guns when she's surrounded by such naughty temptations?

Weylin must convince the beautiful Gwendolyn she's the only woman for him.

Can she handle the reformed playboy and deal with his furry side, too?

PROLOGUE

DIRE WOLF MATES

Gwendolyn stared at her phone as she stood in the parking lot of *Serious Moonlight Roadhouse & Bar.*

The neon pink sign cut a path across the dark night skies, and she shivered despite the jacket she wore. It was September in Blue Valley, and that meant mother nature was going through her moods. It was like the seasons had menopause. But that was typical New Jersey weather.

She wished she was looking at a message from a boyfriend or reading an email with good news for a change. Unfortunately for Gwen, it was another bill she couldn't afford. But this one had the not so subtle subject line "last warning" in bold red letters.

Dang it.

She'd already been to every restaurant and bar in a five-mile radius, which was the farthest she could go in a U-drive rideshare car with her limited budget, to apply for open positions. So far, she'd struck out.

Serious Moonlight was her last chance. With Pop's medical bills piling up, and the fee for the assisted living facility he lived in almost doubling this year, Gwen needed every dollar she could earn.

"Don't worry, Pop. I won't let you down," she whispered, pulling up a selfie she'd taken of herself and the man who'd raised her.

Pop had taken her in after her parents abandoned her and did his best to raise her with the same morals and ethics that as a deacon in the church, he valued. She did her best to abide by his rules and managed fairly well, except for a wild streak in college.

Attending art school in Manhattan meant plenty of changes for the small town Jersey girl, and Gwen had lost her heart and almost lost her virginity to a fast-talking man at the restaurant where she'd gotten a job. He'd done a number on her, and after two years, she'd come back home with her tail tucked between her legs.

Pop had welcomed her, of course, with open arms, and she finished her degree at a local school, getting her teacher's certification as well. For a couple of years, everything was fine. She avoided men, of course, but Gwen was building a life she could be proud of.

Then Pop got sick, and they had to sell the condo to keep up with the bills. His dementia had advanced to such, she had to stay home with him, losing her teaching job in the process. The time had finally arrived where she could no longer give him the care he needed, and with a broken heart, she had him placed in the best assisted care center in the area. The price was hefty, and she hocked everything they had. But the thing about money was no matter how much you had, it never seemed to be enough.

The facility had given her thirty days to come up with the latest late payment. It was money she did not have, but she would do anything to get it. Well, almost anything.

There were things a good girl like Gwen would never do. Even if she'd sunk to an all-time low. No matter. She could live on cold cereal and instant ramen if Pop needed her to.

"You can do this," she murmured, putting her crossbody bag to rights, shoving her phone inside. "It's just a job. At a bar. A biker bar."

Her eyes went wide at the row of gleaming motorcycles lined up outside the place.

Holy crap.

She'd heard from a waitress at the last place she'd filled out an application that Serious Moonlight was the best game in town if you needed to earn money fast.

The owners were a close-knit group of friends, all drop-dead gorgeous. The latter info seemed irrelevant to Gwen, but it had been given as a sort of a warning.

Apparently, prospective employees were ferreted out if their interest in the owners was too blatant. From what she had gathered, the owners, listed as the DWMC, were so gorgeous, people just threw themselves at them.

Whatever.

Sex was not one of her motivators. Gwen was just not in the market for a fling. She'd survived one horrible relationship, and that was all the experience of the opposite sex she intended to have until the day she got married.

The owners seemed to have a good reputation, far as she could tell. Apparently, they treated their staff very well. Paid well, too, not to mention the tips, which was all Gwen needed to hear. She did not care about the other stuff.

Just then, the doors open, and music poured out into the lot. Her eyes went wide as an enormous bald man covered in tattoos held a smaller, skinnier man over his shoulder and was muttering something about *crazy females* and *jealous mates*.

Mates? Maybe he was Australian.

She watched for a moment before biting the bullet and heading inside. It didn't matter. She was there for a job. That was all.

"Gimme back my strippers!" someone, *a woman*, yelled from inside. Then, an older blonde woman, followed by an older man, came rushing out of those same doors.

"Patricia! You get back here!"

Oh my. What am I walking into?

Didn't matter. Gwendolyn Hoffer needed a job, and according to the Blue Valley patch, Serious Moonlight was looking for staff. It was a match made in heaven, far as she was concerned.

CHAPTER ONE

DIRE WOLF MATES

Disco music blasted from the speakers and Weylin grinned like a maniac as the bachelorette party kicked it up a notch.

There were women everywhere, in all stages of dress or undress. The air was saturated with female smells, like hair product and body lotion—nothing too strong since most were Shifters. Glitter and confetti rained down from above as balloons popped and noisemakers went off.

Hell yeah. The place was simply jam packed. Women were talking, shouting, singing, and shaking their groove things all over the place. As for Weylin, well, he was in his element.

What could he say? He simply loved women. Loved flirting, making them smile. Dating was his thing, but he kept his options open. He was a free bird, *er,* Wolf, anyway. Weylin simply loved variety, and he had a whole contact list full of possibles for every night of the week.

Fun lovin'.

That was the best description Weylin had ever heard of himself. Of course, there were those who were not all that entertained by his lifestyle choices. But whatever.

Weylin could not make everyone happy. He was a Dire Wolf Shifter, not *Nutella*.

Lord, he loved the chocolate hazelnut spread! Ate it right out of the jar with a spoon if there was nothing to spread it on. Though, he had to confess, it was even better when he had a warm, willing female who didn't mind a little creative snacking.

Hmm. I am kinda hungry.

Speaking of which, it had been a few weeks since he'd gone out with a member of the opposite sex. And by going out, what he really meant, of course, was staying in. Yep, that was just what Weylin needed.

An evening with some fine, feisty woman who appreciated his brand of humor and was down for some no strings hanky panky. Even his Wolf perked up at the mention of some smexy fun times.

Grrrr.

The big, red-furred beast was easily double the size of the average Werewolf, though smaller than his Alpha, and Thor, that monster. He could more than hold his own, though, but lucky for him and everyone else, he was more lover than fighter.

Whine.

His Wolf whimpered in his mind's eye, and that brought Weylin up short. He slammed a glass down a little harder than he meant to and shook his head. Fuck. His damn beastie was getting all mushy because of all the matings going on in the Pack lately, but that sort of thing was not for him.

He was into happy endings, not happy ever afters.

Snort. What? You think guys really mature after junior high? Ha! Not likely.

Weylin's inner musings were cut short by a loud voice demanding attention. He grinned at his Pack mate, turning towards her expectantly.

"Blow jobs for everyone!" Sheila Rand, *soon-to-be-Crowley,* shouted.

As the only Dire Wolf female in their Pack, and the Alpha's actual cousin, she was something like royalty to the males who'd grown up with her. The fact she was about to become actual royalty, marrying the one and only Lion prince of the Blue Valley Pride, was just kismet.

Damn, but she was pretty as a picture. Red hair flowing around her shoulders, eyes bright with happiness. Weylin could not be more thrilled for her if he tried. Hell, he even liked her mate. Leo was a down-to-earth kind of prince, even if he was a tad bit obsessed with his hair.

Felines and their manes. Grrr.

"Shake a tail feather, Weylin! My girls are thirsty!" she crowed, slamming her hands on top of the bar.

"I'm hurrying, girl."

"Good. Make em extra strong, and for fuck's sake, do not allow Patricia near any of the drinks," she mock-whispered.

"I heard that!" yelled the sassy older Lioness.

"No worries, Sheila. I know better than that," Weylin replied and lifted the shaker up to mix the drink.

"Like my party?" Sheila asked, looking around happily.

"I do, but can I ask a question?" Weylin inquired, considering his words carefully.

"Shoot," Sheila said.

"What is with the disco? Did we fall into a hot tub time machine and zap back to the 70s again? Lord, it was hard enough the first time," Weylin teased.

Dire Wolves aged slowly, and though his true age was nearer to seventy, he looked all of thirty to anyone else. Sheila was younger by far, and he was honestly curious about the whole direction of this bachelorette party.

"Ha! That was my future step-mama-in-law's doing," Sheila confided with a snort.

"I see," Weylin replied, and shook his head.

The Goldens had arrived a little while ago, toting a couple of male exotic dancers wearing platform boots and bell bottoms, but not much else. Patricia, their matriarch, led them, as usual.

The older, golden-haired female was Sheila's soon to be step-mother-in-law, having mated and married Leo's dad, the King of the Blue Valley Pride, Donovan Crowley. She had a gaggle of daughters, like four if Weylin could count, but he was not promising anything, and one son named George.

The crew of outrageous Lionesses were regulars at Serious Moonlight. Three of them were mated now, one to a member of the Dire Wolf MC. Brock and Ariella had a rocky start, but the sweet Lioness made his friend happy, so he didn't see a problem with it.

"Uh oh. Patricia is fondling the strippers again!" Sheila wailed.

A ruckus ensued, but before Weylin could do anything, Thor was on it. The male was a fucking giant, even among their kind. He had the stripper over his shoulder and was hauling his skinny ass outside before King Donovan could kill the bastard.

"Dammit Thor! Bring back my stripper!" Patricia wailed.

"You sure you want to marry into that family?" Weylin asked, only half-joking.

Sheila's smile was so wide as she watched the Goldens and Crowleys tug-o-war over the Lion matriarch. She grabbed the shot he offered and downed it with a shrug.

"I am sure. Leo is all mine, buddy. The Fates picked a good one," she said and winked.

Weylin just shook his head and continued mixing alcohol. Fated mates were like unicorns in his world. Shifters believed the Fates were the only ones responsible for delivering matches made in the heavens —*literally*.

Weylin never bought into all of that, but he had to admit. Something was happening among their Pack.

The Dire Wolves were dropping like flies, getting mated, and in some cases, married, too. And wasn't that just fucking redundant?

Being mated meant more to Shifters than any human piece of paper. But what did he know about it, anyway?

He was more than happy to remain footloose and fancy free. Able to sample the wares of many a female without shackling himself to any single one.

Yep. That was the life for him.

Lonely, you mean, his Wolf grumbled, and Weylin frowned.

The fuck? No. I do not mean lonely! I mean awesome.

"Come on, dude. Where are my blowjobs?" Sheila asked impatiently, clearly, she wanted to join in the fun.

"On it," he said, and got to work double time.

Sheila started tapping her fingernails impatiently. She was giggling, sure, but that didn't mean anything. Weylin knew a hunter on the prowl when he saw one, and his Pack mate was on the hunt for a good time.

No way in hell was he standing in the way of that. He looked at her hands while he shook up the shots she'd ordered, noting the dayglo pink paint. Weylin wondered if she did that on purpose to match their logo. The Serious Moonlight sign was the same shade of neon. Sheila's design, of course.

"There you go, a dozen blow jobs for you and your ladies," Weylin said, handing her a tray filled with the silly little cocktails served in the extra-long shot glasses and topped with a dollop of whipped cream.

"Oh, and that one is a virgin for Lucy," he added with a wink, mentioning their Alpha female, who was currently pregnant and none too happy about being excluded from the more randy shenanigans.

"Perfect. Thanks, Wey," Sheila said and snatched the tray.

The disco continued to pound through the speakers and after another hour, he was ready to strangle someone. Good thing the boys weren't around, since the exotic dancers were on stage, gyrating their man bits in scandalous glitter thongs with banana hammocks in front.

Oh, it was just a bit of fun, but Weylin would hate to see what would happen if Derrick walked in and found his pregnant mate stuffing singles in some dude's panties. Let's face it, they were panties.

"Excuse me," a timid voice said.

Tingles started up Weylin's spine at the dulcet sounds of the stranger's voice. His heart thudded and time seemed to slow.

Not a stranger, his Dire Wolf whispered.

Weylin shook his head. He'd been facing the other direction, but that would not matter to a Shifter like him. With his supernaturally enhanced auditory senses, he would have recognized the speaker if he knew them.

Nah. His Wolf must be crazy. No way did he know that voice. And yet, even though his human side didn't recognize the shy, husky tone, his beast sure as fuck seemed to.

But how? There was just no way Weylin would have ever forgotten it. The voice was clearly female.

Sweet. Husky. Mine.

Wait. What?

Blood rushed through his veins, and thunder pounded in his ears. The whole bar went silent, and the only thing he heard was his own damned heartbeat. His Dire Wolf was clawing and snapping, snarling to break free of his human skin. Weylin grunted as he wrestled with the animal, determined to keep control.

Mine.

His Dire Wolf sat, ears perked in that metaphysical realm where the beast waited to be called. It had been a long time since he saw the animal so clearly inside his head without calling him. It was like the Wolf was in control and Weylin was frozen.

No. No fucking way.

He wiped a hand over his face, blocking out the disco blaring from the speakers as he reined in his inner animal. Shit. This was not the time nor the place for his Wolf to go apeshit over a woman.

"I said, excuse me," the female stranger spoke again, closer this time.

Danger. Danger.

He was already sweating, and shaking like a leaf as Weylin turned slowly, prepping himself for whatever might greet him. Then he saw her, and his breath whooshed right out of his lungs.

She was leaning over the bar, trying to get his attention. Her clothes were normal, nothing special. Just a black shirt and a pair of jeans, but man oh man, the body they covered.

Holy. Fuck.

Petite and curvy, with hills and valleys, soft secrets and treasures, she was true perfection, all wrapped up in cotton and denim. His heart beat double time and the air seemed to sizzle with desire. Confidence and temptation. That's what she was.

Weylin didn't understand why women chose clothes that looked close to torture devices to him, but not this one. She was clearly dressed for comfort, and that alone made her more stylish than any of the females in skintight couture dresses at Serious Moonlight tonight.

She didn't even have on makeup. Her smooth skin looked freshly scrubbed and when he sniffed, yep, he noted she'd used plain old-fashioned Ivory soap. A coating of sheer lip gloss covered her mouth, and he thought he scented strawberries, but that could've just been her natural scent.

Yum. Yum. YUM.

He was thunderstruck, and though Weylin knew a mere moment had passed, it could have been a millennium. Damn. She was beautiful. Her heart-shaped face was mere inches from his. Like a plump, ripe apple hanging on a low branch.

Tempting. Sweet. Seductive.

Clever eyes peeked up at him through short, thick lashes and she seemed unapologetic in demanding his attention. The woman was a walking, talking dare, and he was man enough to give in, no questions asked.

"Hello? Can you hear me?" she asked, nose scrunched up as she raised the volume of her voice to compete with the relentless disco beat pouring out of the speakers.

"I hear you, baby," Weylin growled.

Unable to resist, he caught her face in his hands, stealing a kiss that was just too damn sweet for words. He had no idea who this beauty was, but she was definitely in the right place at the right time. His Wolf howled inside his mind's eye, so loudly it damn near deafened him. Only one word rang clear throughout it all—*mate.*

Mate. Mate. MATE.

CHAPTER TWO

DIRE WOLF MATES

As his Dire Wolf howled with the realization that he had found his one and only true and fated mate, Weylin's entire body hummed with joy.

He'd found her. His mate. The one woman in the entire universe who belonged to him, as he belonged to her, body, heart, and soul. But getting back to the body part, he mused, tilting his head and angling for better access as he delved his tongue inside her hot little mouth.

A million and one questions begged entry to his mind, but Weylin pushed them aside, wanting only to bask in his newfound happiness. Of course, it lasted only about a second and a half, which was right up until a loud *SLAP,* followed by an annoying sting on the side of his face, broke up his rose-tinted musings.

"OUCH!" Weylin yelped in shock.

His eyes went wide as the gorgeous creature backed up from the bar, wiping her mouth with the back of her hand like he had cooties or something.

What the fuck?

"Ohmygawd! What the heck is wrong with you?"

The outraged woman spat—*actually spat*—into a napkin she grabbed from the bar, wiping her mouth like he'd poisoned her.

"Me? Why'd you go and do a thing like that? I just sucked on a peppermint," he shrieked over the music, which, of course, had stopped right at that moment.

Dozens of Shifter eyes watched him and his mate, *er*, the mystery woman have their first lovers' quarrel. At least, that was how he was choosing to see it. Even after slapping him, Weylin had to admit his desire for her was a strong—*if possible, even stronger*—than ever.

"A peppermint? What does that have to—*ugh*," she muttered, a moue of disgust on her pretty little face.

"If you don't like PDAs you just have to say so," he grumbled, signaling the DJ to put the music back on.

"PDAs? Public displays of affection? OMG! Didn't anyone ever teach you any manners?"

"Of course they did, but I'm not the one slapping people," he growled, confused as fuck.

"Well, of course, I slapped you! I came in here for a job not to get manhandled by some puffed up playboy bartender who thinks he's God's gift to women," the woman retorted.

Sassy. Clever. And still cute as hell.

"Never said I was a gift, but you can unwrap me anytime," he replied and winked.

Unfortunately, the woman who would be his mate was not amused. His Dire Wolf snapped at him, but Weylin was at a loss. Usually, women found him charming, handsome, and easy to be with.

She looked at him like something she had accidentally stepped in. It was playing havoc with his ego, but even worse, his animal was starting to get pissed. The Wolf wanted out, figuring he could do a better job than the man. Maybe that was the issue. He just had to get her to understand what his animal already knew. They were fated to be together.

"Weylin, what is going on here?" a very pregnant, and somewhat amused, Lucy, interrupted.

A second hush fell over the crowd of partygoers, but at least the DJ kept playing. Still, Weylin's face turned bright red under their evil grins. Sheila was watching the byplay like it was an instant replay of the last disappointing Giants game.

Go Big Blue. Or don't. Sigh.

Damn human football league had nothing on the unofficial Shifters games he and his Pack loved to attend. Still, he was a loyal fan of the NY Giants, even if they had yet to meet their potential.

Weylin hated being the object of attention, especially when so many of the females at Sheila's party were evil. Okay, fine. Maybe not evil, but since he had dated a fair number of them, he imagined they were more than happy to see him get his ass handed to him by one of their own.

"Look, love, just let me explain—"

"Hi, I'm Lucy, and you are," but Lucy's eyes went round as she gave a delicate sniff of the stranger.

She flicked her gaze to Weylin, who followed suit. *Sniff*—well fuck, that explained it. Here he'd been thinking the little morsel was a Shifter who knew about mates and instant attraction, but the hottie with the body was a normal. A human.

My mate is human. Really?

Yes. Really, his Dire Wolf supplied.

"Gwendolyn Hoffer, nice to meet you, sort of," the woman replied.

Gwendolyn, he thought, sounding it out in his head. It was a nice name. Old-fashioned and sweet. He liked it. Hoped he'd get a chance to use it. If she let him.

Gulp.

Oh fuck. He'd really messed this thing up. Weylin's face fell as he watched the stranger cross her arms over her chest as she gave Lucy the lowdown. Well, her version of it. As Weylin listened, he learned she was from town and had come in looking for a job not to get felt up by some sleazy bartender.

Shit.

Hey, wait. He didn't even feel her up! He wanted to, sure, but he didn't. Hmm. Maybe he should have led with a *how are you* and not a lip lock? But damn, who could blame him? She was spectacular.

The woman was all of five-foot three, give or take, with a curvy little figure that made the beast within him wild for the woman. Weylin just couldn't stop staring at her. She had an ass that wouldn't quit, causing his Dire Wolf to growl and other parts of him to perk up as visions of those luscious globes backed up against his naked thighs swam around in his head.

Fuck yeah.

Weylin could not wait to get lost in that body. It had been a good long while since he'd been this worked up, and so damn fast, too. He thumped a fist nonchalantly against his dick just to settle the damn thing down.

Meanwhile, his eyes ate her up from the top of her head, covered with long, dark hair down to her warm, clever brown eyes, and that figure—*good gods*. He could come just looking at the creature.

He was practically panting for her, and for all his years, that was saying something. He'd become an addict in a moment, but he was Wolf enough to admit it. If only he could go back in time and start over.

"He meant well, I am sure. You know how it is, good-looking guy gets over-confident, assumes every girl is into him," Lucy was trying to explain away his bad behavior.

He hoped she would forgive him, let him start again. Hell, he needed her to, but when Gwendolyn looked at him, it was not with the same heated glow he knew was shining in his own poignant stare.

In fact, the woman looked at Weylin like he was a cockroach crawling across her shoe. Equal parts fear and revulsion. Shit. This was not doing any favors for his self-esteem.

Not good, dude. So not good.

He never had a woman hate him on sight. Never mind, one he was decidedly interested in. And this was more than a cursory interest. If his Wolf was right, and the animal had never been wrong, the female was his. As in *HIS*—all caps.

Mine. Mate.

"Whatever. I am sure he is used to women falling over themselves to get to him, but that's just not me," Gwendolyn said to Lucy.

"I am so sorry about that. He is housebroken, I swear," Lucy replied sympathetically, as she patted the woman on the arm.

"Look, I am sorry about the slap, but he deserved it. Maybe I made a mistake coming in."

"No!" he shouted, biting his tongue when both women jumped.

Shit.

"I'm sorry," he grumbled.

"I just came in for a job, not to get involved in whatever this is with you guys," she said, signaling between the two of them.

"What? Ohmygawd! You think we are together? No. We are not an item," Lucy hurried to explain, and he could have kissed the Alpha fem.

"You're not?" Gwendolyn asked, eyebrows arched.

"Hell no. Um, Weylin is like my brother. My very poorly behaved brother."

"I see," Gwen replied, a tight smile on her face. She looked like she wanted to bolt.

Fuck.

"Well, Wey, what do you have to say for yourself?" Lucy hissed the question, and he could tell the Alpha fem was pissed.

"Uh," he mumbled, and glanced from the angry pregnant female Shifter to the shocked and maybe pissed off human. Rubbing the back of his head with one hand, Weylin shrugged and said the only thing he could think of.

"You're hired?"

CHAPTER THREE

A few minutes earlier...

Gwen swallowed back her fear, trying for courage when she approached the bar where a dazzling redhead stood smiling at the group of dancing, giggling women.

Hmm.

That was odd. The entire crowd was female. Well, except for a few gyrating, almost naked men.

What the heck?

Gwen looked around. All women, almost all nude men thrusting their hips on stage, speakers blasting 70s disco—fuck. She'd crashed a party.

Oh well. She was already there. What did she have to lose?

Famous. Last. Words.

Fast forward to Gwendolyn being grabbed, kissed within an inch of her life, and almost vaulting over the bar to jump the six foot whatever hunk of redheaded hotness before her mind came back to her.

What the heck am I doing making out with some stranger?

Sure, the man could kiss, but why was he kissing her? And why was she letting him? That was it.

SLAP!

"OUCH!" the man grunted in obvious shock.

"What is wrong with you?" Gwen grabbed a napkin, wiping her drool to her utter embarrassment.

"What the heck was that for? I just sucked on a peppermint!"

She had no idea what he was talking about? But yeah, now that he mentioned it, she felt a minty coolness in her mouth after she'd swapped spit with the dude.

"Didn't anyone ever teach you any manners? I came in here for a job not to get manhandled by some puffed up playboy," Gwen hissed.

Then she was being petted and placated by a pregnant female who was also scolding the red-headed, hot boy. She was so mixed up, she could hardly follow their byplay. But two words managed to break-through her kiss-addled brain.

"I'm hired?" she asked, gaze going from the pregnant woman's to the man who'd kissed her stupid.

"Um, yes?" he said.

"Definitely!" the woman replied after glancing at the man.

"Whoooоeeeee! YASSS!" Gwen yelled, balling up one hand and fist-bumping her other one, making a complete ass out of herself.

But what did she care? She'd just been hired! Ignoring the sexy redhead would not be a problem, she told herself, determined to keep her vow and help her Pop.

"Um, are you okay?" the woman asked.

"Yep. I am great. When do I start?"

"Um, come back tomorrow and we will begin training!"

Gwen nodded at the woman, ignoring the man as she gathered her wits and left the place. She would be back the next day where, hopefully, she would find herself with a job.

Fingers crossed.

What the heck am I doing back in this place? Dear Lord, if Pop could see me now—he'd probably ask for a beer.

Gwendolyn's thoughts raced from one thing to another so quickly they were liable to make her sick, but she just couldn't slow them down. At least the roadhouse was on the outskirts of town, and no one she knew would see her.

She doubted many members of the small church she belonged to, where her Pop had been a deacon, attended the raucous bar. That was one saving grace. But what did she really care? She needed money and bartending was an honest living.

"Hi Gwen! What are you doing here?" a somewhat familiar voice called out.

Dang it.

She turned her head and saw Kelly Vanderbilt running up to greet her. She'd been one of those annoyingly perky teenagers at Maccon City High School. Not one of Gwendolyn's small circle of friends, but they'd had some classes together.

"Hi Kelly. I'm training to be a bartender here," she told her, with a tight smile on her face.

Kelly was tall and blonde with a svelte physique and flawless skin. She was gorgeous in a way Gwen could never compete with, so she never tried. Why bother? She knew her limitations, and she was perfectly happy with the face and body God gave her.

"You? I thought you were like super religious?" Kelly said, though it sounded like a question to Gwen.

"Nothing against bartending in the Bible, Kelly," she teased, and the other woman laughed.

"I suppose not. Anyway, good luck. It's a good place to work, just don't break your heart on any of the guys. These boys are all dogs!" she said cheerfully and ran inside.

Gwen shook her head after the woman, tapping her fingers against her pocketbook as she followed much more slowly. She thought about what Kelly said about her being religious and supposed she had earned that rep back in school.

Oh, there were plenty of things about the church she did not agree with, but that was neither here nor there. Pop was a deacon, and she had attended services with him every Sunday. She even taught Sunday school classes when she was younger. Later, she was giving art lessons at the local preschool, but after circumstances, she'd lost that job.

She'd been so happy when Pop had been accepted into Hope Springs Senior Residence Center in Blue Valley. It was rated the best assisted living facility in three counties, and Lord knew Pop deserved the best.

After her parents skipped out on her, Gwendolyn was left with nothing and no one. Pop was her father's father. He hadn't seen his son in years, and he didn't even know Gwen existed until a kind woman who worked for the Division of Child Protection for the state of New Jersey had tracked him down.

He'd come down to the home where the DCF agent had taken her like an avenging angel. His wife, the grandmother she was named after, had passed from cancer a few months earlier, and Pop, aka John Hoffer, had thought himself alone in the world. She could still recall the first time he came to see her…

Gwendolyn had a cut on her knee from where an older girl had shoved her on the playground and it was still oozing blood. Pop kneeled down in front of her and took a clean white hanky from his pocket and introduced himself.

"What happened there?" the old man had asked her.

"I got pushed. Who are you?" Gwen asked in return, clutching her ratty old teddy bear to her chest.

The old man had a thick mass of white streaked gray curls on top of his head, kind brown eyes, and a smile she sort of recognized.

"I'm your grandfather. You can call me Pop, little Gwenny. Your father is my son," he explained as he cleaned my scrape.

"Dad went away with Mom," Gwen whispered, her little six year old brain trying to wrap around the enormity of what that meant.

"I see. Well, your Granny went away to Heaven a little while ago."

"Heaven? I don't think that's where Mom and Dad went. I'm sorry Granny left you," she whispered.

"Don't be. Heaven is a wonderful place where we get to see and be with all our loved ones. I will join her there someday. But not for a while."

"Oh. Maybe I could go there too."

"To Heaven? Sure you can, but not for a very long time, Gwenny. You still have stuff to do here," Pop said and smiled kindly.

It was the first time anyone had offered her such a sweet expression. Her own troubled parents were too involved with whatever had brought them down so low to pay any attention to her. She was just something extra to them.

"I'm scared. Don't wanna stay here," she confessed.

"I bet you are, but I am here now. You know, I got a big house with plenty of room for a little girl, a yard, too. I was thinking we could keep each other from being lonely. So, what do you say?"

"Okay."

"Well, okay, then," Pop said and smiled, offering a hand.

The two of them had been inseparable since that moment. He'd been a deacon at the small church on Main Street, and Gwen had attended services with him. But all her religious studies had done nothing to curb Gwendolyn's wild side. In high school, she'd been a tad rebellious, sneaking off to the Big Apple to take in the sights and museums. Yeah, she might have danced her butt off a bit, too.

In college, she did more of the same. Majoring in art, she had hoped to work in a museum or gallery. She just loved the multicultural climate and the bright lights and artistic richness of city life. Then her heart got stomped on by a boyfriend and she'd run back home.

That was almost eight years ago. Gwendolyn had done her best to stay optimistic and true to her promise ever since. It was easy. She'd simply sworn off men.

"Hey, you coming in?"

Gwen looked up to see Lucy standing by the bar's front door, hands on her belly. She wore a pair of black leggings with a tight shirt pulled over her stomach and a loose flannel she'd left open on top of that. She looked comfortable and cute as a button, Gwen thought, and secretly wished she had the nerve to wear tight clothes when she was pregnant someday.

"Yeah, I'm coming," she said, jogging, so the expecting mother did not have to wait in the fall breeze.

"I gotta say I am happy you came. I wasn't sure you would be back," Lucy said as she showed her the way to the employee breakroom.

There were a few lockers against one wall, and Lucy gestured to one Gwen could use. She thanked her and hung up her thin jean jacket and purse.

"So, where do we start?"

"Well, first we have some paperwork, but I am starving. How about lunch?"

"Lunch?"

Gwen's stomach was rumbling at the mere mention of food, and she could have died of embarrassment. Ever since Pop got sick, and she found she needed more and more time off to care for him, she'd been living paycheck to paycheck.

Food was a luxury these days, curvy body or not. Her eating habits had become heavily dependent on what she could afford. She didn't regret spending all her cash on her grandfather's care, after all, she would not have him forever.

"Um, I'm sorry I am on a budget—"

"What? Oh, no. It's on the house. Derrick, he's my man and the big boss, anyway, he insists all the staff be acquainted with the menu, and I have a hankering for a double bacon brisket burger with brie, caramelized onions, and fig jam!"

"What?" she laughed at what was clearly a pregnant woman's fantasy burger.

"Don't knock it till you tried it," was all Lucy said as she led the way to a table by the kitchen doors.

A big man with blond hair held back by a bandana came out of the kitchen, mumbling beneath his breath. He stopped short when he saw Lucy and Gwen.

"Hey Lucy, is this the new hire? I'm Brock," the man said, introducing himself.

"Gwen," she replied, trying to keep her eyes inside her head.

The man was gorgeous. Then again, so was everyone she'd met so far. Of course, Weylin, the redhead who'd kissed her last night, was by far the most handsome. Not that it mattered, she reminded herself firmly.

"What can I get you ladies?" he asked, as Sheila, the stunning redhead whose party it was she crashed the night before, came over.

"Brie burger for me rare," Lucy said without hesitation.

"Same!" Sheila said, sliding into a chair beside her.

"Got it, and for you?" Brock asked.

"Um, I don't know—"

"Come on, Gwen. You have to try it," Lucy said encouragingly.

She imagined the tiny pregnant woman could entice the devil to drink holy water with those puppy eyes of hers and that wide smile. She was positively beguiling.

"Okay fine, I will have the brie burger also, but medium rare, please."

"As you wish," Brock replied and winked before stalking back to the kitchen.

"So, what are we doing?" Sheila asked when a third woman came running in and joined them at the table.

"Hey girls!"

"Tracey! When did you guys get back?" Lucy asked, hugging the woman up tight.

"About ten seconds ago," a tall man answered for her, his smile wide and indulgent as the woman, Tracey, hugged Sheila next.

"Hi, I'm Tracey. Who are you?"

"Um, Gwen, I'm going to be working here," she replied, smiling back at her.

How could she not? The woman exuded joy, and her grin was contagious. The man with her was clearly one of the owners of the bar, tall, muscular, and hotter than a rockstar, Gwen mused with a shake of her head.

"I'll be back. Have to check in with Derrick," Phoenix said, kissing Tracey quickly before he walked away.

"Hey Brock, put on another burger for Tracey," Lucy screamed, smiling like a maniac. "I am so glad you guys are back. I thought you were going to miss the birth!"

"Not on your life," Tracey told her.

Gwen sat, just absorbing their energy, and listening while trying to remain unobtrusive. As if sensing it, Lucy steered the conversation to include her, and she had never felt such gratitude.

They were really something. This group of beautiful females and their equally beautiful men, Gwen thought. Each of their guys checked in on them at some point during their hour long lunch, either texting or physically dropping by. It was not something she had much experience with, and Gwendolyn was intrigued.

"Okay, I have a question," she asked, tummy full of the unsurprisingly delicious burger and hand-cut fries she'd gorged herself on.

"Shoot," Lucy asked, going to town on the triple crème raspberry and white chocolate cheesecake she was eating for dessert.

"Did you guys like special order your boyfriends from a catalog or something?" she asked point blank.

The three women blinked, looked at each other, then busted out laughing. Tracey was wiping her eyes while Lucy held onto her pregnant belly and chuckled.

"Why do you ask that?" Sheila wanted to know.

"Well. I just never saw such good-looking men be so attentive and caring to their significant others. Seems too good to be true," she said with a shake of her head.

"Okay, there's a story there, woman, spill," Lucy commanded.

Well crap. Of course, that happened. Gwen should have known better than to open that can of worms, but she was trapped now.

"Usual story. Small-town girl moves to the big city, becomes infatuated with a fast-talking handsome man, who uses her, empties her bank account, and breaks her heart."

"The rat!"

"Got a name? I can have his legs broken by midnight," Lucy growled, and Gwen laughed, stopping when she realized no one else was.

"Oh, um, no, that's okay. I was raised by my grandfather, who was a deacon at our church. He taught me you reap what you sow, and believe me that, pardon my French, asshole is going to get what he deserves," Gwen told the three women who seemed to settle a little after that.

"So, you were raised by your grandfather?" Sheila asked.

"Yep. Pop is all I have. He's older now, and I couldn't care for him anymore. I got him a place though, at the Hope Springs assisted living facility. It's truly the best place for him with his advancing dementia and osteoporosis."

"I've heard of that place. It's a fortune if you can get in," Tracey said, nodding.

"Yep. That's why I'm here. I need this job desperately, but I swear I will work my butt off. Please don't think I told you that because I am looking for sympathy. I am a hard worker and I used to tend bar in the city, so I am sure I can keep up," she blurted.

"Hey, easy girl. Look, I have really good instincts about people, and I believe you, Gwen. Besides, Weylin already said you were hired," Lucy stated, eyes sparkling with humor. "After he kissed you silly."

"He kissed her!" Tracey whisper-screamed, and Gwen felt heat rush to her cheeks.

"He did. But it was a mistake," she explained, tucking her curly locks behind her ears.

"A mistake? How is kissing you a mistake?" Sheila asked loudly, just as *he who should not be named* walked into the bar.

The girls all giggled from where they sat in the dining room section, and Gwen whished the floor would just open up and swallow her. What was she getting herself into?

He nodded a hello to the table at large, and she felt curiously sad that he didn't come over to say hi personally. But why should that be? It wasn't like Gwen wanted him to single her out or anything.

"Alright, let me get this straight. Weylin kissed you when you came in for a job during Sheila's party and now you are going to work here, but you don't want him to kiss you anymore—is that right?" Tracey asked.

"Yep. She is here to work, not make whoopee with that redheaded he-slut," Sheila quipped.

"Is he a slut?" she asked before she could close her mouth.

"Um, no. Not really. I mean, it's not like any of us are virgins, right?" Lucy asked.

Gwen's face really flamed then. Seemed like she was way out of her league with these women, and not just because of their attractive boyfriends, but because they understood men on a level she did not.

"Oh my, are you a virgin?" Sheila asked at a decibel that made Gwen cringe.

Seemed the entire bar went quiet at the impromptu announcement, and Gwendolyn steeled herself for the blowback.

"Ladies, that is no one's business but Gwendolyn's," Lucy announced, and her glare seemed to reach everyone in the place.

Thank goodness it was early and there were less than half a dozen folks. Unfortunately, many of them were staff. It wouldn't be long till the rumor mill got finished hurling that chunk of info around.

Sigh. Might as well own it, Gwenny.

"Yes, Sheila, I am still a virgin. My choice. I made a vow to stay celibate until I found the man I was going to marry. I just haven't met him yet," she replied with a shrug.

"But I thought you said you had a boyfriend—"

"I did. In college. We had several very embarrassing discussions about my promise to wait to have sex until marriage that were very painful for me. Then I found my boyfriend in bed with my then roommate solidified my belief that I did well not to partake in anything of the kind with him."

"What a jerk! I don't blame you," Sheila said.

"Yes, he was," she replied. "But I suppose I should be thankful. If he hadn't cheated, I might have wasted more time and I would not have returned home, even if it was with my tail between my legs. See, those extra years with Pop still lucid were worth the heartache."

"Wow. Good for you," Sheila said.

"Yeah. The heck with him. And I am glad you found your way here," Tracey murmured, patting her hand.

"Bottom line, I am not here for a guy. I am here cause I need money, and I need it now. Pop's insurance plan refuses to pay for Hope Springs, they want him in a state home. I went to look at the place nearest us, and I just couldn't leave him there," she whispered, eyes filling with tears.

"Oh honey, no, don't you worry. You already got the job, now we just have to get through the formalities of training and paperwork," Lucy said, nodding her head.

"But what if Derrick doesn't think I am right for the position? I haven't met him yet, and he is the big boss, right?" she asked.

Gwen had to admit, just hearing about the man made her nervous. Meeting him was not something she was looking forward to. But with the job market being absolute crap, she had little choice.

Gulp.

CHAPTER FOUR

DIRE WOLF MATES

"For fuck's sake, Weylin. We do not manhandle potential employees!" Derrick growled at him from across his desk.

The Alpha obviously did not know he'd spent ten minutes wrestling his Wolf when he'd walked into the bar and saw Gwendolyn with three of the Pack females surrounding her. Fuck. She looked so beautiful. Curly brown hair, big inviting eyes, totally kissable lips just sitting there so perfect, waiting for a guy like him to come and worship at her altar.

Mine.

The animal wanted to claim her right there, but his human half recognized the obstacle to his own *happily ever after* ending. His mate was a normal. She knew fuck all about his world, and there was no way for him to explain what she meant to him without outing them all.

The problem? It wasn't his decision to make. At least, not alone, it wasn't. Which led to why he was in his Alpha's office having his ass handed to him by one angry as fuck Dire Wolf.

"I didn't know she was a potential employee, Derrick. Shit, I was completely unprepared, I know, and I apologize," Weylin explained, eyeing the enormously pissed off male.

He thought better of it and dropped his gaze as his Alpha growled menacingly. The guy was super touchy ever since his uber-pregnant wife refused to give up her hobbies despite being so late in the pregnancy. Overprotective? Maybe, if she were a typical pregnant woman, but Lucy did not do things like knit booties or bake cookies.

Her hobbies included bartending till three in the morning, dancing on bar tops despite her swollen feet, and stealing her mate's motorcycle for middle of the night rides with Sheila and those crazy Golden Lionesses. All the Shifter women he knew were hardheaded and sassy as fuck. But that's what made them so damned lovable, or so he assumed.

It drove Derrick bonkers, and that alone was worth it in his not so humble opinion. His Alpha seemed to have it coming, trying to tell that Feline what to do. Hell, that was like taking his life, *make that his balls,* in his own hands. Poor Derrick. He might be the toughest Dire Wolf of them all, but his petite mate had him wrapped around her furry little pinky.

Personally, Weylin did not see what the big deal was. Lucy was a Shifter. If she wanted to ride motorcycles, dance on a pole, and shake her sass all night long, so what? She could handle herself just fine.

Easy for him to say as an unmated male. Suddenly he pictured Gwendolyn—*damn he loved her name, it was every bit as cute as she was*—taking part in the same activities Lucy preferred, and his stomach twisted in knots.

Fuuckk.

Weylin hadn't even mated her yet, and already the woman had his balls in a vise. And this was why he was not looking for a mate! But even as he had the thought, Weylin took it back. He might not have been searching for his mate, but she landed right in his lap, and dammit, he wanted her. Fuck yes, he did! He wanted the female with every fiber of his being.

"Look, I get it, Weylin. You're single, good-looking, and you haven't met your mate yet, but at your age you should know better than to just grab random normals and shove your tongue in their mouths! For fuck's sake, I am telling you, this gigolo lifestyle of yours has to end!"

"Actually Derrick, I don't think that will be a problem because, you see, I have met her. My mate. I mean, I have met my mate," he said, feeling tongue-tied.

"Your mate? Fantastic! Wait. Fuck, please tell me it's not that other loopy Lioness, right?"

Derrick's face went from happy to horrified in the span of a millisecond. Loopy Lioness? Weylin was utterly confused.

"What or who are you talking about?" Weylin asked.

"The last single Golden girl from the Blue Valley Pride. Those females whose names all start with A! It's not her, right? I don't think I can handle another one of them in the Pack," Derrick grumbled, and ran a hand over his face.

Rigghhht.

Weylin barked a laugh, clapping his hand over his mouth at the angry glare from Derrick. The man was apparently not kidding. Weylin figured it made sense, though.

The Goldens had quite the rep, but they were fine females, if a little rascally. What did anyone expect with a mother like Patty? The new Queen of the Pride was well known for her shenanigans—*most of which involved catnip, alcohol, and dancing on top of bars or swimming naked in fountains.*

King Donovan was one lucky or unlucky male, depending on how you viewed his current cup. Weylin was a half full kinda guy. With a mate like Patricia, the Lion King would never be bored. There was something to say about that, for sure!

Now, Brock, the Dire Wolf Pack Beta, was mated to Ariella Golden. Her sister Annabeth had found her mate in a Falcon Shifter name of Hank Garret. While Antonetta had recently mated a Tiger Shifter from the Maverick Pride. If Weylin's calculations were correct, Adrianna was the last sister standing. And while they were each of them fine looking felines, alas, the last Golden was not his mate.

Besides, Weylin figured Derrick was only kidding about that whole *please let it not be her* thing. Right? Well, maybe mostly kidding.

"No, man," he told his Alpha. "My mate is not a cat. It's the woman. Her. She's it."

"What are you talking about? Who is it?" Derrick barked.

"*Her,* man. The potential employee," he whispered.

His super sensitive hearing had picked up a pair of footfalls in the hallway. The scent of berries and sweetness reached his nostrils, and he knew she was almost there. The beast in him rumbled, and Weylin coughed to cover his growl.

"The human? Absofuckinglutely not, Weylin. You can't let her know what you are," Derrick attempted to whisper.

The man was too damn loud for his own good and Weylin winced. That was so not the way he wanted to tell her about him. But it was all good, he hoped.

"Shh! They are coming," Weylin said, realizing his error in shushing his Alpha when the man growled.

"The fuck, bro. No humans. Got it?" Derrick ordered.

"Sorry, Alpha," he mumbled, baring his throat a second before Lucy opened the door.

A pair of warm brown eyes met his, and Weylin's inner beast stirred. Damn, she was beautiful. That long, curly hair fell down in ripples and he was dying to get his hands on it. Wanted to test the softness of each strand. He wondered how it would look strewn across his bed, all wild and perfect, like a dark river he would willingly wade into.

Yep. It was official. Weylin was a goner. Gwendolyn cleared her throat. Her pouty lips made a small frown as she turned her head to avoid his gaze. Damn, he hoped she didn't already hate him for what he'd done before. Maybe she was just shy, though his heart sunk at the thought of the former.

"Hey there, kitten," Derrick rumbled to Lucy, interrupting Weylin's reverie.

The Alpha's icy stare was riveted to his mate's swollen form as she walked over and dropped her cheek for a kiss. Their love was palpable in the small room. Weylin was moved beyond words as they embraced, Derrick resting one big hand on her protruding abdomen, while the other cupped Lucy's neck.

For the briefest of moments, they were as one. Heads bowed, lips touching, eyes closed. Even better, there was complete and absolute joy radiating from the pair, and it brought a rumble to Weylin's own chest. He wanted what the Alpha couple had for himself.

A mate. A family. A reason.

"Gwen, this is my, um, my guy, my fiancé, actually. Um, Derrick Rand, meet Gwendolyn Hoffer."

"Who?" Derrick asked dumbly.

"Honey, this is our new bartender, Gwen. She'll be filling in for me," Lucy said.

The Alpha stilled, hope seemed to radiate from him like rays from the sun. Watching the relief spill across Derrick's face was quite the revelation for Weylin. He was happy for the couple, but again, there was that deep longing to have that sort of bond with someone for himself.

Can have. Mate.

Shhh, he silenced his Wolf. This was not the time or place for mooning over the woman. He needed to clear the air and apologize. If he could only find the words.

"You mean it, kitten?" the big, bad Alpha asked Lucy, snagging Weylin's attention once more.

"Of course, I do—oof! Derrick! You can't just carry me off—sorry, Gwen! Weylin will finish the tour and get you the forms—oooh," Lucy yelped the last bit.

She'd been hefted in the air by her mate, who was even then nuzzling her belly with his lips, as he carted her off to another, more private, location. Weylin cleared his throat and rubbed the back of his neck. That was gonna be a hard one to explain.

"Um, wow. You know, Tracey's boyfriend did the same thing, sorta, to her after lunch," she murmured. "Does that kinda thing happen a lot around here?" Gwendolyn asked, clearing her throat.

Was he mistaken, or was that a hint of longing in her voice as she watched the Alpha pair leave? If she wanted to be swept off her feet, all she had to do was ask, he mused, a Wolfish grin spreading across his face.

"I could lie and say no, but actually, yeah, it does. All the mates, *er,* couples, are like that with each other," he began.

"Mates?"

"Oh, it's just a word we use," he said, rubbing the back of his neck harder to hide his discomfort.

"Like a club word?"

"Club? Oh, you mean motorcycle club, right? Yeah. That. Sorta," he mumbled, hating even the pretense of a lie.

"Well, where is he taking her?"

"Who? Lucy and Derrick? Oh, he's taking her somewhere to, um, show her the proper, *er,* appreciation, for her choice to stop working. You see, she's nearing the end of her pregnancy, and he's been worried sick about her. Lucy has been overdoing it with the long hours and whatnot," he said, watching the play of emotions cross her pretty face.

"Wait. Proper appreciation? Do you mean? *Ohmygah!* But isn't he worried he could, *you know,* hurt her?" Gwen asked, her nose scrunched up adorably.

"Hell no," he said and chuckled. "Derrick would cut off his arm before he hurt Lucy. She means more to him than his own life."

His blood heated looking at the woman, and the clear understanding dawned on him she could mean the same thing to him. Mates were revered in Shifter culture, Dire Wolves especially since theirs was such a long lifetime.

Mine, his Wolf growled.

CHAPTER FIVE

Fuck. Shit. It is her.

Gwendolyn Hoffer was his fated mate.

Well, she could be someday. It was her choice, of course, but it was too soon to broach that subject. Still, the words felt right. This was too new and Weylin wasn't quite there yet. But he would be. Hell, he could see it approaching fast.

Gwendolyn Hoffer was important to him. Really important. His entire future was in her hands. Swallowing down his fear and nervousness, he nodded towards the pile of papers on Derrick's desk and grabbed them. Weylin stood, scrounged for a pen. He handed the whole bundle to her, shivering when their fingers touched, and little shocks of lightning zipped through him.

"Um, well, here are some forms you'll need to fill out. But you can do that at home and bring them in when you start."

"When's that?" she asked and seemed anxious.

Hmm. Why did she want to start so soon? He was curious. Weylin couldn't help it, but Weylin wouldn't hound her for answers. He'd overheard her mention financial obligations to her grandfather or something like that, but he'd stopped listening as soon as she started talking about her ex-boyfriend.

His Wolf hadn't liked that bit at all. Double standard? Maybe. But he wasn't a saint, he was a Dire Wolf and a possessive one at that. Still, it wouldn't be right to steal her story by eavesdropping, so he'd gone in search of Derrick.

Of course, Weylin hoped, in time, she would confide in him. Maybe even lean on him for support. Yeah, he would like that. For her to trust him, to think of him as more than some shmuck who'd accosted her in a bar.

Shiiitt.

"Um, how about you start tomorrow, Gwendolyn?" he asked, liking the way her name rolled off his lips.

She looked around the hallway as he led her back to the bar. All traces of the bachelorette party were gone, but Sundays were still good bar days. Gwen's eyes nearly popped out of her head as Patricia Golden arrived and jumped on the stage, where bands usually set up, leading a horrific rendition of the macarena.

"Wow. I mean, it's only three o'clock in the afternoon," Gwen murmured.

"Yeah, well, some folks start early, but uh, Patricia there is like family," he tried, then gave up when the first scarf came off the older woman's neck.

"Oh, I see, well, I am not judging. It's nice to see a woman having fun," Gwen replied, surprising him.

"Yeah, uh, oh damn, excuse me one moment, I have to stop her before she takes any more clothes off," he murmured.

"Ha!"

Gwen covered her gaping mouth with her hand. Weylin wished he could watch her some more, but he had to fix this first. He shrugged apologetically and ran past her to the stage where he hoisted the older female Lioness off the thing before she could do more than shimmy out of one bra strap beneath her blouse, thank fuck. Really, it was way too early for the Lioness' shenanigans, but maybe she was still in party mode from the night before.

"Give her here!" shouted a loud male, and Weylin willingly handed the woman over to her mate.

"Yes sir," Weylin replied automatically.

King Donovan looked pissed as hell, but he nodded his thanks. Then, he tossed his errant bride over his shoulder, smacked her on the rump, and chuckled loudly as he hightailed it out of the bar, whispering something about a stripper poll and her repeating that little dance in private.

Whatever. It was just way more info than Weylin ever wanted to hear, especially about those two. Shit. Now, where did his mate go? He jumped when she appeared before him, offering a bottle of cold water in her extended hand. Weylin took it, thanking her automatically.

"Wow. I guess stuff like that really does happen all the time in this place," Gwen murmured, worrying the chain around her neck as she sipped from her own bottle.

Weylin glanced down and saw it was a gold chain with a tiny diamond cross she held between her fingers. Pretty. He wondered where she got it. Damn, he was on fire with wanting to know more about her.

"You're staring."

"Sorry. Um, I like your necklace. That a cross?"

"Um, yeah. I got it for my Confirmation."

"So, you're religious."

"Well, my Pop is a deacon for St. Anne's on Main Street, well, he was before he got sick. Anyway, he raised me with his beliefs, I guess."

"That's interesting, Gwendolyn. I'm sorry about him being sick though," he said, truly concerned.

"He's getting on in years, and I sorta expected it. But I was raised to be a good girl, you know, boring," she said with a self-deprecating laugh.

"I don't think you're boring, Gwen."

"You don't know me," she replied, shaking her head.

"That's true. But I want to," he returned.

Gwendolyn bit her lip, then gave him a small, tight smile, before feigning interest in the papers he'd given her. That was alright. She needed time. He sensed her withdrawal and nodded his understanding. Last thing he wanted was to make her feel trapped or bamboozled by him.

"So, I should fill these out, then bring them back tomorrow, you said?"

"Yep. Come in around three and we'll start your training," he said, walking her to the door.

He noticed her checking her phone and pulling up a ride share app, and the beast in him went nuts.

Shiiitt.

"Um, I will walk you to your car. Where'd you park?"

"Oh, um, I don't drive. I was just gonna grab a U-drive," she said, naming the most popular ride share app in town.

"Um, actually, Sheila here was about to leave. I am sure she can give you a ride, right Sheila?" he called out, knowing full well his Pack mate had been eavesdropping no less than ten feet behind him.

The only other redheaded Wolf in their Pack came jogging over, a big smile on her face. Beside her was Leo, her mate and soon to be husband.

"Gwendolyn, this is Sheila and Leo, her fiancé. He's a cop," he told her, and she visibly relaxed in the big man's presence.

"Very nice to meet you, Gwendolyn," Leo said, all teeth and smiles, and Weylin had the sudden urge to punch him right in those too-pearly whites.

"Oh, I don't want to put the two of you out," Gwen said in a rush.

Too late. Sheila had already commandeered her arm and was gabbing a mile a minute about errands she had to run and how tuckered out she was and other girl shit, like where Gwen got her hair done.

Good Pack, that Sheila. She must have read his concern through their Pack bonds and would make sure the fragile human got home safe. Gwen looked as if she would argue, feisty little thing, then she got caught up in whatever Sheila was talking about.

It amazed Weylin how quickly females could become friends, but it also warmed him to know Gwen was getting home safe tonight. The knowledge settled his beast. She paused in her tracks and her brown eyes found him instantly.

"Oh, thanks Weylin. I'll see you tomorrow," she called out and gave him a shy little wave.

"Have a good one, Gwendolyn." Weylin replied, his gaze never leaving her back for one second.

When the door finally closed, Weylin took off like a rocket, ripping the shirt from his body as he hauled ass outside a moment before his Wolf came ripping out of him.

The dark-red-furred beast was a hulking mass of muscle and angst. He followed the sound of the engine of Leo's custom '65 Stingray.

The Corvette was a work of fucking art, and being a Shifter, the Lion had it customized. A bench seat had been added in the back for when unexpected guests happened upon him, along with a titanium reinforced frame, extra absorbent shocks, and a suped up engine to name a few.

A part of Weylin was grateful the fragile human female was tucked up in the back of the big man's car with Sheila there to protect her from, well, whatever. Another part of him was barely hanging on to reason. That part was all animal. The beast didn't want Gwen in Leo's car, regardless of the fact the male was already mated.

Weylin was a Wolf. He wasn't perfect. While he accepted his imperfections as run-of-the-mill type stuff, he sure as shit didn't know he had feelings like this lurking inside him. Turned out he could be quite the possessive asshole.

Mine. Mine. MINE.

The Wolf growled and scratched. He wanted out. And he wanted out now.

She's in good hands, Wolf. Fucking relax.

But knowing all that didn't stop his animal from demanding he follow them. Weylin grunted and swayed on his feet the further she got from him. He couldn't stop himself if he tried, and why bother? He could use a run, anyway,

His transformation was fast, real fast, and his big, dark beast followed the vehicle closely as he could from the shadows of the forest beside the road. His fur was much darker than the flame colored hair that topped his head when he wore his human skin, but the hint of red was still there.

He had to be extra careful when hunting at night so humans didn't see him. Damn red fur tended to reflect in the light. Lucky for him, they tended to write him off as a large fox or stray dog. Humans didn't understand the paranormal world, and they usually ignored the things they could not comprehend.

He only hoped he didn't frighten Gwendolyn if she happened to catch a glimpse of him. Monster that he was, he'd likely scare the crap out of her. His Wolf didn't like that idea. Not one bit. But Weylin knew better than to go into this thing blind.

She was a normal. A human. And from what she'd told him, she'd been raised to be religious, moral, ethical. Shit. What the fuck did a rounder like him have to offer a woman like her?

Sweet, innocent, good girl. She deserves better.

But even those dark, disturbing thoughts did not stop his paws from moving. Oh no. He tracked her using all his skill, watched from the shadows as she got out of the car before Leo could help her—*good.*

His Werewolf senses were heightened, and he listened as she refused to go indoors until she saw them pull away. Leo had balked, but Gwen was adamant but polite. She insisted Leo and Sheila leave first and even watched them drive away.

Strange, he mused. Watching and waiting to see which house on the small residential block was hers. Only, where he would have expected her to choose a walkway, she didn't.

Gwendolyn wrapped her arms around her waist and hurried fast as her two tiny feet would take her curvy little body down the street. Weylin growled softly. Something was wrong.

He followed her for three more blocks, almost lost his shit as she turned down a road to the seedier side of Blue Valley. Right off the highway, there was a gas station, a twenty-four-hour roach coach, and a cheap motel.

His heart thudded as he watched her walk through the parking lot of the cheap motel, ignoring the catcalls from a group of guys leaning against a beat up Toyota and drinking beers from bottles wrapped in paper bags. Hell, it wasn't even dark yet.

Oh, fuck no.

Weylin snarled. The sound had been loud enough to bring a couple of heads swiveling in his direction. The distraction had allowed Gwendolyn to haul her cute little butt straight for the last room on the left side of the lot.

Shit.

If sweet little Gwen was staying here, her situation was far more dire than she'd let on. Weylin bristled beneath his fur. He wanted to bust open the door, pick her up and throw her over his shoulder, take her to his den. But he had no right to her, and he knew it.

Didn't mean he liked it, but he was not about to violate her space. Instead, he walked to the small patch of cement outside the beat up maroon painted door. Cheap black stickers with the numbers 394 were stuck on top of the paint.

He sniffed, revulsion filling him as he recognized urine from both humans and animals, chemicals, rotting food, and other revolting odors surrounding the place. The least of which was not death.

Fuck.

Gwen didn't belong there, but Weylin could not do a thing about it. Not yet, anyway. He paced back and forth, listening to the sounds of her going about what he assumed was her nightly routine.

The sun had just set, and the creeps in the lot were still lurking. It was the usual suspects, winos, and users, maybe one dealer. All human as far as he could tell, and the fact she was there was like a beacon to the evil inclined.

Weylin hated thinking of her in such a place. The lights were off, and the din of the television was low enough to suggest she slept with it on. In a place like this, he didn't blame her.

Admiration filled him as he imagined her struggle. She was smart, educated, beautiful, and she did not have the air of someone who'd grown up in a situation like this. So, this was new, he surmised.

His respect for her grew. Here he thought the woman had grit just walking into the bar to get a job. But it was more than that. Looked to him like she had given up a lot to pay for her grandfather's care. Her staying in the cheap motel, taking rideshares, and wearing simple clothing were all because she was likely putting everything she had into caring for the old man.

He didn't think people did things like that anymore. Gwendolyn Hoffer was just full of secrets and surprises, and Weylin wanted to learn them all. In due time, he told himself. For now, he would simply watch over her. Make sure she was safe.

Brave, tough girl. You can sleep tight, now. I got you.

CHAPTER SIX

DIRE WOLF MATES

"No pets on the premises," the manager of the *Merry Time Motel* barked at Gwendolyn as she emerged from her room at nine o'clock the next morning.

Mr. Jacobs was about sixty years old, if she had to guess, and he had on the same dirty coverall he seemed to wear every single day as he slithered past her. He was dragging two large trash bags towards the dumpster in the back, or so she assumed, and though Gwen had heard him, she had no idea what he was talking about.

"Pets?" she asked dumbly.

"Yeah. No pets. That monster dog you got has to go. Got three complaints this morning, folks scared walking by here last night," he grunted, not bothering to look at her.

"Monster dog? And why were people walking here if this is the last unit and you are the only one who has the key to the dumpster gate?" she called back, not at all surprised he ignored her.

She tucked her still damp curls behind her ears. Crap. She was gonna be late. Gwen had no time for the strange man's delusions. Pop was getting the results back on his latest round of tests, and she needed to be there with him. She grabbed her phone, checking the app to see how long before her car would arrive.

Another two minutes. Ooh. Maybe she would have time to run to the vending machine. Gwen had forgotten to run to the all night dollar store on 3rd Street last night. They had all sorts of snack bars and things real cheap, which was basically all she could afford, and she'd eaten her last granola bar last night.

Thank goodness for Lucy's kindness yesterday. That burger had been the best thing she'd eaten all month. Who knew brie and fig jam were amazing when paired with applewood smoked bacon, and two grilled ground brisket patties with caramelized onions on top? Yep, that Brock was a certified genius in the kitchen.

Living with little to no budget meant she'd been surviving on twenty-five cent packages of instant ramen noodles and granola bars from that same dollar store for the last two months. A girl could live on less, she supposed.

Ever since, she had gotten Pop into the assisted care facility. She'd gotten kicked out of the apartment they had leased and sold off every single thing they had worth anything to pay for his treatment, care, and residence. Pop didn't have very long. Another six months or so, the doctors had said, and Gwen was determined to work her fingers to the bone to ensure he had the best care for every single minute of those six months.

Her heart squeezed in her chest as she pictured life without her Pop, and a tear came tumbling down her cheek. Stupid tears. She hated crybabies, but this was hard, and she was left all alone to deal with it.

Gwendolyn loved her Pop more than anyone on earth and she was so sad to think of him being gone, let alone to have to face the big bad world alone without him in it. The wind rustled the yellow and red leaves on the scraggly looking trees behind the motel and Gwen pulled the old cardigan she had on tighter around her body.

She wore black jeans and sneakers, and a plain charcoal t-shirt with Pop's soft gray sweater on top. Fall was unpredictable in Blue

Valley, but that was typical of all New Jersey. Hot one day, frigid the next. Today promised to be temperate with a high of sixty-nine degrees.

She snorted at that and rolled her eyes at her lameness. Somewhere inside of Gwendolyn lived a 12-year-old boy, she was sure of it. Her sense of humor certainly supported the theory.

The blast of a horn had her looking up to see a red SUV with the license plate DWM394W. Yep. It was her ride. She clicked the little checkmark on the U-drive app that told whoever needed to know she'd been picked up, and Gwendolyn walked to the passenger seat.

"Morning, Gwendolyn," a familiar voice said as a big hand beat her to the door handle.

Gwendolyn startled, a hand on her chest as she turned to find bright, familiar green eyes locked on hers. It was him. Weylin. The sexy hot bartender from last night. What was he doing here?

"Sorry. Didn't mean to scare you," he murmured, opening the door.

"No, it's my fault. Um, I'm just naturally jumpy. What are you doing here?" she blurted, hating to sound ungrateful.

"Picking you up. You ordered a car from U-drive, right?"

"Um, yeah."

"Then that's why I am here. I drive for them sometimes," he said.

But that was odd, right? Didn't he co-own Serious Moonlight? She was almost certain Kelly had mentioned all the sexy members of the DWMC all had a piece of the pie.

"Oh, I see. Sorry, I just thought you were part owner in the bar—"

"I am that, too, but anyway, *er,* what are you doing here?" he asked as he seated himself in the driver's side, waiting until she buckled her seat belt before pulling out into traffic.

Gwen didn't want anyone to know her living situation. Shame and pride warred within her, but maybe she could play it off like she'd spent the night there with someone.

Like who? A man! Sure. She could just tell Hottie McHotterson that she'd shacked up with some rando on her way home. As if doing that was better than admitting to being poor, somehow.

Yeah. Right. Soooo believable. Ugh.

She looked down at herself and snorted. So sexy. Ugh. Gwendolyn was hardly a femme fatale and certainly not a girl who rented motel rooms with strange men. She mulled it over for a minute before settling on the truth.

"I'm, well, actually, I am staying here for a while just until I can afford someplace else," she said, pride stinging her eyes.

She waited for him to judge her or criticize, but he didn't. Weylin just nodded and drove, his glittering emerald eyes on the road. My oh my, but he was handsome.

"So why are you here, Weylin, um, what was your last name?" she asked, uncertain if he'd introduced himself last night.

"Scott, it's Weylin Scott. And you are Gwendolyn?"

"Hoffer. Gwen to my friends."

"I like that. Can I call you Gwen?" he asked, a small smile tugging at the corner of his lips.

She mulled it over, getting the distinct impression he was asking for something else. Without any red flags or warning bells ringing in her head, Gwen nodded.

"You can. After all, I think it's only fair since we'll be working together."

"Good. Friends then, huh?" he asked, and pursed his lips.

Lord, help me, she thought and hid the sudden urge to fan herself.

He had the most kissable lips she had ever seen, and the fact he had actually kissed her was something she could not wrap her head around. Gwen didn't exactly garner that kind of attention from men.

Well, that was not entirely true. She had her share of admirers, but they usually gave up once they heard her hangups about sex. As in, she wasn't putting out for just anyone.

Where was she again? Oh yeah. Weylin's lips. They were a reddish pink against his pale skin, plump and softer than they appeared. After all, she had firsthand knowledge, she thought with a blush. Surprising they were so soft, she mused. Not that she went around collecting info on boys' lips or anything. But there was just something about him she found positively intriguing.

"You have the right address?" she asked.

Weylin nodded and tapped the screen on the console of the SUV to show the GPS. He had Hope Springs typed in and they were about thirty-minutes out.

"So, who's at Hope Springs? Your Pop, right? He okay?" he asked, then blanched when she stiffened. "I'm sorry. I should not have asked you that. It's none of my business."

"No, it's okay. It's just new, you know? Yes, Pop is here, and they are making him comfortable. It's about all they can do now. He has dementia, and it seems to be advancing. With his osteoporosis, the chances of him falling and getting hurt were too great to keep him home, though I tried for a long time to manage that way."

"Is there no other family to help?" he asked softly.

"Just me. My parents left when I was about six, and I didn't even know I had a grandfather. He came down to social services the second he heard about me. Bundled me up, carted me home, and took care of me."

"Gwen, you don't have to talk about this if you don't want to," he replied, giving her an out.

"I don't mind. I mean, this is my reality."

"I appreciate that, but it's okay to need a break from reality now and then, you know? I'm sure he would want you to take care of yourself, too. From what you've said, he sounds like a good man."

"Yeah, he is the best."

Weylin reached over and patted her leg, the brief, platonic contact left tendrils of awareness racing through her, and her breath caught. Of course, her stomach chose that exact moment to go off like a bullhorn, growling loudly in the cab of the SUV. She bit her lip to hide her embarrassment.

"You hungry? I got snacks," Weylin informed her.

He leaned over to open the glove compartment where a small

basket filled with trail mix, protein bars, and little bags of cheese crackers sat.

"Help yourself. There's a water right here, too," he murmured and nudged the armrest where an unopened bottle sat.

"Sorry. I didn't have time for breakfast," she said.

It wasn't exactly a lie. The whole truth was, she ran out of snacks. But this looked good. Oh well. A girl had to eat. Gwendolyn grabbed the trail mix and opened it.

Ooh, this was good stuff, she mused, eyeing the slivers of almonds, peanuts, craisins, and the little dark chocolate chunks with delight. She ate some and offered the bag to Weylin, who smiled and said thanks before snagging a handful.

He chewed with his mouth closed, which was a huge plus in her book, made small talk, and sang along with the radio. He had a nice, pleasant voice, and he knew the words to her favorite Bon Jovi songs, a must if you lived in New Jersey, and Gwen was a Jersey girl through and through.

The minutes sped by, and she found herself relaxing in his company. It was easy with him, for some reason. The interior of the SUV smelled like something woodsy and masculine, his cologne perhaps. She'd never smelled anything like it before. Pop had liked Old Spice, and she was allergic to most other scents. But not this one. This one was just fine, she mused and breathed in another gulp.

"Something wrong?" he asked, sniffing the air after her.

Shoot. She'd been caught. Gwen's face really started to burn just then, and she bit her lip. How embarrassing!

"Um, no. Sorry, it's just I have allergies to most air fresheners and perfumes, but it smells good in here and it's not bothering my sinuses. I was just trying to identify the brand."

"Oh," he said, sounding surprised.

"Um, what is it? The fragrance, I mean," she murmured, wishing a hole would open up and swallow her.

"I dunno. I don't like strong scents, so I stay away from them myself. Could be my deodorant, I guess."

Weylin lifted his arm and Gwendolyn barked out a laugh, was he smelling his own armpit? Sure enough, he did. Even offered her a go, but she just laughed it off and shook her head. It wasn't too long before he joined her in a deep, throaty chuckle.

"Guess that's silly of me," he said, and seemed embarrassed.

For some reason, that made her like him even more. Maybe there was more to Weylin Scott than met the eye. She hadn't known many men, but Gwendolyn liked to think she had a good intuition.

Danger. Danger.

The man is dangerous, Gwenny. He's a bartender and likely has a million phone numbers saved in his contact list.

She felt a stab of jealousy at the thought, but she shook it off. Gwen had no reason or right to be jealous of the man. They weren't dating or anything. She had no time for that nonsense at all. With all her hangups, it would take a man with the patience of a saint to break through her barriers—figuratively and literally.

Weylin Scott didn't strike her as a saint. Too bad really. She wouldn't mind getting to know him better. Not at all.

Why would he need to be a saint, Gwen, when a man is all anyone could ever want?

"What are you thinking about so quiet over there?" he probed.

"Oh, nothing. My mind just wanders," she said, offering him more trail mix. "You know, I never shared snacks in a U-drive with a boy before," she blurted, and her cheeks heated with embarrassment.

Weylin's grin got bigger, and he held out his hand for more of the stuff. Gwen obliged, wondering why she told him that little tidbit. She watched him pour the handful of salty sweet goodies into his mouth without spilling a thing.

He chewed and swallowed, winking at her when he caught her staring. She was making an idiot of herself, but she couldn't seem to stop. He was intriguing, and Gwendolyn was curious by nature.

"So, the bar must not be doing well if you're moonlighting with U-drive, huh?" she asked, worried now that she thought about it.

"What? No! The bar is doing great. I just do this sometimes when I am feeling bored," he said, smiling tightly.

"Oh, okay."

Hmm. Was he lying? He had no reason to, but she had a feeling he was holding something back from her. Odd. Very odd.

"We're here," Weylin announced, pulling into a parking spot.

"Okay, well, thank you very much," she began, but he was already out of the truck and opening her door.

"You are fast," she murmured.

That brought another pink blush to his cheeks, and she watched mesmerized as Weylin lifted his arm and rubbed the back of his neck. His biceps looked likely to shred the t-shirt he wore, they were so dang big. Holy cow. He must work out like a madman to be so fit.

Looking down at herself, Gwen could only shake her head. No one would ever accuse her of being a gym rat. But she was who she was, and she liked her body just fine. She just wasn't made to be one of those slender females. Gwendolyn had curves on her curves, even with the lousy diet she'd been on, but you could blame the FDA for that.

The United States of America allowed way too much garbage in their food, and that alone accounted for the increase in obesity and disease among the poorest of its citizens. Other countries did not have that problem, something Gwen had become aware of after she'd gone to England with her high school with her honors history class.

Whatever.

She and Weylin were not an item. It didn't matter if she was chubby and poor, and he was a veritable demigod. Not that she cared about money or looks. What the heck was going on with her? She had more important things to attend to than worry over a nonexistent relationship with her new coworker.

Wake up, Gwenny.

"We going in?" Weylin asked, waiting for her to speak.

"Well, I am. I mean, I'm sure you have another person to pick up or—"

"Nope. I logged out. Figured you could use a ride back anyway, and besides, who else is gonna feed me trail mix on the way back?" he asked playfully.

Gwendolyn bit her lip and nodded. He was kind, sweet, and really freaking hot. But why was he so interested in her? She frowned.

"Look Weylin, I appreciate the ride and the fact you turned off the tipping option, but if you are here with any ulterior motives, you should know a few things about me from the start. I am not in the market for a one-night stand. I do not put out. I am not interested in playing games or being a notch on your bedpost. My Pop raised me to have a strong moral compass. I promised myself when I was sixteen that I was going to save my virginity for marriage, and I meant it."

She waited, but Weylin stood stock still, no expression on his movie star handsome face. Gwendolyn sucked in a breath before she continued.

"I am not playing hard to get or throwing down a gauntlet. Understand? I truly believe intimacy is meant to be intimate and I am not judging anyone else for their lifestyle, but this is my body, and it is my choice to be celibate until I find *my him*."

"*Your him?*"

"Yes. *My him*. My person. Someone I love, who loves me, who respects me and doesn't want to change me or ridicule me. So, if you are hanging out here cause you wanna bang the new girl, you are better off leaving. Got it?"

Weylin's green gaze seemed to glow in the crisp autumn morning, and Gwen sucked in a sharp breath. He took a step toward her, then another, and another, until Gwendolyn was backed up against the SUV.

"I can't say I've lived a celibate life, because frankly, I've been living the opposite. But I don't play with people or hearts, and I never ever stepped over the line unless someone asked me to. You don't know me yet, and you don't trust me, and that is fine. You'll learn I mean what I say. And I do respect you, Gwendolyn Hoffer. I'm just asking you to be open-minded about me. Can you do that?"

"Can I do what?" she asked, trying hard to catch her breath, but it was a little difficult with him being so close to her.

"Just don't rush to any conclusions about me you aren't sure of yet. Neither of us can tell the future, Gwen. But I can tell you this, and it is the truth, I wanna get to know you. We can go slow or fast as you like."

"Weylin—"

"Gwendolyn, I just wanna spend some time with you. Just some time, okay?"

"Why? I just told you it's not going to end in the bedroom like your other conquests. There's no point in pursuing me," she stated bluntly.

It took a sledgehammer to knock down walls. But Gwendolyn imagined she'd need a battering ram to fell this particular rampart. Of course, Weylin smiled just then, and her heart thudded even louder.

He was just too handsome. Red hair in a thousand different shades from the deepest auburn to the lightest golden flames danced in the morning breeze. Copper-colored eyelashes, so long they were positively sinful, brushed his skin with every blink of his hypnotic green eyes. Then there were his muscles—*so many muscles*—all fighting against the ridiculously tight cotton t-shirt he wore.

Whoa. Down girl!

Butterflies turned into fighter jets inside her stomach. She just could not catch her breath. The man was hot. Smokin' hot. Much too much for a chubby little homebody, goody-goody like Gwenny.

"Oh, baby, you are so worth it."

"Weylin, I mean it. I won't sleep with you," she said, but she didn't sound so certain.

"I won't push you into anything you don't want, Gwendolyn. I promise and I am a man of my word," he said, looking more serious than she had ever seen him.

"Ha! You'll get bored in a week," she snarked.

It was only the truth. Guys had come on to her before, thinking she was playing hard to get with them. But with Weylin, Gwen felt conflicted. Sad even.

What the heck?

Why should the truth make her feel so miserable? Yes, she'd made her vow very young, after a terrible teen romance that had ended the only way it could have—utter heartbreak. But Gwendolyn had never questioned or regretted her decision to abstain from smexy times.

Until now, her inner voice whispered. Gwen gasped, gaze flicking to Weylin's own questioning stare, and she shook her head. She tucked a lock of hair behind her ear, pretending not to notice the charged atmosphere between them. The wind whistled through the trees, the fall sun was still shining, but Gwen couldn't tell which way was up or down or sideways.

"Think what you like, baby. I'm not going anywhere either."

Just like that, her anxiety abided. She frowned hard, angry at herself that he should affect her so. It just wasn't her way. Despite his handsome face and pleasant demeanor, the fact remained Weylin Scott was a scoundrel. Relying on a man for her own inner peace was a foreign concept to Gwendolyn. That he should settle her upset with some words was decidedly uncool.

Heck no. That was not gonna fly.

"Well, it's your time to waste," she mumbled, giving him her back as she hoofed it through the parking lot.

His woodsy fragrance was like a drug, she thought as he caught up to her easily. Damn the man for reading her so well. It was like he knew he was getting beneath her skin.

Gwen had to actively stop herself from taking that one tiny step that would close the space between them. Her heart pounded, and her body heated. She never felt anything like it. Like she was dying for him to kiss her, but somewhere in her mind, she knew better than that.

Warning bells sounded inside her head. This man was dangerous on several levels. For one thing, he was the first guy to make her regret her promise in, well, ever. For another, just being near him made her think of all those dirty little things that happened in those naughty little romance books she liked to read in private. Only, in her version, she and Weylin were the main characters.

Sizzle.

"Are you okay?" he asked, and she realized she had stopped walking.

"What? Of course," she retorted and continued on her path.

Weylin Scott was too sexy for his own good, never mind hers. She closed her eyes and held her breath, seeming to sense the minute he backed off.

"Come on. Let's get you to Pop's appointment."

Gwen nodded and allowed him to lead her inside. She was not sure what had just happened. But it was big. Really big.

Weylin spent the morning with her at the center. He listened when she needed him to, stayed with her after the doctor left, held her when her emotions got the best of her, and even joined her when she read passages from the Bible out loud to Pop.

If she didn't know any better, she would think Weylin Scott was trying to make her fall for him. But that couldn't be. He was drop dead gorgeous, and she was, *well,* her. Men who looked like him wanted a sure thing, and she just was not that. She had told him so in no uncertain terms.

Looking at his profile now, Gwen suddenly wished she was different. Her heart squeezed. She swallowed back her regret and tried to focus on the hurt that was inevitable. They were just too different, and she was not in the market for any heartache. Gwen was not sophisticated enough for a man like Weylin.

He'll get bored and move on. Just wait it out.

Sound advice, but for some reason, it did not make her feel any better.

CHAPTER SEVEN

DIRE WOLF MATES

I'm losing my mind.

The woman was driving me bananas. Or maybe it was just being close to her and not being able to do a thing about it.

Days had passed and Weylin was no closer to Gwen than he'd been since their first meeting. Okay. Not true. He actually got closer back then. At least she'd let him kiss her. Sort of. Fine, he stole that kiss.

Grrr.

His dick thumped in his jeans, and he growled in frustration. He watched her move and bit back his moan. The woman had the most glorious ass Weylin had ever seen. And he meant that in a totally non-creepy stalkerish kinda way. He just could not stop stealing glances at the thing. She was on a whole other level of fuckable.

Shit.

His jeans were too damn tight. He'd even gone commando, but that provided no relief at all. Another bite of his lip and a stifled growl as she bent down to retrieve a new bottle of simple syrup from the bottom shelf behind the bar.

Wanna bend her over. Snuggle in behind. Grab those thick thighs with my hands. Spread em wide. Fill her so deep. Yes. Yes. NO!

He should not be thinking things like that about his future mate. Well, his *would be future mate if he could only get her to pay attention to him* might be a more apt title. Problem was, the little human didn't even seem to notice.

"Weylin, I mean it. I won't sleep with you,"

Her words replayed in his head, but what could he do about it? She was not kidding when she talked about her promise to stay a virgin until she married. In his relationships before, when words failed him, Weylin had been a fan of using kisses to make up for it. Well, more than kisses, but if Gwen said no to sex, then what was a guy to do?

Not to mention the fact that Derrick had all but ordered him to stay away from her. He was to give no hint or suggestion that she was his mate. Fucking Alphahole had pretty much decided to cockblock Weylin for life!

He thought having a human mate might fuck things up for the Pack, and he wasn't having that with his own mate being ready to drop her pup any day now.

It wasn't fair. But again, what could he do about it? Weylin just wanted the same opportunity to have his own happily ever after ending that Derrick and several of the other Dire Wolves in their former MC had found. Was that so wrong?

"One part vodka, then add fresh lemon juice," she murmured, probably thinking she was speaking too low for him to hear.

If he was human, that might have been true. But he wasn't.

And therein lies the rub, he mused, with an expression of distaste on his face.

Still, it was cute the way she recited each recipe as she worked, even if she presumed it was to herself. Gwendolyn was going over a list of signature cocktails featured at Serious Moonlight that Sheila had given her when Weylin walked into the bar.

Technically, he was not supposed to work today, but he'd asked Derrick to switch his schedule, so he had every shift she had. It was the least his Alpha could do. Lucy had supported his request, for which she had his eternal gratitude. The Alpha fem was a hopeless romantic, and she'd argued that Gwen could hardly fall for Weylin on her own without being near him.

Smart lady.

Three days had passed, and so far, nothing. That meant Weylin had seventy-two hours of staying within her periphery. It damn near killed him being so close, and yet so far. Sure, Derrick took pity on him, giving him the same schedule just to get him out of his hair.

But that wasn't enough to get the sexy as all get female to look his way. Weylin stifled a yawn. He was running himself ragged following her home and standing guard outside her door in his Wolf form every night.

What else could he do? That place was a hellhole frequented by all types of unsavory folks. Humans were bad enough, but he scented one or two supes in the area, and that did not sit well with him at all. He wished he could just take her home with him to the Pack House, but that was a no-no.

Even if Derrick allowed it, Gwen wasn't anywhere near ready for him to reveal the truth about himself, let alone what she was to him.

"You got this," Sheila said.

Gwendolyn nodded and lifted the cocktail shaker, mobbing it back and forth at ear level. She was in the process of prepping one of every cocktail. Something all new bartenders had to do before they could pass muster.

He was pleasantly surprised watching her work. She had real potential. There was music pumping through the speakers, country western tonight, and there was already a pretty nice early dinner crowd. Some dudes were seated at the bar drinking beers, and a group of older women were having martinis and sharing a tapas tower. But none of it seemed to mess with Gwen's concentration.

Weylin had been keeping a close eye on her, and for a religious woman, she was not easily shaken. Thank fuck. When she'd told him that about herself, he thought maybe he had misheard. Why on earth would the Fates match a rounder like him with an angel like her?

Someone messed up, or maybe Derrick was right, and he got it all wrong. But nope. Weylin spent the last few days trailing her on two legs and four and he was more certain than ever. Gwendolyn Hoffer was supposed to be his.

"Weylin, can you take over? I'm going out for a bit with Leo to check our venue," Sheila called, breaking his train of thought.

He blinked, gaze shooting right over to where Gwen was pouring her next drink. She didn't even bother to glance at him. Shit. What was wrong with him? Did she find him unattractive? Too burly? Maybe she just didn't go for redheads.

Sad and dejected, he walked over to where the two females worked, staying on the opposite side of the bar. He just didn't trust himself to be any closer to her than that.

"Yep, I got it," he replied softly.

He sat down on a barstool and watching Gwen with a steady gaze. She glanced at him. Barely. It might have been a trick of the light. But he thought he saw her brown eyes widen for a moment. His Dire Wolf hummed with approval. Maybe she was aware of him on some level, at least. Even if she'd been doing her best to act like the other day hadn't happened.

He'd practically spent the entire day with her. After a friend of the Pack set him up with an established U-drive account, it was nothing at all to wait for her to order a car. He'd been surprised at the destination, but it did not matter. He would've driven her to Timbuktu if that was where she wanted to go.

She didn't know it, of course, but the feisty female was safe as could be with him. The fact she seemed to relax in his presence after some initial awkwardness warmed the beast within him. She hadn't expected more from him than a ride, but when he walked her inside and voiced his intentions to stay with her, she seemed grateful.

Poor thing, having to go through all that alone. He didn't know how she did it. Being born in a Pack meant you had people with you to back you up, bolster you, and offer support whether you wanted it or not. It was a choice sure, but Gwendolyn did not have that option.

Now she does. We'll be her Pack, his Wolf inserted.

His mind kept wandering back to that day, and he wondered what he'd done wrong to make her keep her distance ever since. Maybe Weylin had been too much, forcing his company on her by waiting in the hallway while Gwendolyn went inside Pop's room. Or perhaps, he hadn't done enough. The not knowing was eating at him, and the Wolf was getting antsy.

He didn't mean to eavesdrop, he couldn't help but overhear the doctor's prognosis. It was not good, but the older man was comfortable at least. No pain, that was what she'd begged, and Weylin's Wolf had raged at that.

"Well?" Gwen's soft voice asked the doctor, and Weylin heard the plea behind her words.

"No change, Ms. Hoffer. He is comfortable for now, but the most recent scan showed a series of minor strokes. It is highly unlikely Mr. Hoffer will get out of bed again. I am very sorry," the doctor stated.

"Oh no. Poor Pop," she'd murmured, tears in her voice.

Weylin had heard all he could take without moving into action. In half a second, he was beside her, wrapped his arm around her waist, and miracle of miracles, she'd leaned into him for support. The doctor waited for her to nod, and she did, then he went ahead and explained the test results in more detail.

He was so fucking relieved when she didn't back up or push him away. In fact, her tiny hand latched onto his as she allowed herself to rest against him. Taking comfort in his body was a gift he never expected, and fuck was it beautiful.

"Thank you, doctor," she had said when the man had finished his long speech.

Weylin had tried to listen to his words, but being so close to her had filled his senses. After hearing the news about her grandfather's condition, Gwendolyn had a moment of pure despair that was so heartbreaking all he could do was hold her while she cried.

Seeing her so upset was super hard, but hearing her plead with someone made him want to kill things. Lucky for the doctor, the man had been gentle when explaining their standard of care was to ensure all patients were very comfortable as they transitioned from this stage of life to the next.

Afterward, she sat by her grandfather, read to him. She cared for him and spent some time with the staff as well. Weylin waited in the hall, not wanting to intrude, but he heard everything, and his heart swelled with respect and affection for this intriguing woman.

Strong. Passionate. Loyal woman. Soft heart. Good heart.

They'd stayed a couple of hours, and when she was finished, he'd led the way back to his SUV, allowing the silence to envelop them like a safety blanket in the vehicle. The emotional and physical toll of seeing someone you loved suffer that way was unthinkable to him.

Dire Wolf Shifters lived very long lives, and illness rarely played a part. After a moment, his Gwendolyn with the pretty brown eyes had turned to him and thanked him—*him, Weylin Scott, newly reformed playboy who no one takes seriously*—for just being there with her. Like that was a hardship.

His heart thudded at the memory, and his Wolf bayed like a wild thing inside him.

"I'm so sorry for what you are going through, Gwendolyn. I know my opinion might not mean anything to you, but I think you're an incredible person. You care so much, sweetheart. I have never met anyone like you. And, this might not seem like much, but I am here for you if you need a hand, or a shoulder, or an ear, or anything at all."

He thought for sure he'd blown it. His Wolf was about to chew him a new asshole, but then she smiled through her tears. It was one of those tentative ones, watery, and kind of trembly. But maybe that was why it struck him like lightning.

Precious. Fleeting. Honest. Gift.

It was a moment he would never forget. Even now, he coveted it, cradling the memory to his heart and mind. Burying it deep so no one could ever take it from him.

"Thank you, Weylin. But you're wrong, it does mean a lot. You don't seem like the kind of guy who makes promises like that to just anyone, and I am touched, even if maybe I don't deserve them."

"What do you mean?"

"Despite what you saw, I'm not especially good or anything. It's just, he's my Pop."

"We can agree to disagree on you being especially good. Now, wanna go grab something to eat with me?"

He'd asked her to get food with him, even held his breath, waiting for her answer. Thank fuck, Gwendolyn had said yes. Driving an hour out of his way to feed her hot dogs from a famous hole in the wall grill that'd been serving the same deep fried dogs for over seventy-five years was fun.

She had scoffed at first, doubting any hot dog was worth the ride, but after her first bite, the girl was hooked. Damn, she was special. He had never had so much fun with a woman. She was even cute when she belched behind her napkin after she had polished off her third hot dog loaded with house-made relish and a tall, cold birch beer.

Gwen had been mortified until he let one rip out his mouth, then she just laughed till she almost fell out of her chair. Afterward, they shared a huge slice of cherry pie, covered in real whipped cream, and then he brought her to the roadhouse to get ready for work.

Fun woman. Sexy, too.

CHAPTER EIGHT

Dire Wolf Mates

Everything had been going along just fine. Or so he'd thought. But overnight, something had changed. Gwendolyn had started avoiding him in earnest after that day. He felt raw and confused, his Dire Wolf, too.

Weylin hated to admit it, but he was a little bit butt hurt by the whole thing. Fuck, he didn't know how to do this. What she needed was someone with patience and understanding, but what the Fates stuck her with was him.

Weylin was OG love 'em and leave 'em type. He never had a serious relationship, flitting from bed to bed like a bee flying from flower to flower. At least he hadn't bedded any of their staff.

Oh, he'd had some minor flirtations with one or two waitresses. But that was as far as it went. Even he knew not to shit where he ate.

Then there was the biggest impediment to his pursuing Gwendolyn, and that was the fact she was human. How he was going to get over that obstacle was a mystery to all, him included.

Weylin was a damn monster. These days, he was barely keeping his animal under control. It was way too soon for any normal to understand, but Gwendolyn Hoffer had already burrowed her way into

Weylin's untried heart. Bottom line was he never felt this way about a woman before.

Warm. Fuzzy. Possessive. And yes, horny as fuck.

But it was more than that. He was curious about her. Wanted to learn what made her tick. He just had to get near her first, but she'd bolstered her defenses and was locked up tighter than Fort Knox.

It was hell on his nerves. He felt as smooth and suave as a pimple-faced virgin at the school prom whenever he was around Gwen. This was not his usual MO, for fuck's sake.

Weylin had his share of hot women. But not one of them held a candle to Gwen. Now that he had met his mate, they were just bodies in the dark. He had been open and honest with them, of course. He was Wolf, not a dog.

Dire Wolf Shifters never stayed in one place long enough to form permanent attachments. Until now. Hell, when Derrick had announced his intentions to settle down in one spot, plant roots, Weylin had initially balked.

Note to self: Send the Alpha a beef jerky bouquet and a thank you card.

Well, if he claimed his mate, maybe he would. For now, he would keep that notion under wraps. Derrick was being too much of a cock-blocker to deserve any meaty goodness.

Second note to self: Send myself a beef jerky bouquet because I am awesome, and I am gonna win my mate.

Yeah, that was more like it! Weylin could not be more grateful for his Pack setting up shop in this little slip of a town in New Jersey. This place had presented him with something to work for. A goal. His mate.

Mine.

Gwen's natural strawberry scent reached his nostrils, and his lips flexed in an easy smile as he breathed her in. So tempting. Sweet. Fresh.

"Ready," she said, excitement ringing in her voice.

"All done?" he asked as she finished pouring the last drink into a martini glass.

It was a twist on a lemon drop martini made with a brand new local label, Crescent Moon Gin. It was a new branch of the Bite label owned and operated by Mason Lane, a member of the Macconwood Wolf Pack. Good people. Good Shifters. And the guy made fantastic spirits far as the Dire Wolf Pack was concerned.

"Yep. All done. Lemme know what you think," Gwen replied, biting her lip as he sipped drink after drink, washing his mouth out with water between sips.

Weylin was a consummate professional. Fated mate or not, he had to take his job as a co-owner of Serious Moonlight, *er*, seriously. He opened his senses before each sip, allowing the depth of the flavors, the essence of the alcohol, and the ratio of sweet, tart, and bitter to filter through as he tried each one.

Holy, Fuck. The woman was a rockstar.

Mine.

"Shit."

"Shit?" she asked, frowning hard.

"No, no," he blurted. "I meant it like, shit, girl, these are fantastic!" he told her with a grin.

Just like that, his sassy sweet Gwendolyn lit up before him. He'd be a liar if he said it meant nothing to him, that way she had of glowing at the smallest of compliments. He'd bet she wasn't used to them, and damn, but he wanted to change that. She deserved compliments. Lots of them.

"Really?" she asked, her lips turned up in a mirror image of his own expression.

Weylin nodded, his heart warming at her obvious pleasure. He liked she was so happy when he complimented her. Wanted to see what else he could say or do to bring that look of joy to her face, that hint of radiance to her caramel eyes.

"Truly. You nailed them!"

"Yes! Okay, so do you think I can handle the back bar tonight?" Gwen asked.

The back bar was Lucy's usual haunt, and since Gwen was filling in for the Alpha fem, Weylin did not have an issue with it. She'd been tending bar the last three nights beside Sheila and the she-Wolf had nothing but glowing reports on how the curvy little normal had handled herself. Apparently, her sassy mouth was a source of amusement with the females of the Pack.

Takes one to know one, he mused. Not that he'd be saying that out loud. Those Pack females scared the shit out of him. Any sane man would say the same, of that he was certain.

"Think you're ready to go it alone? It's Saturday, you know. Our busiest night," he told her.

"I'm ready, and you know I need the tips," Gwen replied, no guile in her voice.

He knew she was working hard to pay for her Pop's care. Hell, he wished he could just give her the money, but it was too soon for that. He tried hinting at a loan and she damn near turned to ice. He read between the lines. Gwen would not take any handouts from him.

"Alright. You can take the lead in the back bar. I'll be checking in on you from time to time, but don't be afraid to call out if you need something."

"Okay, but if you come back here, who will handle the front?" she asked.

"Saturday, remember? Me and Cole will both be at the front bar, but I'm manager tonight. If there is an issue, I will deal with it."

She had her hands on her hips but was listening to everything he said. If he didn't know any better, he would think she was a Shifter the way she practically growled at him with her normal little voice. She had grit, that one. Grit and sass, and fuck, was it sexy!

"You'll be keeping tabs on me. Got it," she said. "I won't let you down."

"You couldn't if you tried," Weylin whispered and rubbed the back of his neck.

Tonight was going to be a long one. He probably needed to let the Wolf out before the crowd started coming in. Weylin was shifting into his Wolf every night, but he was staying outside her room and that was not the same as running.

The animal needed to let off some steam. Usually, his choices were to shift and run in the woods or find some woman to fuck when he got this antsy. He didn't want anyone but Gwen, and she was nowhere near ready for physical intimacy, so shifting to his monster won out.

"Oh, my shirt came in," Gwen told him with a grin that stopped him in his tracks.

She was so damn pretty. Her hair was down, and curls were raining down her back and shoulders, so bouncy and sexy. He was dying to feel them between his fingers. Wondered if they were coarse or silky. He would bet on the latter, but damn, wouldn't he love to find out for sure?

His attention was snagged by Gwen as she held up the teeny weeny excuse for a t-shirt that Sheila had ordered her. Weylin frowned hard.

Fuck.

There he was, hoping he wouldn't have to smack anyone upside the head tonight, but it looked like that plan was flying right out the window. The woman was fine as fuck in baggy tees and cotton pants. But he had forgotten all about the Serious Moonlight uniform—*if you could call it that.*

Thank you very much, Sheila. Fuck.

"Hey, you don't have to look like that. It will fit me," Gwen retorted.

Her posture had gone ramrod straight, and the scent coming off her was bitter, like she was angry or hurt. Fuck. She was obviously mistaking his momentary pause for something it wasn't. But that was all his fault. He should have explained better.

"Hang on a second, Gwen—"

"No need. I understand by your expression what you are thinking, but let me tell you something, people come in all shapes and sizes."

"Gwen, I think you misunderstood, and I know that's my fault, but if you just let me—"

The woman was not letting him get a word in edge wise, and fuck, it was difficult for him to stay focused. Her eyes were bright, and her hair was flying as she waved her hands around as she spoke in true New Jersey fashion.

"I know the shirt looks small, but Sheila said it stretches. And yes, I realize I am a big girl, but that is no one's business, but mine. I have tended bar before, and let me tell you something, Mr. Body Beautiful, my boobs usually detract from my belly, so you don't have to worry about me. I will do just fine with your customers. The rest of me will be behind the bar. I won't embarrass you or the business," she said each word with a hushed fury that both startled and turned him on.

Damn, but she was feisty. Gorgeous in her fury, too, but she had it all wrong.

"Gwen, I gotta tell you, I have no idea what you are talking about," he growled.

"Listen up, because I will only say this once. Words have power, and I believe in being kind to my body and my mind. Now, I realize I don't look like you all, but can I help it if I wasn't blessed with whatever superior physical genes your entire friend circle was blessed with? I mean, I have never seen so many tall, muscular, good-looking people in one place in my life. But that doesn't mean I will shame you when I put on the uniform—"

"Hang on a second," he pleaded louder.

His heart was pounding, the Wolf clawing at hm. Fuck! He fucked this all up. Weylin felt like was about to explode, but wait—*did she say?*

"You think I'm good-looking?"

That little doozy seemed to stop her tirade, and Weylin's grin grew wider. Her arousal teased his senses, adding even more sweetness to her natural strawberry scent. Weylin's chest rumbled with his beast as he watched her like the predator he was.

"Oh, like you need me to tell you that you're hot. Fish for compliments somewhere else, buster. Besides, I heard all about you from the waitstaff. You're a regular heartbreaker, aren't you?" she replied, hands on those damn delightful hips of hers.

What? Shit. The staff was talking shit about him. Well, that sucked.

"Gwendolyn, I don't know what you heard, but I never fooled around with someone who didn't know the deal, alright? And never with any of the staff. Besides, I already told you, that's behind me now," Weylin said, narrowing his eyes at her.

"Whatever," she replied.

She placed her hands on her hips, and fuck if that didn't emphasize her sexy little curves. Her brown eyes seemed to glow amber, spitting fire as her temper fluctuated. Sassy, sweet, and so damn pretty his heart was liable to stop if he kept on staring. Call him a glutton for punishment, cause he simply could not look away.

Her chest lifted as she sucked in a deep breath, and he closed his eyes. The longing he felt was fucking painful. But if he failed at every other thing, he had to at least clear the air between them.

"Just for the record, Gwen, I wasn't staring at you because I thought the shirt was too small. I was staring at you because the thought of anyone else seeing you in that is making me lose my damn mind," he ground out, gritting his teeth to try to hold in his animal's snarl.

The Wolf was damn near crazed with the idea he had hurt her. Even unintentionally, it ripped him up inside to know he had caused her any bit of hurt.

"I'm sorry that was unprofessional and unkind," Gwendolyn replied, eyes downcast.

Well, shit. He didn't want her feeling bad or anything. Fuck. he was not cut out for this. She was better off without him.

Grrrr.

"No need for apologies. I'm the fuckup here. You are gonna rock the shit out of that uniform, baby," he murmured, the endearment natural as it slipped from his lips.

He was always calling her baby or sweetheart or something cute cause he thought she was just that. Cute as a dumpling and ten times as tasty.

Mine. Want. Grrr.

Ha, you don't have to say that," she started.

Her cheeks were turning pink, so he knew she liked the compliment. Good. That was good, right? His animal let him breathe easier, but he was still scratching to get out.

Fuck.

Weylin needed fresh air. He needed space.

"Alright, um, why don't you go on and get ready? I will meet you at the back bar later on, okay?"

Weylin waited for her nod before letting go of the breath he'd been holding. She was still frowning, and he felt like a total piece of shit. The woman was so damn beautiful it hurt to look at her and not touch her, but she didn't know he felt like that. How could she when he wasn't even allowed to tell her?

Fuck. Fuck. FUCK.

He left her there, hauling ass to the side door down the hallway. He had to slow his breathing. He felt his Wolf clawing inside, and it hurt like hell. There was not much time before shit got busy, but Weylin had to make it outside, to the woods at the end of the lot. Then he could shift and run and get rid of some of his animal's angst. A sound brought his head up, and he turned with a snarl on his lips.

"You alright?" Cole asked, hands raised, and Weylin shook his head.

"Nah. I am far fucking from it," he growled.

"Look, you need to relax. I think Derrick is right. Forget the normal, man. Maybe you should go out for a ride or something. Grab your bike and take off for a few months?"

His Pack mate stared at him like he was fucking crazy, and Weylin wanted to punch him in the face. Asshole. Forget her? Was he insane? Gwendolyn was ingrained in his very soul. Cole and Derrick could just fuck right off. He was not giving her up. He just needed a plan to woo her, that was all.

"She's not just some normal, Cole," he growled. "Gwendolyn is my fated mate, okay? I felt it the first time I saw her. My Wolf knows it.

I'll lose my mind without her, man. She is it for me," he confessed to his Pack mate.

Cole scowled, hands on his hips. Weylin knew what he was thinking. It was the same thing Derrick had said. They finally had a place of their own after wandering around the world for decades without roots or ties.

It was no simple thing. The Dire Wolf Pack had settled down, and they did not want to risk it. Outing what he was to a normal was always gonna be risky. Even worse, if she rejected him, his beast would go mad, and Derrick would have to put him down.

Fuck.

His Alpha did not want that on his plate, and he could not blame him. Neither did Weylin. But what choice did he have?

His sensitive ears picked up on the sounds of the band arriving. They were a Shifter group, all women, and they usually packed the house. Sure, the bar's customers tended to be mostly supes, though the odd human came in from time to time.

He could hear them loading their instruments onto the stage. Other sounds filtered through to where he and Cole stood by that side door. Brock shouted orders from the kitchen, the nighttime wait staff was slowly filing in, and Thor, another Pack mate, had taken his place by the door as the bouncer for the night.

It was just another Saturday night, and Serious Moonlight promised to be packed.

"I can't pretend to know what you're going through, man," Cole added. "But maybe just take it day by day."

"Yeah," Weylin nodded, clapping the male on the shoulder as he walked past.

Not like he could take the days two at a time, anyway. Slow and steady won the race. But Gwendolyn wasn't just some race he wanted to win. She wasn't a challenge he needed to notch his bedpost. She was his whole damn future. For a Dire Wolf who never took things seriously before, and enjoyed living in the fast lane, slow and steady was a helluva change.

"So, shift if you need to. I will cover you for a while. But bro, is she worth it?" Cole asked before he walked away.

"Fuck yeah," Weylin replied automatically.

As if on cue, Gwendolyn entered the hall, dressed in the bar uniform. Her brown eyes found his across the way, and he was struck dumb.

Holy hell.

She must have brought her own ripped up jeans because they hugged her curves like a second skin, accentuating the dip of her waist and flare of her hips. That little cotton t-shirt with the neon pink Serious Moonlight logo splashed across the front didn't look like it had a prayer of containing her ample bosoms for the duration.

Strategically ripped and cut low in the front, exposing the trim of the sexy lace bra she had on underneath. It was enough to make his mouth water. A growl left his throat at the mere thought of anyone else looking at her this way, but he had no right to be so damn protective.

The truth of that statement did nothing to settle his beast down. Hell, she deserved compliments and stares. She was gorgeous. Weylin shouldn't be worried about anything. Whatever woman magic females used when it came to turning men into obsessive nincompoops, she'd done her bit alright. Weylin was a fool for her and right then, he did not care who knew it.

His eyes ate her up as she slowly walked confidently across the floor, high-heeled boots on her feet making a *clack clack clack* sound as she went. The beat was in time with his heavily pounding heart, not to mention the thumping erection below his belt. He'd never seen such a tempting woman in all his life.

She ducked her head down, as if steeling herself, then found his gaze once more. The smile she gave him then was bright, and he felt one echoing across his face. Lifting her arms, she did a little spin for him, and he grinned even wider.

Heartbreaker.

Damn, she was sexy as fuck with that little strip of skin around her navel peeking out as her raised arms lifted the tight shirt. Her confidence and obvious enjoyment made her even more attractive.

"Holy hell. Little normal is smokin' hot!" Cole mumbled from beside him, followed by an, "Ooof!"

Whatever. It was only a little punch. Weylin tried not to grin as the fucker gasped. Cole went in for a punch, but Weylin blocked him easily, all without turning his head. He twisted the man's arm, and Cole whimpered.

"Ouch!"

"Fuck off, Cole."

"Stop staring at her so we can have a decent fight," grumbled his Pack mate.

"Not on your life," Weylin grunted.

If he had the choice, he would never stop staring at her. Gwendolyn frowned over her shoulder at the two men before walking to the back bar. What a pleasant view it was, watching her butt sway from side to side in her new gear. The woman was killing him, but he had a plan now.

Slow and steady. Fuck what his Pack mates thought. Gwendolyn Hoffer was going to be his.

Mine.

CHAPTER NINE

DIRE WOLF MATES

It was only eleven, and the place was jampacked. The band was really rocking, and she had to hand it to them, they were the best all-female group she'd ever seen, except for maybe clips of the Go-Go's on YouTube. She'd been juggling customers between sets, and so far, so good.

"How are you doing back here?" Weylin asked.

Gwen froze from where she was bent over, retrieving more long-necks to fill the coolers lining the back of the bar. Beer and shots had been the standard so far.

"Great!" she said too brightly as she spun around to face him.

Weylin Scott. Sexy, confident, growly, redheaded alpha male. Great, there she went, waxing poetic on the guy again. The man had been taking up way too much headspace lately.

"Awesome, Gwen. So, what do you think?"

Did he have to be so damn cute? She wrang out a rag over the sink, and shrugged, determined to keep things light. Maybe if she hadn't been such a hardass about that promise she'd made, she wouldn't feel this way.

Ugh.

It was one thing to vow to save yourself for marriage because you believed in love. Quite another to hold on to that vow because you were betrayed by a boy you had no business dating, anyway. If only she could go back in time and warn her college self that bitterness was a joy killer. Holding on to one thing because a bad thing had happened was probably not a good idea.

But that was what she'd done. Held on to her virginity, like it was some prize. Now she was a thirty year old virgin with a crush on a playboy bartender who would likely laugh at her ignorance of the most basic bedroom shenanigans. What a mess!

And telling him she wouldn't sleep with him? Why had she done that? He probably thought she was just playing hard to get and saw the whole thing as some game! This was so messed up.

"Um, you were right," she said, realizing she had to reply. "The bar is really crowded, and I can see why. The band is fantastic. The food is even better."

"And the drinks are flowing from the fingers of a pretty and expert mixologist at the back bar," he added with a grin.

"What?" Gwen asked, shock making her eyebrows arch.

"Seriously, some of your customers are complimenting your skills."

"Yeah, right?" she snorted but couldn't hide her pleasure at the unexpected compliment.

"Why shouldn't they? There's nothing like getting a good cold drink from the hands of a pretty professional bartender."

"Compliments will get you nowhere," she mumbled.

Good thing the music was loud and bar full, otherwise he might have heard the catch in her breath when she spoke. It was just so unfair. If only she knew more about the opposite sex. Maybe then she could have just casually flirted back with him, and ignored all the butterflies and fighter jets flapping against her insides.

"Don't I know it, Gwen," he replied, but his eyes were all glittery and his gaze direct.

Shivers.

The man gave her chills. Gwendolyn had worked in some pretty popular places when she was in school in Manhattan, and in her opinion, Serious Moonlight could rival any of the bars and restaurants in the big city.

It was just that good. Of course, there was also the eye candy. She had never seen so many gorgeous people in one place. Of course, no one could hold a candle to Weylin. Not that she cared.

Liar.

Whatever. Gwen knew she wasn't in his league, and she even understood him kissing her meant nothing to him. It couldn't. She rolled her eyes and went back to stocking the coolers, but he took the case of beer from her and went to work as another customer called for her attention.

She smiled at the young man, nodding as he ordered a round of tequila shots, and went about setting them up. She fully expected Weylin to leave, but he didn't. Her skin tingled with nerves every time she brushed her arm against his. It was close quarters, but it wasn't like she could order him to leave. He was her boss, after all.

Every cell seemed aware of him, and it was wreaking havoc with her nervous system. Maybe it was the atmosphere, but every time she got a look at the big sexy redhead, Gwendolyn had the naughtiest visions of him trapping her in his arms and nibbling on her skin.

Yes, please.

No. Down, girl.

Lord, this was so not good for her. She knew better than to be tempted by sins of the flesh, but holy crap was he gorgeous. Yes, he flirted, and she appreciated she was just one of many females following him around with her eyes like a lost puppy. But a girl could dream, right?

"Tips good?" he asked, coming behind the bar and lifting the case of beer easily for her.

"Uh, yeah. Better than I expected," she told him.

Truthfully, they were awesome. If she made this much on one Saturday, then she'd have the next payment for Hope Springs sooner than she thought. That was good. After all, that was why she was there. To pay for Pop's care. Not drool over a man.

"That's terrific. I'll finish filling these for you and I will check the hard stuff too, okay?"

"Yep. Thanks," she replied tightly.

Get a grip, Gwenny.

"Here you go," Gwendolyn said, returning to the bar and lining up the six shots of tequila, complete with a couple of saltshakers and six slices of lime in front of her customer.

"No, baby, here you go," the young flirtatious male retorted, pushing one shot back her way.

"Oh, thank you, but I don't drink hard liquor," she replied, shaking her head but smiling to soften the blow.

"You have to. It's like bartending rules, if a customer buys you a shot, you drink," he said, and there was something in his eyes she did not quite like.

Gwen smiled and shook her head, politely refusing the drink. The man had some buddies who were finishing their own shots, slamming the glasses back down on the table. The rowdy group of guys lined up next to him, chanting for her to *drink drink drink.*

"I'll buy this round, how about that? You all have a good night," she said, trying to keep the customers happy.

"I said drink," he snarled, grabbing her wrist when she would have turned around.

Gwendolyn winced under the man's surprise strength, and before she could do more than open her mouth, Weylin was there. He vaulted over the bar gracefully and had the man by the throat faster than she could blink.

Her wrist was suddenly released, and she staggered back, hardly realizing she'd been pulling to get away. Oh, but Weylin looked furious. His nostrils flared and eyes glittered like emerald ice as he lifted the man up to eye level. Totally in control, he dragged the jerk closer and whispered something in a voice way too low for Gwen to hear.

"You alright here?"

Gwen turned around and yelped at the image Thor had made beside her. The man was huge, even bigger than Weylin, with a shaved head and a dozen tattoos that she could see.

"Did that guy hurt you?" he asked.

All she could do was shake her head. The guy was a prick, but he hadn't hurt her. He was young, and a little buzzed, clearly trying to show off in front of his friends.

Thor's eyes were dark as midnight, and just as scary, she thought as he nodded over her head. When she turned, it was to see Weylin dragging the handsy jerk and his buddies out of the bar. Anger coursed through her. He didn't have to do that!

She would have been fine. Maybe. But anyway, he had no right to just swoop in and treat her like some dang damsel in distress.

"Hey, Thor?" Gwen shouted as the man turned to leave.

She knew she shouldn't be doing this. She should leave well enough alone. But it bothered her that Weylin thought her so weak. She could have handled that idiot customer. Plus, she didn't need him messing with her brain this way.

Weylin was her friend. That was all. He didn't get to go all protective boyfriend on her for no reason. Besides, she didn't inspire that kind of reaction in men. Besides, that whole thing with her uniform earlier just confused her even more. She couldn't afford to think things that were not real. Especially since she kinda sorta maybe had a developed the tiniest crush on the guy.

Fine. She had the hots for him. The full-blown, thinking about him all the time despite certain vows she'd made as a teenager kind of hots. Shit. Gwen needed to clear the air for sure.

"Yeah?" the big man asked.

"Can you watch the bar for a moment? I need to tell Weylin something."

"Uh. I really don't like talking to people, Gwen, you see, I'm more a bouncer—"

But she was already taking off the tiny waist apron she had on and walking after Weylin. He'd gone through the front door, so it was going to take her a moment to get through the crowd. NO. She could get to the back lot faster through the side kitchen door.

Good plan.

"Thanks, Thor!" she called back, not even listening to what he said.

Her heart was pounding, and she did not know why, but it was like her whole being was focused on getting outside. Getting to him. Right now.

Once she stepped into the night, Gwen was taken in by how dark it seemed. The neon sign broke up the deep purple skies, and the air seemed tense, full of mystery and magic.

Oh what fanciful nonsense, she mused, shaking her head.

"Weylin?" she called softly, walking around the building itself.

It was dark with the odd light here and there, but Gwen couldn't see anything. She listened a moment, hearing strange popping noises, and followed them to the end of the parking lot.

"Weylin?"

Weylin's Dire Wolf was scratching at his insides. He needed to change into his fur before he fucking lost it in front of the entire bar. Seeing that bastard's hand on her wrist had damn near made him lose it completely.

Good thing the asshole punk was a Shifter because even in pulling his punch, Weylin had clocked him harder than he'd meant once he had him outside. Little fucker deserved it. What kind of man tried to force a drink or anything at all on a woman? Well, he and his buddies had learned their lesson after tonight.

But even that didn't do much to calm his beast. Asshole punk Shifter kid should have known better than to do that kind of thing to a female. And not just any female, but a human one. It was all he could manage not to change inside and tear the asshole a new, *er,* asshole.

That would have broken every Shifter rule there was, including the main one which was absolutely no exposing themselves to humans. Gwen was a human. She knew nothing about him or his kind, and so far, he had yet to convince Derrick to allow him to tell the woman who would be his mate the truth about himself.

Weylin was in a tight spot. How was he going to convince her he was serious about her? He only kissed Gwendolyn that one time, and her consequent smacking of his face was not an encouraging sign she was meant to be his. At least, that was what the Alpha thought.

He believed Weylin was jumping the gun. But this was no mistake. Regardless of Derrick's expectations that Weylin would move on to the next female as he'd done before, he knew that was so not happening. It was different with Gwen. She was it for him.

Weylin felt it down to his marrow. The Wolf inside him knew it, too. He just had to stay the course. But it was not easy. With her religious upbringing and moral compass, and the promise she made to herself regarding her—*Christ, Weylin could hardly think the word without going cross-eyed*—virginity, Gwendolyn was skittish around him, to say the least.

Every time he thought of the line she'd drawn in the sand between them, he wanted to howl at the moon like a wild thing. His desire for her was fierce, but the tenderness he felt, that was the real surprise. She needed patience, so he would give her that. But that didn't mean it was easy.

Being near her, smelling her, seeing her every day was the best part of his world right now. Also, the worst. How could he be so close and not tell her she was his? It was torture having to keep how he felt hidden, like a dark, dirty secret when it was none of those things.

Sure, this was new and scary. But from what he knew of her already, she was fierce and brave. Strong woman. Beautiful, loyal, and brave. She'd made a vow to save herself for marriage, and he wanted to honor that vow.

Weylin knew she was meant for him. Hell, he would marry her right now if he thought she would say yes. The idea of spending forever with her warmed his heart, made his blood pump faster.

Too fast. She's human. Slow it down.

He was stuck between a rock and a hard place—*a very hard place*—waiting for her to give him a sign she was interested. Add to that his Alpha's order to stay away from the human and bam! You had one very frustrated, whiny, pining Dire Wolf.

Weylin felt like he was being torn apart. He took his shirt in one hand, ripping it over his head. The side door by the kitchen slammed, but he paid it no mind. Brock was always sneaking off for a moment of silence when he was in the kitchen. The Wolf was a master chef, but he could be a damn lunatic about how he ran his ship.

By the time he heard who had really followed him outside, it was too late.

"Weylin? Oh my God! You're a-a WEREWOLF!"

Fuck. Shit. No. GWEN!

"Awoooooooooooooooooooooooooooo!"

CHAPTER TEN

DIRE WOLF MATES

"Is she alright?" Gwen did not recognize the man's voice.

"She looks like she's coming around," came a soft reply, maybe from Tracey.

"What the fuck did you do, asshole? I told you to stay away. She's human, for fuck's sake!" Derrick's angry voice reached her ears.

"It's not my fault, man. Some guy grabbed her, a Shifter dick, at the bar, and I lost it. Needed to change," Weylin murmured, his voice sounding all gritty and sexy.

"Guys, shh!" Lucy whisper-screamed and Gwen wanted to smile.

Instead, she closed her eyes tight.

"What happened?" she asked, and her mouth felt like she had just eaten a wad of cotton.

Her memories came back slowly, replaying in her mind. Earlier, Gwen had been going through the list of signature cocktails, practicing them for tonight. It was her first time handling the back bar alone, and she'd been so excited.

Saturday nights were reportedly jampacked, and she had been looking forward to the tips. She ran her hands over her body. She had on ripped jeans and a tee, so she was already in uniform. That was right. She'd been working the back bar, and it was going well.

Gwen blinked her eyes open, slowly at first, and warm light filled her vision. Weylin had come to the back, was helping her restock. She had a customer. He wanted shots. He got a little mean, then Weylin jumped over the bar and *–what next?*

"She's waking up. Hey, Gwen. How are you feeling?" a petite blonde—*Lucy*—asked, helping Gwen to a sitting position.

Her mind was hazy. She turned and looked at the two huge men in the room. One she recognized as her new boss, Derrick Rand. The other was him. Weylin Scott. The redheaded hottie who'd been filling her dreams with naughty visions and causing several sleepless nights over the past week.

He wasn't wearing a shirt, and his rippling muscles were a huge distraction to her addled brain. Wowza. He had a bunch of sexy tribal tattoos crisscrossing his body that Gwen hadn't known about. Why would she? Not like she had that kind of relationship with him—or anyone since, *well*, ever.

"Ouch, my head," she mumbled as she pressed her feet firmly to the floor.

"Here, drink this," Lucy said, handing her a glass of ice cold cola.

"Thank you. Mm, that's sweet," she murmured.

"I figured the sugar and caffeine would help," Lucy, who was very pregnant, replied and shrugged.

"Oh, the bar, I should get back to work—"

"Honey, the bar is all closed. Everyone is home. Now you just take as long as you need," Lucy murmured.

The bar was closed? Crap. That must mean it was after three. Gwen closed her eyes and took a steadying breath. They were in Derrick's office again, and she was on the big couch he kept there. Still, she was starting to feel a little like a pinned butterfly.

"Do you all mind not staring?" she asked.

"Sorry," Lucy whispered, grinning at her for some reason.

"Gwendolyn, what do you remember about what happened?" Derrick asked.

"Um, I don't know. I was at the back bar. Tending it like Sheila taught me and keeping the crowd happy. Mostly beer tonight, but some shots too. Oh, Weylin helped restock the cooler. Then I think I, um, had a customer and I disagreed with him about something, maybe?" she said, searching his green eyes for clues.

She had only ever seen Weylin Scott looking cocky or earnest, but right then, he appeared concerned and a little freaked out. What the heck had happened?

"He wanted you to take a shot," Weylin inserted carefully.

"That's right. Tequila. Um, I don't drink hard liquor straight," she explained to Derrick. "It makes me sick. Especially, shots. I'm sorry, I know it is customary for bartenders to drink sometimes with customers—"

"That's alright, Gwen. You never have to drink if you don't want to," Derrick replied. "What else do you recall, if anything?" he pressed.

Lucy rose from her seated position and eyed her man strangely. What the heck was going on here? Gwendolyn blinked, shaking her head to clear it. Oh boy, that was a mistake! She pressed her fingers to her temples.

"Ouch! Is this a bump?" she mumbled and pressed gently around the tender area.

"Fuck, Gwen. I am so sorry. You hit your head when you fell, and I wasn't fast enough," Weylin confessed, looking worried and sick as he gripped the back of his neck with one hand.

"I fainted?"

"Shut up, Weylin," Derrick growled, and for some reason, Gwen really did not like that at all.

"Hey, I don't mean to be out of line, but what is your problem, Derrick? Weylin just apologized for something that doesn't seem to be his fault, like at all. That customer grabbed my wrist, ouch, look, he even left a bruise! Weylin got me out of a tight situation, so why don't you give him a break?" she said, staring at the big man until it got uncomfortable.

Derrick's chest was rumbling, and she did not know why, but Gwen dropped her gaze. Weylin had stood up at this point, body tense as he moved between Gwen and Derrick. What the heck was going on?

"It's okay, Gwendolyn. He's just doing his job," Weylin murmured, tilting his head oddly and avoiding Derrick's glare.

What the heck?

"Wait," she said, turning back to Weylin. "I don't remember tripping. How did I fall? What happened?"

"Gwen, maybe you should take the night off—" Derrick said, but Lucy clamped her hand over his mouth.

"Baby, I have a craving for a cheesesteak. Take me to Tony's, would you?" she asked, rubbing her protruding belly and pouting at her man.

Gwendolyn felt sort of like a voyeur, watching the obvious chemistry between them. Even with her belly swollen with his baby, Derrick seemed to find her irresistible. Wasn't that something?

"Lucy, I am in the middle of something here," Derrick began in a growly voice that sorta scared Gwendolyn.

Lucy didn't seem to mind. In fact, the woman swayed closer to him. Weird. But it must be nice, Gwen mused.

Oh sure, Gwen talked a good game about being fine alone. After one lousy little heartbreak, she'd been hiding behind her promise to save herself for marriage. But that imaginary future husband was just that—*imaginary*.

Truth was, Gwendolyn never planned on finding a guy who could measure up to her book boyfriends. How could she? Folks thought Walt Disney was responsible for unhealthy expectations of what true love was supposed to be like, but she knew better.

That man had nothing on the romance writers of the world, especially the indies. There was nothing Gwen liked more than to find a brand new favorite author pioneer in the indie publishing world.

"Fine. I will take myself," Lucy growled, slapping her hands against the mountainous man's chest, and pushing him back.

He moved, too. Though Gwen was certain that was only because he wanted to. No way could a tiny thing like Lucy move that giant of hers. Lucy tossed her blonde hair over her shoulder and narrowed her eyes at Derrick before grabbing the keys off his desk.

With a sharp nod, she waved goodbye to Gwen with a wink, then stomped out of the office, big booty swaying as she went.

Uh oh.

"What? Dammit. No! Wait! Weylin, fix this!" Derrick snapped before running after Lucy. "Not the Harley, Kitten, come on. We'll take the truck! It's better for the cubs!"

"Did he say cubs?" she turned her head and asked Weylin.

"Um, let's talk about what happened for a minute, then we will get into that," Weylin said, standing up.

He started rummaging through the cabinet behind Derrick's desk and pulled out a clean, black t-shirt with the bar's logo on it. Gwendolyn frowned at the loss of all those tattooed muscles, but she supposed it was for the better. After all, her adult life had been all about avoiding the kind of temptation a man like him presented.

"Look, I owe you an apology," he began, turning to face her as he pulled the shirt over his head.

Gwen gulped down a whimper as she faced his pure masculine perfection. Yeah, he had some scars on his pale skin, but they did nothing to deter from his male beauty. His tattoos were many and so intricate, the detail was just beyond anything she had ever seen. He was a living work of art, and Gwen's heart fluttered in response to that realization.

"Why do you owe me an apology?" she asked.

"I seem to put my foot in my mouth whenever I try with you. I keep giving you the wrong impression, Gwendolyn."

"How? When? I mean, we hardly know each other," she murmured, but even saying that felt wrong.

Ever since she wandered into *Serious Moonlight*, something about the place, the people, just seemed to call to her. Gwendolyn's world wasn't so big, she wasn't so lonely when she was with them. This strange group of beautiful people had made her feel like she belonged to something, even as dumb as that sounded, she realized she was right.

"Since day one, I've been keeping secrets."

"Secrets? Why?"

"All I wanted was to know you better, but you told me to stay away, and I just couldn't, beautiful—"

"Stop," she said, angry now that he was trying to play her. "You don't have to say things like that to me. Sheila is beautiful. Big as she is with her baby, Lucy is beautiful. Not me. At the most, I'm cute. It's fine though, I am happy being cute, but what does that have to do with why I woke up in here?" she asked, tucking her hair behind her ear.

"Maybe to some people you are cute, but I called you beautiful because you are to me, dammit," he growled, stepping forward and invading her space.

Eyes wide, she backed up instinctively. He was just so big. So much man. She could feel heat rolling off his body, warming her in the cramped office. Gwen gasped as her back met with the wall, but he'd already put his hands there, cushioning her from it.

"You scared the crap out of me, woman, fainting like that. Fuck, I've never been that scared," he mumbled.

"Sorry," she murmured, reaching out with shaky hands to touch him.

She was acting on instinct, and it was scary. She'd never touched a man like that, with long, slow strokes down his chest. She wanted to calm him, soothe him, but had no idea if it was right.

He sucked in a breath, then big, tall, too handsome Weylin just shuddered. He closed his fiery emerald eyes, giving her a reprieve from their intensity, and leaned into her touch.

Dammit if she didn't miss the intensity of his stare almost immediately. Honestly, she loved being caught up in the emerald fire of his gaze. Then he pressed his forehead to hers in a gesture that felt like it meant something bigger than what it was, and her insides just melted.

What was happening? She should stop this, right? Pushing him away or slapping his face for presuming to touch her without permission, but her hands seemed frozen in place on his body, and wild horses couldn't pull her away.

There is something different about this one. Wait and see. Give him a chance.

Gwen didn't know what to do, or how to quiet the voice in her head she attributed to the naughty angel on her shoulder. So, she let go of all feigned control, and just let it happen.

Yeah, she had very little experience with men, and whatever she might have promised herself, it looked like her body had other ideas. Desires and needs were flaring to life. Secret hidden ones she hardly ever expected to feel at all.

It was scary and wonderful, and for once in her life, she felt like the heroine in one of those romance novels she loved. Weylin smelled so good. That woodsy scent she'd started associating with him alone seemed brighter now, stronger with him so close.

Weylin's eyes seemed to glow in the dimly lit room, and for one moment, she swore she saw swirls of something else deep within the emerald depths. Like there was another consciousness present in his gaze, and this one watched her, too. The idea should have frightened her, but all it did was kindle her desire.

Gwendolyn shivered, her breasts flattened against his chest as he leaned down. She saw something outside. Just before she fainted. It was right there in her memory. Something impossible. Scary even.

Fur. Fangs. Claws.

The sounds of bones cracking and tendons snapping ringing in her ears.

Impossible.

It had to be a trick of the mind. Gwen's breath caught as she tried to force the memory, but Weylin was leaning in closer, so much closer. His body felt good against hers. He was hot, hard, and heavy.

She was hypnotized, confounded, and desperate for whatever came next.

Please, oh please, let there be more.

"Everyone keeps telling me to wait, to give you time. But I don't think I can wait another minute," he murmured in a voice so low she hardly heard him.

"For what?" she whispered her reply, holding her breath as anticipation reached a crescendo.

"This."

Then he was kissing her, and Gwen could not think at all. Well, nothing except, oooh, was he good at this. So good. So much better than that first time.

"Gwen," he moaned her name, angling her head as he deepened the kiss. "Christ, you're sweet."

Lust glazed eyes blinked down at her, and she knew her own stare must have looked just as dreamy. Weylin smiled that slow panty-melting grin of his before capturing her mouth again. His tongue delved between her lips, and she moaned her response.

Hot boy. Sexy boy. Turning her head. Making her feel.

He ground his hips into hers and she felt him there, in that place she had neglected so long. Yearning built and built and built until she was moving with him.

He's making a fool of you. Using you. That is what he's doing—No! Shhh!

Gwen shushed that nasty little voice in her head and held on to the moment. To Weylin. To the man right in front of her. His eyes opened, the green was so bright they were neon and a shiver raced up her spine. He could see straight into her soul with those eyes. And he was, wasn't he? Seeing all her secret needs and wants. All her hidden desires and fantasies.

Suddenly, her memory came plowing back into her brain like thunder and with her two hands on his chest, Gwendolyn pushed, forcing Weylin away from her. Fuck. She missed his heat, his scent, his strength. But no. This could not be. Horror, confusion, and dread filled her.

"What is it? Did I hurt you?" he asked, baffled.

In her mind's eye, she saw the memory she'd tried to block out. Weylin naked, stopped over by the edge of the forest. His body bent, face contorted with pain as he broke apart.

Skin tore, bones snapped, and fur sprouted where it shouldn't be possible. His body shifted and changed from the most handsome man she had ever seen, the gentle giant she had grown to care about, and lust for, to something out of a nightmare or a dream.

Weylin Scott was no ordinary man. Gwendolyn's breath caught in her throat as she raised her finger, pointing it at him. Then she shouted.

"WEREWOLF!"

CHAPTER ELEVEN

DIRE WOLF MATES

F*uck.*

Weylin winced as the sound of her shout did some serious damage to his supernaturally enhanced eardrums. He shook his head, waiting for her to continue with her freakout. Hell. She'd earned it.

But, to his surprise, Gwendolyn's face went from scared to pissed. She slapped his chest, turning on a dime with her hands on her hips and began talking so fast he could hardly catch up.

"You jerk! Here, I thought you were just some he-slut, trying to get into my pants and I was working damn hard to keep you firmly friend-zoned, but really, you were just trying to keep me from learning about this supernatural secret? I am such an idiot!"

"I was forbidden to tell you by my Alpha. He gave a command! Never mind the fact the Shifter Council would have my head if I told a human we existed without claiming her. But, I mean, if it helps, I do want to get into your pants," he mumbled, utterly confused.

"What? Hang on, we will circle back to that," she said, blinking slowly.

Her brown eyes seemed to darken at his words, and the Wolf in him rumbled appreciatively. Damn, she really was a knockout. Sassy as all hell, too, but he found that just as attractive.

"So, what you are saying is Werewolves exist?" she asked, moving away from him.

One minute he had his arms full of wiggling, sexy, curvy woman. The next they were cold and empty, and she was pointing and screaming names at him. Now, she was asking him questions when all he wanted to do was kiss her stupid.

"No. Yes. Sort of. We don't really call ourselves that," Weylin tried miserably to explain.

"Dude, what did you do to her?" Cole Mingan, his Pack mate, asked from the doorway.

The others had left, but this fuckhead had come running the second he heard Gwen's scream. Now the ponytail wearing asshat wouldn't leave. He'd been growing his hair out, and right then Weylin hated it.

"Why don't you get out of here? I got this," Weylin grunted.

"He can stay, maybe he can answer some stuff too," Gwen replied.

Well, damn. That was not what Weylin wanted at all. The thought dawned on him that maybe she was afraid of him. Like his Wolf would ever hurt her! Hell no. The monster inside him was loyal to her now. She had him, she did, mind, body, heart, and soul. He would do terrible things to make sure this woman felt safe and sound.

Hmm. Come to think of it, maybe she was right to fear him. He was a monster, and apparently, he had no scruples when it came to her. What kind of man would put one woman's needs above all others?

Him. He would. Gwen above all else. Always.

Grrrr.

"I think you better start from the beginning," Gwen said, head high, even if he could hear her heart hammering inside her chest.

"Okay. Well, the world is bigger than you think. Everything is not all black and white, Gwendolyn."

"I know all about religion and the soul. I was raised by a deacon, remember?"

"Yeah, but you see, that's the human world, the human soul, Gwen. I live in the supernatural world."

"The supernatural world?"

"Weylin! The fuck, man?" Cole hissed.

"Shut up, Cole. She is my mate. She has to hear the truth from me. I never should have tried to hide it! For days, man, I have watched on the fringes, waiting for the ideal time to try to talk to this woman, and it has been eating me alive."

"Shut up, man," Cole warned, grabbing him by the collar, but Weylin grabbed him right back.

"Do you know what happens to a Wolf who doesn't claim his fated mate? He loses his fucking mind, Cole. I can't take not knowing. Gwen deserves to know what she is to me, and I deserve to know if I have a shot at this," Weylin snarled, rejecting everything Derrick and all the rest of them had told him from the beginning.

"Stop! Wait! Is this all true?" Gwen asked, interrupting the two snarling Wolves.

Cole was still in Weylin's face, and he was growling at him. The bastard was at the same dominance level as him, and if he didn't back off, they were bound to scuffle.

Stop. Dangerous.

"You can't tell her about us man!"

"She's already seen, Cole! It's not a fucking secret anymore. Now, let's take it outside or you need to walk the fuck away," he grunted.

Weylin's Wolf was pissed off. Here was this asshole, grabbing onto his t-shirt collar and starting all kinds of shit just inches away from Weylin's mate. He could smell her anxiety and emotions, and it was making him even madder. He wrapped both hands around Cole's wrists and shoved the man away.

"Weylin, think man," Cole growled.

"I am thinking."

"You are threatening to out us all over some human, man—"

That was as far as Cole got. Weylin had enough of that fucking word, he punched his friend right in the jaw, just as the sound of glass smashing and the scent of whiskey filling the air.

"Stop it! Both of you!"

What the fuck? Weylin and Cole both turned to see petite and curvy Gwen waving a broken bottle at the two of them. Eyebrows raised, the two males separated, hands in the air. Shit. He didn't mean to scare her, but his Wolf was out of sorts, and Cole was pushing him too far.

"Whoa! Easy now, baby, why don't you set that down on the desk, so no one gets hurt," Weylin suggested.

"Call me crazy, but I feel better with it in my hand. Now, excuse me for being *some human,* but someone better tell me what the fuck is going on!" Gwendolyn shouted.

"Language," Cole growled.

Weylin went to elbow him in the stomach, but the fucker dodged it. This was not at all how he'd imagined telling his mate about all this, but it looked like he had no choice.

"Cole, get the fuck out of here! Me and my mate need to talk."

"But I think—"

"Stop thinking and go," he growled.

"Weylin. Explain. Now." Gwendolyn's chest was heaving, but she was lowering her hand. That was progress.

"Shifters, that is what we are called, not Werewolves, exist, Gwen. I am one," he said, eyeing the broken glass in her hand.

Her shoulders slumped as she absorbed his words, and with a shrug she threw the thing on the floor. Thank fuck. he was worried she would hurt herself.

"Okay. So, you are a Wolf Shifter?"

"Dire Wolf Shifter, actually. Our beasts are bigger, more powerful, older," he murmured, carefully observing her as he spoke.

"So, Shifters exist. Dire Wolf Shifters. Are you alone? Are there others?"

"Like me? Derrick, of course, he is our Alpha. Sheila, Cole, Thor, and Phoenix."

"Not Lucy?"

"Lucy is a Shifter, but not a Dire Wolf. She can tell you about that someday, maybe," he explained.

Gwen just nodded. He had to hand it to her. She was taking this all really well. Any other woman might have broken down, needed a drink, a pill, a week's paid vacation—but not Gwen. She just asked her questions and listened to his replies.

Not demanding. No hysterics. Yeah, she smashed a bottle, but he had a feeling that was more because he and Cole were seconds away from brawling at the time. Not now. Now she was almost eerily calm.

"So, there are other kinds of Shifters?"

"Yes. Shifters, supes, heck, there are many creatures in this world, Gwendolyn. Many levels of reality in the universe, or multiverse, even."

"Okay, hang on, I don't know if I can take all that right now," she said, biting her lip. "Ugh. It stinks in here like whiskey. I made such a mess," she mumbled.

"Don't worry about it. Someone will clean it. Did you want me to take you somewhere?"

"Home. Take me home, I need to think."

"Alright," he murmured, walking carefully behind her to his big SUV.

Worry gnawed at him. She seemed to be in a state of shock, all docile and quiet, which was hardly her norm. The drive to the motel took minutes, but Gwendolyn didn't speak during that time. She just looked out the window, her brown eyes clear but withdrawn.

Weylin cut the engine, pleased to see the usual group of shady characters were nowhere to be seen. Gwen remained seated, her eyes on the small concrete patio outside her front door.

"You've been here, haven't you? At night," she said.

"Yeah."

There was no point lying now. Fuck, his heart was breaking. Was this it? Would she say goodbye to him forever before he even got to know her?

"The, uh, manager told me my dog had to go. I was confused, but now it makes sense. He meant you," she said, turning to face him.

Weylin nodded, words failed him. The moon was almost full, its light shining in from the passenger window seemed to cast her in an ethereal glow. His mouth went dry, body straining, heart pumping as he stared helplessly at her.

He had never seen such raw, unspoiled beauty in a woman. So pure and with so much unrealized potential. Gwendolyn held all the cards here. She could end him with her rejection. Did she know that? He wondered, but kept the words to himself.

"Why? You never said why," she whispered.

"Why what?"

"Why me?"

"A million reasons, Gwen. The Fates paired us, for one thing. But more than that. I've been watching you since that first day and I've never seen anything like you," he murmured.

"You mean, you've never seen an old maid like me," she said with a self-deprecating snort.

"You choosing to wait is nothing to scoff at, baby. It means something, the value you placed on yourself. Your body is yours to share with who you choose when you're ready. I admire you so much for your choice, Gwen, I mean that," he told her, sincerity ringing in his words.

If only she could hear the truth as he spoke, he mused. Bodies were cheap these days, but not Gwen. She knew her value, and he wanted to honor her for it. What a woman to stand against the current of what was popular and trending. She was an enigma. A wonder. A marvel.

Mine.

Not yet.

Hell, if he was ever lucky enough to have Gwendolyn choose him, he wanted it to be on her terms. Not his. He wanted her to pick him of her own free will. That would really be something.

Earning her love and trust? Fuck yeah.

That would be everything.

CHAPTER TWELVE

DIRE WOLF MATES

Shifters existed. Dire Wolf Shifters, to be exact. Weylin Scott, the sexy, hot man who'd kissed her twice now, was one of them.

Holy. Crap.

She sat in his SUV outside the shitty motel she'd been living in, and she knew she should get out, leave him in peace. But she couldn't. Her body just wouldn't listen, and her mind had so many more questions.

"I, uh, that is, you probably have to go," she mumbled.

"I don't have to do anything, Gwendolyn. What's on your mind?" he whispered, careful to keep himself small, she realized.

Oh, he was good. Aware of her emotions, it seemed, and tender with his actions. Weylin Scott was a mystery to her before she knew his big secret, and now, well, now he was a total enigma.

Why would a big, powerful man like that be interested in a curvy little nobody like her? Only one way to find out. Turning herself to face him, Gwendolyn straightened her shoulders, drawing in a deep breath.

"Why me?"

"Why you what?" he asked, green eyes wide.

"The kiss, well, both of them. The keeping guard at this shithole motel. You look like a man who has his pick of women, so why me? Is it because of what I said about saving myself for marriage? Am I just a challenge to you?"

"Hold on," he said, exhaling slowly. "First off, why not you? You're gorgeous, Gwen, and that's just a casual observation. Second, even if I could have anyone I want, I only want you. We have a legend," he began.

Gwen really started listening now. She was not going to be side-tracked by those emerald eyes, or his multifaceted hair, the muscles straining beneath his clothes, and his incredibly soft, exceptionally skilled pink lips. God, she could get lost in those lips.

His kisses were consuming. They were the kind of thing she'd read about but never expected to find in real life. It was like all his attention was on her when he pressed his mouth to hers, and her promise to remain chaste until marriage abiding, Gwen was dying to indulge again.

What would it be like if she let go of that vow she made? If she gave herself to a man, no, *a Shifter,* like him? She'd had her heart broken before, and sex had had nothing and yet everything to do with it.

Would Weylin break her heart? Even if he did, she'd bet the farm he would make it worth her while. There was something so primal about her need for him. Gwen could not help her reactions to the man. The way he looked, the way he smelled, the way he moved—everything drew her to him like some invisible magnet.

Wait. Was he talking? What was he saying?

"I said, we have a legend," he murmured, a hint of a grin playing at the corner of his mouth. "That is, *supernaturals* have a legend."

"About what?" she asked, curious about legends that had their own legends.

"About fated mates," he said, his voice so deep and rumbly it sent chills traveling up her spine.

"Fated mates. What's that?"

"A fated mate is like a soul mate. It's the one person or persons the Fates created just for you. The soul that can make yours complete. Fated mates are everything to each other."

"Wow. That's a fantastic notion," she said.

"Yeah. It is. A lot of folks believe it is pure fantasy, and it gets confusing, and lines get muddled. People think having a fated mate means you have no choice, but that isn't true. And it isn't just a supernatural thing, humans have fated mates as well. Supes are just better able to spot them, is all."

"So, are you saying I have a fated mate?"

"Yeah, you do, Gwen," he whispered, eyes glowing in the darkness of the vehicle.

"What about you? Do you have a fated mate, Weylin?"

"Yes," he hissed the word.

The air seemed electrified, with whatever awareness was sizzling between them. Her skin burned, seeming to want his touch. Gwen swayed slightly towards him. She was so close, tiny specks of gold glittered in his green gaze, dazzling her with their depths.

"My Dire Wolf knew the second I spotted you. You were always meant to be mine, Gwendolyn Hoffer."

"How can you be sure?" she whispered, scared to raise her voice lest it break the spell weaving between them.

"Oh, I'm sure. It was like the whole world had been slightly askew my entire life, then you came into it, and everything was right, for the first time ever. The Fates set you right in my path, and I am so fucking grateful. You make everything right, Gwen."

"But where's the choice in that?" she murmured, swallowing softly.

"It's not enough for me to see you and know what you are to me. You have to want me, too."

"I see," she replied softly.

Their heads were so close now, one small move and she'd be touching him, kissing him. God, she wanted to. How she wanted to! But what would it mean, giving her heart to a monster? Listening to her gut instincts about him, she suddenly knew this was right. Weylin Scott was different from the rest. He was special.

Safe. Tender. Caring. Real.

"Yes or no, Gwen. I have to know if you want this, baby. Tell me, please," he whispered, his plea tender, endearing.

The soft, warm tickle of his breath had her trembling in the passenger seat. Gwen inhaled the woodsy scent she'd come to associate with the giant redhead, and she felt her insides warm with recognition.

"I trusted a boy with my heart once," she began.

Weylin cocked his head. He listened to her, and that was a marvel in and of itself. She felt his confusion, but his patience outweighed it, or overruled it, and that was one of the things she was starting to love about him. It was way too soon for that word, she thought, and winced, but went on with what she had to say.

"He betrayed me. He just wanted someone to warm his bed, and when I wouldn't, when I told him I had made a vow to save myself for marriage, he found someone else who didn't have the same hangups as me."

"I'm sorry," he replied, brows furrowed.

"After, he told me I wasn't worth the wait. He said nobody would want to wait for a frigid little fat girl and I'd better think twice before life passed me by."

"Where does he live now?"

"Oh stop," she laughed. "I don't need you to avenge me, Weylin. What I want to know is what do you think?"

"About you? I know for you it's been a few days, but for me, it's been decades. But Gwen, you are worth the wait. My fated mate, Gwen, that is what you are. I'd spend forever waiting if I knew you were going to be there in the end."

"You would?" she asked, and when he nodded, something inside her just clicked.

Gwendolyn believed him. It was like her heart had taken a leap of faith, and now it was pounding like a herd of buffalo through the plains. Holy crap. Could she die of this?

"No. I wouldn't let anything hurt you, baby. Not ever," he whispered just before she crushed her mouth to his.

Fireworks exploded as their lips melded to each other. And oooh, but he was even better at this than she'd thought. There went the earth, just like he described it, spinning out of orbit, then righting itself again.

He was a patient teacher, cupping her face tenderly in his hands until she got used to the way their mouths fit. He reached back with one hand, holding onto her neck, moving her just so. Then his tongue was sliding past hers in a dance old as time.

She reached out with shaky hands to steady herself, clutching his wide shoulders, which was damn hard to do in the confines of the car. The center console was in the way, but Weylin pushed on something, a button maybe, then slid the thing back, and pulled her flush against him.

She felt the power he kept so tightly contained, and it moved her almost as much as his skilled lips and tongue. Oh God, she had no idea what she was doing, but he was a good leader. He cradled her head with one hand, holding her there, while the other threaded in her hair as he worked his tongue in and out against hers.

He tasted good, she thought as she swallowed him down. Licking and lapping at one another like they could not breathe without the other. Maybe they couldn't. Is that what fated mates meant?

Her body heated, nipples hardened, and that place between her legs ached with a need she had never felt. It was like fantasy and biology were taking over her mind, some magical combination of the two and they were causing her to soak her panties. Or maybe that was just him.

Gwen thought she knew how to kiss, but this was a whole other level of lip locking. Weylin was a god here and for the first time, Gwen couldn't wait for what came next. She wanted, *no*, she needed more. She needed him.

"Gwen," he moaned, pressing his forehead to hers.

"Come inside with me," she moaned.

"I don't wanna rush you, baby. We can take our time," he growled, but she instinctively knew this was hurting him.

That was the last thing she wanted. Truth be told, ever since meeting him, that fateful night when she'd walked into the bar, Gwen hadn't been able to stop thinking about him. Weylin Scott had taken more of her time than she cared to admit. But maybe she could now that she knew what she was to him.

Mate. You are my mate.

"You're not rushing me. I told you I made a mistake before trusting a boy, I think maybe this time I try trusting a Wolf."

Mine.

CHAPTER THIRTEEN

DIRE WOLF MATES

He almost fell getting out of the SUV, her smile was blinding and the hardness in his jeans was making it difficult to think. But the second he did manage to exit the vehicle, Weylin snarled.

The scent of urine and feces, filth and degradation surrounded them. He wanted to claim Gwendolyn as his own, but not there. Not in that awful place. He got back in the car and started the thing.

"What are you doing?" she asked, confused.

"Need you somewhere safe. Gwen. Need to take you to my den," he growled, more Wolf than man.

She nodded, but he could scent the shame coming from her. Fuck. He was being a dick, and that was the last thing he wanted. He stopped the car at a red light, grabbed her hand, and kissed her palm.

"I'm sorry I know that place—" she started.

"Don't you dare apologize. Brave, hardworking, loyal, humble woman. You steal my breath with your strength."

"I thought maybe you were ashamed," she whispered, and he heard her gasp, the soft sound breaking his heart.

"Ashamed of you? Never. My beast won't let me claim you inside that place. Monster that he is, my Wolf wants me to burn it to the fucking ground. You're so good, Gwen. So worthy, love, can't you see? My animal would have me rope the moon for you if you said so," he murmured, wiping her tears.

She laughed then and kissed his palm, and fuck, it was like lightning striking through his body. Already he felt his bond to her growing. Amazing, since they'd only ever kissed.

Oh, but she was magic, this sassy, curvy human with her warm eyes, and curly hair. Pure magic, and it thrilled him to the marrow that she was saying yes. That she trusted him with her most precious gift—*herself*.

He drove back in the direction of the bar, past the Pack house, to where he'd built a small cottage for himself. It was just five rooms—*bedroom, bathroom, kitchen, living room, and a small closed-in porch*—but he had plans to increase that should he ever find himself in need of more space.

"This is perfect," she said, and he heard the smile in her voice before he turned to see it.

"Wait there."

The almost full moon was low in the sky as he ran around the car to open the door. She grinned shyly as he scooped her up in his arms, loving the weight of her. Slight thing she was and always concerned about her size. Weylin shook his head. She was perfect for him, and he was going to spend every day loving on her until she believed him. Even then, he had no plans to ever stop.

Gwendolyn laced her arms around his neck, resting her cheek against his. Fuck, his breath caught in his throat as her strawberry scent grew sweet with her arousal. The woman had him hotter than a firecracker, and he was bound to go off any second if she didn't stop pressing those sweet little kisses to his throat.

Don't ever stop.

He walked straight through to the bedroom, dropping her gently on the coverlet atop the king-sized mattress. Gwen squeaked, and he cursed himself for being an oaf.

"Sorry," he murmured, nerves causing him to freeze in place.

Where had all his prowess gone? Fuck. he was no green pup, and yet one look at his gorgeous, *and virginal,* mate sitting on his bed had Weylin at a complete fucking loss as to where to start.

"Come here," she murmured, using the crux of her finger to lure him closer.

How was she so cool? So calm? She was the virgin here. Not him. And yet.

"Kiss me," she whispered, cupping his cheeks, and Weylin loosed a soft growl as she pressed her mouth to his.

Virgin or not, there was no question who was in charge here, he thought, moaning as she slid her fingers beneath the hem of his shirt. Gwendolyn sat on the bed, legs splayed while he kneeled on the floor in front of her.

Fuck, she was tiny. Sweet, petite, and so damn hot. His growl was almost constant now as she lifted his shirt, with him helping to remove the confounded thing from his too hot skin. Goosebumps broke out across his sin as she ran her nails up and down his abdomen, chest, and shoulders.

"Gwen, my Gwen," he whispered, licking intently at her lips, chin, and neck.

He cupped her breast territorially, claiming the soft flesh as his, swallowing her moan when she pressed against him. Thunder roared between his ears, and he pressed his covered cock against the apex of her thighs. Fuck, he couldn't get close enough. He was on fire for her. Body aching, pulse racing, heart hammering, when he opened his eyes from this last kiss to see Gwen's own molten chocolate gaze boring into his, he knew she was more than ready.

"Mine," he growled, gripping her shirt and waiting for her brisk nod to proceed.

He undressed her slowly, like the gift she was. Kissing every inch of flesh revealed, Weylin memorized every freckle and beauty mark, every touch that brought with it a whimper or sigh. He tried to go slow, really, he tried, but Gwendolyn was more passionate than he could have ever dreamed she would be.

"You drive me wild, baby," he murmured, leaning over her on top of the mattress.

Their kissing and heavy petting had raised the temperature in the cabin, so hot it might as well have been a sauna. Not that he minded. The woman conjured fires inside him to the depths of his soul, and he was more than willing to follow her into the flames.

"Oh, Weylin," she moaned his name, sending shivers through his body at the hushed sound.

She was magic, this woman. Pure, unadulterated magic, and every cell in his body was attuned to her pleasure.

Weylin captured her nipple between his lips, kissing and sucking the bud until it hardened for him. Strawberries and cream, he thought with a growl as he licked a trail from one breast to the other, coveting her, worshipping her like the goddess she was.

His cock thumped against his briefs, hard as steel and begging for release, but he couldn't go to her like this. Like some rutting animal, even if it was half true. She was virginal and untried, and the last thing he wanted was to scare her or, gods forbid, hurt her in any way. But like everything else about her, Gwendolyn was surprisingly forward in her carnal desires.

She clutched at his shoulders when he slid down her body, kissing her breasts, belly and thighs as he did. He loved how soft she was, how smooth her skin felt. The short crop of curls that topped her sex were dark and silky, he parted her slick folds with his fingers, keeping her gaze on his as he placed a kiss on her nether lips.

"You can't—oh, yes, you can," she moaned as he kissed and suckled on her womanly flesh, nibbling her pink bits until she writhed mindlessly beneath his ministrations.

He sounded positively feral as he ate her sweet pussy. His growl built and built, reverberating in the bedroom as he licked and sucked, adding one than two fingers as he worked and stretched her, readying her for his possession.

Gwendolyn cried out, pulling his hair as her first orgasm took over. He moved quickly then, sliding up her heated body, positioning himself at her entrance, and pressing home as she came harder with the first flex of his steely cock into her core.

"Weylin!" she cried out, and he snarled and held still.

Fuck. She was tight. Tight. Hot. And his.

"Mine," he growled, heated stare capturing hers, holding it as he started to move.

"Yours," she replied, nodding even as she welcomed him with a desperate whimper.

Fuck. She was new to this. He had to remember that. It was easy once his animal understood, and he coveted her so. Beautiful, brave, strong woman. Slick, sexy, wet heat surrounded him, and Weylin lost himself in loving her.

My woman. My mate. My everything.

Rearing up on his knees. He pulled her body with him, wrapping her legs around his waist. Weylin crashed his mouth to hers, lifting her up and down on his cock until she was gasping with another, stronger climax.

"Weylin!" She gasped, eyes wide with shock and awe as he took her even higher.

Now! The time was now. His beast demanded it. He had to claim his fated mate right then and there. She wanted commitment, well what he was giving her was more than even she might have bargained for.

"Gwendolyn, I claim you here now, mine, mate," he growled, his body moving urgently now.

"Yes. Oh, yes!"

And that was all the permission he needed. Weylin slammed Gwen down on his cock, lifted her hair off her shoulder, and sunk his teeth into her flesh, marking her with his bite and claiming her as his own for now and all time.

"Mine!" he roared as seed spurted from his cock, coating her walls, and filling her with his scent.

Weylin cradled Gwen in his arms, cuddling her closely as they both tried to catch their breaths. Thirty years she'd held onto her virginity, only to give it away to a, *well, make that to her,* Wolf man.

Did she have any regrets? None. Weylin was everything she could have ever wanted in a lover and more. So much more.

"Are you alright?" he asked, his growly voice kindling something in her belly.

She turned to face him, loving the way he could not seem to stop touching her. He was really so handsome, she mused, tracing a line from his thick, silky red locks, down to his copper eyebrows and lashes, past his straight nose, and stubborn chin. Smiling, she leaned into him, kissing his lips, loving the way he seemed so ready with a kiss just for her.

"Does it hurt?" he asked, and for a moment, she wondered what he meant.

"I feel good, actually, not sore like the books said," she replied, then realized he was looking at her shoulder.

Oh yeah. He bit her.

"Why did you bite me?" she asked, as she looked down at the already healed puncture wounds his teeth made.

"Sorry I didn't tell you first, baby," he murmured, kissing her booboo, and then pressing his forehead to hers. "It is part of the claiming ritual. I thought I could wait till, well, that is to say, until the next time we, er—"

"Made love? Had sex? Did the dirty? Boinked? Fucked like bunnies?"

"Gwen!" he said, shocked. He was laughing as he tickled her mercilessly for her description of what they did. Truth was, it went beyond words for her. Even as she landed on top of him, heat began to stir in her nether regions, and she opened her legs just to feel his rigid length against her core.

"Gwen, I want you so badly," he murmured, but for some dang reason, he was holding back.

"Want you too, please," she moaned, finding him with her hands.

"Don't wanna hurt you, baby," he confessed.

So that was why? Well, she might not know a lot about this, but she wanted to know more, With him. Maybe Gwen was just lucky or something because there was no pain, only pleasure. She placed his head at her entrance, thrilling at the size and hardness of him as she slid down, taking him deep, so deep inside.

"What do you want? Anything, anything at all, I will give it to you," Weylin growled, fingers digging into her hips.

"I only want the truth from you."

"You have it, Gwen. I swear."

"Good. And you have me, always," she replied, then she started moving.

CHAPTER FOURTEEN

Waking up with his mate in his arms, in a tangle of sheets, with the sunlight streaming in through the blinds, was definitely up there on Weylin's top three things to do of all time. First, was kissing her. Second, was making love to her.

Hmm.

Maybe there should be a fourth thing too. Like when she smiled. Fuck yeah. Weylin loved it when she smiled.

"Morning, baby," he grinned when she stirred.

"Good morning," she replied, her cheeks pink with exertion, sleep, or perhaps a tendril left of shyness.

Though, after everything they'd done during the night, he would be hard pressed to ponder that one. He'd kissed, touched, and loved on every inch of his delectable little mate. And she'd done the same to his delight and her unending curiosity.

Leaning down, Weylin slipped his hands beneath the sheet covering her hip and traced her curves. She gazed up at him with lusty, soulful eyes that stole his breath. Sexy woman, looking so well-loved and perfect in his arms, in his bed, in his life. He kissed her quick, wanting to make her breakfast since he'd heard her stomach growling almost an hour ago. But she was so warm and comfy, he didn't want to jostle her until she woke up herself.

"How's a dozen pancakes sound to you?" he asked, loving the way her eyes sparkled as she bit her bottom lip and nodded.

"Sounds amazing. Got any blueberries and lemons?"

"Yeah. Why?" he asked curiously.

"Cause we are gonna add some lemon zest and a cup of blueberries to the batter and you are gonna love it."

"Oh, I am, am I?"

"Yep."

Forty-minutes, and some tussling on the bathroom floor later, and Gwendolyn was sitting down at his kitchen counter beside him, a stack of blueberry lemon pancakes between them. She giggled and fed him the first bite, which Weylin took too fast, almost dying in the process. Fucking things were hot.

"Oh my God, you should see your face right now!" Gwen chuckled. "You are breathing smoke like a dragon."

"I'm a Dire Wolf, baby. We are way cooler than Dragons."

"Wait, those are real?" she asked, eyes wide.

"Gwendolyn, how many times do I have to tell you the multiverse is a big place filled with wonders," he said, feeding her a normal-sized bite.

She made a little chomping sound as she chewed, and fuck, it was cute. He grinned, watching her, falling for her more with every passing second.

"So, we're mated now, right?"

"Yep."

"And no weird side effects, right? Shifters aren't like Werewolves in the movies," she said, and Weylin's heart started pounding.

"Um, well, far as I know. It has been a long time since a Dire Wolf mated a human," he murmured.

"So, I might get a tail?" she asked, stunned.

"Nah. Um, I mean, I don't think so," he mumbled, making a mental note to talk to Derrick. "Hey, I promise, anything happens to you, and I will be right here, okay?"

"Okay, yeah," she murmured and sat up straighter.

It was Sunday, but they were going to visit her Pop after breakfast. Weylin had a little surprise, he hoped she wouldn't mind.

He was nervous about the awkward conversation they'd had at breakfast, but after a while, she seemed to relax. The drive went by quickly, and soon they were headed inside Hope Springs.

"Where's Pop?" Gwendolyn gasped, walking right to the old room her grandfather had shared with another patient.

"I hope it's alright since we're mates now," he told her, placing his hands on her shoulders and turning her around. "I had his package upgraded. I know you want him to have the best care, Gwen, and it is the least I can do for the man who raised my mate."

Weylin paused, trying to gauge her reaction. She was looking over his shoulder, her big brown eyes glassy with unshed tears. His stomach turned in knots and he rubbed the back of his head.

"Gwen, fuck, I am so sorry, I should have asked—" he started, but she jumped on him, hugging him so tight he could hardly breathe.

"Thank you," she whispered, and he felt warm tears seep into his shirt where her face was pressed against his shoulder.

"It's alright. Shhh, hey, come on. Let's go see him," he said, cupping her pretty, heart-shaped face in his hands and dropping a kiss on her lips.

It was too soon, but his heart glowed with love for her. Love? No. Yes, his Wolf pushed. Stupid, red-furred monster was preening with it. Fuck. The realization dawned so suddenly, Weylin tripped on his way down the hall.

"You okay?" she asked, turning her head to check on him as they followed the directions on the map to the private suites.

"Yep. Fine," he replied, but was he?

Mating was one thing, but falling in love was something else entirely. Some folks were built for love, he knew. Like Derrick and Lucy, even though the Alpha fem had been reluctant at first. Kind of like Sheila and Leo, who rejected the Lion before she finally accepted his claim. Their relationship sure was weird.

Brock and Ariella were a loving couple, though he'd had some psychological issues to get past before they got together. And Tracey and Phoenix, though she had some personal shit too, from what Phoenix said.

Maybe love wasn't for people who were perfect. Maybe it was just for couples who were willing to give it their all. Folks who knew the value of their partner and wanted to honor and keep them safe and happy. That was all he wanted, and he was more than willing to work hard for it.

Watching Gwen walk down the hall in her jeggings and white crop top made Weylin realize it didn't matter if he thought he was worthy or not. He was already in love with the woman.

She was the keeper of his heart. The other half to his soul. She had the fealty of his beast. And he would live every day just to see her smile. Oh yes, loving Gwendolyn was easy as breathing, and even more rewarding. It was necessary. Vital. And he would not have it any other way.

"You coming?" she asked, excitement in her voice as she waited outside the door to Pop's new room.

Mine.

"Yes."

Weylin joined her inside the spacious suite, standing back while she greeted her grandfather. The older man seemed to be having a good day as recognition sparkled in his warm chocolate eyes. So like Gwen's, Weylin thought as he shook the man's hand.

"I see my Gwennie has a fella. You do right by her, boy, or I'll come looking for you," Pop warned, only half-teasing.

"Don't worry, sir. I promise to take care of her."

"You guys, I am standing right here," she complained, but her eyes were glossy and her smile wide as she held Pop's hand with one of hers, and Weylin's in the other.

"You did good, Gwennie," Pop said, and prided filled Weylin as he watched her give her grandfather a kiss on the cheek.

They would not have the old man forever, but with his mood improved, and Weylin's new connection to his mate, he could see the familial bonds tying the old man to Gwendolyn. Without knowing if it would work, he tried pushing a little light into that bond, hoping for the best.

They stayed there, playing cards, and later, Gwen read aloud to Pop from one of her infamous romance novels. Weylin had to remember to ask to borrow that one, since she skipped the steamy scenes. The three of them remained together until a nurse shooed them away with a report from the doctor that Pop's health was improving, and he was quite comfortable in his new room.

It was early evening by the time they got back home, and Weylin growled contentedly as he lifted Gwen from the passenger seat. Sweetheart that she was, she'd worn herself out making sure her grandfather had enough of his favorite foods and easy access to the TV remote and nurses' call button. She'd dozed off almost as soon as she got into his car.

"Mmm. Are we home?" she asked.

"Yeah, baby. Hey, do you feel okay?" Weylin asked, suddenly on alert.

Her skin was on fire, and his wolf had perked up almost immediately upon touching her. A cool, fall breeze rustled the leaves near his cabin, but Weylin took no time to enjoy the scenery. Something was wrong here.

"Derrick!" he shouted, knowing full well the Alpha would hear him across the patch of grass that sat between the Pack house and his cabin.

He hustled inside, placing her down on the sofa. Weylin started by removing her jacket, shoes, and socks. He ran a clean washcloth under the faucet and came back with it in his hands, pressing it to her head. Gwen moaned, curling up on the couch with her hands across her stomach.

"What's happened?" Derrick asked as he pushed his way inside without knocking.

"I don't know. She's sick or something. My Wolf is freaking out," Weylin growled, kneeling down on the hardwood floor beside Gwen.

"Hey," Lucy said, hands on her belly as she walked over to them and felt Gwendolyn's head. "She has a fever."

Weylin growled helplessly as Lucy doctored his mate. Worry consumed him, and the beast inside was raging.

"Did you claim her?" Derrick asked sternly. His eyes glowed with his Wolf as he followed Weylin's nod.

"Yes. But I'm not sick, Alpha. Fuck, we don't get sick! Are humans allergic to the bite?"

"You bit her? Even though she's human?"

Weylin nodded, swallowing down the bile threatening to out itself from his lips. Fear clenched his stomach, and his Dire Wolf was shredding him from the inside out. After everything, he'd finally claimed his mate, and what—he made her sick?

Shit. No. This couldn't be happening.

Please, please be okay.

"I'm calling Thor. He might know something," Derrick grumbled, pulling his cell phone from his pocket.

Weylin nodded, sweat dotting his brow. Gwendolyn moaned loud. Lucy was still holding her hand, her big blue eyes darted from Gwen's prone body to Weylin's drawn face.

"She feels so hot, Wey. I don't know what this could be," the Alpha fem said, looking concerned.

The pounding of footsteps reached the cabin, and Weylin moved in front of Gwen. He couldn't help it. His Wolf was going nuts.

"Easy," Derrick commanded, using his Alpha voice. But something freaky was happening.

Weylin growled at his Alpha, lowering his gaze, but snarling, nonetheless.

"You bit her when? Last night? During a full moon?" Thor asked, entering the house.

"It wasn't full yet," Weylin growled.

"Close enough, brother," Thor replied, his eyes glittering like black onyx as he moved towards Gwen.

Weylin snapped his teeth, grabbing his Pack mate's beefy arm as he tried to pass. He could not help it. The Wolf was out of his mind with protective instincts, and Pack mate or not, he did not want anyone near Gwen save for the Alpha fem.

"I must assess her, brother Wolf. I will not harm your mate. I swear it," Thor told him in a voice deep with his animal.

Thor was perhaps the quietest Wolf among them. Weylin trusted the man with his life but asking him to trust him with his mate's life. Well, that was something else.

Something pushed its way through the Pack bonds, his intentions, Weylin realized, and his Wolf rumbled approvingly. The Dire Wolf MC was more than a Pack, it was a family. They had built their bonds on friendship, trust, and affection.

"Sex, blood, a full moon, and your sacred vow to love this woman have all converged to make the impossible happen, my brother," Thor said in a rumbly voice.

Thor looked at Weylin, just as Gwen's back arched and she roared a loud, horrible sound full of pain that tore at his heart. Thor growled, then he gripped the waistband of Gwen's pants. Fury hit him hard, but before Weylin could move, Derrick and Cole were tackling him as Thor tore the clothes off his mate's body a single moment before a wave of power knocked them all on their asses.

Next, the impossible happened. A dark brown Wolf ripped out of his mate, and she was ferocious. The animal lunged for Cole, nipping him on the ass and forcing the idiot to let go of Weylin. Derrick did not have to worry about that. The Alpha was smarter than he looked, releasing the male who was already on his knees and reaching for his incredible mate.

"Gwendolyn?" he asked, wonder lacing his raspy voice as the huge she-Wolf butted heads with him.

I thought you said no secrets, Weylin.

"I didn't know, baby, I swear," he said, smiling through tears of wonder as he ran his hands over her fur. "*Ohmyfuck!* Are you talking in my head?"

I think so. Weylin, come with me. Let's run.

Gwendolyn yipped, making a circle in the living room, and knocking Cole over in the process. The butthead had only just found his feet. Oh, well. He had it coming, Weylin was sure.

"I think your mate wants to run with you, brother," Thor said, a smile on his usually somber face.

CHAPTER FIFTEEN

The entire world had changed, or maybe it was just Gwen.

She raced through the Blue Valley forest with her new eyes keenly taking stock of the land. Her mate was hot on her heels, but this new body was fast and strong. She vaulted over a creek, landing in a pile of freshly fallen autumn leaves with a happy bark.

She'd gone from alone to mated to the most handsome man she had ever seen, with a beast of a Wolf inside her in less than a week, but if you asked her if she had any regrets. Gwendolyn would have to say no. It was only the truth.

For what seemed like hours, she and Weylin ran and walked through the forest together. When her fur started to tingle and her muscles twitched, she turned scared eyes to her mate, whose own emerald gaze was calm and knowing.

It's okay. You just have to change back, he said, speaking through their matebond.

She had learned so much that night. Things she had never dreamed of back in her Sunday school classes, or even in college in Manhattan. The world was a lot bigger than she knew, but instead of feeling scared and lost, Gwen felt good. IN fact, she felt better about it than ever before.

There were infinitesimal mysteries out there, but she belonged right here. With Weylin, with the Pack, with her Pop for however long she had him, and that was all she really needed.

How do I change back?

Just picture your human self, Gwen. Hold on to that image in your mind's eye and let the magic wash over you.

I can't! I, but before panic set in, Weylin was there in his skin, on his knees before her.

"It's okay, baby. Just picture her. You got this. I'm here," he murmured encouragingly, and Gwendolyn allowed her trust in him to fill her.

Lord, it was amazing having someone believe in her besides her grandfather. The way Weylin looked at her, a mixture of pride, love, and possession, warmed her to her marrow. Heated her insides, made her body tingle with anticipation.

She did as he said, held onto the image of her in her human skin. Just Gwendolyn. With him. Her mate. Her bones began to snap, muscle tearing, reknitting itself into her other shape. It took a few minutes, and she knew it wasn't pretty, but he stayed right where he was.

Good mate, that new inner voice, her she-Wolf, growled in a huskier version of Gwendolyn's voice.

Yes, she had to agree. He was good, and he was her mate. Earnest green eyes glittered down at her, hands hovering but not touching, as Weylin waited for every last tingle and ache to fade from her shivering skin. But Gwen wasn't as patient as him.

The second she could move on her own, she was reaching for him, crawling into his lap as she placed a thousand kisses on his skin and sighed against him. Love like she never even knew was possible filled her to the brim.

"Was this how you felt all along? Was it just like this?" she asked, eyes wide with wonder as she cupped his face and kissed him with everything she had.

"Yes, and no. I'm not as brave as you, fierce, bold, sassy thing that you are, my Gwendolyn. I was afraid to even think the word I can hear from you. Fuck, it's filling my head, and it is so damn beautiful," he whispered, holding her face and kissing her hard. "Love you so much, Gwen. Love you, my mate. My fated for me and only me, mate," he growled.

"I love you, too, Weylin. So damn much I can't breathe without saying it. It's like nothing I ever felt," she whispered in awe of this wonderful man who'd given her so many incredible gifts.

"I will spend the rest of my life making sure you never feel even a moment's regret," he growled.

"Let's start now," she said, moving her hips against him, loving the way his body reacted so readily to hers.

Weylin's eyes glittered with his Wolf, and she felt hers rear up to meet him through her stare. Oh, she loved his beast, loved the man, too, and was desperate to show him. Gwendolyn was still new to the physical side of loving, but it was fun with him. He made it all seem easy as breathing.

"That's it, baby. Take me. Take all of me," he growled and positioned her over his ready cock.

Her head fell back, hair a hopeless tangle, but Gwendolyn was beyond caring as he filled her with his hardened length. The man really was a god, she mused as he lifted her and pulled her down again, filling her to the hilt until they were both panting, desperate with the need to come.

He was turning her into lava from the inside out. Creating wildfires with every touch and brush of his skin against hers. Gwendolyn gasped, digging her fingers into his wide shoulders and arching her back. Weylin roared a little then, flipping them over so that she was flat on the bed of moss he'd somehow found for them.

She mewled, needing him to move again, but he sat there, buried deep and staring at her, running his hands over her body from her neck, over her breasts and soft belly, to strum that tiny nubbin peeking through her curls. Gwen hissed, and he growled his reply, flexing his hips and sliding that deliciously long cock in and out, all the while flicking his thumb over her nubbin.

Pleasure danced along her skin, anticipation of what was to come, *mainly her*, sizzled up her spine. Yes, yes, yes. She loved what he was doing. Every sound of his body sliding out of hers. Every welcoming slap of skin against skin as he pushed back in. Each breath, grunt, groan, whimper, and sigh. She loved all of it. All of him.

"More, please," she begged, and her mate did not make her beg again.

Though, to be honest, Gwendolyn would not have minded. His dick was heavy and hard, wet with her pleasure as he pumped, pumped, pumped, bringing them higher and higher until she thought she would burst with it. She loved the feral expression on his face, the fierce glint in his eye as he grabbed her hip with one hand, stroking her clit faster with the other.

"Come for me, mate. Now," Weylin growled, more Wolf than man.

Gwen was already there. But with his command, her body broke apart. Flying into the sun, that was what it felt like. Her orgasm shot through her with all the heat and power of that enormous star, creating a gravity field all of its own, pulling Gwendolyn and Weylin right into orbit.

Weylin's body spasmed jerkily as he rode out his orgasm with her, dragging hers out in the process until she was too weak to move. He slumped over her, careful not to crush her with his tremendous size, though she would have welcomed his weight. Instead, he curled on his side and pulled her back, cuddling her close.

"Mine," he murmured, still trying to catch his breath as he kissed her shoulder and her neck, sniffing deeply where they met.

"So, do I smell weird now?" she asked, only now processing some of her newfound powers, which included one hell of a sniffer.

"Not weird. Good. You always smell good, Gwen. Like strawberries. But now you smell like me, too," Weylin told her.

She could hear the smile in his voice as he said, and something animalistic inside her approved of his possessive snarl. Gwen smiled contentedly, realizing she was a tad bit psycho, *er,* proprietorial herself. Her eyes grew heavy, and her breathing slowed as she found peace beside her mate. The steady beat of his heart soothed her nerves, and she dozed off in no time.

"Come on, baby. Let's get you home," he said, after what seemed like minutes.

Gwendolyn sat up, realizing she was off the ground already and in Weylin's strong arms. The evening had turned to full on night sometime after she had closed her eyes, and she yawned, glancing up at the full moon smiling down on them.

"Mm. I am pretty heavy, you know. You sure you got me, mate?" she asked, rubbing his shoulders and kissing his neck.

"I got you, Gwendolyn. Always," Weylin growled, slapping a kiss across her lips and carrying her home.

Home. That sounded nice to her ears, and she smiled, knowing Weylin was her real home. The Fates had brought them together, and Gwendolyn had never felt so whole before. It was going to be some adjustment from what she was then and what she was now, but with Weylin, and the Pack, she was confident it would be okay.

"What's going on in that head of yours, love?" she asked Weylin, noting the Cheshire cat grin that seemed stuck on his face.

"I was just thinking, you know you have to marry me now, right?"

"What?"

"Yep. You were saving yourself for marriage, and you gave yourself to me, so you gotta marry me! Ha! We're gonna beat Derrick and Lucy to the altar," he said, seeming to find that amusing.

"What are you saying? Who says I'd even have you?" Gwen teased.

"What?"

"You didn't even propose, Weylin. Now who's to say some handsome man might not come along and get down on his knees and ask to marry me tomorrow?"

She looked over her shoulder at him, crossing the room as she opened the bathroom door. Poor man had his eyes glued to her ass, but they shot up when he realized what she said. Too bad she was already headed for the shower.

"What? Gwen? GWEN! Open that door, Gwendolyn," he growled, pounding on the thing.

She turned on the water and started humming over Weylin's shenanigans. Of course, she was going to marry him. But when she said, not the other way around.

Silly man, thinking he held the strings.

The shower curtain flew back, and Weylin stood there, chest heaving, eyes glittering, and finger raised at eye level.

"Gwendolyn Hoffer, you are my mate and I absolutely forbid you marrying anyone but me!"

"Is that so?" she asked, brows arched as he growled at her. "Then might I suggest you get down on your knees, mate?" she growled, bottom lip between her teeth, as he finally understood what she was suggesting.

"Yes, ma'am," he growled and slid to the floor, large hands wrapped around her thighs.

Weylin's green eyes danced with delight as he lifted one, slinging it over his shoulder, and kissed her right on her needy little sex.

"Mine," he snarled, and Gwendolyn gripped his hair, nodding her head.

Yes, she was his. And tonight, she planned to claim him right back.

Mine.

EPILOGUE

DIRE WOLF MATES

"Honey, I am home!" Gwendolyn shouted as she entered the cabin she shared with her mate and her husband.

They really had been bad, running off to Atlantic City to get married over the weekend, but that was what they both wanted. It eased something inside her that had held onto her vow for all those years, even though her new Wolf side understood being mated was just as important as being married.

She spent the last couple of hours changing her name at the DMV, and the nearest Social Security office, and all she really wanted was to go for a run with her mate, then dinner, and some celebratory love making under the stars. Not necessarily in that order.

"Weylin?" she tried again, but he wasn't answering.

Gnawing her lip, she walked to the kitchen table, smiling when she saw a single red rose and folded letter written in his handwriting. The sexy scrawl made her heart flutter, and she sighed like a lovesick teenager when she opened it.

Dear Gwendolyn,

I have a surprise for you. It's good, I promise. Meet me at the Pack house.

Love always,

Weylin

Gwendolyn crushed the letter to her chest, smiling widely as she grabbed the rose too, dropped her keys and bag, and raced across the lot to the Pack house. Everyone was there, and she frowned, wondering if she missed a Pack meeting.

Something about how she came to be a Dire Wolf Shifter meant her bonds were more solid to Weylin than to anyone else. Still, she scented him among the others, and knew he was inside. But she wasn't prepared for the sight that met her eyes when she walked inside.

Weylin, sans shirt, was on his knees, head bowed. The entire Pack stood shoulder to shoulder in a circle around him. Only Thor was with him. The bald giant seemed different, as if he wasn't seeing anything through his impossibly black eyes. At least, nothing she could see.

"What's going on?" she asked, and Weylin's head snapped up, his emerald eyes boring into hers.

"Gwen," he breathed, and smiled.

"Weylin?" she said again, uncertainty cracking her voice.

Her inner beast wanted to tuck tail and run. There was magic there, ancient and powerful. Something strange was happening, strange and important, she realized, taking in the somber atmosphere.

Thor began chanting in a language she did not recognize. The enormous man moved quietly, taking what looked like sticks and a jar of something murky out of a box.

"Come," Lucy whispered, and the woman looked incredible considering her tummy dropped, and her pup was going to be born any day now.

"He's speaking in an old, forgotten tongue. Those markings are the ancient glyphs of the original Dire Wolf Pack, the first ones," she whispered, explaining what was happening even as Sheila placed her hand on one shoulder, Lucy's on the other.

Eyes wide, Gwendolyn looked at everyone there in the circle. It was not just Dire Wolves, but their mates, too. Some faces were streaked with happy tears, others stoic as they watched Weylin prepare for whatever ritual this was.

"This is a sacred ritual from ancient times. That ink is special, magicked by friends of the Dire Wolves. It's the only ink strong enough to mark their skin," she continued in a whisper-like voice.

"Has Weylin talked to you about our origins?" Sheila asked, and Gwen shook her head.

"The Dire Wolves MC has a long history, a long brotherhood. We are all connected to our past, Gwen. To our present. And to our future. Thor can see it. The map of our lives through his bone deep connection to the ancients and our devotion to one another. We are descendants of the original wanderers, and before we came to Blue Valley to settle down, we were nomads."

"He didn't tell me," she said.

"It's different now. In settling down, the Dire Wolves have found their mates. They found *us*. We are their homes, and they are ours," Lucy said, bringing tears to Gwendolyn's eyes.

"But what is this? What is wrong with Thor's eyes? What is he doing to Weylin?" she whispered in awe as Thor's chanting grew louder.

Just then, the big bald man placed his hands on Weylin's shoulders, and Gwendolyn tensed. Only Sheila's and Lucy's hands steadied her. He slowly turned her mate until he faced her. Still down on his knees, back to Thor, Weylin's emerald eyes flicked to hers, and he gave her a thin-lipped smile.

Thor slapped his hands, commanding everyone's attention as he lifted something that looked like a pen and stuck it in the jar filled with a swirling, glittering substance. Weylin's gaze remained locked on Gwen's, not even flinching when Thor cut into his skin with the pen-stick.

"Thor is what we call touched by the Fates. His talents run deep, just like his Pack bonds."

"I don't know what that means, but he scares me a little," she murmured, eyes wide as the bald Dire Wolf's chanting changed pitch.

"See, he's using a set of ancient bamboo tattoo pens to mark your mate with your story, Gwen. This is all for you," Sheila told her.

Tears ran down Gwen's face, and she sniffed loudly. Her heart was beating a million miles a minute. Oh, this was big. She knew it was. Felt it down to her bones. Even her new furry half was in awe of what was happening.

Peace, happiness, and love pulsed through her, and she gasped, raising her watery eyes to the smiling ones of those men and women surrounding her and her mate. Gwen was still so new at this. She wasn't sure if what she was feeling was coming from her, or Weylin, or everyone gathered inside that special space.

"I don't want him to hurt," she began, gasping as she watched.

"It's tradition. You see, our tattoos tell the story of our Pack and our MC. But our backs we save until we find our fated mates. Those tattoos tell the story of us. Right now, Thor is inscribing the story of you and Weylin on your mate's back. It's an honor. A tribute. A way for him to show his love."

"I love you," she whispered.

Gwen touched her hand to her lips as she watched Weylin, straight and sturdy as an oak, despite the pain she knew he felt with every prick and slice of the bamboo needles as he got tattooed by Thor. Her heart felt so full in that moment, and Gwen finally knew what it meant to be loved.

Oh, she'd promised herself she was going to save her body and her heart for the man she was going to marry, and she did, well, in a roundabout kind of way. But she had no idea in doing so it meant she was going to step into a world of magic and mystery.

Secrets were not her favorite things, but she understood why Weylin had to keep this one. The truth about Shifters, the supernatural world, Dire Wolves, Pack, magic, and bonds were her secrets to keep now, too. And Gwen realized how precious a gift that truly was. Living with this kind of knowledge would be hard sometimes, but she felt strong here, with her Pack, with her mate.

She would keep their secret, because it was hers now, too. Gwen was loyal right down to her innermost secret heart. The one she'd gifted to Weylin. Just like he'd promised to keep her safe and protected, she vowed to do the same for him. Not just for him, but for all of them.

Gwen's heart squeezed as she finally understood the depths of what he'd done for her in choosing her as his mate. Weylin had taken a poor woman whose last living relative was a shell of himself inside a care facility to a woman who was mated, married, and had friends. She had Pack now. And Pack was family.

"It is done," Thor announced, slumping down on his haunches as he tried to catch his breath.

"I got you, brother," Derrick, her Alpha now, blurred across the room, catching the big, bald Wolf before he keeled over on the spot.

"Is he okay?" Tracey asked, and Phoenix answered with a nod.

"It takes a lot out of him," Weylin grunted, falling forward, and catching himself on his hands.

Gwen raced to him. She wasn't sure where to touch him, didn't know if he was still hurting, but her mate caught her gaze and, thank heavens, she didn't have to wait another second to be in his arms.

"Love you," he growled into her neck, kissing her there, cupping her face, then slamming his lips to hers.

"That's nice ink, bro," Brock announced, standing with his arm around his mate who was smiling and nodding her agreement.

One by one, the Dire Wolves and their mates walked around Weylin and Gwen, commenting on his new ink.

"Well?" he asked. "Don't you want to see it?"

"I do. But I'm a little scared," Gwen whispered.

"Don't be, baby. Thor is good at what he does, and this is our story. Come on, tell me what he saw for us," he whispered, kissing her palms.

Still trembling with emotion, Gwen crawled around to see Weylin's back and sobs wracked her body at the vivid scene Thor had etched into her mate's skin. Weylin froze, asking her if it was okay, and she nodded, unable to form words for a full on minute.

"Baby?" he asked, sounding panicked.

"Oh, Weylin. It's incredible. There's a silhouette of a woman, *me*," she murmured, her voice wobbly. "I am standing beneath an almost full moon, with colors purple, green, and gold swirling around, but the image is like a progression. A woman on two legs, turning, shifting, falling to the floor and then there's my Wolf, and I am running to meet you. You're so bold and beautiful, good mate."

"I am? You think I'm a good mate," he whispered.

"Heck yes, I do. You are," she replied earnestly. "Anyway, your Wolf is welcoming me and, in the distance, there are cubs. Three cubs circling the trees in the back. A floating figure is watching from above with angel wings. And way, way off are more Wolves, and Lions, and a bird. Oh Weylin, it is beautiful!"

He turned around and caught her to his chest, the two of them overcome with feeling. She heard the rest of the Pack shuffling out of the room, joy and happiness pulsing through their Pack bonds, floating in the air. Weylin kissed her then, and everything else just faded away.

He was it for her. She knew it as surely as she knew the sun rose and set each day. Weylin was meant to be hers, and she was meant for him. The world might not be what she thought. There was so much out there Gwen didn't know. But this right here, this was all she needed to know. This was everything.

"I love you, mate," she whispered, nuzzling him with her lips.

"I love you too, my sassy little Wolf," he growled playfully, nipping her lip between his teeth.

"Hey guys, sorry to interrupt. Um, did you see Derrick?" Lucy asked.

Weylin and Gwen whipped their heads to the side to see Lucy clutching her stomach with one hand, and the sofa with the other. She was sweating and her voice was strained as she held on to the furniture for dear life.

"Lucy? You okay?" Weylin asked and stood, offering his hand to Gwen.

"Oh, I'm fine. But I think it's time, and I would really, really LIKE MY FURRY-ASSED MATE!" she roared the last as the couple raced to her side.

"Ohmygawd! She's in labor," Gwen shouted, holding Lucy's hand while she helped her onto the sofa.

"I'll get Derrick!" Weylin offered, running from the room.

"Tell him to haul ass and find a preacher! I better be married before I give birth, or he is in the doghouse for good!" she grunted.

"Easy, Lucy, just breathe," Gwen said, lips curled up in a grin.

Sheila came running in with a bowl of hot water. Ariella was hooking up speakers and starting Lucy's birthing playlist, which featured a lot of 80s rap, oddly enough. And Tracey was on the phone with the local church, trying to order a preacher.

"Lucy? Kitten! Are you alright? It's too soon," Derrick growled, scrambling into the room and kneeling at his mate's side.

"Derrick, I'm scared," she wailed as another contraction hit.

"You got this, kitten. I know you do," he told her.

The entire Pack gathered around, moving from kitchen to living room to help with the birth in shifts. Even Thor, who should have been unconscious, came downstairs brandishing an online certificate that stated he had the right to marry the Alpha couple.

"Are you sure?" Derrick asked Lucy one more time.

"Hell yeah, Derrick, hurry up," she grunted.

"Get on with it," the Alpha snapped at Thor, who started the ceremony immediately.

Fifteen minutes later, Derrick and his new bride, Lucy Rand, welcomed the first of their cubs into the world. There were three in total, all girls.

"Oh man, three girls? He is going to lose his mind," Sheila snarked, laughing gleefully.

"Lucky man, I say," Phoenix chimed in.

"What about you? Do you think he's lucky?" Gwen asked Weylin.

The lot of them were gathered on the porch, drinking cold beer and soda, looking up at the full moon. They were celebrating the arrival of their Alpha's cubs, and just enjoying living in the moment.

Weylin's smile spread wide across his handsome face, striking Gwen in the heart like lightning. Oh, but the man was special. Handsome as sin, and tender as a rose petal.

"Any male who finds his fated mate is lucky, baby. But three female cubs at once," he paused, and she narrowed her eyes at him. "Hell, Gwen, it's better than hitting the lottery, especially with all these sassy aunties to help raise them up right!"

Gwen joined him in his laughter, and soon everyone else did as well. Weylin took her in his arms and spun her around under the stars, and Gwen giggled and hugged him tight.

Life was scary sometimes. But Gwen finally understood the bad was necessary. It helped you recognize the good. Weylin was a good one. And he was hers.

"Mine," he growled, dropping a hot kiss on her lips.

"Yours. Mate."

 *he end...*

KISS MY SASS

DIRE WOLF MATES

BLURB

DIRE WOLF MATES

Can a Dire Wolf with *the sight* find his future with a wanted female?

Rare Raven Shifter Domenica Corvo is being hunted by her ex, the leader of her former Murder, when she stumbles on her knight in shining fur.

Thor Ulger is not just the Enforcer for the Dire Wolf MC. He is also their Seer—an ancient and feared position gifted by the Fates to those strong enough to hold it.

Part of his job is to see the paths of those Wolves he calls Pack, and to mark their skin with their stories once they have found their fated mates. If only he was destined for the same future as those he cares about.

Resigned to living his life alone, Thor's entire world turns upside down when a Raven with a broken wing crash lands at his feet. She needs sanctuary, but this sassy little bird is no one's pet project.

He thought falling in love wasn't in the cards, but the Fates work in mysterious ways. Thor is on the fast track to losing his heart with every passing second.

When her ex demands she return to him, there's only one answer as far as Thor is concerned.

Anyone coming for his mate can *kiss his sass*!

PROLOGUE

DIRE WOLF MATES

Thor's head pounded, and exhaustion filled his veins. He could hardly muster the strength to return the cheers and congratulations floating about the Pack House tonight.

It was always the same when the sight took over. Thor was present, but not. The tattoo he'd inked across Weylin's body showed a promising future for the male and his newly awakened she-Wolf mate.

He was glad for Gwen and Weylin. Just as he was glad for his Alpha and Alpha fem. He'd even performed the ceremony, marrying the couple just minutes before Lucy and Derrick welcomed their three precious cubs into the world.

Tonight was a good night. Fuck yes, it was. But instead of being happy, Thor felt completely and utterly drained. He ducked out of the Pack House for some much needed quiet time, walking to the end of the paved lot that bumped up against some woods.

He still could not believe this was all theirs. Their bar, their house, their land. At first, when Derrick had suggested pooling their resources and settling down to establish roots, Thor had been uncertain. The Dire Wolf MC was built on the belief that their kind did better on the road.

Sure, there were different branches, and yes, they technically still belonged to the main MC, which was a human term for the motorcycle loving Shifters. Really, their MC was a Pack. An ancient, powerful Pack made up of prehistoric monsters like Thor, whose Dire Wolves needed the freedom of the road lest they be drawn into petty wars with other supernaturals.

It was the nature of the beast, he knew. Shifters, especially, were nothing if not predictable. Volatile creatures, they thrived on physical violence and the establishment of a hierarchy. Everyone wanted to be the toughest, strongest, and most lethal. Reputation was everything, and fortunately or unfortunately, depending on how you saw it, the Dire Wolves had quite the rep for being badasses. Which made everyone and their motherfucking uncle want to challenge them.

So far, so good.

The Dire Wolves hadn't had to deal with any threats, but that could also be because the Wolf world was blowing up left and right with the demand for a High Alpha. So involved in their own politics, the local Macconwood Pack Wolves had left the Dire Wolves to themselves. Their Alpha was a good male, a worthy male, and the one meeting they'd had established the fact he was uninterested in challenging Derrick for anything.

Settling down had been a good move on Derrick's part. Perfect, really. Most of the Pack had paired up and Thor had his job to do. But nothing could fill the hole he felt inside him. Thor crouched down, trailing his fingers across the ground as he sucked in a long, deep breath.

Fuck. What a day.

SO much for being a Seer. Thor had no inkling his long time Pack mate and friend, Weylin, would come to him to perform their most sacred and ancient tattooing ritual. A good thing, for sure, but typically he had a clue when he was about to dive into the ether.

But the decision was not up to Thor. It was up to the Fates. This was the way it happened for their kind. When a Dire Wolf found his or her fated mate, it was up to the Pack Seer to convey the story of them on the Dire Wolf's back.

Thor used special magicked ink gifted to their MC by friends of the Pack. It was the only kind strong enough to penetrate Dire Wolf skin, and bamboo pens to inscribe the picture as was given to him by the Spirits.

He was touched by the gods. One of the few Dire Wolves to inherit *the sight.* He was the Seer. That meant it was Thor's job to perform such duties. But communing with the spirit guides of their ancestors took its toll on him, and each time he went under, he felt the desire to return to the natural world lessen more and more.

If it wasn't for his bonds to his Pack and Alpha, Thor might still be there in the *other world,* walking and talking amongst the ghosts of the past. He shivered involuntarily, looking up at the bright September moon.

The month was almost over, and soon fall would be in full effect. No more lazy summer nights and warm breezes. Fall and winter would be especially hard this year. He should know. His grandfather, Bjorn Ulger, had told him all about it on this recent visit with the old graybeard's spirit.

Ghost wasn't a term the deceased liked, and Thor knew better than to use it to describe the corporeally challenged. Bodies turned to dust, but spirits were eternal. If anything, Thor had that to comfort him.

Still, he rubbed his chest, the feeling of something coming heavy on his mind. Funny, really. He figured the *something coming* had happened already. After he'd tattooed Weylin and subsequently passed out, Derrick's mate, Lucy, had gone into labor.

Good thing Thor had bookmarked that webpage he'd seen on how to get your license to perform marriages in under ten minutes. Derrick had also done his part, getting the license ahead of time, knowing the fury of his mate if he failed to marry her before their cubs came into the world.

He grinned tiredly as he pictured a panting, grunting Lucy with tears in her eyes and a curse for her mate on her lips as he presented her with the document. She'd just had to sign then repeat after Thor, and bam! The two of them were married. A couple of hours later, three brand new cubs were born.

Three cubs. Three precious lives. Three girls.

Thor shook his head. He didn't know whether to laugh or cry for Derrick. The man was one lucky sonovabitch in his opinion. But of that feeling of some impending doom or greatness—*it was still a toss-up which*—hadn't ebbed with the coming of the triplets.

"What is it?" he grumbled.

Asking his grandfather for help on this plane was pretty pointless, but he did it anyway, keeping his voice low and deep. Thor stood, knowing there were no answers incoming.

He turned away from the woods, about to head back to the House, to his room where he would spend yet another night tossing and turning in his big, empty bed. He paused. Frozen mid-step, Thor noticed something hurtling towards him from the sky.

"What the hell?"

The thing was small and dark and traveling unbelievably fast. He squinted, watching its progression before it nosedived a few hundred feet away. Thor didn't know why, but he took off running towards the falling object. He had to get there, had to help.

It was a biological imperative. Thor growled, pulling on his Wolf's strength to up his speed. He slid the last fifteen feet just in time to catch the thing before it could crash into the hard asphalt. He was out of breath, heart thundering, when he opened his big hands to see a giant black bird cradled against his body.

A raven. A female raven.

CHAPTER ONE

DIRE WOLF MATES

She smelled like clean rain on a crisp Autumn day. Like freshly baked bread and sweet summer jam. The Raven smelled good. Too good.

He frowned as he looked at the small creature. Impossibly dark, glossy feathers trembled as the animal loosed a pitiful cry. She was in pain, and the knowledge caused something dark to grow inside of his mind. Something or someone had hurt her, and Thor's Demon Wolf snarled in fury.

The bird was covered in scratches and blood. His growl escaped his lips. He noted the odd way the Raven's wing was bent and was careful not to jostle her unnecessarily. How had she flown with that?

Fuck. Worry replaced his anger at whoever had done this to the creature. He could not imagine the pain she was in.

Poor, brave, determined thing.

"Shhh. It's okay. I got you," he whispered, needing to console the sweet-smelling bird.

For some reason, his voice would not come out any louder. He didn't think too deeply about that. Just held her gently, crooning stuff and nonsense, trying to settle the animal.

Not animal. Ours, his Demon Wolf murmured inside his mind's eye.

Thor froze, then he felt it. Magic. Shifter magic. The vibration was familiar, and his eyes narrowed, zeroing in on the Raven in his hands. The black bird's body was larger than a wild raven's would be. She was already warm, but started growing warmer as the vibration grew stronger.

He narrowed his eyes, taking in the blue black aura swirling around her body. Oh fuck. Surprise and awe filled him when, suddenly, instead of a bird, Thor was holding a woman. Her lush body felt good in his arms, but he wasn't about to overstep any Shifter niceties by paying attention to the side of his brain screaming at him to look his fill.

Instead, his eyes remained on her face, willing hers to open. Finally, they did, and stole his very breath from his chest. Clear and blue, her eyes flashed up at him, and Thor sucked in another sharp breath. It was like he'd forgotten to breathe.

His lungs were burning, but he couldn't seem to get any oxygen. Her eyes were gorgeous, stunning, rooting him where he sat. They reminded him of October mornings, full of promise and beauty. But that dream was short-lived. Too soon, her pretty eyes clouded over with pain, and he mourned the loss of that brightness. He wanted to punish whoever had taken it from her.

Forcing his gaze from hers, he noted a motley of bruises across her face and body. That wing, now an arm in her human skin, was dislocated if not broken. She had dozens of scratches on what was otherwise clear, smooth, fair skin with a hint of freckles on her shoulders and the bridge of her nose.

One eye was red and swollen, she would undoubtedly have a shiner by tomorrow. Her nose was bruised, and her lip cut as if she'd been punched in the face repeatedly. The fury he felt before had amplified tenfold by the time he was done cataloging her injuries.

Someone had worked her over, and his Demon Wolf snarled with the need for vengeance. The beast was not like the others in his pack. With one paw in the other world, his ideas of vengeance and loyalty were a bit more intense. But that was what happened when you were touched by the gods themselves.

"Who hurt you?" Thor asked, his voice a guttural rumble that sounded harsh to his own ears.

The female gasped as she opened her eyes. She met his bravely, and he knew he looked like one scary motherfucker with his size, his many tattoos, and his shaved head, but she didn't flinch.

Bold, beautiful, brave female. Worthy mate.

Shut the fuck up, he told his Demon Wolf.

The animal had crazy ideas about getting himself paired up, but Thor knew better. He was not made for a woman's love. His life was one of service to his Pack. That was no life for a mate. How could he ever justify putting her after the needs of his Pack mates? No. He was meant to be a lifelong loner.

"Hide me. Please, hide me," the Raven Shifter begged.

Her voice was scratchy and hoarse, as if she'd been choked, and, *motherfucker,* one look at her throat confirmed she had. Thor's rage went from simmer to boil once again, and he had to work to rein in his beast.

"Who?"

"Please, please, you have to hide me. They'll come looking!"

She gasped, panicked and in pain. Still, she leaned on him, and that puzzled Thor. A woman who'd been roughed up by some lesser males would surely push him away, but she didn't. Instead, she used her one good arm to cling to him instead.

Good. Ours.

Thor ignored his animal. Focused on the woman, he needed to know more about her situation so he could protect her.

"Who? Who is after you?" he asked again.

Thor watched helplessly as those gorgeous eyes rolled back inside her head as she passed out in his arms. Shit. What was he supposed to do now?

"Fucking hell," he growled, not for any other reason than because he wanted to protect her.

He didn't understand why, but the feeling was damn near overwhelming. Thor stood, holding the woman in his arms. She moaned softly, and he moderated his pace to not jostle her any more than necessary.

The rest of the Pack was likely just getting to bed after all the excitement, but he needed them now. Pulling on his bonds, he called on Brock, the Pack Beta. By the time Thor got to the pack door, the male was there waiting with it open.

"Who is she?" Brock asked, carefully averting his gaze away from her naked body.

Good. Thor was feeling volatile as fuck, and though Brock technically outranked him, he was glad the man was already claimed and mated to a curvy little Lioness. The fact he had looked away was clearly him trying to assuage Thor's stress.

Fuck. Don't get attached. She is not mine.

Yes, she is, his Demon Wolf disagreed.

"Bro, you need to calm down," Brock said, brows furrowed.

"What?"

"Stop growling before you wake the whole house."

Damn. Was he actually growling? Thor shook his head and followed Brock to the tiny spare room they used for medical emergencies and placed the woman on the bed. No sooner had he done that than he grabbed a sheet and draped it over her naked form.

"Thor, man, who is she? We can't just let some stranger in without asking Derrick and he's finally asleep with the triplets and Lucy—"

"Mine," Thor barked his answer, cutting off his Beta.

Oh fuck.

His Demon Wolf growled, smiling Wolfishly in his mind's eye. His shocked eyes met Brock's, and he realized the man was just as surprised as he was. Now that he said it aloud, he knew it was true.

"She's a Raven Shifter. She fell from the sky, and I caught her," Thor explained, running a hand over his face.

"What? Mates are just falling from the sky now?" Brock asked, scratching his head.

"She is not my mate," he argued, more for himself than Brock.

Oh yes she is, Demon Wolf argued back.

"Well, whoever she is, her arm looks broken. We need to call someone—"

"Me. No one else sees her. No one else touches her. I can set it," Thor replied, and somehow, he simply knew he could.

That was another thing about having *the sight,* Thor could sometimes glean information from the spirits. Right then, a healer ancestor was sending him instructions on how to feel for breaks and dislocation. Luckily, it was the latter.

Still, he knew it would hurt when he popped her shoulder back into place. Thor directed Brock on how to assist him. Though he hated the other male's hands on her.

Grrrr.

Get the fuck over it, he told his Wolf.

Thor needed Brock's help. Jealousy was not a good look on him, and he would have to figure out how to handle the tidal wave of emotions hitting him and knocking him off balance. Thor pushed all that from his mind. He needed her all healed up so he could decide what to do about all this.

And he did not just mean the part of him screaming at him to mark, claim, and keep the woman. He also meant the undeniably possessive alphahole side of him that wanted to find whoever did this to her and remove that shit stain from the face of the earth.

"Dude, easy," Brock rumbled.

He realized he was still growling, even after the Beta had released her shoulders after Thor had re-set her arm. If the pain from that didn't wake her up, she would have been hurt more than he realized.

The thought did nothing to calm his beast, who was desperate to rip out of his skin. It was that fiercely loyal side of him that made him a good Enforcer, among other things. But even with the need for vengeance burning in his veins, his Demon Wolf could not bring himself to leave her. Not until he knew she was out of harm's way.

Her eyes fluttered open just as he put some salve on one of the dozens of scratches across her flesh. Thor paused, unmoving, while caught in her line of sight. The blue of her eyes was clearer now, and something inside him warmed at the fact he'd helped.

"Thank you," she whispered.

Her eyes were still laced with exhaustion and pain, but there was something else, too. Maybe relief.

Too much pain. Never again.

"You don't have to thank me," he whispered.

Unable to help himself, he moved closer, reaching up to brush back her wild curls from her face carefully. He'd covered her with a sheet to protect her modesty. Her comfort was tantamount to everything right then.

"Thank you anyway," she whispered, wincing with the effort.

"It's no problem. But I need you to tell me who."

Thor was aware of Brock lingering in the periphery of his vision. The Beta looked on, concerned as the fragile woman moaned softly, shivering as her body pushed her to heal. Finally, her gaze focused back on him, and it was laced with such sorrow, Thor's heart damn near stopped altogether.

"Who did this to you?" he repeated, intent on her answer.

"My mate," she answered, right before her eyes rolled up.

She had passed out again, and it was a good thing. Thor's heart seized in his chest, unadulterated rage filled him.

Her mate? No!

She could not belong to another. She just couldn't. What kind of man would do this to his woman? What kind of cowardly sack of shit could hurt the one person he was to protect and cherish?

Mate? No. Fuck that.

She was his, dammit. How could the Fates be so cruel?

Mine, snarled his Demon Wolf just before the animal tore out of him.

CHAPTER TWO

DIRE WOLF MATES

Three weeks.

That was how long she'd been hiding out with the Dire Wolf MC in Blue Valley, a suburb in south Jersey. Three weeks. That was when Domenica Corvo, Nica to her friends, had plummeted to what she'd thought was her death from the sky. Only she did not die.

Nica didn't even hit the hard, black asphalt that had been getting closer and closer as she lurched into a panicked freefall when the last thread holding her wing in place came undone with an agonizing snap. Something had stopped her fall. No, not something, but someone.

She'd been saved. Caught in the arms of a hulking brute who should have scared the poop out of her. But there was always something a bit off when it came to Nica and her sense of self-preservation. As in, she simply didn't have any.

Instead of being frightened by the tattooed giant with the shaved head, she couldn't help but admire him. Even if only from afar. Sigh. Three weeks. That was how long since she'd first spied her savior. It was also how long he'd been avoiding her.

She wasn't beautiful like the other women in the Pack. She was short, curvy, and a bit of a tomboy, really, with her lack of finesse and fashion sense. Maybe he preferred tall, sophisticated blondes or something.

Gods knew that was not her. Disappointment filled her and regret whenever she thought of the type of woman who might attract Thor Ulger. But even if he hated her on sight, at the very least, she'd expected some questions about her situation and how she'd landed there.

But other than the Alpha couple, no one else had asked. So, she just hadn't bothered to tell anyone her story. Derrick and Lucy Rand were wonderful, easy to talk to, and sympathetic to her plight. They'd offered her sanctuary, and she took it.

What else could she do? Nica had nowhere to go. Plus, she was curious. She wanted to know more about the big, quiet man with the dozens of intricate tattoos covering his arms, chest, belly, and even his neck. He was not bald, as she'd first thought, but rather, he shaved his head with a long, sharp knife. She knew this because she'd walked in on him once in one of the several bathrooms in the Pack House.

It was more like a compound now that they'd added suites and wings to it, keeping in line with the oldish design out front, but affording the Pack some privacy by dividing the rooms up. She was staying in an unoccupied bedroom, but it was located in Thor's wing.

She'd been startled at first and offered to move to another room. But he'd canted his head in that animalistic way he had about him and replied with one word, one very important word.

Stay.

That was all he said. *Stay.* And Nica did. Of course, she didn't let it go to her head. Thor said very little in general, and his wing had three bedrooms and a bathroom. Clearly, there was enough space for her.

No, she didn't make it weird. Or at least, she tried not to. He couldn't be interested in someone like her, anyway. But sometimes, to her secret pleasure, she found his eyes on her. Oh yes, sometimes he seemed to track her movements with intense, dark eyes.

It flattered her when she caught his attention even for a minute. Thor was something else. Something other. The rest of the Pack treated him with a mixture of respect and awe, and it was easy to see why.

Part of her living with the Pack deal was that she would work to pay her way. Nica didn't mind at all, in fact, she loved working. As a Shifter, she had oodles of energy, and as a bird, well, she could get a bit flighty if that energy wasn't properly channeled.

So, yeah, working was a no brainer. And working at Serious Moonlight, the roadhouse she remembered hearing about from people in her old life, well, that was a thrill in and of itself. The place was renowned for their excellent dining, which she got to sample from world class chef, and Pack beta, Brock Laurent himself. The bands were phenomenal. And she had the best view whenever she worked at the front bar.

Sigh.

Nica's eyes darted across the room to where Thor sat, watching the door in his position as bouncer. He wore fitted jeans and a tight black t-shirt, his permanent scowl already in place. Boy, but he was fine. The man was enormous. Taller than the rest of the Pack, with huge cords of muscles roped around his body. She'd seen him without a shirt once and had dreamed about it for days after.

His shoulders were immense, pecs curved and hard, and his abs had abs before they tapered off to his trim waist. And yes, he even had that elusive V she'd read about in some of the racier novels she once borrowed from an online library. Still, for all his size and strength, Thor managed to not look bulky.

He looked perfect, *er*, well, he looked good. Just as she thought it, his black eyes flashed at her, and Nica squeaked, dropping the bowl of lemons she was currently slicing for drinks. Darn it. He always seemed to know when her thoughts started taking a naughtier turn than normal. But Nica couldn't help it. At least, not when it came to Thor.

Crud.

She really needed to find a better hobby than Thor-watching. She was becoming something of a stalker, she mused, shaking her head. Too bad the big, bad Wolf didn't seem to notice her at all. Derrick, the Alpha, couldn't have picked a better man for the job. His aura seemed to scream Enforcer, even if that secret part of her, her Raven side, who sometimes saw more than it should, whispered to her when no one else was around.

He's not just an Enforcer. He's much more. Mine.

Eek! Nope. She was not going there. Besides, it didn't matter what the bird thought. Thor Ulger might be one badassed motherhumper, strong, loyal, handsome as sin, especially with all that marvelous body art, but there was one more thing he was. And that was not interested in Nica Corvo.

Not in the least.

So yeah, she could admire his body, and his gorgeous and intricate tattoo work, but only from afar. Thor wanted nothing to do with her, obviously. When all was said and done, Nica would leave someday soon, and that would be that.

Speaking of tattoos, she wondered why his back was the only part of him that seemed free of ink. Maybe it was because he couldn't reach it. She'd learned from Sheila, the Alpha's cousin, that Thor was responsible for all the body art in the Pack, and the thought of that man as an artist stole her breath away.

Her favorite piece was a wreath of flames circling his thick neck. Fire had never looked so hot as it did on him. The man simply had too many muscles for one person. It was hardly necessary, for Pete's sake. But there it was.

There he was. Like some Greek, or in his case, Norse god, looking down on the rest of the mortals from his lofty perch, *er,* barstool. Muscles rippling with every move, he seemed oblivious to all the female eyes coveting him, and Nica felt her jealousy rise in response.

Sighing, she went back to cutting lemons after having retrieved them from the bar top. She had no business feeling possessive about the man. Thor wasn't hers.

"Take a picture, honey. It lasts longer," Sheila said, surprising her.

She winked as she wiped down the bar where Nica was supposed to be working, slicing lemons, and filling the condiment trays. Her cheeks burned at being caught staring. She was just glad the pretty she-Wolf could not read her train of thought.

Nica would have sounded like a crazed female in heat, the way she was panting after the man who clearly was not interested. Besides, there was no reason for this other than maybe some misplaced hero worship.

Raven Shifters did not experience a heat cycle. Not like Felines or Canines did. Bad enough she'd fallen from the sky to land in his lap, literally. The last thing she needed to do was walk around, giving him puppy eyes.

But it was more than that, even she was not ready to admit it aloud. Thor was the first male she had ever really felt connected to. Her Raven croaked, the deep guttural sound making her animal's preference for the male known.

CHAPTER THREE

DIRE WOLF MATES

The music got louder as the band switched from a power ballad to something faster, so folks could dance. Nica tapped her foot and shrugged, slightly embarrassed at being caught by her peer.

"I wasn't staring exactly," Nica mumbled, but Sheila just gave her a look.

"Yeah, right, but Nica, you can look all you want. Still, you should know that Demon Wolf right there is not like the others. Thor is deep. He's got power and a temper, too," Sheila informed her.

"Demon Wolf? Like he's evil or something?" Nica asked, confused.

"Hell, no, girl. He ain't evil," the redheaded she-Wolf continued. "Thor is touched by the gods. He's our Seer. That means he has the sight. You know, ancient Vikings didn't use the term Demon like Christians do. You see, Demons were simply otherworldly beings. Folks like Thor, who have a foot on either side of the veil."

"I knew he was special, but I had no idea," Nica mused aloud, wonder lacing her tone.

"Yep. That Demon Wolf is pretty special. Look at those shoulders and thighs. No doubt about it, the man is *s-p-e-c-i-a-l*," she spelled it out, thrusting her hips with each letter.

Nica rolled her eyes and laughed at Sheila, who giggled, and play bumped her on the shoulder. It was strange, but she felt a sort of camaraderie with the Dire Wolves she'd never felt with anyone back home.

No, not home, Nica corrected herself.

The place she'd been kept for close to six years had never been her home. She shivered, wishing things were different, wishing she were different. Her gaze wandered back to where Thor was checking the IDs of a group of young women, all giggling and pretty.

The females looked happy and free, confident with their tight clothes and made-up faces. Just out for a good time, she supposed. Nica could not help envying their easy looking lives. One even dared to flirt with the unusually large and somber male. Thor's black gaze was on the blonde as she leaned in and spoke to him, her eyes smiling in invitation.

Something ugly and dark twisted in Nica's gut, and she frowned, recognizing that feeling for what it was. Jealousy. But she had no cause for that. She didn't have any claim on the stoic Dire Wolf Shifter. Behaving the fool was something she couldn't afford nowadays. Nica had other worries, serious worries, but she couldn't help but watch as he dealt with the trio of blonde beauties.

All three of them had the same golden stare and lithe physiques. They moved with a grace she identified as belonging to Feline Shifters only. Lionesses, if she had to guess. Serious Moonlight, the Dire Wolf MC's roadhouse and bar, was located right on the border of Blue Valley, prime Pride territory.

They wore skintight jeans and crop tops with strips of tanned skin revealed through expertly cut rips in their clothing. Yeah, they looked good. Confident, too. Perky boobs and tight butts were on display, with their tiny little waists showing off belly button rings and chains.

Nica felt downright dowdy by comparison. She was short and leaning towards the chubby side, despite being a Raven Shifter. Where her animal form was fine-boned and capable of flying, her human body was thick and stocky, with more soft curves than sleek muscles.

She had dark brown curly hair that she usually pulled back into an untamed puff on top of her head. Unless she had hundreds of dollars to spend on conditioning treatments, which she did not, the frizz was a constant in her life. Then there was her face. She had smooth skin, clear of blemishes save for a few freckles on her nose.

But Nica was allergic to most makeup, so she never bothered with the stuff. Her eyes were nice. A bright, clear blue that was attractive, if not pretty. Still, Nica was the kind of girl who'd rather stay home in yoga pants and a t-shirt watching reruns of old sitcoms and eating ice cream out of the carton than get dressed up and go bar hopping.

Yep. That settled it. Nica would never attract a man like Thor. Still, she watched him as he handled the randy Lionesses without moving off his barstool. He was smooth and professional, allowing them entry but not entertaining any of their flirtations. The leader seemed determined. Bold, that one was, for sure.

Thor mostly ignored the female, and for some reason, that made Nica feel better. Her Raven croaked again, a rumbling sound that showed her animal's content. At least the Demon Wolf, as Sheila had dubbed him, was as indifferent to the pretty Lioness group as he was to Nica.

She recalled how he'd reacted when, to her undying shame, Nica had sought him out after she'd recovered. Her healing sleep had lasted for nearly thirty-six hours after she'd fled her former Murder. Of course, her flight was on the heels of the Crow King's cruel punishment that had left her naked and bleeding, tied to a post outside like an animal.

No. Not mine. They were never my Murder.

In the wild, a group of ravens was called an *unkindness*, but even then, they were rare. Ravens tended to live solitary lives, sometimes in pairs, but only that. There were so few Ravens, they often flocked to other Flight Shifters who were more common. Like Crows.

A group of Crow Shifters was called a Murder, and aptly so. The last one she belonged to held just about as much warmth as the word itself. Harsh and cold, the Crow king was a liar, but duty kept his good little soldiers in line, and no one had helped Nica while the male had beat on her. Some had joined in under his orders.

That memory was forever burned into her brain, destroying any kind thoughts she might have ever had about the Pine Murder. After Nica had finally woken from her healing sleep, she'd been full of sweet thoughts and gratitude towards the man who literally caught her before she could crash land on the unforgiving asphalt.

Thor was her savior, and she had to tell him how grateful she was. So, Nica had cornered him that very afternoon, gushing with emotion when she tried to thank him. His reply to her thankful praise echoed in her ears, and embarrassment filled her once more.

"Stop saying thank you. It's done."

No doubt about it. Thor Ulger was no fan of hers. He was ice. Frozen through to the bone, that one. Just a statue where a warm, breathing man should be, and she would do well to leave him alone. Some men were just like that. Cold, unfeeling brutes, incapable of affection and unwilling to form lasting relationships.

More memories swarmed inside her mind, sending shivers through her body. She'd learned her lesson about men the hard way. The first time she'd seen Jack Branwen, King of the Pine Murder, Nica was barely twenty years old. Green and gullible, she'd believed the older male when he told her he was in love with her and wanted to make her his queen.

Her widowed mother had been thrilled at the news and could not wait to ship her off. After a brief ceremony, Nica and Jack promised themselves to each other beneath a blooming cherry tree with his Beta, Emmet, and her mother as witnesses.

Oh, he'd been sweet then. Paying her compliments, the first she'd ever gotten from a man. Jack was never handsome, but he was so commanding, with his sharp features and fathomless eyes. He'd read her poetry, brought her roses and sweet cakes from the market near the place where she'd grown up in Maryland.

Jack was tall and lean, his face too hawklike to be truly handsome with his large nose and long black hair. He looked like something out of a Vampire romance. But he was no Vampire, he was a Crow. A King to his people. And Nica was so lucky he chose her. Wasn't that what her mother said?

"You should be grateful, child, looking the way you do. Too fat to land a regular man, but he sees value in those wide hips of yours," she snapped when Nica had hesitated about accepting his proposal. "You will not get a better offer!"

So, Nica accepted him at face value. She allowed him to court her, took his gifts, and believed his lies when he said he loved her and wanted her. She hadn't questioned a thing.

What a foolish girl I'd been. I deserved what happened.

She shook her head, wiping a tear that escaped her eye before anyone could see it. Jack had done a real number on Nica. He loved playing his little games, making her apologize for things she didn't even know she did wrong, and always making it feel like it was her fault when they disagreed or when she had a difference of opinion.

It was never about anything important until he wanted more than the chaste kisses she offered him whenever they returned from a date.

"I'm a man, Nica, not a boy. I need more from you."

"I'm sorry, Jack. I don't know how—I'm a virgin," she'd confessed one night, guiltily.

"I see. You want a contract first. Fine, I'll meet with your mother tomorrow.".

True, they hadn't done more than kiss, but she didn't know what he meant by contract until her mother explained she was Jack's the next night. Then she told Nica to wear her one good Sunday dress, and she drove her to the cherry tree where Ravens had been making their intentions known for years and years. Nica had heard stories about the promising ceremony, but she never expected to have one for herself.

Fear and excitement warred within her, but the sharp look on her mother's face was as much incentive as the idea of finally getting out of her small hometown and the house she was raised in. Nica's mother was never affectionate with her, and she wanted more from life than waiting tables.

Jack's offer seemed too good to be true, but she wouldn't learn about that till much later. After she'd signed the papers he'd thrust at her, and they spoke their promise to mate one another aloud as per the ceremony, Jack drove Nica to a cheap motel where he took her virginity with Emmet waiting outside the door—what a horrible disappointment that night was. Eye opening, too.

Sex was painful and messy, and over too damn quickly for her to do more than wince and gasp. Jack was angry at the way she'd received him, her lack of warmth. But she was a virgin, and he didn't seem to care.

"Christ, that was rough. Let's fuck off back to the trailer park. Maybe Ella and Denise can teach this little puritan something about sex before I have to bed her again."

Oh, yeah. She'd heard every scathing thing he'd growled about her to Emmet while she'd been in the bathroom, using a damp washcloth to clean the blood from between her legs and soothe the hurt he'd left there. When she was finished, he demanded she get in the car, then Jack and Emmet drove her to the trailer park where he and the others in his Murder lived.

Nica was almost relieved when he put her inside a trailer with two other females and told she would have to wait her turn to marry the King. She didn't understand, but when she questioned him, Jack told her the promise ceremony they'd had in front of her mother was just that, a promise to marry in the future.

"You ain't the only one in line. Let's see if you can hold my seed better than the others," Jack said, nodding at her stomach.

Nica felt as if the floor had dropped out from under her. Not growing up in a Murder, she did not understand the politics. Apparently, Jack wanted her pregnant before he mated her. That was news to her. Nica wanted to finish school and maybe spend some time getting to know him first.

Thank goodness Ella and Denise had been kind upon her arrival. Ella was ten years older than Nica, with blonde hair and a tall, willowy frame. She was a Crow Shifter who had been promised to Jack since they were teenagers.

Denise was shorter than Ella, but still taller than Nica, with bronzed skin and sharp features and straight black hair. She had been brought in about two years before Nica. The Crow King was apparently desperate for an heir, and after failing to get either of them pregnant, he was still looking for a fertile female to be his Queen.

Lucky for Nica, she had started birth control back in high school to help regulate her period. Still, her reality had hit her hard. She was no treasured mate and there was no impending marriage.

Jack Branwen was a liar.

What she'd thought was the happiest time in her life turned out to be the worst. She was the third in line to mate the Crow King, and she paid her way by cleaning and cooking, doing laundry and other housework the females were told to do. She was made to quit her classes and all outside activity. Her life was to be dedicated to the Murder.

Funny thing was, pathetic as it might sound, Nica could have handled that. She would have done the dishes and washed the clothes, hell, she would have scrubbed the windows and the floors till her fingers bled, if only he loved her. But Jack never loved her. It didn't take her long to realize that. Unfortunately, there was a reason a group of Birds like them was called a Murder—*death was the only way to leave.*

Unlucky at love. That's what you are, Nica girl. Terribly unlucky.

CHAPTER FOUR

"Nica? A Word," Derrick poked his head out of his office and called out to her from down the hall.

She turned her head, placing the last of the lemon slices in the condiment tray. Raven Shifters might have an inferior sense of smell when it came to other Shifters, but her hearing was just fine. And her sight, well, that was even better.

She placed the clear plastic cover back on the tiny tray, taking a second to enjoy the rainbow of sliced lemons, oranges, limes, cherries, and such, before she wiped her hands and headed to Derrick's office.

"Yeah, boss?" she asked, knocking before entering.

"Sit down, Nica," he invited, patting the back of the baby he held.

Nica smiled. The triplets were the most beautiful babies she had ever seen. At almost one month old, they were triple the size of a human baby, and alert in the way of Shifter offspring. She was delighted with the way the entire Pack pitched in to take care of the cubs. It wasn't something she was used to growing up with just her mother.

Catherine Corvo was the opposite of what Nica thought of when it came to maternal instincts. Her mother saw to the necessities like keeping food on the table and a roof over her head, but she never witnessed the kind of utter joy she saw on the faces of Lucy and Derrick when they held their precious young. If only she should be so lucky someday, she mused, laughing as the baby let out a surprisingly loud burp.

"That's my girl," Derrick murmured, grinning as he kissed her head.

"She's just perfect, Alpha Derrick," Nica said, smiling at the infant.

All three cubs were perfect, in her opinion. Their cherubic faces were as pretty as their names—*Eden, Astrid,* and *Selena.* Nica watched the new father as he gently placed the now sleeping babe in a bassinet, just in time to retrieve another, who was already fussing, as if she knew her sister was settled, and her daddy's hands were free just to tend her.

"Lucy is napping," he explained and nodded his head to a door where the Alpha couple had set up a mini nursery, complete with a rocking recliner and a daybed.

Nica smiled and reminded herself to speak softly so as not to wake the exhausted she-Cat. That was another thing she found interesting about this pack. They accepted everyone into the fold without issue. These Dire Wolves were mated to various Shifters and supes, even normals with no protests from the rest of the Pack. That was not something that would ever happen in the Pine Murder. Bad enough she'd been a Raven among Crows. After she'd refused to mate Jack, her status had dropped so low she'd been little more than a servant for years.

"You've been with us three weeks now—"

Oh, no!

Fear gripped her, and her stomach clenched. She should have seen this coming. Derrick stopped speaking to rearrange the baby's bib as he patted her back and burped her. But Nica was too nervous to be entertained by the homey scene now.

"I am so sorry if I'm wearing out my welcome, Alpha," she began. "I swear, I will leave as soon as I have enough saved, but if you can see your way to giving me some more time."

She did not know how she would find the means to move on, but Nica was determined to not be a detriment to those who had helped her.

"Do you want to leave?" he asked suddenly, and Nica ducked her head.

She could not lie to the man, after all, he would smell it on her. But she was embarrassed by how much she actually wanted to stay. Her feelings were a mess lately, and part of that was due to the broken bonds she had with Jack and his Murder. She had to find some way to get rid of the remnants, so they couldn't find her before she even thought about leaving.

"No. I don't want to go," she said. "But I don't want to put you or your mate and cubs, the whole Pack, in any danger, either."

"Danger?"

"Well, so far, Jack and the Murder have stayed away, but there is no guarantee he will keep his distance, is there?"

"Do you know something you aren't telling me?" Derrick asked, eyes narrowed.

Nica swallowed. She knew Jack and his men were out there watching, just waiting for the right time to strike. That's what Crows, and sometimes Ravens, did. They were the best spies, inconspicuous and seemingly harmless. But Nica knew better than that. She suspected they'd been scoping her out these last few weeks, and her blood chilled at the thought.

"Not for sure, but I, I think they might be watching me here," she whispered, ashamed of herself.

"I see," Derrick replied.

Nica was a coward for hiding behind these Dire Wolves. She despised that side of her that was just too weak to run. Isn't that what Jack had said about her all those years ago? She was too small, too meek, too fragile to make it on her own. So what that he had other women? Her feminine sensibilities had been affronted by his assumption she would simply obey his decrees.

After that first time in the motel, and once she'd known about his other mates, Nica refused his attentions. Oh, he punished her for it in different ways., but her resolve was rock solid. Sometimes his punishments were as simple as withholding food for the night or access to the trailer park's communal showers. But it got worse.

After six months of polite refusals, she was forced to leave the trailer where Jack's other mates lived. No longer under that protected status, he'd reduced her rank and shoved her in a rundown shack instead.

She shivered, remembering the cold winters and sweltering summers in that four by six hovel. It was used to house lawn care equipment back when whoever had run the trailer park took care of things like that. By the time the Murder moved in, there was no grass to speak of.

Just a dusty lot with a smattering of trees surrounding it and the loud highway beyond an ugly, tall, brown wall that served as a noise barrier for the community. The stink of oil and gasoline had permeated the walls, but it didn't matter. Nica was spared Jack's drunken advances for a good long run as she cowered and hid behind her duties and her rank at the bottom of the Murder.

It wasn't until Ella got sick that it all started again. She frowned, thinking of the frail female who was the only one in the Murder who had maintained a friendly smile whenever she saw Nica hurry by. She hoped Ella was all right, prayed that Jack got her some medical attention, though it was unlikely.

Once his first mate fell ill, he'd tried courting her again, giving her extra rations at mealtimes, and sending her flowers. He'd just finished moving her stuff out of the shack and into a nicer, newer trailer one afternoon after washing the Murder's clothes at the local laundromat.

Nica was suspicious, nervous even. The man did nothing for anyone, not without a reason. She soon found out what he wanted that night when he let himself into her small bedroom, naked and stinking of booze. Nica had fought him like a wildcat, scratching and clawing anywhere she could reach.

That was the first night she'd tried to run, but Jack was so fast and strong. He'd caught her, beaten her, and let his Murder take turns attacking in their bird forms. Oh, they were just toying with her. They could have easily killed her, but he wanted her broken, not dead.

One of his soldiers had unwittingly cut the binds tying her to the pole Jack used to bind whoever was being punished. Nica hid the torn tethers until they gave up on her torture for the evening or just plain passed out. Once they were gone, she did not hesitate. She broke free and wound up here with the Dire Wolves.

For the first time, Nica had felt a spark of hope ignite inside her chest. She'd found a place she felt safe, wanted. Still, she would leave if Derrick told her to. She would have no choice.

"I am sorry I didn't say anything sooner," she fretted.

"Don't be sorry. Look, I am not chasing you away, Nica. You let me and the Pack worry about the Murder."

"Do you mean that?" she asked, surprised.

"Hell yeah," he whispered, the baby in his arms stirring slightly. "Truth is, we are so lucky you came to us when you did. With the cubs arriving early, and Lucy's replacement at the bar, Gwendolyn, still learning to control her new Wolf, your help here has been a godsend! I know it's unconventional, but I'd like you to seriously consider staying on with us as long as you want," Derrick said, surprising Nica into smiling.

"Well, all right then," she replied. "As long as you need me, I'll stay."

CHAPTER FIVE

DIRE WOLF MATES

"W*ell, all right then. As long as you need me, I'll stay.*"

Thor released the breath he was holding, and his entire body seemed to relax after hearing Nica's reply to Derrick's statement about needing her. Recently, he'd started to suspect she was growing restless. He had tracked her with hungry eyes. Saw the way she started watching the trees and the skies when she thought no one was looking.

Oh yeah, Thor had been clocking the curvy little Raven as she went about her business, picking up slack at the roadhouse and even taking on extra chores at the Pack House. How many times had the tiny female done laundry that wasn't hers? Or washed up after dinner when it wasn't her turn?

The other females made damn sure the men in the house knew they were not there to wait on them, but Nica seemed cut from a different cloth. She took on chores without complaint, so much so, he intervened when he thought others were taking advantage. Like when he caught her cleaning Cole's bedroom. He'd put a stop to that shit real fast, reminding her the single male was perfectly capable of washing his own bedding.

He'd also had a one-on-one conversation with Cole, which ended with the man wholeheartedly agreeing to never take advantage of Nica's kindness again. Thor didn't even have to say anything. He'd just tossed the pile of wet sheets he'd taken from Nica, she was about to hang them to dry on the outdoor line, right onto Cole's lap, followed by a single punch to the male's jaw.

But aside from throwing herself into her chores, Thor noticed something else strange about Nica. Not once in the three weeks that had passed had she shifted into her animal. But maybe it was odd to him because his own Demon Wolf had been acting like a total fucking lunatic.

Thor was so amped up with her around, he was shifting into his beast nightly. It was the only way to contain the animal's anger, lest he hunt down and decimate the first Murder he came across. Thank fuck she was a Shifter, and those bruises she'd arrived with were long gone by now. That was enough to placate his beast. Mostly.

Not a day went by that Thor didn't have a flashback of her broken wing, cuts oozing blood, and the black eye that had swollen so much by the time she woke up, she could hardly open it. Those first few days had been hell on him, and yeah, he realized he was whining like a cub, but fuck. He couldn't really explain it save to say it hurt him to see her hurt.

Thor's blood boiled with the thirst for revenge. He hungered for it. But revenge was not his to take. Finding her at last, Thor had given everything he could to help fix her battered body. He couldn't bring himself to leave her side, at least not till she told him the only thing that could have moved him.

Nica had a mate.

A right bastard for sure, but still her mate. The beautiful Raven was not free for Thor to claim. She just wasn't. Knowing it made his heart feel like someone had tried to rip it right out of his chest.

So, he'd done what any besotted fool, who had no chance in hell of claiming the woman the Fates told him was his, would do. He'd stayed away. Hid in the background. Watched from afar. And he cursed those same Fates for showing him something he couldn't have.

Why did she have to be so perfect? With her dark curls and bright blue eyes, and her fresh baked bread and sweet summer jam scent.

"You should talk to her, man," Weylin said, suddenly beside him.

The younger Wolf had been walking by, carrying a couple of cases of beer up from storage, but Thor hadn't been paying attention. He hadn't realized Weylin stopped beside him until the man opened his fat mouth with his Captain Obvious observations.

Gods dammit.

Could he really blame him, though? Weylin was still in that honeymoon phase with Gwendolyn, his somehow newly turned Dire Wolf mate. Newly matched up and just about as annoying as every other mated pair in the Pack, Thor could give two shits what Weylin thought.

"Don't go getting all growly and shit, all I'm saying is instead of stalking her like some giant psycho, you might try talking to the woman—hey!"

Thor tried to make it a point to hate as few things as possible in his life, but there were a few he just could not help but loathe. One of them was unsolicited advice. However, staring down at the mess he'd made of Weylin's perfectly coiffed red hair after dumping the glass of water he'd been holding was extremely satisfying.

In fact, Thor felt better than he had in days. Of course, that was probably because of his eavesdropping ways and overhearing Nica tell Derrick she was planning on staying for a while.

Good. Mine. Mate.

No. She belongs to another.

Grrrrrr.

Fine. Maybe Weylin had a point. Gifted, or cursed, with the sight as he was, Thor knew better than to just toss away something the Fates had so purposely thrown at him. He didn't pretend to understand the motives of supernatural deities and power players, but he knew enough that the shit they did was for a reason.

If Nica had fallen into his lap, so to speak, it was likely because he had a hand in her future. Thor wasn't the type of man to mess around with another male's mate, but perhaps that was the part he had wrong. Fact was, he needed answers, and he could only get them from her. So, yeah, maybe he should try talking to her. He grunted and nodded at the still sputtering Weylin. His advice was unsolicited, but useful.

Hmm. Imagine that.

Thor placed the empty water glass on top of the cases of beer his drenched Pack mate was still holding and walked away to mull things over. Perhaps he'd commune with the spirits tonight, see if they had any advice for him. It wasn't his favorite pastime, and it took fuck all out of him, but he needed to proceed with caution.

Could be he was mistaken, and Nica wasn't his fated mate, after all. But judging from the way his cock turned to steel behind the tight denim jeans he often wore every time he saw her, he doubted he erred in his assessment. As if to emphasize the fact his cock also disagreed, the damn thing thumped inside his jeans, filling with lust at the mere mention of her.

Yep. He really fucking doubted he was wrong. He needed to bide his time until she had a spare moment. So, Thor kept busy most of the night, working the front door, just business as usual. He didn't mind checking IDs and making sure the supernatural members of the mixed crowd Serious Moonlight attracted knew he was there to keep the peace. As the Pack Enforcer, it came with the territory.

Dire Wolves had a reputation for being tough, and sometimes folks liked to challenge them just on the off chance they might win a fight. Not that it happened very often. Still, his senses were on high alert, the Demon Wolf inside him riled for whatever reason.

More than likely it had to do with the fact that Sheila, his redheaded Pack mate, and his Alpha's cousin, was teaching Nica how to tend bar. Sheila was mated and devoted to her man, but she could flirt with the best of them. Still, she was a spitfire and could hold her own where Nica was shy around most men.

He was concerned Sheila was going to push her outside her

comfort zone, so he waited, poised to intervene. But he shouldn't have worried. Nica was holding her own. Pride, the likes of which he never felt for anyone, sprung inside him like a well.

Go on, girl. Show 'em how it's done, his Demon Wolf growled.

The curvy little goddess was grinning and pulling beers on tap with almost zero foam to the praise of their patrons. She was wearing a pair of skintight jeans strategically cut to show tantalizing swatches of smooth, unmarred skin. On top, Nica wore one of Serious Moonlight's famous logo tees, the deep V revealing her fantastic cleavage, making Thor's mouth water, and drawing the eyes of the male customers at the bar.

Grrrr.

It was part of the deal with bartending, but those guys could fuck right off if they wanted to keep their eyes inside their heads. They served mostly Shifters, so when one male leaned over, checking out her ass as he bent over to grab something from the cooler behind the bar, Thor sent a snarl his way. The young male blanched, sat his ass back down and treated Nica like she was his Sunday school teacher after that.

Good, but let's bite him, anyway, growled his Wolf.

But Thor knew better than to throw his weight around. Saying he was a big man was like saying Texas was a big state—at the very least, it was a bland way of describing something that sizeable. The Lone Star state was the second largest state in the country after Alaska. It was fucking vast.

In the same sense, Thor was not simply *big*. He was the biggest motherfucker in the bar, including a couple of Grizzly Shifters and that fat-headed Lion mate of Sheila's. Leo was okay, but what was with that fucking hair? The man used more conditioner than all of Thor's sisters combined, and he'd grown up with three. They were all spread out now across the world, mothers, the lot of them, and happy as little mated clams. But he'd still bet Leo used more hair product than any of them.

It had been a while since he'd checked in on them, and he made a mental note to do that. The line outside was growing, and he calculated the numbers before allowing the next group in. There were legal limits to how many they could have under their roof at one time, and Thor was highly conscientious of that.

He growled at a group of underage Bears, turning the rascals away by pulling his top lip away from his teeth, revealing enormous fangs. Those cubs couldn't run away fast enough. The next trio were of age, and female, even better for the bar. It might be sexist, but it was the business. Women brought in men, which added up to a packed house, and that added up to paying customers. Sure, their money was mostly made on the market, and gods knew, the Pack had plenty. But there was something about making Serious Moonlight a success that meant a lot to each of them.

Thor didn't think it would happen, but Derrick had been right about all this. Settling down, growing roots, making a home. Thor had to agree. For the first time, he found contentment in a patch of land. Blue Valley was turning out to be ideal. Now if only he could have a conversation with a certain curly haired beauty, then maybe, just maybe, his Demon Wolf would be okay, too.

Tonight's band was thumping, some local Wolves singing country rock with a little hip hop thrown in. They were pretty good, but he just wasn't paying enough attention to really judge. There was a sizeable group of normals amongst the crowd of mostly Shifters, but they were all right, too, seeming to just want to have a good time.

Thor kept an eye on everyone. It was his job, but there was more to it than that. As a Seer, he picked up on auras and inklings, things the Spirits were trying to tell him, messages, and warnings. It was like he was always on, constantly reading from ten different books, in ten different languages. He had to pay attention not to lose track of one or the other.

It was a unique dance he did, keeping steady, maintaining balance. Keeping watch over the Pack and those who meant the most to him was a most sacred duty. For years, he assumed that was why he was not mated. How could he focus on one and the other at the same time? It worried him, even now.

When he wasn't watching Nica, of course. She was so damn pretty. Far as he could tell, she didn't seem to know it. Her heart-shaped face was free of makeup, save a little lip gloss. He never really liked artificial things, and Nica was anything but fake. She was more beautiful than anyone he had ever seen.

Thor was a spiritual guy, and he wasn't all that fond of fake things and materialism. Didn't matter to him if a person lived in a mansion or a cardboard box, he made up his mind about someone based on how they acted. So far, Nica had been sweet and kind, patient, and hardworking. She was a good one. He could tell.

Suddenly, her head snapped towards him, and Thor froze, thinking he'd been caught staring. But she wasn't looking at him. Her gaze was fixed beyond where he stood a few feet away from the front door and his usual barstool perch. Her face blanched, and those blue eyes he'd been obsessing over widened with fear. That's when he smelled them.

Feathers.

Thor turned and spotted them immediately. Six tall, thin Shifters, Crows he was betting, walked into the bar, fanning out and taking up way too much space as far as he was concerned. His Demon Wolf snarled deep inside the metaphysical plane where the beast waited to be called.

Enemies, the animal growled.

Yes, Thor agreed.

Animosity and anger seemed to roll off the males in waves, but it would take a fucking tsunami to knock Thor off his substantial feet. The one in front looked the most dangerous. That had to be the Crow King, Thor assumed. He had a broody expression, muddy eyes, long black hair, and a big nose.

Good. Easy to break, the Demon Wolf inside him snarled.

They advanced, but Thor stopped them, positioning himself in front of the leader. One of the lackeys held their IDs, but Thor did not give two shits about that. He ignored him, focusing on the so-called King. Thor's Pack bonds lit up, and he felt his Pack mates easing next to him, Cole on his left, and Weylin on his right.

"Pardon us, friend." The man smiled, but it did not reach his eyes.

"No." Thor said. His voice had been clear, so he was mildly confused when the fella replied.

"Excuse me?"

"I said, no. You are not welcome here, Crow. Leave. Now."

"Show him some respect," one of the lackeys said, stepping forward.

All Thor had to do was flick his gaze in the male's direction to stop him in his tracks. That laser like focus, and his uncanny ability to see into the minds and hearts of people, was often enough to halt whatever tomfoolery was about to happen. Thor was used to leaving folks shaky and vulnerable when he gazed upon them with the *sight*.

"Fuck. Off." Thor growled.

This Murder was tainted. He knew it. They knew it, too. But they were too scared or too lazy to do anything about it. Unfortunately for them, that was not Thor's problem. The Crows would have to work out their issues themselves. But not here. Not anywhere near Nica.

"Gentlemen, calm yourselves. Our Wolf friends require an introduction," he explained and raised his hands in a fake gesture of peace. "I am Jack Branwen, King of the Pine Murder. And I demand to speak with your Alpha about returning something he has of mine," the Crow King sneered.

"There is nothing for you here, Crow. And you are most decidedly unwelcome," Thor grunted, unfolding his arms.

His chest was heaving and the growl in his chest grew louder with every passing moment. Before he could advance on the hawkish King and his smarmy grin, Cole got in front of him. The gray-eyed Dire Wolf opened his arms, hands spread and nodded to the door.

"Look, tonight we have *mixed company*," Cole explained, his intention clear. There were humans in the bar. It was not an ideal time for a fight.

"However, if you would like to arrange a meeting for a later date? Who has a card? No one? No matter. Here is mine," he said, handing a business card to one of the Crows standing beside the King. "I suggest you leave now and call tomorrow after ten."

A few more minutes of the Crow King trying to stare Thore down resulted in nothing but frustration for the man with the big nose. Thor could have kept that shit up all fucking day. He even knew the second his eyes bled to black by the way the man startled. The Crow even swallowed a loud gulp full of fear.

Grrrr.

That was a foolish thing to do in front of a predator. Thor pulled on his powers, calling on the Spirits to delve into the man's mind and heart. Likely, the Crow King did not realize what Thor was, never mind how much he wanted to end him. Blackness and evil intent came back at him, and the Demon Wolf snarled again. The Crow King did not just want Nica. He wanted to break her.

Fuck. No. That was so not going to happen. Thor refused to look away, even when the Crow broke eye contact.

"Fine. Tomorrow," clipped Jack Branwen.

Then he left with his men, and Thor closed his eyes, trying to rein in his beast. It wasn't easy when all he wanted to do was follow him outside and tear the piece of shit limb from limb. Derrick would not approve. But as far as the Demon Wolf was concerned, Jack Branwen's number was up. It was merely a matter of when.

Grrrr.

CHAPTER SIX

Damn. Damn. DAMN.

Nica waited until after the bar was closed to have her first freak out in the weeks since she'd come to be there. She'd been on edge ever since she escaped Jack's clutches and despite Derrick's assurances the Pack could handle a bunch of Crows, she didn't want to bring that kind of heat down on them.

Crows fought dirty, and the Dire Wolves were just so different from the other predatory Shifters she'd been around. They were loyal and honorable. They seemed to have the deepest respect for community and family, and well, Nica just didn't know what to do with that. How did you show gratitude for something you never even knew was a possibility?

After the Murder appeared in the bar, she expected the shit to hit the fan, and for the Alpha to rescind his invitation. But that didn't happen. In fact, no one said a word to her. She'd watched as the guys filed into Derrick's office after that tense little meet and greet. Nica even stayed close, waiting to be called in. But she wasn't.

If this situation were reversed, and she'd brought trouble to the Murder, Jack would have had her tied to that horrible post in the trailer park and beaten in front of everyone. That was his go to form of punishment. He'd done it to others, and he did it to her after the countless nights of her refusing his advances.

"Nica, what was all that about?" Sheila asked, sliding up next to her. "Look, I know we haven't really talked about your past, but that was pretty intense."

"Crud. I am sorry, Sheila. Derrick and Lucy know everything, but I just didn't think anyone else cared—"

"Oh, honey, no! We care. We were just waiting for you to open up."

"Really?" Nica was shocked, but it was time for a break anyway, and Sheila dragged her over to a small table where she had some appetizers waiting.

"Come on, spill," the redheaded firebrand said.

Ariella, Tracey, and Gwen were there, too. All the women looked concerned, and like they wanted to help. Tears pricked Nica's eyes, and before she knew it, she'd spilled. Like *everything.*

"Look, no matter how much you liked or felt sorry for those two women, Ella and Denise, you were right to refuse to become like them," Tracey remarked, her brows furrowed in anger, but not at Nica.

"They're just Jack's possessions," Gwen added, but she was more upset than she was judging them, Nica could tell.

"Ella was sick when I got away. I feel bad, like I abandoned them," she confessed.

"No, that is not on you. You had to do what you needed to survive," Ariella replied, her hand on Nica's arm, reassuring her. "I don't know anything about the way Murders are run, but my sisters and I would have torn those Crow males limb from limb. I am glad you got away, Nica, no matter how you did it." The Lioness nodded, and the others seemed to agree.

"Oh my, thank you all so much. I mean, I never had a lot of friends growing up, but I always imagined what it would be like, and you ladies are blowing it out of the water," she said, her cheeks burning with embarrassment.

"Hell, honey, we like you too," Sheila replied, and Nica felt her own wobbly smile on her face in return.

"Are they dangerous, though?" Gwen asked, and Nica could not dishonor her new friends with a lie.

"Yes. Crows are dangerous, but not in the same way you and your mates are. Oh, they are plenty strong, but worse than brute strength is how they think. You see, Crows are wily, sneaky, and cruel. Very, very cruel," she replied and worried her lower lip.

They divvied up the last of the mozzarella sticks before break time was over. The next half hour went by quickly, and she mulled over what the Pack females had said. Maybe she was wrong to feel guilty. One thing she knew, this was like a second chance for her, and she was wasting it being idle. She had to speak to Thor.

Sooner than she knew it, closing time approached and Nica was wiping down the bar while most of the Pack males were still inside the Alpha's office. She moved on with her spray and rag, cleaning every available surface in the bar, and was just tying up the trash bag when she saw them leaving. Of course, her eyes zeroed in on him.

Thor Ulger came out of Derrick's office, oozing confidence, and barely muted fury. His face was normally a mask, hiding all of his emotions—assuming he had any. And tonight, that assumption was correct.

Nica gasped as he walked into the room. She could practically feel his rage, and it was stunning in its purity. His dark eyes flicked to hers for one poignant moment, and it was like he sucked all the air out of the room before he mercifully looked away.

She inhaled, hardly aware she was trembling till she looked down at the spray bottle in her hand. Forcing herself to be still, she placed it on the table nearest her. Music played low in the background, some hip-hop song one of the guys played while they cleaned up. But Nica couldn't name the song or the artist, how could she? When Thor walked into a room, the man simply commanded all of her attention. Every. Last. Bit of it. Like he was a superstar or politician or something.

There was never any opportunity to go to concerts or the big city, despite being so close. Not for Nica, anyway. But she imagined this was how she would have reacted to seeing one of her favorites up on stage or maybe in passing outside of some posh little café in the Village. Her reactions, of course, were grossly embarrassing.

Nica got tongue-tied and turned into a quivering mess whenever Thor was in the same room as her. Liquid pooled between her legs, and her nipples turned into pebbles. She didn't know why or how to stop it. All she knew was that when he was near, her stomach tensed, breathing grew erratic, and she felt hot all over, like her skin was too tight. Something sparked, and it spread through her veins like molten lava. Even her clothes irritated the hell out of her. It was sort of like when she needed to shift, but different.

Yes, different, her Raven pushed the thought at her, and she exhaled slowly.

Thor was gone. She didn't have to look up to know that for sure. Nica could tell he'd left by the ease with which she took her next breath. Of all the males in the Dire Wolf MC, Thor was the only one who made her chest feel tight and the baby hairs on the back of Nica's neck stand up whenever he was near. Her inner Raven watched him, always. But her animal had always been more curious than was good for her. Still, she knew what she saw, and she knew it was bad.

Jack had found her. The Crow King and his men had tracked her to Serious Moonlight. To Thor and his Pack. Damn it. It was time for her to run again. But she couldn't go yet, not without knowing what the evil man said to Thor about her.

Usually, her hearing was good enough that the distance wouldn't have mattered, but the bar had been crowded and their speech too low for her ears. Her Raven croaked deep and low, this time the sound was anything but content. Grabbing her courage, she rushed out the side door.

Determination filled her. She needed to track Thor to find out what happened before she took her next steps towards freedom from that horrible Crow. Only, she'd sort of forgotten the very real physical reactions she had when she was near him and rushed to the building where she sensed he'd gone.

"C-can I talk to you?" she asked, her voice barely above a whisper.

Nica should have put something on, a sweatshirt maybe, anything to cover herself up. She was highly aware of the low-cut t-shirt she'd worn to tend bar and the fact it revealed way more skin than she was used to showing off. But it was too late now. Nica shivered involuntarily, hovering by the open door of the enormous garage that sat on the other side of the parking lot across from the bar.

Actually, it was a barn the Pack had converted into their own personal garage. A place where they could work on the dozens of motorcycles they owned, and usually displayed in front of the roadhouse to attract other enthusiasts. It was nothing like the Murder's old trailer park or the shack where she'd spent so many nights in her bird form. Her stomach was all clenched up tight, and she wondered where she had finally found the nerve to approach him.

Meek, weak, small, insignificant thing. Who are you to bother him?

She closed her eyes to quiet those ugly voices inside her head. Jack and the Murder had loved to break down any female who dared speak out. Especially the ones who turned down offers to share their beds. They'd called her stuck up and conceited, a cock tease who needed to be broken. They just couldn't even see the real problem was with themselves. She shivered again, hating the idea of going back.

No. I won't go.

They'd have to kill her first, she vowed with renewed determination. Thor still hadn't looked up from what he was doing, but she'd seen him these past weeks and knew he would answer in his own time. The man simply would not be rushed.

That was okay. She could wait. Besides, she enjoyed looking around at all the bikes and parts. It sure didn't smell like any garage she had ever seen. Not that there had been many. To Nica, it looked like some sort of motorcycle museum.

Shelves were immaculately kept, row after row of parts new and refurbished, some still inboxes. They had powerful looking tools, dozens of them, each cleaned and put in its place. That was how everything was inside there. Everything was either new or clean, kept with the utmost care, and returned to its proper place. Everything but Nica.

Always the odd duck.

She bit her lip, waiting for him to acknowledge her. Finally, he turned to face her, and Nica damn near swallowed her tongue. She normally had to bend her neck back just to look at him, but not this time. She was about eye level with him almost kneeling on the floor.

Even that didn't stop her from feeling so small compared to him. Thor was crouched down, working on his enormous Harley. Nica had asked Cole about the makes and models one evening when she'd been hanging the wash on the outside line.

Before the Alpha fem had given birth to her triplets, she'd been obsessed with the scent of laundry freshly washed and hung outside to dry. Since Nica didn't mind the work, she'd kept it up for the weeks she'd stayed there.

Happy to help.

"What is it?" Thor clipped.

His deep, gravelly voice cut through her reverie and Nica startled, clutching her throat and he stood up swiftly, running a hand over his shaved head and cursing to himself.

"Fuckin hell," he muttered.

"You shouldn't cuss."

"I shouldn't cuss?" he asked, head canted to the side.

"Yeah, you shouldn't cuss."

"Is that why you came in here? To tell me not to cuss?" he asked, eyes wide with incredulity.

"What? No! Um, w-what did they say to you?" Nica asked, averting her gaze.

Staring into Thor's impossibly dark eyes was almost too much for Nica to bear. The tight black t-shirt he wore did nothing to hide the rippling muscles corded around his chest, arms, back, and abs. Same thing went for the well-worn denim clinging to his rugby player thighs.

He was a powerhouse of a man. The few times she'd seen him without a shirt had left her tongue-tied and aching in a way she hadn't felt since those days when she'd thought Jack Branwen was the sweetest thing in the world. Actually, that was not true.

This feeling eclipsed her first tastes of carnal hunger. But Nica knew better than to let it show. There was no way on earth a man like Thor Ulger would want anything to do with her. And that was what she'd been telling herself every day for the last three weeks.

Hide your feelings. Keep your heart safe.

"What did they say? They who?"

"Them, the, uh, the Crows," she murmured, hating even saying that out loud.

"You mean your mate," he growled the word and raw fury flashed in his black eyes.

Nica shook her head. Thor looked furious. His expression was thunderous as he slowly turned towards her. The muscles on his chest and abs flexed as he tried to control his breathing, but they were mesmerizing. Instead of being afraid as she should have been, Nica felt bold and curious, warm all over.

"You've got that wrong," she explained, and started towards him. "Jack's not my mate."

"You called him mate."

"When? Anyway, no, I mean, he was supposed to be, but h-he lied," she blurted, trying to catch up.

Thor went still, lifting a hand to halt her advance, and Nica fumbled. What the heck was she doing? Why was she so intent on getting closer to a man who could not stand her? Her Raven cawed, and she shook her head, trying to clear some of the fog.

"You said your mate hurt you. The day you fell," he grumbled.

"I did? Well, I mean, we were supposed to be mated, but he already had two mates when he brought me to the trailer park, and, um, I j-just couldn't," Nica replied, racking her brain for more of an explanation.

Thinking was hard with Thor staring daggers at her. Hell, the man must truly hate her to look like that, and the thought made her sad. He seemed to wait for more from her, but the truth was, she simply wasn't used to talking about herself. And after a couple of years of living as an outcast in the Pine Murder, she was unaccustomed to talking period.

"I'm going to need you to explain what you mean by that, Nica. Start from the beginning."

Nica swallowed. A cool Autumn breeze swept in through the open door of the garage and she shivered involuntarily. Thor stood there, eyes glittering darkly despite the fluorescent overhead light. He wanted an explanation from her. But why? Curiosity got the better of her, and Nica couldn't have walked away now if she wanted to. And she didn't want to, she realized as the word he'd spoken to her the first night after she woke from her healing sleep echoed inside her head.

Stay.

CHAPTER SEVEN

DIRE WOLF MATES

Fuck. Fuck. FUCK.

Thunder roared in Thor's brain, and he wanted to hit something just to make it stop. He was angry, furious at himself, at Derrick for ordering him weeks ago not to seek retaliation against those hateful fucking cowards who'd hurt her. Only an Alpha's order could have stopped him from going after the stain, who so richly deserved the vengeance Thor wanted to reap against him.

Should've hit that prick. Should've given him a nice shiner like he gave our Nica, his Demon Wolf snarled.

Thor expelled a harsh breath, the growl in his chest never ending as he tried to control his emotions. The second that Crow motherfucker had left the bar with his lackeys, Thor had to use all his strength to stop his beast from going after them.

Oh, he knew what the man really was. King of his Murder to all his cronies, but he was nothing but a coward. A phony with a crown and Thor didn't give a fuck about his position. His beast was old school when it came to revenge, and he demanded blood for the bruises that asshole had put on Nica's sweet face.

Weeks wasted, snarled his Demon Wolf.

The animal was right. He'd spent weeks dancing around his feelings, staying away from the only woman he had ever wanted. A woman he'd thought was already mated. But here she was, standing in the otherwise empty garage and facing him down bravely. It seemed Nica wanted answers, too. But he kept his mouth shut until he knew he could speak without snarling at her. Only then did he speak.

"You said your mate hurt you. The day you fell."

"I did? Well, I mean, we were supposed to be mated, but he already had two mates when he brought me to the trailer park, and, um, I j-just couldn't."

"I'm going to need you to explain what you mean by that, Nica. Start from the beginning."

He watched her process his request, waited until she nodded her head in agreement. Thank fuck. he didn't know what he would have done if she refused him. Her assent was step one in the quest to find out more.

Of course, it was made that much more difficult since the movement of her head had the long curls down her back and around her shoulders flutter about like magic. She was pretty before, but fuck, right then, she was beautiful. He didn't know when she'd pulled the elastic band from her hair, but he preferred it this way. All loose and wild and perfect.

He had to work hard not to reach out and run his fingers over it, not through it. Curly hair demanded a different approach. Despite shaving his head, Thor understood her curls worked differently than waves or straight hair, and he would never want to hurt her.

Not ever.

"I guess it started with my mother," she finally began after some seconds of careful consideration.

"Your mother?" he asked.

Thor was incredulous. How did her mother have anything to do with this? Patience, he reminded himself. Nica was not like the other women in his life, and he would do well to remember that.

"Ravens are different from most Shifters. We tend to live solitary lives, unless paired up. And only then do we live with our immediate families. We don't gather in groups because there just aren't very many of us," she explained.

"Ravens and Crows don't usually live together?" he asked.

"Sometimes, but not always. There aren't that many Crows either. Not like Wolves and Bears. Anyway, when Dad died, it was just me and Mama for a while. She worked at a small diner waitressing, and after I finished high school, I worked there too after my community college classes. It was a tough couple of years. Quiet, boring, until the Crows came through."

"Came through how?"

"Motorcycles. Not like that, though," she said, nodding towards his hog and he thought he saw excitement light her gaze for a moment. "They aren't wealthy, and well, I hate to speak ill, but they don't take care of their things like you all do."

Thor's Wolf looked on approvingly, but he needed to reserve judgement for when she finished. So far, it had been nothing but the truth. Even if his supernatural senses couldn't hear a lie, there was something so innately honest about Nica. Even when she was hiding something.

And yes, there was something else she was trying to keep hidden. He wanted so badly to use his sight, to ferret it out of her. But there was another side of him that wanted her truths freely given.

Wait. Don't force it.

So he stood and listened to her talk. Her Maryland accent was subtly different from the Jersey girls he was used to hearing, but he liked it. Like her tone and the cadence of her speech. Nica was naturally soft-spoken.

Sweet girl. Pretty girl.

"Then he started coming to the diner more often, and one day it was like he was there every afternoon during my shift after my classes," she mumbled through that part.

"You went to college?" Thor asked.

"Yep. I know I don't sound very educated, but yes, I did. I liked school. A lot."

She shrugged as if it were something to be embarrassed about, and Thor frowned. She deserved a chance to follow her dreams. If that meant going back to school, then why the fuck not?

"First, I think you sound just fine, Nica. Real fine. Smart, funny, caring. I've been watching you for weeks, and I don't think you've ever said an unkind word about anyone," he murmured.

"That's not true. I called Leo a fathead one day when he criticized my shot pouring."

"Leo is a fathead. So again, you were just being honest," he told her with a grin he couldn't hide if he wanted to. "Second, how old are you?"

"Oh, I'm twenty-six. I know it's still young, but I feel older sometimes. Much older," she mumbled, and his heart squeezed for another reason.

Twenty-six. Fucking hell. It seemed the Fates were more fucked up than he'd thought. Dire Wolves aged even slower than other Shifters, and Thor was almost twice Nica's age, though he looked about thirty tops.

"Third, what did you study?" he asked, scrubbing a hand roughly over his face. He needed to focus on something other than their age difference.

"Well, I had to take some regular classes like English and Math. But I was really into these horticulture classes," she told him.

He watched, interested, as Nica's cheeks turned pink, and she averted her gaze. Was she embarrassed? He grinned and asked her for more details, delighted when she spoke about hydroponics and raised garden beds, experimenting with different soil types and experimental filtration systems. There were so many layers to this woman, he mused. And he wanted to know them all.

"Horticulture? Wow! I wouldn't have guessed that," Thor replied.

He had one hand on top of his head, rubbing the stubble that had grown that day, and the other on his hip as he stood shaking his head and grinning at her. It felt like a present, this little snippet of information she was giving him about herself. Yeah, like a really good present, and he liked it so much, he wanted more. But Nica was just staring, so he dropped his hand.

"What is it?" he asked.

"Nothing," she blurted, and he could scent her embarrassment now.

"Nica, what is it?" he repeated.

"You just have a really nice smile, is all. Like a really, really nice smile. And you don't do it very often. Smile, I mean. So I don't get to see it very often. It surprised me, but like, in a really nice way. You look good when you smile. Well, you look good all the time, but you look fantastic when you smile, and I am talking way too much now, so I am going to shut up," Nica finished with a popping sound on the final *p*. Now Thor was smiling even harder.

"Tell me why you said that Crow was your mate," he said, needing to know before he did what he was dying to do.

"H-he told me he was. That is, he started courting me. He was sweet at first. Said all the right things, brought me gifts, won my mother over right away. She couldn't have said yes to him when he suggested a pairing any quicker than she did. At least, that was what I thought."

"Did you love him?"

"I thought so," she replied honestly. "But understand, I'd never had a boyfriend till Jack. The things I should have questioned, I didn't because I thought maybe I was wrong. Maybe that was what love was supposed to be. He hid stuff. He left for days on end. He told me what he liked me to do, how I should act and what I should wear, and I tried to make him happy. But he would leave, and when he came back, he'd be different. Sometimes happy. Sometimes cruel. I was very green, you see. Jack liked to make fun of me for not knowing about stuff," she confessed.

That black rage inside Thor grew as she told her story, but he held it in. He did not want to make it any worse for Nica. Keeping his Demon Wolf hidden was necessary. So, he zipped his lip and listened.

He wished he could smile for her right then, the way she'd liked, but that grin was nowhere to be found.

Not then, anyway.

"Mama conducted a promise ceremony that spring under a cherry tree in the local park. He gave me a ring, and I was floating on air, thinking I was gonna be married and mated. We went to a motel, and we, well, you know," She muttered, cheeks red now, and he could scent her discomfort. "Jack was so angry after. He made fun of me, said I didn't know a damn thing about being a mate. After that humiliating experience, he brought me to the Pine Murder trailer park, where I was placed with two other women. I didn't know till after he took off that they were his mates, and that I was going to be his third."

By the time Nica finished speaking, Thor was trembling with rage. That motherfucker. He'd taken something precious from her, and instead of being grateful and easing her into it, he'd humiliated and abused her trust. Thor's fury intensified. And her mother! How could a mother give away her innocent young daughter like that? It was revolting, and more black fury filled him. But there was something he didn't understand.

"He had other mates. Living mates and he wanted you, too?"

"Yes. Ella and Denise are both alive and both wear his mating mark. Crows don't bite like other predatory Shifters, they scratch and offer a token. He got Denise on the right side of her face, and Ella on her left. Used to call them a matched pair," she whispered, shivering before she continued.

"Poor Ella was not well when I got away. He broke them, and he wanted to break me." Horror leaked into her voice.

"Nica," Thor said her name and took a step closer to her.

"They're both just broken shells of the women they once were. I thought I was lucky when Denise got pregnant. He left me alone for years, but then she lost the baby, and then Ella got sick. He still has no sons, you see. So suddenly, he wanted me again, but I refused him. I swear to you, I refused him. I was so afraid Thor, so afraid would break me, too," she confessed, tears running down her cheeks.

"He didn't break you, Nica," Thor interrupted, taking her by the upper arms.

He couldn't stand to see her pain, but she needed to see the other side of it. He had to help her see. And he would if it took him all his life, he would. That was his vow to her, though he didn't voice it.

"You got free, Nica. You aren't broken."

"I ran. I was afraid, and I ran, and I just left them!"

She hiccupped, her blue eyes were wild, and her tear-stained cheeks were ruddy. Nica trembled beneath his fingers and something darkly possessive grew within him. His protective instinct went into overdrive, and he growled deep and low before reining back the Wolf. When his eyes met hers again, she was no longer crying, but shivers seemed to run through her and into him.

"Listen to me, Domenica Corvo, you are not broken. You did the best you could in a terrible situation. You got the fuck out, Nica. You got out! And I am so fucking proud of you," he told her, and pride filled his veins, lacing his voice.

Brave. Fierce. Badass female.

"You shouldn't cuss," she whispered, eyes glued to his mouth, and that warm feeling inside him grew some more.

Thor couldn't have stopped what was going to happen next even if he wanted to, and he had to be honest with himself, he did not want to stop it. Not at all. He closed the space between them, lifting one hand to cup Nica's cheek. Her big, blue eyes stared, unblinking, as he slowly lowered his head to hers. He needed to make sure she had ample time to step back, to tell him no if that was what she wanted.

Please don't tell me no.

Thor continued his advance, nuzzling her nose and tipping her head to the side before pressing his lips ever so softly to hers. That warm buzz he felt whenever he was around her was focused now, right on their meeting lips. Then he kissed her harder, pressing against her mouth, waiting till she parted her lips on a sigh, and he delved inside.

Mine.

CHAPTER EIGHT

DIRE WOLF MATES

He's kissing me. Thor Ulger is kissing me.

He closed the space between them. Those hard, hot muscles she'd been coveting for weeks pressed into her soft body, as he ever so slowly pressed his lips against hers with soft, tender kisses. Her whole body teetered on the edge, but she didn't move. Didn't want to scare him away. Thor kissed her sweetly, as if he was waiting for her to push him away.

Yeah, right.

Like she was going to do that. Didn't he know how much she wanted this? To be the woman who got to kiss a man like him? Those first few kisses were everything to Nica. She sensed him holding back, though, and that was not okay. She wanted all of Thor, not some watered-down version. Nica needed more.

She didn't have to wait long, thank goodness. As if sensing her desire, Thor growled, crashing his mouth against hers, and Nica moaned, helplessly accepting him, and holding on for dear life. It was all she could do while the man himself plundered her mouth like his Viking ancestors did to villages in the not so distant past.

Yes. More.

His scent enveloped her, Wolf, wood, and some musky spice that made her want to climb him like an oak. The kiss turned rough, demanding as he backed her against the wall, and she wondered what he would say if she told him she wanted him to strip her clothes off and make love to her just like this.

Her emotions were all over the place, and something inside told her this man could wreck her. It was nuts. She'd been living in fear of one man breaking her for so long, but a few weeks with the Dire Wolves, with him, and she was ready to throw all caution to the wind.

Nica had felt anchorless, helpless for so long, but in this moment with Thor, she felt grounded, truly grounded for the first time in her life. Thor's chest reverberated with that ever-present growl as she clung, kissing him back for all she was worth. True, she was unpracticed, but he did not seem to mind at all. She clutched his shoulders, tangling her tongue with his while pressing herself more fully against his body.

He was so big, so hot and hard. And so very good at this, she thought while he kissed her till her toes curled. Again, as if he'd read her mind, he lifted his head, ripping his shirt off so she could feel all those wonderfully warm muscles pressing up against her. Her shirt came next, then both their shoes and pants.

"Fuck, we should stop. I should slow down. Get you to a bed or something, at least," he growled, but she pulled him back down to her.

"Let me have this," she whispered, almost begging. "Let me have you just like this, Thor. Please, I need, gods, I need," she moaned, rubbing herself all over him wantonly, but unable to help herself.

"Fuck, you are so sexy. What do you need, angel? Tell me," he commanded.

Nica gasped when she felt the cold wall against her back. Thor growled, lifting her like she weighed nothing at all. She moaned, wrapping her legs around his waist, loving the feel of his hardened length against her core. She was wet with need and embarrassed by it.

How long till he realized she was dripping for him? Would he shame her like Jack did that first and only time she had been with him? Of course not. Nica should know better. Trusting her gut, she decided to own the way he made her feel. This was something good, something rare, and beautiful. She wouldn't cloud it with thoughts of Jack. The foul man deserved zero seconds of her time.

"Your scent is driving me wild. But you gotta tell me what you want," Thor growled, and she moaned as he slipped her panties to the side and found her sopping wet secret. "Fuck, you're so wet for me, angel. So hot and tight. S'good."

Nica could hardly believe what was happening. Somehow, he'd gotten through all her hangups with his magic kisses and skilled hands. He was moving now, inside her panties, those thick fingers parting her slick folds, Thor was doing what no man had ever done. Thor was giving her pleasure.

He used his thumb to caress her swollen nub while he pushed one, then two fingers into her core. It had been so long since anyone touched her, and never, never ever had it felt so good.

She was wound so tight, her mouth opened as she clung to his neck. Thor seemed to love it, though, and he kept on stroking her with her panties pushed to the side. The fabric was hopelessly soaked now. He growled, sucking in her neck and back to her tongue, moving his hips in time with his efforts.

"Oh gods, Thor, that feels so, oh gods!" Nica cried out and moaned, unable to finish her thought as pleasure exploded, pulsing through her veins.

"One," he grunted.

He kissed her again, rewarding her, it seemed. Nica continued to ride his hand, embracing the sharp pleasure and the mini aftershocks he had so thoughtfully gifted to her. Through her lusty fog, she realized he was counting off her orgasms.

Holy cow.

Her experience with men was pretty nil, but she had to admit, it was a mighty turn on for a guy to exude such utter confidence in his ability to pleasure her. Nica's eyes widened, a disappointed groan sounding from her lips as her sex clenched on air, missing his invasion once he slid his fingers from her channel.

"Fucking delicious, angel," he growled.

Thor slipped his two fingers, still glistening with her pleasure, into his mouth and sucked them dry. Holy hell. She had no idea how hot that would be, and watching his eyes dilate with hunger sent pools of moisture flooding her crevice.

"You ready for two?" Thor asked, backing up a step but holding her still against the wall.

She looked down to see his engorged cock in his fist. Thor watched her watching him as he placed the broad head against her needy sex. She'd only ever done this once, and it was horrible, embarrassing, but even acknowledging that, she had to admit she never wanted Jack the way she wanted Thor.

"If you want me to stop, Nica, tell me now. Once I do this, there is no going back," he growled, black eyes burning into hers.

"I want this. I want you," she said automatically, owning her truth the only way she knew how.

"Mine," he growled.

Then he fed her his cock inch by delicious inch until he was seated all the way to the hilt. He pressed his whole body against her, cupping her face and holding her still. He was so big, but patient with her, giving her time to adjust to his size and girth.

"Damn angel, you feel better than I thought you would," he grunted, kissing her then as if she were something precious to him.

Had he been thinking about her like this? Holy cow. This big, beautiful man had been imagining sex with Nica, and suddenly she felt like a goddess instead of a silly girl with almost zero skills to offer the sexy as sin male. Sensations flooded her system, he was so big stretching her till it burned. But it was a good feeling, very good.

She wanted him to move so damn bad, but the beast of a man would not be rushed. Oh, she felt his animal inside him, knew the Demon Wolf was there, waiting just as she was. Then suddenly, he pulled out, pushing back in, taking her in long, deep, hard strokes.

Nica had no idea people could do this standing up, let alone for as long as they did. But his strength was immense and his stamina double that. In the end, Thor made her come three more times. Each time was better than the last.

Hours later, he carried her outside with a clean towel draped over her naked body and didn't stop moving until he laid her down on the king sized bed inside his room in the Pack House. Once there, he crawled up her body, kissing, nibbling, tasting her flesh until she was panting and moaning beneath him.

"You taste so good, angel. Sweeter than the sweetest strawberry jam," he growled, kissing her *there*.

"Thor," she yelled, pulling on his head, his ears, whatever she could grab.

Nica yelled, moving up on her elbows, eyes glued to him as he parted her folds with his tongue. Her heart was beating so hard it was liable to come right out of her chest with the things he was doing to her. Big hands pushed against her thighs, holding them open as he ravaged her pussy with his mouth.

How did he know how to do that? She couldn't even imagine another man impaling her on his tongue, making her see stars. Jealousy slapped at the recesses of her mind, but she pushed those hateful thoughts away. They had no place there with them. Just because she'd had an unfortunate past didn't mean he had.

She couldn't fault him for having women before her. He changed angles, filling her with his fingers while lapping at her clit. It was not long before she was moving again, grinding her sex on his face as she screamed his name, chasing her orgasm this time. It was too much.

He was licking her with steady swipes of his tongue until she thought she would fall apart into a million pieces. She couldn't do that, could she? Fear and curiosity filled her, and Nica pulled on his head. Thor stopped, looking up curiously at her.

"Did I hurt you?" he asked, his lips glistening with what she knew was her essence.

"No," she shook her head. "But no one ever, I mean, I never—"

A wicked grin split his face, and Thor kissed her pussy again, the same way he did her mouth. He lifted his mouth, eyes fixed on hers.

"You taste so good, angel. This is natural. It's good. I love the way you taste and I'm gonna make you feel so good, I swear it. Lemme have you. Lemme make you feel good," he growled, and she nodded, helpless to do otherwise.

Thank goodness for that. Trusting him was easier than it should have been, but Nica never felt anything as miraculous as Thor feasting on her pussy. His entire body seemed to reverberate with the steady growl he hadn't been able to dismiss, and the resulting vibrations had her flying over the edge sooner than she ever could have imagined.

In all her life, she never orgasmed multiple times in one night. Not even with the tiny clitoral stimulator she'd gotten in a swag bag from a birthday party she went to when she'd turned seventeen. Hiding that from her mother had been tricky, but she did. Otherwise, she might not ever have known what satisfaction felt like.

Of course, nothing compared to Thor. Her sex clenched around him when he finally reared up and gave her his dick. So long and thick, he hit all the right spots as he pressed inside. Nica moaned at how good he felt, filling and stretching her to capacity. It was like she was made for him. Her body was designed to fit his to a T.

"You were made for me," he growled in her ear as he rocked into her with deep, powerful strokes.

"You. Are. Mine. Nica, do you hear me? Mine. Now, tell me. Say it, angel," he grunted, and she nodded.

"Yes. Yours," she murmured, wishing with all her heart he meant those words for always and not just right now.

She felt like his. At least, she did right then. But Nica knew better than to hang her hopes on dreams of the future. This time, she would be smarter. This time, she would just live in the moment.

Enjoy the ride but hold on to your heart.

CHAPTER NINE

DIRE WOLF MATES

Words of wisdom she'd heard somewhere, though she could not recall who'd said them. Nica wasn't the type of woman to hop from bed to bed. This was special. This was big. She would never forget the way Thor made her feel, even after he inevitably walked away. She would always remember this and him.

Regret was not something Nica was fond of. Though she regretted Jack and the Murder, she would never regret this or her time together with Thor. Living in the moment was something she strived for, and this right here was one helluva moment.

Tension started once more in her core, and Nica's whole body began to tighten around him. Every move he made pushed her closer, closer, closer, until she was right there in the middle of a torrential downpour of pleasure.

"Thor!" she yelled, scratching his shoulders, followed by a loud, "ouch!"

Her Raven cawed inside her mind's eye just as a sharp pain stung her shoulder. But that feeling was soon overshadowed by another, second building of pleasure threatening to explode inside her until suddenly—*it did.*

White lights danced behind her eyes as she skyrocketed into oblivion, holding onto Thor for all she was worth. Thor reared up, his eyes completely obsidian, with no hint of white. It should have scared her, but Nica was too stunned by the sharp beauty of his face as he pounded into her.

The things he was doing, the feelings she was feeling, Nica just couldn't verbalize it. It was impossible for her to comprehend, but so damn poignant. Tears pricked her eyes as her pleasure intensified and Thor's rhythm turned jerky. He threw his head back and roared as the most intense orgasm she ever felt encapsuled them both. Thick jets of warm cum filled her, and Nica gasped at how right this felt.

Everything that happened before seemed to fall away. Her past. His. All of it. Nothing else mattered except for what was happening between them. Thor cupped her cheek with one hand, using the other to hold himself up so as not to crush her, but she wished he would. She welcomed his weight, loved the feel of his heavily muscled body pressing her down onto the mattress.

His black eyes glittered down at her, the look on his face as he worked to even his breathing was so serious, so full of awe, and she wondered if she looked the same. Everything was different now. She felt it in the air, a sort of charged energy that wrapped itself around her. Ravens didn't have a lot of lore about mates, but right then, she wished Thor was hers.

"Nica," he whispered reverently, dipping down to kiss her gently.

It was the smallest of touches, really, but it sent her heart pounding. He didn't seem done with her. Not yet anyway. A spark of hope ignited in her chest. Her experience with Jack had been hard and cruel, nothing like this. But it had left her so jaded.

She had to let that go. It was the past, and Thor was here in the now with her. He wasn't Jack. And she wasn't the same naïve girl she'd been. It was not wrong for her to want Thor. And she did want him.

Even more, she wanted him to want her back for longer than just this night.

"Want you," he whispered. "Want you so damn bad. Always."

His words were like music to her ears, and her body reacted to them predictably. Heating, warming, wetting just for him. She'd never felt so connected to another person, and she realized she was all in with him. The man could have her body, heart, and soul if he wanted her. What a frightening and wonderful thought that was, she mused.

Nica wanted him again, hoped he would take her fast and hard. That way, she could try to reconcile these new and scary emotions. The responding rumble in his chest and hardening of his cock still buried inside her told Nica he felt the same. But then someone knocked on the door, intruding on this sacred moment.

"Thor, that Crow came by with his lackeys. They're waiting across the highway behind the gas station, man. He says it's neutral ground. Says he wants his mate back, too," Cole told them. "Derrick wants you there," the Dire Wolf finished.

Thor and Nica remained quiet, but the moment was gone. She listened to the sounds of Cole's heavy footsteps walking away. That and the silence filled her ears, but he was gone before she even had time to protest Cole's use of the word *mate* in relation to her and Jack.

Nica was never the Crow King's mate. Not when he was courting her, not when he bedded her, and not when he beat her. Not ever.

Nothing could have told her that more than the way she'd responded to Thor's touch. The second the man known as the Demon Wolf of the Dire Wolf MC touched her, it was like a switch had gone off inside her. Nica's entire being seemed to recognize him.

His manner of speaking, the way he told her in no uncertain terms, he wanted her, was something she had never had from a man. Then there was her response. Her body welcomed his in a way she would have never thought possible. Thor was big and sexy, and rough around the edges, but with her he was direct, tender, and attentive.

Her skin heated, thinking about what they'd been doing together for hours now. She would have given anything to spend the entire night wrapped around him like a boa constrictor if only Cole hadn't knocked on the door. Just like that, the burning emotion she'd seen in Thor's eyes was extinguished.

He pulled out of her, leaving her cold and bereft as he got out of bed. Whatever passion had burned so brightly between them moments ago had dulled now to a muted flame. Nica sat up, watching him with sad eyes.

"Where are you going?" she asked.

"To deal with this," he growled.

"It's not your problem, Thor. I'll go—"

"Not my problem? Nica, you're mine."

"I can try to reason with him," she said, avoiding his statement and hating the hope that rose within her. *Yes,* she wanted to say, *I am yours, but for how long?*

"No," Thor grunted, shaking his head. "I don't want you near that fucker. You stay here."

He pulled on jeans and a shirt, and she watched the play of muscles helpless to do otherwise. Her body was sore in places she didn't even know she had, but Nica would not have traded the last few hours with him for anything else in the world. Everything was all a jumble. Still, she refused to sit still and stay like an obedient puppy. Nica was a Raven, not a dog.

"Look, this is my mess. If you go, I go."

"Fucking hell, Nica," he growled, and turned to her so quickly he stopped her in her tracks.

Thor's eyes bled to black, and she felt a sudden weight pressing down on her. Nica's shoulder burned fiercely while he glared at her, his powerful body flexing as he tried to keep his control in place. She looked down at her aching shoulder, finally taking stock of herself. Nica gasped at what she saw.

"You bit me," she whispered, shocked that she hadn't realized it.

"I told you. You are mine. You agreed, Nica." he growled, and her heart squeezed tight.

"Biting is the same as claiming to Wolves, right?" she asked, still trying to wrap her head around it.

"Fuck, I thought you understood," he cursed, rubbing the top of his head.

"Explain it to me," she demanded, wondering where she found the gumption to question him like that.

"Explain it to you?" he asked, his eyes blazing, that growl echoing in the room. "You. Are. Mine. Explanation over."

Nica knew she shouldn't like it when he said that. Something about feminism and being independent. It was all the females of the Dire Wolf Pack talked about. And a sassier group of females Nica had never met. Still, something primal and deep inside her recognized his claim, and reveled in it.

Lucy was the best. The tiny Alpha fem was always giving her mate hell one minute, then making goo-goo eyes at him the next. Sheila was the same with Leo. Though Ariella and Brock were slightly more complicated and openly worshipped each other, while Tracey and Phoenix were all about traveling the globe and visiting when they could. Gwen was still managing her new Wolf, and Weylin was a surprisingly kind mentor, but their love was off the charts.

Nica had spent the last few weeks getting to know this close-knit Pack, and she'd been pleasantly surprised to find the females all had a say in what went down. That was the total opposite of how the Murder was run.

But back to his possessive declaration, honestly, Nica had heard the others say similar things to each other, but she never understood it. Now, with Thor standing in front of her naked and proud, his thick erection jutting out from between his legs, staking his claim with words as he had with his body, Nica just about melted into a puddle of goo at his enormous feet.

And why shouldn't she? Sassy or not, none of the females there seemed to mind it one bit when their larger-than-life mates came in, dropping proclamations of outright ownership and hauling them off to ravage them well into the night. Nope. In fact, those lucky women seemed to live for those moments.

You can too, her Raven whispered. *Mine.*

"But what does being yours mean to you, Thor?"

"There's no time now—"

"The heck you say! Look, Mr. Tall Dark and Tattooed, you said I'm yours. Tell me what that means!" she demanded, chest heaving with her sudden anger.

Thor paced a moment, then turned to her, those Demon Wolf eyes of his glittering dangerously. He was so damn handsome. So big and powerful. Thor just took up all the space in the room, leaving her with one helluva view, she had to admit.

"Okay, you want to know what it means? Fine," he grunted, freezing her in place with his laser like stare. "It means you let me have you, angel. Now, you're mine. And I have no intention of letting you go."

"Okay then," she mumbled, swallowing hard. "I'm yours.," Nica agreed aloud, her voice stronger. "Now, let me go to the meeting with you."

"No!" he snapped. "Fuck, Nica, I am sorry. I don't mean to yell. But it is dangerous."

"I don't understand, Thor. I want to be with you to clear this up. Why can't I come with you?"

She started towards him, but Thor stopped her with one hand and ran the other over his face. The air felt heavy again, and she swore she saw the air around him shimmer and pulse. He blinked a few times, his eyes returning to normal before he looked at her again.

"Thor?"

"Nica, please understand the Demon Wolf is feeling fiercely protective of you right now."

"Your Wolf wants to protect me," she replied, and she almost dropped the sheet she had wrapped around her body.

"If you go out there looking like you do, hair tousled, lips swollen, smelling of sex and me, I'll tear the throat out of every one of those motherfuckers before Derrick could even think to stop me. Understand?"

Truth.

Shifters had an ear for lies, and every word out of his mouth rang with the truth. Nica swallowed hard. Thor was trying to protect her from his Wolf, from the one everyone called Demon. But Nica wasn't afraid of him. His animal was possessive of her, and something deep inside her approved. She nodded her head, wanting to offer him comfort. But Nica didn't say anything. She didn't have a chance.

Thor was already crossing the room, looking powerful and determined. He slammed his lips into hers, taking her mouth in a fierce, savage kiss that hurt her lips, but in the best way possible. Those big, strong hands she loved gripped the back of her neck as he kissed her, stamping himself on her one more time before he had to go.

"Wait for me here. Say it," he commanded.

"I'll wait."

"That's my angel. I'll be back soon," he murmured, turning around before he could see her swoon.

Why was that such a serious turn on? She had no idea. All Nica knew was she was squirming by the time he adjusted himself in his tight jeans and turned. The man sure knew how to fill out that well-worn denim. His jeans were so tight, they were molded to his long legs and fit perfectly. The tight, long-sleeved shirt he wore was black, as usual, and clung to his musculature like a second skin.

Nica's mouth watered. He looked like a Viking warrior, all tattooed and scarred. They called him Demon, and she knew why. But to her he wasn't a Demon, he was an avenging angel. Her avenging angel. But Thor didn't look at her as he slipped his feet inside his boots. She waited for him to say something, but his hard lips remained closed.

Her heart squeezed, and she felt unsure and anxious. He'd claimed her with his bite, but she still did not understand the full meaning. Crows and Ravens didn't mate for life, but Nica would be crushed if he let her go. How was she going to survive this? How would she ever survive him leaving her?

Darn it. She was thinking too much. Over complicating things with her runaway thoughts and lack of confidence. The man called her his, that must mean something, right? Should she leave while he was gone? Go back to her room?

She had no experience with this kind of thing. Had no idea how to act. She wanted to make him happy but had no idea what he was expecting from her. Right when she was about to fly off into a full-blown panic, and before he walked out the door, he turned to face her. Thor's dark eyes found hers, and Nica stilled. Her Raven settled down, even as emotions flooded her system. Nica wasn't going anywhere.

Thor asked her if she understood what he meant with his oddly specific account of what he would do should she walk across the street to the meeting place. In his eyes, she saw his Demon Wolf, saw the possessive beast staring at her with hunger in his impossibly dark eyes., and something else. Something dark and deadly.

Somehow, letting Thor between her legs and wearing his bite mark had turned the Pack's Enforcer into a giant murdery powder keg. What else was there to understand?

Okay. Nica swallowed, certain now she understood what he meant.

Kinda. Mostly. Gulp.

CHAPTER TEN

DIRE WOLF MATES

The Demon Wolf snarled and snapped inside of him. The giant brindled beast wanted out. He wanted to savage the motherfucker who'd put hands on Nica. The animal was dying to punish the assholes who participated in that cruel and savage beating she'd received, along with the cowards who stood by and let it happen.

Grrrr.

Of course, he couldn't do that. Derrick would not allow it. His Alpha was already there. The true image of leadership, standing tall and strong, his power obvious to everyone there. But Thor was not concerned with Derrick or that piece of shit Crow at the moment.

He was busy battling the *other* as he traipsed across the semi-busy highway to the lot behind the gas station. Dark images of shadow spirits floated around him as he walked to meet with the Pine Murder and their cowardly leader. Their desperate pleas and gravelly whispered bargains pounded against his head.

Whispers full of evil suggestions slithered in his ear, and he fought with his Wolf for control. Unlike his human side, the Demon Wolf had no qualms about gutting the men who'd hurt what was his. But

Thor did not live in his fur alone. He could not give in to those spirits whose cries and moans he decidedly ignored whenever he crossed the veil.

They were the cursed ones. The ones who wanted vengeance and threatened to pull him down into the darkness forever. It was a battle sometimes, to return to this side of the veil where the living ruled, and the spirits whispered to those few who had the sight. But not anymore. Thor belonged here in the light with Nica. He just had to make sure these assholes understood she was his now.

Not theirs. She would never be theirs.

Thor canted his head, watching the two groups of males face off behind the gas station, just across the road from the Pack House and their bar. Neutral ground. That was what they thought they had by going there, but Thor had a surprise for them. He didn't give a fuck whose land they stood on. If they came for Nica, he would gut them all.

He walked over to them unhurriedly, listening with all his senses. No one had spoken a word yet. They just stood, waiting he imagined for him to arrive. Derrick stood half a foot taller than the Crow King.

Good Alpha. Strong.

His animal approved of Derrick, always had. He was easily the tallest man there, save for Thor. He knew the male had his back and normally, neither he nor his Demon Wolf would ever think of questioning him.

Until now.

Why the fuck did the Alpha agree to meet with these needle dicks? They hurt his Nica. Demanded she return to them when Thor would never let that happen. Fuck. He was losing it. Thor was acting like a possessive fucking caveman, but he never claimed to be anything else. No, he wouldn't ever send her back, but more than that, he knew she didn't want to go back.

"Great. The giant is here. Now, can we talk about you giving me my mate back?" the King whined like a petulant child.

Grrrr.

"I was not aware we had your mate, Jack Branwen, King of the Pine Murder. Perhaps you have a photo? A description? Anything handy, so we might help you search for this lost mate."

Derrick addressed the man whose neck Thor was itching to break with as much respect as propriety demanded. But he did not bother to disguise his loathing for the woman beating piece of shit. And that was why Thor loved the man.

"You listen to me, Wolf. She's here, I saw her—" Jack said, spittle flying from his lips.

A fierce growl interrupted the byplay, and Thor stepped forward, forcing the man to back up. He was rude and disrespectful to their Alpha, and the beast in him would not tolerate such blatant discourtesy. His Pack mates loosed similar growls, though none held his venom. Thor kept advancing, forcing the King to retreat like the coward he was. No, he was not above using his size to intimidate, especially in these circumstances.

"You will address our Alpha with the respect he is due," growled Thor, holding on to his anger by a thread.

"You can't do this. I came here under a banner of peace, but I will bring this to the Council if I must—"

"Peace? You beat a woman for refusing your bed. You came here with your men, walked into our bar to force her to go with you, and you call that peace?"

"Thor," Derrick said his name. "Leave off," he commanded.

Thor was breathing heavily, wrestling with his Demon Wolf, but the beast owed fealty to their Alpha. He stopped short, holding onto the fist he so desperately wanted to bury in that asshole's face. Derrick had saved the man from a broken nose, but there was nothing he could do about the permanent growl in Thor's throat.

"She is m—"

"No. She is not your mate," Thor stated, daring the Crow King to argue.

He did. But not with Thor. The pitiful excuse for a man couldn't seem to meet his eyes. Thor's growl got louder, and the Crow King stuttered. He imagined his eyes were full black now, glittering, and dangerous looking. Having the sight meant sometimes Thor could see a person's true nature. When he looked at the Crow King all he saw was darkness.

Grrrr.

The Crow blanched, the color leaving his face faster than rats fleeing a sinking ship. He looked back at Derrick, as if Thor's Alpha would take his side for some reason. Stupid, entitled coward that he was, he probably did think that. Thor just shook his head.

Of course, he can't look at us. He knows we want to rip his black heart out of his chest, his Demon Wolf grinned inside his mind's eye.

"*Alpha,*" Jack sneered the title. "Domenica Corvo is my mate. She is a liar if she says otherwise! I signed a marriage contract with her mother for her hand, and it is binding. By Crow law, Domenica Corvo is my claim," Jack said, handing one of his men an envelope.

One of his Crows, a lanky, thin male, held the envelope out to Derrick with shaking hands. Fucking guy had to be twenty years old, if that. Cole stepped forward and took the thing, handing the envelope to Derrick. Thor made no effort to move. His black eyes stayed pinned on the Crow King while the slimy, unworthy male continued to argue his so-called rights.

"I will look this over, but Mr. Branwen? You should know I don't give two fucks about Crow law. The Dire Wolf MC lives outside of Shifter Council law, as we have for hundreds of years."

"Yeah, well, you broke off from your MC, *Wolf,*" the Crow King replied with a smirk. "You can't claim their privilege anymore."

"You know, it's interesting you think those ties are so easily broken, Crow. You think because we settled here, we are no longer part of the greater Dire Wolf MC, but you could not be more wrong. If I were you, I would think about that before deciding what route you wish to take with us," Derrick commented, inclining his head to the Pack.

"I will have her back!" the Crow King shouted, and Thor paused, only moving forward when Derrick slapped a hand on his shoulder.

The rest of the Dire Wolves walked behind the two of them, giving the Murder their backs in the ultimate *fuck you* someone could give to another Shifter. Thor wanted to be the last to leave, but it turned out to be no simple thing to walk away. His entire body trembled with pent up anger.

His *other* pulsed and growled. That part of him watched hungrily, waiting for him to act. The shadow spirits grew louder, egging him on to do something foolish. His Demon Wolf allowed him to commune with the spirits and granted him use of his *sight*, but it was not always good.

Right then, Thor's other was a hungry thing. It craved vengeance, demanded he pay back the Crow King for every scratch, bruise, and for the dislocated arm he had given Nica. But his good Alpha had given an order, he'd bolstered him up, and led Thor away. Yes, he would find peace and solace in obeying that command. Didn't want to return to Nica with blood on his hands. Not when their mating was so new.

"The Council will hear about this, Wolf. If she is not returned to me by tomorrow, I will be back and I will bring war with me. She is mine, do you hear me? My mate," yelled the soon to be dead motherfucker.

He did not know how or when, and yes, Thor would obey his Alpha always, but that Crow was pushing him too far. Thunder roared in his ears. It was too loud for Derrick's newest Alpha command to take root.

"Thor—"

Too late. He blurred across the street the same second the Crow had stopped speaking, lightning fast, Thor moved, facing off with the piece of shit. He snarled, snapping his teeth as he grabbed the Crow King by the throat, dangling the male a good three feet off the ground.

"Let's get one thing straight, Crow. Nica is mine."

Mine, grumbled his Demon Wolf.

Derrick and the rest of the Pack jogged back to his side and the Alpha's hand clamped down on Thor's shoulder once more. He felt the man's innate power pulsing through their Pack bonds at his touch. Lucky for the Crow King, he still recognized his Alpha as his leader before he went and tore his head right off. A regret he felt immediately as he loosened his hold.

"Come on, man. We gotta go."

Thor completely released the male's throat and watched with more than a little satisfaction as the fucker hit the ground. He muttered a curse in the ancient language and spat on the floor next to where the Crow King gasped and struggled to catch his breath.

Once he was back on Pack land, the tension in his shoulders lessened a tad. He felt everyone's questioning eyes and concerning glances, but he shook them off. There was only one thing that could help him release his stress now. He needed to change shape, to run in his fur.

Without a sound, he let the Wolf take him. The clothes shredded right off his body as his enormous beast burst from his skin. Thor meant to run through the woods, but the soft gasp he heard from the side door had his big, lupine head turning around. Fuck, she saw his uncontrolled change. Worry over whether she would fear him now spiked his heart, but her eyes held nothing of horror as she watched him. Only wonder.

Nica. Mine.

Brave and beautiful, she stood watching him. His mate. A deep, satisfied rumble made its way past his lips as he trotted over to her. She had her hands over her mouth, her big blue eyes eating him up. Her happiness intensified the freshly fallen rain scent that seemed as much a part of her as the fresh bread and sweet summer jam he often associated with her.

"Oh Thor! You are so beautiful. I've never seen anything like you. A brindle Dire Wolf, well, I'll be," she murmured softly.

His animal preened under her warm praise. The beast liked her eyes on him, hungry and proprietorial. He liked them so much he wanted more. No, Thor demanded more. He needed her hands on him, so he bumped her gently with his head, allowing her sweet laughter to wash over him as he nudged her towards the door, away from prying eyes.

He never thought of himself as a jealous man, but there was something wildly possessive in how he felt about Nica. She closed the door to his bedroom behind them and kneeled on the rug by the recliner he had against the wall. He didn't know where she found the shirt she'd put on, but he liked her in his clothes.

"Can I touch your fur?" she asked, her eyes glowing with her animal.

To answer her question, Thor got down on his belly and crawled over to her. He knew he was big, and the last thing he wanted was to scare the woman. She squealed happily, reaching out with tentative hands, and running them over his back and neck.

Then he dropped his head in her lap and licked her elbow, making her giggle until she was giving him a good, long petting. She was wearing his shirt, so he didn't mind dirtying it, and even better, the little minx had nothing underneath it. He discovered that sweet little tidbit after he pushed his head down farther to investigate.

"Hey! Bad Wolf," she said, swatting his nose.

Thor's Wolf sneezed. He felt the air surrounding him shimmer as he swapped his Wolf's brindle fur for his human form. She was so fucking beautiful it hurt to look at her, but he couldn't turn away. He wouldn't. Not for anything. Nica was part of him now. Somehow, the curvy goddess had gotten beneath his skin. She was big now, important in a way he never knew possible.

"You swatted my nose, angel. Time for payback," he growled playfully.

"No fair! You were sniffing my hoo ha!" Nica yelled, but she was also laughing, and her eyes were sparkling with humor and something more.

"Gonna do more than sniff it, angel. I'm gonna lick that delicious little pussy until you're coming all over my face, begging for my dick. Then I'm gonna fuck you real good, just like you like, until you're screaming my name," Thor promised, his voice thick like gravel as he ran his hands up her luscious curves, divesting her of his shirt.

Her eyes grew hooded, the scent of her arousal perfumed the air. Thor could not wait a second longer. He tackled his sweet little mate to the ground like the predator he was, but he made sure she didn't get bumped or bruised. He wasn't a total asshole, after all.

"Thor,": she moaned his name, and he was a goner.

He kissed her until she clung to him in submission, opening her thick thighs and cradling him with her soft body. After a while, after Thor was finished driving them both crazy with only kisses, he slid down her body, ready to feast on her sweet strawberry jam flavored essence.

He knew the old cliché about cats liking cream. But the thing was, Thor was all Wolf. He was the total fucking opposite of a cat. But he also knew one thing for sure, he fucking loved eating her pussy. Loved lapping at her cream. And he would never stop licking at her until he'd downed every last drop, with his woman screaming his name and coming on his face.

Mine.

But it wasn't enough to lap at her. He needed to feel her come. So Thor fucked her with his tongue, using his nose to grind against her clit. Naughty girl that she was, Nica arched and tried to move against him, but he held her down with one hand on her hip, while keeping the other busy squeezing her sumptuous ass. Her pleasure was his only goal, but he was the one in charge. And from the way she panted and moaned, he knew he got that right.

Fuck, this woman was everything to him. For someone who knew virtually nothing about sex, she was more passionate and responsive than any of his previous experiences. Even thinking of sharing his body with another made him cringe and his Wolf snarl, but there wasn't anything he could do about it. Those women were in the past. Nica was his present, his future. She was everything.

"Thor, Thor, THOR!" she moaned his name, pulling on his head.

Her orgasm crested, making him feel like a god as she quivered and clenched around his tongue. Nothing was better to Thor than seeing the expression on Nica's face when she came and knowing he was the reason for it. He wanted to see it at least half a dozen times before the sun came up.

"One," he growled, and her blue eyes widened as he slid up her heated body.

"It's already five. You must be tired," she whispered, confused, but still accepting his mouth when he reached for a kiss.

"Not telling the time, angel. Counting your orgasms. So, how many you want before we go to sleep, angel?" he asked, ignoring her observation.

Thor didn't wait for her to answer. He was already pushing into her, feeling her walls clench and ripple as she started to come again, almost immediately. Fuck, he loved this woman. It was too soon, but so what? He was a Wolf with the *sight*, and for the first time in his life, he saw a future for himself. A future that revolved around a woman with curly dark hair, eyes like an October sky, and a heart of gold.

"Mine. Mine. Mine," he growled in time with his thrusts.

And when she came a third time on his cock, he followed suit. But still, it wasn't enough. Thor's cock grew hard again in seconds after he'd finished spewing cum into her womb. This time, instead of rutting her on the floor like a beast, he carried her to the bed. He needed to go slow. Needed her to feel what he felt.

"Damn, Nica. You really changed everything, didn't you?"

"What do you mean?"

"You're a miracle, you know that. You make me hope," he murmured, kissing her cheeks, her mouth, her neck.

"How, what do you hope?" she asked.

"You just give me hope, angel. Like there's a future for me now, here with you," he confessed, kissing her hard and deep.

Fuck, he was talking too much. He thrust his tongue into her hot cavern, mimicking what his cock was doing to her tight little pussy.

In and out. Slip and slide. Flex and withdraw.

And all he could think every time he had her was more. More.

More. MORE. He wanted all of her. Even as he stamped himself all over her, he still wanted everything. The thought of that Crow bastard coming there and demanding Nica as his claim made Thor's blood boil.

Fuck him.

Thor would not let that happen. Not ever. He needed a plan. A good one. Because if the Council came sniffing around for his mate, there would be trouble and it would be big. The only thing certain was Thor would never give Nica up. Not without a fight.

Mine.

CHAPTER ELEVEN

DIRE WOLF MATES

Nica woke to the sounds of hushed voices and a bright light. What the heck? Oh, someone had opened the window curtain. But who? Wait, her bedroom window was on the other side of the room, wasn't it? She yawned, taking a moment to reconcile where she was.

Dire Wolf Pack? Check.

The bedroom they gave me? Nope.

Thor's room? Yep.

Smiling with memories of how she'd spent the night filled her as she rolled over, dragging the sheet with her as she stretched. Sitting up, Nica blinked herself awake, then screeched like a crazy person. Not one, but four, four pairs of eyes were looking at her with matching expressions.

"Look who finally decided to join us!" Sheila barked, clapping her hands.

"Come on, darlin'. Upsy daisy. Your man has everyone up in arms this morning, and I am grumpy as fudge."

"Huh?" Nica asked, confused as all get by several things.

The least of which was not figuring out why the Alpha fem should be grumpy. She was gorgeous, had a mate, and three cubs, and a totes perfect life from Nica's point of view. The other females sighed in commiseration, But Nica just blinked.

"Well, what do you expect since this little mama still isn't allowed to have coffee?" Lucy grumbled.

"Oh," Nica muttered.

That made sense. Still, Nica grinned as she looked at one of the reasons the horrible *no caffeine rule* was in place. The pretty little cub was currently suckling from Lucy's left boob, while Ariella and Gwen bounced the other two reasons, *er*, cubs, in their arms to calm them while they waited for their turn to eat.

It was a sight, but it still did not explain why any of the women were in hers, *um*, Thor's bedroom. Nica cleared her throat and clutched the sheet up higher to hide her naked breasts from the crowd.

"We've already seen those tatas. Good for you, by the way! Oh, just a word of advice, get your man to shave or at least moisturize before he chaps them raw with that scruff of his," Ariella informed her with a sage nod.

Tracey and Gwen murmured in agreement, and Nica just stared. Were all the men in this Pack as randy as her own sexy as sin mate? Lucky women if they were. Ariella seemed to be waiting for a response, and the Lioness truly was exquisite with her mane of wild curly hair, not unlike Nica's, but that was where the similarities ended.

"Oh, I don't think I could say things like that to Thor. Besides, I like the way his scruff feels when he, *er*," she trailed off.

"Nuzzles you in your most sensitive places?" Ariella suggested.

"What?"

"She means when he's going down on that *poonanie*," Lucy supplied.

That did it. Every female in the room started snickering and giggling at the Alpha fem's use of that word. Even the babies gurgled.

Nica wiped her eyes and tried to calm down before asking them what she really wanted to know.

"Well, that was fun. But ladies, why are you here?"

"Oh, well, the boys are going over that bit of paper that big nosed Crow brought with him, and it looks like the Council has reason to side with that horrible man seeing as how you and your mother signed it—"

"But I didn't know he had two other mates waiting back home. And I didn't love him. He didn't even like me! Jack Branwen is a dirty liar," she replied vehemently.

"Mm hmm, that is what Thor said, but Derrick isn't sure that matters. He is consulting with a Shifter lawyer on loan from the Macconwood Pack. Meanwhile, there is a little something we would like to do while the boys handle this business."

"Shouldn't we stay and help?"

"Nah. They're only just getting through the posturing portion of their meeting. Then will come the brainstorming, and I sure as hell don't wanna be here for the mansplaining," Ariella told her, and Nica had to admit she had a point.

"Okay, then, what do you want to do?"

"Well. After Lucy here is done feeding the triplets, we thought we'd go into town and have a real ladies' day out!" Ariella squealed.

"A what?"

"You know, we'll go into town and have a girls' only day. There is this new place called Heavenly Bodies and they have a full treatment spa. I already called and booked us the bridal party treatment package—"

"Bridal party? But I am not getting married," Nica replied, stunned.

"Oh, honey, it doesn't matter. You just got mated."

"No, I mean, I guess so, but we haven't had a chance to talk," she tried to explain.

But Nica could not get a word in. Those women ran roughshod right over her in the best possible sense, of course.

"Of course you didn't talk. Words still have no place in mine and

Weylin's bedroom," Gwen mused, her eyes taking on a dreamy look as she spoke of her mate.

"Look, Nica, Thor gave you his bite mark, don't you know that means you are as good as married?" Sheila interrupted.

"It's true. Besides, mated is better," Tracey told her with a soft smile.

"I guess, I mean, Crows seem to throw that word around a lot, and even though I am a Raven, I hardly remember what my parents were like together when dad was alive. With Jack, it seemed like Mama picked him before I even had a chance to make up my mind. Everything happened fast, and I was confused, but I am not confused now. I want Thor. He's the only man I ever really wanted."

"Well, it's settled then. Congratulations," Lucy said, grinning as she swapped babies and boobs. "You should know, Dire Wolves are different from other Shifters. They are more powerful, they follow ancient rules, and when I tell you they mate for life, I mean it, honey. Thor is never gonna let you go. Anyway, come on. It'll be fun," she coaxed.

That was a lot to swallow, and though Nica had misgivings about what they'd all said about mating for life since those words had not exactly come from Thor, she couldn't help but agree a day out sounded just peachy.

"It will be super fun. Besides, tonight is bikini night at the bar. We need to get our wax on!" Sheila exclaimed.

"Okay," Nica said, finally giving in.

Her head was spinning by the time they stopped yammering. She got in the shower. Well, she was dragged and pushed into the bathroom by Gwen, then had a pair of leggings and a sweatshirt shoved unceremoniously at her when she was done. One by one, they filed out of the bedroom with Sheila practically frog marching her through the hall and into the living room.

"Nica? Are you okay?" Thor asked.

"Um, I think so—" was all she managed to say with Sheila pushing her forward in with a relentless grip on her arms.

"She's fine. We're going out for the day," Lucy replied, handing Derrick one of their babies, while the other women placed the other two in nearby bassinets.

"I pumped this morning, bottles are in the fridge. We should be back by three," Lucy told him before following them outside.

"Wait. What is going on?" Thor asked.

"Ladies' day out," Tracey repeated slowly.

Nica had to hide her grin. Thor looked like he wanted to say something, maybe ask her to stay home. But Nica had no idea what to do. She really could not refuse, what with the entire Pack going to bat for her and all. Besides, Sheila had an iron grip on her.

Nica barely had time to take in the intimidating males sitting in the living room, discussing her life without her. Of course, she knew Thor and Derrick, but the pair of identical twins were strangers. They smelled like Wolf, but different from the Dire Wolf MC.

One had on a charcoal gray suit, and seemed to never smile, while the other wore a t-shirt with a bone on it, and the words *I got a boner to pick with you* strewn across the top. He was grinning at them like a loon. Nica raised her eyebrows and shrugged, but if she thought Thor was going to rescue her this time, she was mistaken.

"Be careful, angel. Come home safe," he rumbled, his black eyes boring into hers.

Twenty minutes later, Nica forgot most of her questions as a large woman with a German accent named Helga started wrapping her body in a seaweed mask treatment. The smell was not altogether unpleasant, and she kind of liked the part where the matronly female had massaged her scalp before applying a conditioning treatment there.

Heavenly Bodies was run by a coven of Eastern European Witches, so they did not have to worry about letting things slip in front of the staff. Helga had assured them their room was private and soundproof, not to mention surrounded by magical protection wards.

The spa was also located smack dab in the middle of town, with tons of normals around, so Nica didn't have to worry about the Murder trying anything with so many onlookers.

Still, she'd felt like someone was watching her while they drove and then walked through the parking lot. But even if they were following her, keeping tabs, Jack was not that stupid. He knew better than to grab her out in public.

"Ohmygawd! I feel like a princess," Lucy squealed when Helga moved on to her.

"Princess of the mud people," Ariella snorted, only to get thwacked by Sheila on the butt.

"Shush it, Miss Kitty. This is the most relaxation I've had in weeks," the she-Wolf told her.

"With the way you and Leo go at it, go figure, Sheila. I mean, I'm surprised you can even walk with all the sexy times you two got going on," snarked Gwen.

"Catty!"

"Ha! As if Gwen isn't getting sexed up every night," Ariella pointed out.

"Damn straight, I am," the new Dire Wolf confirmed.

"OMG! Just look at you, Gwendolyn. A second ago, you were this cute little pious virgin coming into the roadhouse for a job. Now look at you! Weylin sure corrupted you. But now, come on, we're scaring Nica here and today was supposed to be about her," Lucy teased.

"Who me? Nah, I'm enjoying the banter, believe me. I didn't know women could be so sassy and frank and still be friends," she told them honestly.

"Well, damn," Lucy said, sitting up. "Look, Nica, I don't know how you were raised, but in this Pack we females have one solemn rule and that is to always have each other's backs, no matter how outrageously sarcastic and sassy we get!"

"That's right!"

"Preach, Lucy!"

Nica laughed and wiped her eyes as the others all clapped and hooted. These women were like nothing she'd ever seen, and she was so grateful they included her, it was like a dream come true. She joked and laughed, and sipped champagne with them while they got pampered by Helga and her team.

She did her best to enjoy her first ladies' day out, and it was wonderful. Truly, it was. Her mind kept wandering back to Thor and the confrontation with Jack. The last thing she wanted was for the Crow king to bring war to the Pack's doorstep.

These were good people. They'd welcomed her with open arms, gave her a job, and made her feel part of the Pack, even though she was a Raven and not a Wolf. When they returned to the Pack House late that afternoon, Nica got ready for work.

She'd bought a new pair of tight blue jeans and a pale purple crocheted bikini to wear for tonight's theme at Serious Moonlight. It was October, but working behind the bar meant constant movement, besides Shifters hardly ever felt the cold.

Thor was nowhere to be found, but Nica assumed she'd see him at work. It was difficult not to feel a tad bit abandoned, but then again, they'd burned pretty hot and heavy for their first time together. Maybe he needed a break.

She worried her lower lip, wondering if the big beautiful Dire Wolf had grown tired of her already. Jack's cruel words came back to haunt her after the first time she'd ever had sex. He'd said bedding her was rough and called her a puritan. She hadn't satisfied Jack, and he'd been rude and hurtful.

Yes, it wounded her pride, but now she was really worried. Thor had not texted or called her all day. He was nowhere to be found when she got back. Not knowing what to do, she'd gone to her bedroom, *not his*, to bathe and dress. The whole time, her gut felt tight and heavy, clenched with nerves.

What if she was bad at sex? What if she'd turned Thor off with her wanton enthusiasm and lack of experience?

So many what ifs, her Raven observed with a sharp caw.

The animal was tired and weary of being kept locked away, but Nica did not dare free her bird. Not yet. Not until the Murder stopped hunting her. Then another of Jack's favorite taunts flooded her brain.

"No one gets away from me, Domenica. You should know that before you run. I would rather see you dead than let you leave."

She stepped outside, about to walk across the lot to the bar, when she saw it. A single black feather sitting on the porch. Tied to it was a black rose. Nica gasped, picking up the hateful thing. She ran to the dumpster and threw it away.

"Nica? What's wrong?"

A scream tore from her throat before she could stop it. Hand over her heart, she recognized Thor as he came thundering towards her, running his hands over her body, arms, and legs, checking for damage.

"Nica? Talk to me, angel. Are you hurt?" he asked, before tugging her to his warm, hard body and wrapping her up tight in his embrace.

"Thor," she murmured.

Was she hurt? No. She wasn't hurt. She was fine now.

Perfectly fine, she thought as she hugged him back.

CHAPTER TWELVE

DIRE WOLF MATES

"Nica? What's wrong?"

Thor's heart almost hammered right outside of his body when he saw Nica run across the lot behind the bar. He raced after her, calling her name, only to startle her into screaming.

Fuck. He should have been more careful, but his Wolf was riding him hard. He needed to make sure she was all right.

"Nica? Talk to me, angel. Are you hurt?"

"Thor," she said his name, clinging to him once she recognized him.

Thank fuck. He'd never felt this level of concern for another person, and it was downright scary. Hugging her close after he assessed her condition, Thor exhaled the breath he'd been holding.

"What happened, angel? Talk to me."

He kissed her temple before drawing back to look at her face. She was pale and shaken, and his beast reared up, ready to attack whatever had threatened his sweet mate.

"There was a feather tied to a rose on the porch. It was Jack, I know it was Jack. He used to leave that sort of thing for me back when he was courting me. Only this time, the rose was black. It was black," she murmured, and her voice was thick with tears.

"Sonofabitch came on Pack lands," he growled, incensed beyond measure.

"It's worse than that, Thor. A black rose is bad," she whispered, shaking her head.

"What does that mean? It was black, so what?"

"Crows only leave black roses for the dead, Thor. This was a warning. He wants me dead."

Motherfucker.

"Shhh. You're okay. I got you, angel. You're safe," Thor reassured her, kissing her head and holding her close.

Nica was scared, that much was obvious. But there was something else beneath her fear, and Thor was almost afraid to ask. Was she mourning the loss of Jack? Did she want the man to court her sweetly? Did she want him instead of Thor? Even after everything he'd done.

Fuck. His emotions were all over the place, and he didn't have any fucking clue how to calm them. He knew better than to think about such things. Nica was his. There was no denying how explosive they were together in bed. Her body sure as fuck knew who it belonged to, and yes, she'd even said so. But why did this have to be so hard?

"Angel, if you wanna take off work tonight, just tell me and I'll let Derrick know—"

"What? No. I don't want that. I think working might help me take my mind off this stuff," she said and nodded her head.

Pride infused him and he grinned at her, so strong and brave. Did she even know it? Could she even see the changes in her already? She wasn't meek anymore. Not scared or battered. Nica was growing into her confidence, and it was sexy as fuck.

Her soft curls felt nice under his hand, and he tried his best not to get her all mussed. It was super fucking hard, kind of like his cock, which was crazy and thoughtless cause in that moment she needed tenderness, not a rutting animal. He wanted to be the one to give her everything she needed.

"I just need you, Thor. Only you," she murmured, tilting her head up and kissing him with impossibly soft lips.

Had he spoken aloud? Thor didn't think so, but he wasn't worrying about it since Nica was still kissing him, giving him everything he ever wanted and more. He really should stop since he could hear folks pulling up, getting ready for a night on the town. Serious Moonlight was the talk of the town, and every weekend they were jampacked with people, supes and normals alike.

Sheila had introduced these "theme nights" to interest newcomers who might think Serious Moonlight was just a place for brawling bastard MCs, and so far, it was working. Of course, a lot of her themes had to do with scantily clad women showing off their assets and bringing in the crowds, though to be fair, some of the guys got in on it, too.

In fact, he was pretty damn sure he'd seen Weylin saunter off to the bar in nothing but a Speedo and a pair of motorcycle boots. Sheila knew better than to ask Thor to participate. He'd rather die than be caught dead, tending bar in a pair of skintight underwear—*wait a second.*

"Did you buy this today?" he asked, fingering the strap of the teeny tiny bikini top he was only just noticing.

Nica blushed prettily, easing out of his embrace, and looking down as if she was unsure of herself. Fuck no. Thor was having none of that. He never wanted to break his woman down. Not ever.

"Is it all right?" she asked, biting her bottom lip in that way she had, making him wild with desire.

"All right? Angel, you look good enough to eat," he growled and leaned down to kiss her again, fast, and hard.

The soft purplish material was barely big enough to cover her ample bosoms, and his Demon Wolf snarled at the idea of anyone other than him seeing her in the tantalizing little outfit. But he wrestled with his beast, reminding him she was already claimed with his bite, his and no one else's. That helped. A little.

"All right, now that's enough of that. I can't be bouncing with a boner all night," he muttered, adjusting his steel dick in his jeans.

"Ha!"

Nica covered her mouth to hide her laugh, but he liked it too much to let her do that. Thor gently pulled her hand away and kissed her giggling lips again. He just couldn't help himself.

"Ha, nothing, you little minx. You do this to me all damn day," he confessed.

"I do?"

"Hell yes, angel. You look good enough to eat. And I will, later," he promised with a wink. "Now, if you get into trouble behind the bar tonight, just call out and I will be there fast as thunder," he told her, dropping one more kiss on her lips as they eased inside the roadhouse.

"Of course," she replied, smiling up at him.

Gods, she was pretty. All soft skin, blue eyes, pink lips, and curly dark hair. And she was his. That was the part that really got him. Nica was really his, and he was hers. He felt the truth of that down to his soul.

Mine. Mine. MINE.

But there was still a sense of foreboding plaguing him. An unease that started in the pit of his stomach. It made him want to pick her up, toss her over his shoulder, and hide her away from the whole damn world. She smiled at him again as they walked back to the bar, and he knew he could never do such a thing.

His little Raven deserved to be in the light, and he was going to make sure she had the chance to shine. That was his vow, and he swore it aloud in the old language once she was tucked away safely behind the bar with a half-naked Weylin on one side and Cole sporting a cut off wetsuit on the other.

"What in the fuck are you wearing?" he asked the long-haired Dire-Wolf, not even bothering to check Weylin's sanity.

"Sheila said I had to take part in tonight's theme, or else she was gonna slash my tires," Cole grunted.

"Damn, that's cold," Thor replied, knowing the she-Wolf meant business if she was threatening to maim a man's bike.

"You still aren't in compliance," Weylin added, butting in as usual.

"Who asked you, Mr. Banana Hammock?" Cole said, wincing at the bright yellow Speedo Weylin was wearing.

"First off, this is not a banana hammock. That term refers to a thong, which, as you can see, I am not wearing. My buttocks are perfectly covered," Weylin replied, spinning around like a fucking ballerina to show his covered assets.

"Ohmyfuckingods," Cole growled, but Weylin continued unabashed.

"Second, this is a certified Speedo, name brand, and my lady love bought me this for our trip to Hawaii we are taking next month in honor of our mating. Now, don't you all be jealous cause you can't fill this bad boy out like I can," the redhead added, waggling his eyebrows for effect.

"You wanna hit him, or should I?" Cole asked.

The dour-faced Dire Wolf Shifter had leaned back against the bar nonchalantly. With his arms crossed over his chest but Thor knew he was 100% serious in his question.

"Nah. We can get him later," Thor told him with a sharp nod.

"Okay. Then we'll have a couple of beers."

"Sounds good."

"Hey, is that nice? Is that fair? You guys wanna bond over beers and beating me up? What kind of Pack are you?" Weylin asked, running after Cole.

Thor just shook his head and walked back to his post near the front door, grateful as fuck Sheila did not bother to threaten or demand he follow any of her nutty rules about themes. His eyes found Nica adding longnecks to one of the coolers behind the bar, and the Demon Wolf inside him rumbled at the sight of her.

Now, she looked good for tonight's bikini theme in all that curve-hugging denim and the pretty little bikini top she had on. The other females had on similar ones in different colors, and he guessed they all did some shopping after their spa day. Good for them, he mused with a wide grin.

Now, Weylin, on the other hand, looked like a nut job in his lemon yellow Speedo. Come to think of it, so did Cole in his giant wetsuit onesie, even if he cut off the sleeves and the pants at the knees. It would be a cold day in hell before Thor would be caught in either outfit. He was perfectly comfortable in his usual jeans and black t-shirt, *fuck you very much*.

CHAPTER THIRTEEN

Derrick had the night off. Lucky Wolf. He and Lucy were back at the Pack House with their triplets, which meant Brock was in charge. The Pack Beta and head chef was in the kitchen, making sure everything was set up perfectly for the tremendous dinner rush they often saw. Gwen was enjoying the night off, along with Phoenix's mate, Tracey. That left Thor, Nica, Weylin, Cole, Phoenix, and Sheila running the roadhouse.

Once eight o'clock rolled around, people started turning up by the dozens, and there was a pretty healthy line to get in. Thor was working the door, checking IDs, keeping the peace. It was just business as usual. An all-female band of Witches was playing tonight, more of that country rock mix the crowd seemed to like. They were good, but he wasn't much of a judge.

"Hey there, sexy. Can I rub your head for luck?".

The question caught Thor off guard. He frowned, but quickly moved out of the way of the bright pink, acrylic tipped nails the strange woman was reaching for him with. She was wearing a sparkly pink bikini over her spray tanned body and a tiny black skirt. It was possible she was a regular, but he did not recall having seen her. Her companions, either.

"Sorry, ma'am. I have a girlfriend—"

"So? What's that to me, big guy? Besides, she can't do what I can do," the woman purred.

"Sorry, letting other women touch me is a hard no. Best keep your hands to yourself. Have a good night, ladies," he told the forceful woman.

Her eyes flashed gold, and Thor sniffed. She was a Lioness. But no one he knew from the neighboring Blue Valley Pride. The she-Cat and her friends all appeared shocked that he'd said no. But whatever.

He knew their type. They were entitled and spoiled, treated like princesses by the males in their Pride who chased them. Everything about them screamed overdone, and though it was not to his liking, Thor normally didn't have an opinion on how anyone dressed or spoke. Still didn't.

In fact, he remained uncaring of the trio of females who sat nearby and kept giving him long glances that he'd successfully ignored up until Nica came over.

"Hey, I'm on break and I thought you might like a glass of iced water," she said, smiling sweetly at him.

She was so gorgeous with her bright eyes and freshly scrubbed face. He liked she didn't wear any makeup. Liked that he could see the real her all the time and didn't have to dig to find it. Everything about her was so open and freely given. He was one lucky Wolf, and he knew it. Thor took a long pull of the icy water and leaned down to nuzzle Nica's cheek affectionately.

"Thanks, angel. I was parched," he said, one big hand resting on her warm, soft waist. "You didn't have to bring this all the way over, though."

"Oh, that's okay. Weylin is watching my spot, and I wanted to see you. I missed you," she confessed, blushing prettily.

"Is that right? I've been missing you, too. Been standing here, thinking about everything I intend to do to you when we get back home," he replied, touched by her thoughtfulness, aroused by her nearness.

It got to the point where he could not stop his dick from rising at the slightest touch from the woman, even if he tried. She wasn't just a Shifter. Nica was pure magic. And he was falling harder and faster with every second that ticked by.

"Thor, you shouldn't say things like that out loud," she whispered, clearly scandalized.

He had to kiss her again, he couldn't help himself. So he did. Quickly. He wouldn't jump on her in public or anything. Hell, his Demon Wolf was likely to kill one of these assholes if they even caught a glimpse of her wild and moaning in passion. He was too damn possessive to allow that.

Mine.

She deserved better. He knew that, but nothing could ever make him leave her now. His Nica was everything. A natural caretaker, and he had the feeling she was a secret badass, too. Warm, open, and giving, but also beautiful, fierce, and loyal. She was an ideal mate.

And Thor was so grateful he'd been there that day to catch her. He never expected to be on the receiving end of such tenderness. It felt good. She felt good. Hell, the woman was taking up so much space inside him, he could not even imagine life without her. She'd only be there for a few weeks, and in his bed for just days, and she was that deeply ingrained. He needed to tell her how he felt. That he wanted her forever, and that he loved her, even if it was too soon. He was just about to confess it all when the shit hit the fan.

"This is why you wouldn't let me touch your head? Are you serious? She's fat and plain. I mean, damn girl, maybe you should invest in some makeup if you want to keep your man," the hoity toity Lioness came stomping over on her spindly heels, interrupting Thor, and Nica.

Anger rose swiftly and Thor growled a warning, ready to defend his woman to this pissed off predator. But there was no need. Nica put her hand on his arm and turned to face the slightly tipsy female with a concerned expression on her beautiful face.

"Hi, I'm Nica. What's your name?"

"Are you kidding? You wanna know my name now, fatty? Like we are besties or something?"

"Right," Nica replied with a bashful sort of grin as she faced the woman and her friends. "Well, I don't know you, but this is the second time that I am telling you my name is Nica. Not *fatty* or *damn girl*. Just Nica. And wow, I have to say your makeup looks really good, professional even. You're lucky, you see, I have serious allergies to cosmetics, and I can't wear them at all. Lucky for me, I found a man who doesn't seem to mind," she went on, friendly as ever, facing down a trio of Lionesses, who could probably each swallow her Raven with one gulp.

Not fucking likely, his Demon Wolf snarled.

"You're allergic to makeup? Ohmygah, that sounds terrible," one of the woman's friends said.

"Yep. That's me. Allergic to makeup. But wow, I mean look at all you, so thin and trendy. Made up to the nines, and just killing those bikinis," Nica said, nodding.

"Oh, um, thanks," the original aggressor muttered, and she looked as confused as Thor.

"You really do look good tonight, ladies. Did you get those from *Gladys' Swimwear & Care* in town?"

"Oh, um, yeah. That's my aunt's shop," one of the women added.

"Nice. That's where I picked this one up, and I am lucky she carried plus sizes cause these boobs would never fit into a bikini if she didn't."

"You got great boobs," the third Lioness commented.

"Yeah, are they real?" the second one asked, and reached out to cup Nica's left breast.

"Oooh! Y-yep, thanks, they are, *um*, real," his mate stuttered, and removed the woman's hand with an awkward pat.

"Delia, what the hell? Anyway, she is right. Your boobs are great. I mean, I'm so flat, and um, I am sorry she said you were fat. You are just super curvy like a pinup model! I mean, you look really great," the first Lioness, the one who'd tried to grab Thor, told Nica.

Thor frowned. Was this woman hitting on his mate? She had a point about Nica being curvy and having great boobs, but he was not exactly comfortable with the staring or the grabbing.

Grrrr.

Nica pressed back into him, as if she knew her touch would soothe his beast. He put his arms around her waist and pulled her back against his chest. Still, she kept the conversation going with the Lionesses as if he wasn't there, growling behind her.

"Well, thank you," Nica replied honestly. "That means a super lot to me. I never had many female friends growing up, but I always wanted them, and you girls are so lucky to have each other."

"OMG! You are so sweet," one of the blonde Lionesses gushed.

"I don't know about that," Nica replied. "But, I am sure you won't have any trouble picking up men of your own if you want that, and if not, I know you will still have an awesome time tonight just doing your thing. This big guy here, though, is totally off limits. And I know that makes me super lucky. But I also know you all got more self-respect than to try flirting with a man who's spoken for, right?" Nica continued, her smile big and her blue eyes sparkling.

"You're totally right. I am sorry about all the cattiness, Nica. My name is Cheryl. This is Taylor and Delia. Anyway, thanks for being so nice about this," Cheryl told her sheepishly.

"No worries. Now, when you go to the bar, see the guy in the wetsuit? Tell him Nica said to give you a round on me," she finished and waved them away.

Thor stood there in total shock. How the fuck did she do that? The woman had to be magic or something. She had single-handedly turned a group of hostile Lionesses into sympathetic allies in just minutes with that sweet, open way she had about her. She never raised her voice or lashed out. She took their insults and turned them around, complimenting them and making them see the error of their ways as if it were their own discovery.

She was good. Really fucking good. Like pure gold. Pride zipped through his body, filling his veins as he watched her wave them off.

"Ooh, I think I better go help Weylin, he is getting slammed," she said, about to run away.

But Thor pulled her back, catching her questioning smile with his lips as he kissed the hell out of her. Yeah, his jeans were going to be really uncomfortable for a little While, but it was worth it. This woman owned him. Body, heart, mind, and soul, he belonged to her now. She had the fealty of his Demon Wolf—*gods, help them both.*

"What was that for?" she asked breathlessly when he finally came up for air.

"For being you. What you just did? Turning that volatile situation around without violence or resorting to threats? I never saw anything like that. That was fucking awesome, angel. I am so proud of you," he growled.

"I don't know, I mean, I am the lucky one, right? I have you," she said, but it sounded more like a question than a statement.

"You have me, angel. One hundred percent." He kissed her hard before swatting her on the butt so she could get back to work.

Hours later...

"Shit. I'm so tired the bags under my eyes got bags," Weylin moaned, trudging across the lot to the cottage he shared with his mate.

It had been a busy night. Seemed like people really enjoyed the bikini theme, even if Thor had to turn away a couple of enthusiasts who insisted dental floss was acceptable attire.

"Was it mint?"

"What?" he asked Nica, who'd been quiet to that point.

"The dental floss," she said, brows furrowed.

"Nica, I didn't say any of that out loud."

"You didn't?"

Thor shook his head. His mate stopped and turned to face him, her whole expression one of abject confusion. The crisp Autumn air swirled around them, and the sounds of dried leaves rustling was a soft hum in the background. Nica's heart was pounding, and his own matched its pace. He felt like the very air was charged with something *other*.

"I think it's because of our matebond," he murmured.

"Matebond? What is that?"

Thor's Demon Wolf stirred, the animal wanting to be with his mate. Inside his mind's eye, Thor saw the thin strands of their new matebond. It was warm and gold and pulsed as he drew near. His beast staring off into the ether, as if he was waiting for something.

Yes. Waiting. Always waiting.

CHAPTER FOURTEEN

DIRE WOLF MATES

Thor stood on the periphery of the forest with his eyes closed, and Nica knew he was attempting to communicate with the Wolf inside him. Her own beast stirred. The sound of her thick, shaggy feathers rustling filled the inside of her mind's eye, and Nica doubled over. She felt sick with the need to shift.

Not safe. Not safe.

But telling her Raven it was not safe to change didn't seem to do the trick as it had over the past few weeks. Her stomach cramped, and she whimpered. Trying to fight a shift sucked. It was painful in a way she could hardly describe. Like a million tiny needles pricking all over her body, while her gut was twisted, clenched inside a giant vise.

"Nica!" Thor rushed to her, his black eyes glittering at her in the darkness.

"Can't let her out," she grunted.

"How long has it been?" he asked, and panic hit her.

He knew her secret. Knew she'd been too afraid to change. For some reason, she felt so ashamed. He deserved a better mate. Someone who was strong enough to get out of a bad situation before it got to the point of no return. Someone who wasn't afraid of themselves like she was. Tears filled her eyes, and she moaned, falling to her knees. Then he was there, lifting her in his arms and cupping her face, asking her again.

"How long you been keeping her locked up, angel?"

"Since the day I fell, and you caught me," she replied and saw the horror in his gaze.

He would think she was a coward now, for sure. Sadness filled her at the thought of disappointing him, but Thor merely shook his head. He looked determined and powerful. She saw the mists swirling around him again, and the frank proof he was strong, that he was other was like a wake up call. Thor was magnificent, and at the very least, she could try to be brave for him.

"You're safe here. You can Shift here with me," he growled, his response brooked no arguments.

"I can't. The Crows are watching me, I know they are, and Thor, I never want to go back," she told him with feeling.

"You can do this, and I promise you will never go back there," he said, still cupping her cheeks with his hands and kissing her head.

"Look, let me explain, angel."

Thor stood up and pulled her to her feet. He took her hand, his big one swallowed hers, but she never felt as safe as she did with him. He walked her into the forest behind the parking lot. It ran the length of the property, but Nica had never ventured into the woods before. She had no reason to.

"The forest is ours from just beyond the creek to the property here where the bar, the Pack House, and the smaller houses all sit. This land is the property of the Dire Wolf MC, and any trespassers would violate our claims to this territory. We don't fall under the purview of the Shifter Council, but we have a longstanding treaty with them."

"What does that mean?" she asked.

It was good to know, but she didn't understand what it had to do with her very real fear that if she shifted and flew, the Murder would swoop in and attack like the sneaky bastards they were. She frowned, watching Thor as he shook his head, those dark eyes glittering with something that looked a whole lot like mischief and maybe some pride.

She'd seen the man angry, annoyed, serious, and horny, but his teasing face was the one that got her in the gut every single time. Gods, he was gorgeous. Spending the last two days wrapped around each other must have cut into his shaving time, because the two-day-old bristle on his face and head was darker than ever. Nica liked it. A lot. There was something dangerous about a man who looked better the scruffier he got.

"What it means is you can change here any fucking time you want, angel. The same laws that Crow motherfucker is trying to use against us will protect you. I will protect you," he told her with a wicked grin and a promise in his eyes that settled something inside her.

Her Raven cawed. The animal was tired of being cooped up. She was weaker, unused to being kept from the world. And there as something else, too. She wanted to meet her mate in her feathers, not just her human skin. She needed to connect with him like that.

"Is that what you were talking out with those two men earlier? The twins?"

"The Lowell brothers? Yeah. Those Wolves are lawyers for the Macconwood Pack. They're the largest Wolf Pack in North America. You see, he didn't wait for us to get back to him. Jack Branwen went right to the Shifter Council of New Jersey and filed a formal complaint," he told her in a rush.

"Wait. He challenged you?" she asked, wide eyed.

"Fuck no. He's too much of a pussy to challenge me. He is making a claim that by Crow law, you are his mate because of the promising ceremony your mother signed off on. But the Lowell boys said it doesn't hold water. That law is outdated, plus with the increase in female Shifters on the Council, there is no way in hell they'd vote for you to return to a mate you didn't pick. And even if they did, I already bit you, Nica. You are mine. Anyone who says differently can kiss my big ass," he growled.

"So, you were busy working this out, looking for ways to take care of me while I was getting massaged and waxed?" Nica laughed, not realizing tears had fallen from her eyes until he wiped them away.

"Who the fuck gave you a massage, angel?" he growled, but she giggled in response.

"A Witch named Helga at the spa we went to in town. She gave me a bikini wax, too. You want one? I can book her for you," Nica teased.

"Bikini wax?" he murmured, eyebrows high as he mentally pictured what she was saying.

Then he shook his head abruptly, as if he had just processed the rest of what she'd asked him. Nica couldn't stifle her laugh if she tried.

"Hell no, I don't want one. Only woman I want touching me is you," Thor stated, kissing her hungrily, and making her knees weak.

"Good."

"Good, huh? Possessive little thing, aren't you?"

"Sorry," she began, frowning.

"Don't be sorry. I like it. I'm the same way about you."

"You are?"

"Yep. Look, this is big between us, angel. Big and good. I feel it in here," he growled, rubbing his chest.

His focus was so intent on her, Nica's knees knocked. She swallowed hard, unsure of how to respond. Yes, she felt it, but she couldn't just say it. Could she? Her Raven cawed, and the air grew heavy and shimmery, making her shiver. Then Thor just switched it off, his eyes cleared, and he grinned, lightening the mood.

"Come on, I swear this will be fun. Oh, I want to tell you something else, too," he started, heading towards a gigantic oak tree that still had its leaves.

The entire forest was awash in Autumn colors. Greens had given way to reds, golds, purples, and oranges. It was like a painting in a magazine she'd once seen a long time ago. The colors were like a riotous symphony dancing on the early morning breeze. It had to be near four o'clock already, tonight being one of the latter nights that the bar stayed open.

"What did you want to tell me?" she whispered the question.

It felt right to whisper. Awed by all the beauty surrounding them, she turned her eyes back to Thor's and felt his gaze like hands brushing across her skin with nothing less than wonder. He touched her gently, caressing her face as he spoke, turning her insides to mush.

"The thing is, I think our matebond needs help. You know that telepathic link we have sometimes? It isn't truly formed. It's weak, always coming and going, and I believe it is because you haven't changed in so long. Our animals haven't had a chance to sync yet, and it's messing with our connection."

"Oh, I see. That's why I can only hear you sometimes in my head," she whispered, nodding her understanding. "I'm so sorry, I didn't think."

"Don't apologize, angel. You have nothing to be sorry for," he said, kissing her knuckles.

"Do you really think it's safe to shift here?"

"Yes. The Crows have been given strict rules to stay off Dire Wolf lands. As long as you don't go past our boundaries, you will be fine. I'll show you where those are."

"All right, I trust you," she said, and Thor seemed to light up like the fourth of July.

"Gimme a sec to make sure no one else is here," he said, stilling her hand when she went to unbutton her jeans.

Nica's cheeks flamed pink with embarrassment and Thor just swung an arm around her and chuckled deeply. Dang, she loved that sound. She had a feeling the big man didn't laugh very often, and it warmed her to her soul.

Thor let out two sharp barks and whatever stragglers were about, Pack or not, she was sure they skedaddled. It was definitely not a typical response that she thought he was hot for basically threatening to maim anyone who saw her naked body. But whatever. They were Shifters, not normals, so that was okay.

Mine, the word whispered inside her mind, and Nica shivered with delight.

"Yours," she repeated aloud, pressing into his side.

With every step closer to the forest and to her first change in weeks, Nica felt their matebond growing stronger, thicker, more powerful. Her Raven flapped her wings, eager to be let out. Her senses felt heightened and that something else about her, the one that sometimes let her see more than she ought to, was vibrant and alert.

She turned her gaze to Thor, and what she saw stole her breath. The man was magic. Pure magic. His whole body seemed awash in glittery black smoke, swirling and dancing around him like those ribbons on a stick she used to play with when she was little. He was magnificent, and Nica was so grateful he was hers.

After he made certain they were alone, Thor nodded his head, giving her the okay to strip out of her clothes. Oh, sure, she'd had all sorts of fantasies about him taking the little bikini she wore, with his teeth preferably, but this was important. Maybe they could get to all that afterwards.

I hope so.

"Don't worry. You can always put it back on later," he murmured, and her cheeks burned under his knowing stare.

"You're reading my mind again," she murmured, mouth going dry as she watched him shuck off his jeans and his t-shirt.

"Was I reading your mind?"

"Yeah, you were," he said, raking her with his eyes from head to toe.

He got to her clothes next. Thor was careful, gentle, brushing across her sensitive skin with his fingertips and knuckles. She never knew a man's hands could be so damn beautiful, but his were. Strong and solid, with long fingers and intricate tattoos across the backs. There were Wolves and a beautiful rendition of a forest with a full moon hanging overhead.

Nica squinted, thinking she saw a bird sitting in a tree, a raven, actually. But then he touched her again, and she lost her train of thought. By the time he was finished, she could hardly speak. Need pulsed through her veins, a living thing, and Nica swayed towards him unsteadily.

Need. Want.

He made her feel like a goddess when he looked at her and touched her so carefully. Thor was the only man who ever made her come completely undone with just his eyes. Hell, any second now, she was going to drop to the floor to worship at his feet.

Maybe she would. After she shifted, though. Not before.

CHAPTER FIFTEEN

DIRE WOLF MATES

Thor's heart raced inside his chest as he undressed his gorgeous mate. It was early morning hours and all he wanted was to get her back to their room, strip her naked and make her come a time or ten before they fell into a sleep so deep it only happened when you were truly exhausted or satisfied. He was banking on the latter.

But Nica needed this. Her Raven needed this. And if he were being totally honest, his Demon Wolf did, too. The growl building in his chest told him he'd hit the nail on the head, and with one more thorough glance around, he nodded. He tucked their clothes in a neat pile on the floor and gave her one more reassuring squeeze on her shoulders before he turned her around to face the woods. Fuck, the view was even better from behind. Thor's cock throbbed, jutting out from between his legs, letting all and sundry know just how badly he wanted her.

Later, he promised himself. He wasn't a totally thoughtless oaf. His mate needed to feel safe and secure to change, and he would give his right arm to do that for her. She deserved to feel safe. The fact anyone had ever hurt her made his blood boil, but he stilled the growl in his throat knowing she needed this more than he needed to voice his desire for revenge.

Mine.

"Go on, Angel. I got you," he assured her.

Some Shifters had a hard time swapping skins, and Thor braced himself for whatever happened when a woman morphed into a badass bird. Her Raven was large, he recalled, but still much smaller than her human shape. He could not even fathom how it was possible.

Well, that wasn't entirely true. Thor's connection to the *other* brought him a different aspect of what was possible and what wasn't. Shifters had walked the earth longer than normals. Their origins were as deeply ingrained in the multiverse as any of the sentient creatures in the preternatural world.

Knowing all that usually brought him a certain sense of peace, but Thor felt his hackles rise as he noted the change in her scent. She was nervous, anxious, possibly both. He frowned, but held on to his control, batting down on all his protective instincts. On a scale from one to ten, they were at an eleven.

Doubts plagued him. What if he was wrong? What if this was a bad idea? But no. How could it be?

Thor understood her animal's needs. The beast inside her needed to come out so their matebond could grow and blossom. It was a necessary step. Nica had already seen and accepted his Demon Wolf. Besides, he was right there. Thor would never allow her to get hurt. Not for the whole fucking world. Still, he had to force himself to back off. He needed to trust her to know what to do, so he bit his tongue and waited.

The air trembled around them. It started shimmering and glowing with Shifter magic he could see as clear as day. Oh, but it was beautiful. Nica's Raven was black as midnight, and the magic accompanying her shift reflected that. It was all glittering black diamonds and sparkling blue fire. It danced along her skin, permeating the air with the scent of strawberry jam, fresh baked bread, and ozone.

He looked on helplessly, mesmerized, as her human shape began to transform. Limbs morphed, bones broke, and muscles reshaped. Nica didn't shudder or cry as some Shifters did when changing. Instead, she just fell into her other shape with the softest of sighs, like when she was kissing him. One minute she was on two legs, the next she was covered in glossy black, shaggy feathers that extended down to the center of her pointed beak.

Gods, she was beautiful. So much so, she stole the breath from his body. He coveted her with his hungry gaze, wanting her more than anything. But with that wanting came a bone deep tenderness. Once acknowledged, that feeling was so profound, Thor dropped to his knees at her talons right there in the middle of the forest.

"Are you all right, mate?"

Her sweet voice filled his head, and Thor closed his eyes to stave off a wave of dizziness. Oh, he'd heard her before, he realized, but never this clear or loud. Their matebond pulsed around them and when he looked down, he saw it. Their bond was beautiful, ethereal, full of color and magic.

It connected them, tethered them together like a long, fettered rope. If he didn't think she was fated to be his before, he damn well knew it now. Possessiveness, love, and devotion surged inside him. And something more, a need he had never felt before.

Like he wanted to bare his soul to her. Dangerous. She was dangerous. Chipping away at the carefully laid walls he'd placed around his heart to stop anyone getting too close. Nica did all that and more. She made him want to be better. She made him want to try harder.

But there were parts of him that were so dark, so full of fear and rage. Sometimes, when he went past the veil, Thor didn't think he would make it back, and that was the biggest fear he had. He frowned hard, wondering how to explain, if he should explain. He wasn't certain someone filled with such a bright light would understand.

Despite that, Thor still wanted to show her all the grit and dirt that clung to him. He wanted to confess those secrets that were so damn ugly about him, just to see if she still loved him. And she loved him, all right. Just like he loved her. Neither of them had said it yet, but he felt it, especially with her in this shape.

Caw caw.

Her Raven's call brought him back to the present. Thor wiped a hand over his face, forgetting his worries as he simply took her in. She canted her head, black eyes flashing at him, and he grinned.

"Fuck, Nica, you are so gorgeous in your feathers. Wanna run with you, angel."

"Let's go then."

Her reply was short and sweet, and he could hear the smile in her voice. No sooner had she agreed than Thor was swapping his own skin for fur. His change was swift, instantaneous. In the blink of an eye, Thor's human body swapped places with his Wolf. He shook his enormous body hard, chasing away any leftover tingles.

Nica had been right about calling his Demon Wolf brindled, though he hardly gave it a thought. His fur was dark at the roots, like an almost black espresso brown that lightened to pure gold at the tips. His muzzle was the same black brown as his roots, but it was his eyes that usually frightened people. Thor's Wolf's eyes were pure black, holding no white at all.

He was also monstrously huge, of course, like the other Dire Wolves. But Nica had already met his beast, so he knew she would not falter at the sight of him. On the contrary, his sassy little Raven hopped up on his back, ruffling him with her beak behind his ears before cawing and taking off into the sky.

She flew low, dodging trees, and scaring the shit out of him, but Thor kept pace easily. He could feel her happiness, and he loved it. It was addictive, and he was already planning their next adventure like this. Yeah, he would go running with her flying overhead daily if she wanted to. She was something, alright. A true wonder in his Wolf's eyes.

Hours later they fell back into their skin beside the creek, and yeah, it was *hella* cold, but that didn't stop him from picking her up and jumping in the frigid water with her. Just having her curvy, warm body in his arms was worth it.

"Thor!" she squealed, clutching his shoulders when they hit the water.

He kissed her before she could protest again. Like so many of their kisses, it grew hot and heavy in a matter of seconds. She was perfect like this, submissive and aggressive all at the same time. She seemed to know exactly when to demand, and when to give in, writhing her sexy little body all over him, and driving him out of his damned mind.

Before he knew it, Thor was already pressing into her tight heat with her back up against the flat side of a bolder in the shallow side of the waters. Fuck, her pussy felt like heaven. Hot, wet, tight heaven. She clenched around him, sending lightning bolts of pleasure shooting through his veins. He was an animal taking her rough like this, but he couldn't help it. He needed her like he needed air. Maybe more.

Fuck yes, more.

"Mine," he grunted, pushing his hips harder, faster, stroking her walls just right. "Tell me," he commanded, needing to hear it.

"Yours, Thor. I'm yours," she repeated over and over aloud and in her thoughts, pushing the words right into his head.

Hearing her voice in his head was fucking magic. A kind of magic he never thought he would share with anyone, but Nica was not just anyone. She was his heart and soul.

"Harder," she moaned, and he obliged, pounding into her sweet sex until he almost blew without her.

"Need you to come for me, angel. Now, right now," he demanded, and miracle of miracles, she did.

Nica clawed his back like the little hellion she was, crying out his name. There was nothing sexier on the whole fucking planet than his mate's face when she came all over him. Thor roared in ecstasy, her pussy clamping down on his dick right before he exploded into his own spiral of pleasure.

Warm jets shot into her, a direct contrast to the cold water surrounding them, and he could hardly catch his breath. He'd never felt anything so intense. The air shimmered, the veil between worlds and planes disrupting around him as he came and came and came some more inside of his mate.

My mate. My fated one. My one and only.

He didn't deserve her, but he would do everything he could to be worthy. She was precious to him now. Ingrained in his very soul, and branded on his heart. Oh, she had his loyalty. His Demon Wolf's too.

Thor was never going to give her up. Not ever. He was going to love her for the rest of his life, and several lifetimes after that. He closed his eyes, feeling his ancestors cheering him on, offering congratulations, and blessing their union. It was phenomenal. Important. And so damn big, he could hardly think of any words to explain it.

Eons later he felt soft kisses on his face, and his shaved head as Nica tended him, whispering sweetly.

"I got you, mate. I got you."

She did. Heart, body, mind, and soul. Nica had him all right. Thor closed his eyes to slow his pounding heart and, doing so, he saw his Demon Wolf. The animal sat and watched her with hungry eyes in that metaphysical plane where he existed till called, and he wasn't alone. His Raven mate sat with him and their matebond glowed between them, ten times as thick as before.

"I got you too, angel."

And he meant it. He really did.

CHAPTER SIXTEEN

DIRE WOLF MATES

The days sped by in blissful happiness. Those turned into weeks with no word from the Murder or the Shifter Council. Nica was too busy enjoying every moment to give it much more than a passing thought.

She was busy building a life. Days were spent working in the bar, helping with the triplets, and doing chores in the Pack House. It was fall, but that didn't stop Thor from building her a miniature greenhouse in the back. She had been so touched by his efforts, her heart almost exploded when she saw what he was doing.

The others all pitched in, and when the outside construction was done, he'd furnished worktables and shelves, set up the plumbing, and went with her to a huge garden center to place an order for things she'd need.

"Are you sure about all this? It's expensive," she'd said, worrying.

"Of course, I'm sure. I think we should stop by the community college to get some course pamphlets for next semester, see if they have the kind of classes you were taking before."

"Really? You would do that for me?"

"I'd do anything for you," he said, his expression so serious it bordered on bafflement.

True, Nica was a homey sort, and didn't mind housework or any work. But this touched her deeply. Thor listened to her, and if she was not already head over heels in love with the man, that right there would have done it. He was still protective, always worried about others taking advantage of her work ethic. He didn't want her doing too much.

"You don't have to do the dishes tonight, angel," he told her after dinner one evening.

"I know, but I don't mind."

"Here, lemme get 'em. You go sit and enjoy your coffee."

She was still stunned a man like that would do things like the dishes, taking out the trash, and carrying the shopping. But he did things like that often. And not in any *me strong man, you feeble woman* sort of way. Thor was a natural born provider. A soul deep protector, but he had a sweet side, too. She was just lucky and totally happy his gentle side only came out for her.

She'd just finished unboxing an order she'd placed for gloves, hand trowels, sheers, and other gardening tools inside the greenhouse. Next week, she would get her first shipment of soil and seeds. Thor was still working on the heated lights they would need to ensure the seedlings and plants did not freeze during the winter. Once that was finished, he was going to help her build some hydroponic planters. Nica had all sorts of ideas about how to combine hydroponics with traditional gardening to grow things faster and bigger than ever.

For the first time in her life, Nica was truly happy. It was addicting and contagious, she realized, thinking about how much more Thor seemed to smile now. Their days were amazing, but their nights were even better.

It was nothing short of ecstasy, spending each night wrapped up in the man she'd come to love and worship with every inch of herself. Gods, the man was insatiable, and thank goodness, so was she. Thor brought out a side of her she never even knew she had. He might not be demanding in any other aspect of their relationship, but in bed, Thor was the master.

He'd introduced her to more carnal delights, more sensual pleasures than she ever realized existed. Sex was important to Shifters, to everyone, she supposed. When Thor was buried deep inside her, demanding she tell him who she belonged to, well, that was Nica's favorite thing. She loved the way he made her spiral, the way he pushed her higher and higher, demanding more than anyone ever had, and yes, she complied with those demands willingly, desperately even.

Every. Single. Night.

"Tell me you're mine, angel."

"Yes, yes, I am yours. Always. Only yours. Yours. YOURS."

Her body hummed even now with remembered pleasure, and she smiled as she pictured the things he'd said and done to her just hours ago that very morning. Oh yes. No doubt about it. Thor was a dream of a mate. Gorgeous, physically perfect, kind, funny, smart, sweet, with a direct approach that left her gasping.

He paid her so much attention, and he listened to her when she spoke. He offered his opinion, but never forced it. She didn't know a mate could be like that. That men, in general, could be fair-minded and tender with their women. Back in the Murder, the males were like tyrants, dictating what the females should be doing and when.

There were only about half a dozen of them. But a more beaten group of women, Nica had never seen. So different from the females of the Dire Wolf Pack. Even Ella and Denise, who had been kind to her at first, taking her in and helping her adjust to Jack's way of doing things, had changed the way they felt about her the moment they realized she was there to join their ranks as just another mate to the Crow King. Her naïve notions of romance were very short-lived back then. Reality in the Murder was a dream killer.

She'd been so pitifully green, wearing rose-tinted glasses when she looked at the world, so unaware of how badly Jack had abused her trust and innocence. But Nica was not the only one who'd suffered because of his lies. Jack wasn't a heartbreaker in that cute boy cocky sense people often joked about. He was literally a heartbreaker, in that he tore the love right out of a person, leaving them bereft, gutted and hopeless.

"You think you can come here with your young ass and take him from us? Jack is ours! You're just a little slut. He thinks he needs you to get himself an heir, but I got that handled. Don't you worry about it, missy. Just keep your head down and when Jack comes calling, you say no!" Denise had seethed.

It broke Nica's heart to see the tears in the older woman's eyes hidden behind her rage and cruelty. That was part of Nica's curse, though, seeing deeper than most. She only wished she'd seen the truth in Jack's eyes before she'd gone with him all those years ago. But no. she would not regret the past or her decisions. After all, those had led her here, to her true mate.

Thor. My Thor.

Her Raven cawed, the animal as crazy about the man as her human side was. Speaking of the man, he ambled over to her, wiping his hands on the back of his jeans. She saw the smear of grease and grinned.

He'd been working on his bike while she'd been unpacking her boxes. He wanted to get it ready so he could take her for a ride. It'd taken days of begging, but finally, he'd given in. Good mate that he was, Thor insisted on making sure his motorcycle was in top shape before putting her on the back. As if it would be anything but, she mused.

He was meticulous with all his possessions. Careful and precise in his handling of them, including Nica. She supposed it was antifeminist to think of herself as belonging to Thor, but that was just one opinion.

She found belonging to someone was more liberating than she ever expected. Belonging to Thor was a dream come true. Gods, she loved the man. She still hadn't told him yet. Not in those words, but she tried to show him every single day.

"Come here, angel," he growled, his bold gaze raking her from head to toe.

Nica went readily, loving the way he seemed to always want her. It felt so good. It felt so right. After all, she was of the same mind. He kissed her eagerly, with a barely restrained hunger, sending waves of need rippling through her body. She moaned her desire right back at him. Sometimes Nica didn't know what to do with all that stark intensity and masculinity. She returned his desire, was desperate to get closer to him. Nica only hoped it was enough for him. *She* wanted to be enough for him.

"You know you are, angel," he told her, reading her thoughts now that their bond was stronger than ever.

"It's weird with you being in my head all the time," she murmured, clinging to him as he slowed their kiss.

Thor stilled, and when she looked up, it was to see him frowning at her. Nica swallowed. Dang. She hated her insecurities were so open to him, but she didn't want to make him upset, but this was all so new to her. Still, she bit her lower lip and waited for his reaction.

"Do you not like it? I can try to shut it off some of the time at least," he replied, rubbing his head thoughtfully.

"Oh, I'm not trying to shut you out or anything," she blurted, one part relieved he was not mad, and the other part worried he might think she didn't want him.

"No, yeah, I know," he mumbled, not very convincing either.

He also stepped away from her, which was a first. Normally, when they were apart, even for just a few hours, he couldn't stop touching her. But not this time. He moved back another inch, and it might as well have been a mile. Nica shivered, cold without his body heat. But there was another reason. She felt like he was distancing himself from her, and it hurt.

"Thor? It's just, privacy was not something I was really afforded in the Pine Murder. I like that I have the choice here to be private or to share. I do love that we can communicate without words, dang, I am doing this all wrong. I'm sorry," she said, shoulders sagging.

A long, tense moment passed while she waited for him to respond. It was impossible to gauge his reaction, and Nica was on tenterhooks.

"I hear you, angel, and I'm sorry. This is new for me too, but I'll try to respect your boundaries, okay?"

"Okay," she whispered. It was a win, for sure, but somehow, she felt like she'd lost something.

"Um, let's skip the ride, okay? I'm kind of tired. How about we just go for a quick run through the woods right here?" Thor suggested, nodding towards the place that had become like a sanctuary to her.

She followed his gaze to the trail they normally took. Thor missed the look of disappointment that flashed across her face, and she quickly schooled her features to show nothing of her disappointment. By the time his gaze landed back on her, she'd already disguised it.

"Okay. Sounds good."

He led the way into the woods and stepped back to give her some privacy to shuck her clothing. Usually, he helped her remove them, not like she needed it, but it was just something he did. Not today though, and she felt cold without his warm, large hands to heat her.

He was giving her space. Something she hadn't asked for before, and she knew it was her fault. Nica's heart squeezed inside her chest. She normally felt excited about changing into her animal with him, but the joy had been sucked out of the day by her thoughtless words.

She needed to focus on the positive. She was here, now, with her mate, and about to join him in her animal form. That he accepted her was amazing. In her limited experience, Shifters stayed with their own kind. But the Dire Wolves were different. They followed their hearts, and that was amazing.

Thor's brindled Dire Wolf was the most gorgeous creature she'd ever seen, and when she was in Raven form, her eyesight was that much keener. He was all muscle and strength, his black eyes glittering with power. She'd never seen a more dominant and majestic animal.

Nica would fix the hurt she'd caused by asking for privacy. She would mend this minor rift because she wanted to. Yes, being *mate-bonded* was new and kind of scary, but she was stronger than she had ever been. She was a better version of herself with him. Maybe if she explained she just needed time and care, it would be okay.

No maybe, it would be, she corrected herself.

By the time she hopped back to the lane in her feathers, croaking deep in her throat as she searched for her mate, he was already there, waiting for her in his Wolf's gorgeous brindled fur. She cawed, letting him know she was going to take to the air, but the animal stepped forward, blocking her path and Nica stilled.

Nica froze. Nerves kept her from twitching, even though she knew Thor would never harm her, even when he was wearing his magnificent beast's skin. Demon sniffed along her head and back, the nickname she'd given him felt apropos especially since she knew it meant something entirely different from the Judeo Christian definition of the word. He was the descendant of Vikings. A mighty warrior Wolf gifted by the gods to be so much more than she could have ever dreamed in this lifetime.

Demon's growl reverberated in his chest as he rubbed his lupine face against her body, marking her with his scent, letting her and everyone else know she belonged to him. He wasn't mad or disappointed. He still loved her. Nica loosed a deep, satisfied croak. Her human had hurt his earlier, but she would make it up to him.

Boundaries were tough in any relationship, but when one of them was a little bit psychic and the other a little bit sheltered, communication was highly important.

Normally, she would just send her thoughts to him in this form, but when she tried, she just couldn't. Nica cawed, but Thor simply canted his head, waiting for her to take to the skies as he usually did.

Crap. Messing up did not feel good at all. But she'd apologize and tell him how much she cared about him, and how much she wanted to grow their matebond as soon as they finished their run. She was certain now that if they just took some time to explore their bond together, she wouldn't feel so anxious about it.

Truth was, the depth of her feeling for Thor was immeasurable. Scared the crap out of her most of the time. She was in love. Not lust. Not like. But really in love. He was so big. He felt like everything to her.

But what if he didn't want her for keeps like she wanted him? What if this was just a passing thing? Wolves mated for life, but did they still do that if their mates weren't Wolves, too?

She had so many questions. Nica wasn't educated like Thor, who had two degrees in theology and Philosophy on top of his vast world experience. She sure as heck was not on the level of beautiful as him. So, what was keeping him there?

Dang it. She hated feeling inadequate, like she didn't have the right tools for the job. The wind was coming in powerful gusts, blowing Nica to the side, and she righted herself, but it was difficult to focus when her brain was a mess of feelings. All she knew was she loved Thor, and that had to count, right?

Tell him, her Raven insisted.

Yeah. The animal was right. Nica needed to talk to him. The sooner the better. The swoosh of her wings was loud as the passing wind as she soared high above Thor. Looking down, she wished she could tell him everything she was seeing, but with their bond closed tight, she couldn't.

Oh well. It will have to wait.

Thor snarled and barked from below. She cawed a reply, but there was no way for him to understand her. Nica cursed herself for being the reason he closed their link. What was he trying to tell her?

She looked up, shrieking, when she suddenly understood what had her mate in a frenzy. The two tall pines that marked the end of the Dire Wolf territory whizzed past her. Darn it. Nica had been so damn lost in thought, she hadn't been paying attention to where she was headed.

No no no! How could I make such a big mistake?

Thor's growls and snarls grew frantic, and she tried to slow down so she could safely come around again. But before she could turn, something slammed into her from the side. Nica spun to the left, seeing stars explode behind her eyes. She tried to right herself, but she'd been flying too fast and started hurtling towards the ground.

Desperate to slow down, she spread her wings as far as she could, hoping the air would slow her down in a parachute effect.

Please gods, please.

Bam! She got hit again. This time from the other side. Raven cawed in pain as something grabbed her wings and pulled. No, not something, but two pairs of somethings. The sounds of Thor's howls and snarls from down below echoed in her ears, and the realization she might never see him sent icy tendrils of fear spiking through her heart.

Caw! Caw! Caw!

The shortened caw of the Crows filled her head, and she wanted to scream her rage. It was them. The Pine Murder. Four of their Crows had been waiting for her to cross the boundary line. And now, because of her foolishness, they had her now.

Disoriented and scared out of her mind, Nica tried to fight. A viciously sharp peck from the biggest Crow, from Jack's monster bird, had blood dripping down her face. She was immobilized as their sharp talons dug into her wings, forcing them wide.

She cried out, to no avail, as they yanked her far away from the Dire Wolf Pack. Far away from *him*. Thor's howls were further away now. He was following her on the ground, but the crows flew higher and higher, zigzagging until her mate couldn't see them any longer.

The Crows knew better than to lead the Demon Wolf over the forest. Her heart broke for what she could have had as they dragged her away from the first taste of happiness she had ever known. Smarter than she gave them credit for, the Crows headed for the highway, where dozens of normals might overlook a bunch of birds, but not a monstrous Wolf.

Cursing her stupidity, she croaked one more time. A Raven's goodbye to the only man she ever loved. Who knew what Jack would do with her now? She didn't even care.

Oh gods, no. Thor, forgive me. I am so sorry. So very sorry.

CHAPTER SEVENTEEN

DIRE WOLF MATES

Thor raced like a madman back to the Pack House. He didn't even bother to grab clothes as he hunted Derrick down.

"Fuck Thor, put on some pants," the Alpha growled, covering his mate's eyes with his big hand.

"They took her," he growled, barely holding on to his fury.

"What?! They came on our lands?" the Alpha asked, standing up swiftly.

"No. She crossed the boundary in the woods. Fuck, it's my fault. She wanted to go for a ride on my bike, then she said something about our bond being too much and I cut it off. I was stupid and hurt, but then she was flying and I, I couldn't fucking warn her! I acted like a possessive asshole and now my mate is in the hands of the motherfucker who hurt her in the first place!"

Thor fell to his knees, holding on to his head as pain the likes of which he never felt filled him. The shadow spirits were lurking closer, then, begging him to let them in, promising to give him the vengeance he desired. He wasn't strong enough to resist them. Thor couldn't hold on to his grip on this world, his sanity, anything—*not without her*. Nica was his everything, and he'd ben to weak and proud to take care of her. He let this happen. By pushing too hard. Not talking enough. This was his fault.

"Thor? Thor! Stop! Stop it right now!"

The Alpha command snapped him out of that dark place he'd fallen into. When he focused, he saw not Derrick, but Lucy, and she was kneeling in front of him. His face stung, and from the position of her arm, he realized the tiny Alpha fem must have slapped him. Hard, too.

"Nica needs you right now. I don't give a crap what the Council said. Those Crows took her against her will. That is kidnapping. Now, are you ready to get your mate back?" she asked.

"Lucy," Derrick started, but the woman flashed a glare at her mate before turning back to Thor.

"You call the Council or the Lowell brothers or whoever the fuck else you want, Derrick, but Nica is my friend, and I am going with her mate to get her back."

"Fuck," the Alpha snarled, then added. "But put on some fucking pants, Thor. I'm not sitting next to you with your dick hanging out, for fuck's sake."

"We are gonna get her back," Lucy reassured him, before standing up.

Thor nodded, too numb to do much else. He ran to his room, grabbed some clothes, and raced outside in jeans and his boots. He could do without the rest. Dark energy swirled around him, and Thor didn't need to look in the mirrors of his Harley to see his eyes were completely black.

He'd been trying so hard to balance his life, half in and half out of the other world, he never fully realized what that did to those around him. Anger and fury, the rage of restless spirits batted against him, but he had no time for that. Thor had one focus now.

Nica.

He revved his engine, growling in satisfaction as the sounds of his Pack mates bikes echoed his. Together, they hauled ass like bats out of hell, or Wolves on the prowl, he supposed. The Pine Murder thought they could hide behind laws, but the Dire Wolves were a law unto themselves. They had been for eons. No shit stain Crow King was going to change that.

Jack Branwen had fucked with the wrong female. Maybe trusted his men to keep him safe. Or maybe because he hid behind petty rules, he thought they applied to everyone. Fucking scumbag. He had no idea what he was fucking with. Thor didn't care about the rules or man or beast.

He was a motherfucking Seer. He dealt with things small minds like Branwen's could not even comprehend. That asshole had riled the wrong monster. Demon Wolf was coming now. And he was angry as fuck.

"Oh my gods, Jack. Do you have any idea what my mate is gonna do to you when he comes for me?" Nica asked.

She laughed aloud at the pitiful man even as blood trickled down from the wound, he'd given her on her head when his Crow hit her in the sky. Dang. Her body ached, and she shivered involuntarily. Nica was bruised and sore, and her left shoulder screamed in pain. Dislocated, she knew. After all, it wasn't the first time.

"Shut up! *I* am your mate," the pathetic man screamed, pulling on his own hair as spittle flew from his mouth.

"No, you're not. You never were. Hell, Jack, you don't even know what it means to be a real mate," she told him, unflinching when he raised his hand and struck her again.

"SHUT UP!" he wailed, but Nica simply wheezed a laugh.

She was naked, cold, tied to the same hated pole he'd shackled her to all those weeks ago. But unlike last time, she didn't feel alone and scared. She knew better now.

The entire Murder was gathered around, except for poor Ella, whose passing had recently occurred. The same males who guarded the King hovered close, though none looked quite sure about what was happening. Denise was still there, eyes rimmed in red, like she'd been crying for days. Nica's gaze landed on her, and the woman doubled over, sobbing.

"Get her out of here. Useless bitch," Jack snarled, stomping over to the fallen woman, and pulling her hair. He shoved her at one of his men, who carried her away.

There were less than two dozen in the Murder now. Small numbers for a group that once boasted a hundred strong. It was his poor leadership that sent them away. Nica knew that, even if Jack still lived under the grand delusion he was a mighty King.

"Where are all your Crows, Jack? Did they leave their weak King?" she taunted.

"Weak? I stole you back, whore. I took you while your mate was stuck on the ground, powerless to stop me! Who is weak now?" he shouted, arms wide in an attempt to appear triumphant.

"Still you, Jack. You're still the weak one. I can't imagine Thor would ever have to kidnap a woman or trick her into signing some piece of paper to get her to be with him."

"Fucking bitch," he snarled, looking around for something, a weapon likely.

"What's the matter? Can't kill me with your hands?"

"You are just begging for it, Domenica. Keep testing me and I will show you exactly how strong I am. Stand her up!" he commanded.

Two Crows came forward, releasing her from the pole and pulling on her manacled hands till she stood before him. She was naked, dirty, and covered in bruised, but Nica did not care. Jack's eyes raked over her body, sending tendrils of fear and revulsion through her, but she needed to be strong.

She wanted him focused on her. Didn't care about his screams or the slaps he delivered. All she knew was she didn't want him to hear what she'd heard until the last minute.

"I'm going to do what I should have done years ago. I'm going to fuck you in front of the Murder. Claim you in the way of our ancestors, get that Wolf's stink off your skin, whore," he said, undoing his belt and sliding the leather thing off with a sharp clack.

He wanted a reaction from her. She knew it, but the only thing she could do was smile. Jack's face turned red as he sneered, till suddenly, he heard it too. The sounds of half a dozen motorcycles closing in on them. Suddenly, the air was filled with electricity, magic. Power crackling and covering the Murder like a hushed cloud.

Then they were there. Finally! She exhaled, slumping forward. Her Pack had come for her. He had come for her. Just like she knew he would. The two Crows who'd been holding her up let go, and she fell unceremoniously to her knees, tears streaming down her face.

"Crows to me!" Jack screamed, but most of the Murder had already run away.

The ones who'd initially remained changed their minds real quick when Thor stepped off his gigantic motorcycle. Oh, her mate looked lethal. He wore his jeans and boots, and nothing else but acres of muscles and tattooed skin. Fury rolled off him in waves, and from Derrick and Lucy and the others who made a circle around them.

"You took one of us, Crow. Stole our Enforcer's mate," the Alpha started.

"Big mistake. Huge," Lucy added.

"Now you will see what losing really means," Derrick growled, stepping back with his hand on Lucy as Thor walked forward.

He seemed to get bigger with every step he took. The air around him shimmered, and a swirling mass of black smoke slithered up and down around his body. Nica did not think anyone else could see it, but she sure as heck did. It was terrifying in its power, just as he was mesmerizing in all his masculine beauty.

"She's mine. She was always mi—" Jack didn't get to finish his thought.

Thor raised his hand, like a certain Sith lord in her favorite movie did. With a flick of his wrist, Jack's neck was broken, and the threat he posed to Nica was finally over.

"Angel," Thor growled, coming to her at once.

He ripped her manacles off with his bare hands, lifting her in his arms. The others nodded and clapped, and tears were shed as Lucy approached her and slid a dress over her head. Thor tugged it down the rest of the way, cradling her on his lap as he revved the engine on his bike.

"I'm sorry this is your first ride," he murmured, eyes still black as he looked down at her. Nica shook her head, wrapping her legs around his waist.

I'm not.

She knew the second he realized she'd spoken inside their telepathic link because his eyes went back to normal, and a wide grin split his face right open. Derrick was barking orders, and she heard something about the Council and the Macconwood Pack being on their way to clean up the mess Jack made.

Hopefully, they would reorganize the Murder, set up new leadership, but Nica was not concerned. That was not her life anymore. Her life was with Thor. With her Pack.

"Fuck, angel. I was so worried," he growled, holding her tight. "I didn't think I would get here in time."

"That's nutty because I had no doubt. You saved me again, just like I knew you would," she told him, laughing through tears and holding on for dear life as he pulled out of the trailer park.

"You got that backwards. You've been saving me every day since I met you."

Just like that, Thor's confession melted Nica into a puddle of goo. She didn't think it was possible to love him any more than she already did, but every day, he proved her wrong.

"I love you," she said suddenly, whispering it right into his ear.

Thor revved the engine louder, speeding through the back roads to get back to the Pack House.

I love you, too, he said right into her mind.

Good. Now, take me home, mate.

EPILOGUE

DIRE WOLF MATES

Thor carried Nica inside, carefully placing her inside the shower stall. Her arm wasn't dislocated this time, just bruised. Her Shifter healing had already kicked in, but he wasn't satisfied until he bathed, dressed, and saw to every single hurt she'd received at the hands of that thankfully now dead motherfucker.

"I'm not glass."

"What?" he asked, laying carefully on his side so as not to jostle her.

"I said, I'm not glass," Nica murmured, her blue eyes flashing up at him from her position in their bed. "I was taken from you today, but I wasn't entirely blameless. I was scared of our connection. I pushed you away. I am so sorry I did that."

"You got nothing to apologize for, angel. I shoulda been more patient. I shoulda explained what I am better. Having the sight makes all those other things way more amped with me. You don't just get a mate, you get all my crazy quirks, too," he confessed sheepishly.

"I love your crazy quirks. I love you."

"I love you, angel. So fucking much," he growled, kissing her head softly.

But Nica was having none of that. His sexy mate crawled over him, spreading her thighs, so she sat with her naked pussy against his belly. He growled, shivering as she leaned down to kiss him fully, her tongue tangling with his.

"Want you, mate. Need you," she whimpered, sliding down so her hot, wet lips stroked his hardened length.

She had him worked up in no time at all. The need to connect with her on this level overpowered his decision to let her rest, and soon she was riding him like the untamed beauty she was. She looked so fucking beautiful. Her curls cascading down her back as she arched, swerving her hips, sucking him deep, so deep, and squeezing him with her tight little channel. Nothing felt better than fucking his mate, and Thor reveled in knowing she was every bit as wild about him.

"Oh gods, Thor, you feel bigger, deeper, it's too much," she gasped, her movements growing jerky.

"You can take it, angel. You were made to take it," he grunted, holding on to her hips and taking over.

She had his full attention now, riding the cusp of her orgasm like this. Fuck, she was so damn sexy. Her earthy vibe was every bit as delicious as her impossibly strong heart. His hands squeezed her hips, her ass, running over her heavy breasts and back. She was perfection personified. She was all light and pure goodness, the perfect foil for all his darkness. She was everything. And the woman undid him every single time, and she didn't even know it. He was the one riding the edge now.

But there was no way he was going without her.

"Come on, angel. Come for me. Right now," he growled, closing his mouth over the claiming bite he'd given her, scraping the skin with his teeth.

"Thor! Thor! THOR!" she screamed his name, her pussy tightening on him like a vise.

One, two, three more pumps, and he was spewing cum straight into her womb. His dick knotted at the base, traveling up the length until even more of his essence filled her. This orgasm was so intense, Thor might have even passed out for a second or two.

"*Ohmygods*, that was so," she whimpered, both of them a tangled, sticky mess on top of the sheets.

"Yeah, it was," he agreed, kissing her head.

He held her until her breathing steadied, then Thor grabbed a pair of sweats and headed out to the living room. He was not exactly sure how this would work for him, but he took the ancient box and removed the murky ink, shaking it until it started to swirl and glitter with magic. He laid out the bamboo pens side by side as one at a time his Pack mates joined him in the living room.

Of course they would. He'd been pulling on their Pack bonds ever since he felt the urgency to do this now. There were whispers and sniffles, one of the babies cooed, another cried. These were the sounds of life, a good life, and Thor was truly grateful to be a part of it. He worked in silence, allowing those good spirits to fill him, chasing away the shadows that had darkened his sight for too long.

Thor knew the second she walked into the room. Her love was like a beacon in the night, and she shone brightly even from the other world where his spirit currently roamed.

"Thor?" she whispered, as the others parted so she could make way for him.

He smiled then, handing her the first bamboo pen.

"What am I supposed to do?" she whispered, panicked.

Let me in, he whispered into her mind. *Let me in, and I will guide you, show you how to draw the story of us onto my back, mate.*

I don't want to hurt you, she replied, using their telepathic bond. Her love pulsed strongly, and he thanked the gods and the Fates for bringing this woman into his life.

You won't. Just follow my lead, angel.

He was already on his knees, but Thor turned so his back faced Nica. She inhaled a shaky breath, but he was with her all the way. From inside that metaphysical plane where their animals waited together until called, Thor talked Nica through every step of this ancient and most sacred process.

Tears fell from her eyes, and he smiled, knowing they were tears of love and joy as he reached in through their bonds, guiding her hands stroke after stroke as she used magicked ink and one bamboo pen after another to create an image of them on his skin. It took hours, but he was surrounded by his Pack, and they lent him strength, which he shared with his sweet, brave mate.

There was nothing she couldn't do. Oh, she was still finding her feet, but lucky sonofabitch that he was, Thor was ecstatic he was going to be there to see it all. Every step of the way. He couldn't wait.

"It's done," Nica said with a shaky breath, and Thor released the tension he was holding in his back.

She took a damp rag someone handed her and gently blotted his skin, meeting his eyes in the big mirror someone else had placed in front of them. Congratulations were whispered, and the Pack came forward offering gentle hugs and shoulder pats as they welcomed them as a couple for the first time.

"Don't you wanna see it?" Nica asked, and he felt her curiosity.

He'd already seen it in his mind, but she was so sweet, so excited. He wanted her to tell it to him. To see it through her eyes.

Bright, brave, beautiful mate. Strong woman. Good girl.

"Describe it to me," Thor said, after everyone backed off and he was putting away the ink and pens.

"Okay," she whispered, getting behind him. Her hands gently touched the periphery of the image and he growled softly, loving the feel of her hands on his body.

"It's our forest, our trail, and there are dozens of leaves falling from the oak tree where we first shifted together," she spoke softly, reverently.

"Demon is sitting on his haunches, big and beautiful, bold as ever. He's looking up at the sky, and I'm in my feathers, flying overhead. Oh my gods, there are two young Ravens with me, Thor," she said, and her voice grew shaky on that part.

Thor turned around and held her in his arms. She was sobbing now, tears of joy he knew cause he felt them too. Thor kissed her head, her temple, her cheeks, her lips, everywhere he could touch, She'd described their future, and it was more than he had ever dreamed.

"Do you want that with me, angel?"

"A family? A future? Yes, oh yes," she replied, kissing him back harder.

"Good. Let's start now."

"Now?"

"Right now, angel."

Thor stood up, taking her with him, and she sighed, wrapping her legs around his waist. It was going to be a long road, but they had each other. They were the best of each other, and they'd been together through the worst already.

"I love you, Thor."

"I love you too, Nica," he told her before sinking into her sweet body.

His mate was everything he ever dreamed of, and more. She was his anchor to this realm. Nica grounded him, their connection the one thing guaranteed to keep him steady and solid for however long they had on this earth together. And he intended for that to be a very long time.

"Stay," he whispered. "Stay with me."

"Always. I choose you, Thor."

"And I choose you right back, mate."

She was the most important thing. She was everything. And he was going to spend every day of his life showing her. Then Thor kissed her again, and everything else, all rational thought, simply fell away.

. . .

The end…

Did you enjoy this Dire Wolf Mates story?
Enjoy the rest of the series today by going to https://www.cdgorri.com/series/dire-wolf-mates
& don't forget to look for Cole's story in Purrfectly F*cked, part of The Maverick Pride tales located here:
https://www.cdgorri.com/series/maverick-pride-tales/!

READING ON A BUDGET?

Hello Readers!

I am so excited to be able to offer you exclusive bundles available only on CDGORRI.COM for readers using my BUY DIRECT option.

Right now, I have several bundles available at a whopping 30% off the listed prices and there are several series bundles to choose from.

Orders will be delivered via BookFunnel email. Just download to your favorite app and READ!

Thank you for buying direct. Have an awesome day!

xoxo,

C.D. Gorri

JOIN THE PACK!

Looking for a Paranormal Romance series that is loads of growly fun?

Welcome to the Macconwood Pack!

These stories are split into two series, the Macconwood Pack Novels Series, and the Macconwood Pack Tales.
Each story features one or more Pack members their journey to their one true and fated mate. They can be read alone, though they are better read in order, as characters may show up in each other's stories.

Pack is family for the Macconwood wolves, and when you read their tales, you become family too. What are you waiting for?

Join the Pack today!

https://www.cdgorri.com/series/the-macconwood-pack-novel-series/

No cliffhangers. Steamy PNR fun.
Go and read your next happily ever after today!

OTHER TITLES BY C.D. GORRI

Contemporary Romance Books:

Cherry On Top Tales

Her Yule His Log

His Carrot Her Muffin

Her Chocolate His Bar

Wild Billionaire Romance

His Wild Obsession

Jersey Bad Boys

Merciful Lies

***

Paranormal Romance Books:

Macconwood Pack Novel Series:

Charley's Christmas Wolf: A Macconwood Pack Novel 1

Cat's Howl: A Macconwood Pack Novel 2

Code Wolf: A Macconwood Pack Novel 3

The Witch and The Werewolf: A Macconwood Pack Novel 4

To Claim a Wolf: A Macconwood Pack Novel 5
Conall's Mate: A Macconwood Pack Novel 6
Her Solstice Wolf: A Macconwood Pack Novel 7
Werewolf Fever: A Macconwood Pack Novel 8

**Also available in 2 ebook boxed sets*
**Look for discreet editor paperback and hardcovers*

<u>Macconwood Pack Tales Series:</u>
Wolf Bride: The Story of Ailis and Eoghan A Macconwood Pack Tale 1
Summer Bite: A Macconwood Pack Tale 2
His Winter Mate: A Macconwood Pack Tale 3
Snow Angel: A Macconwood Pack Tale 4
Charley's Baby Surprise: A Macconwood Pack Tale 5
Home for the Howlidays: A Macconwood Pack Tale 6
A Silver Wedding: A Macconwood Pack Tale 7
Mine Furever: A Macconwood Pack Tale 8
A Furry Little Christmas: A Macconwood Pack Tale 9
The Wolf's Winter Wish: A Macconwood Pack Tale 10
Mated to the Werewolf Next Door: A Macconwood Pack Tale 11
Wolf's Scottish Geek: A Macconwood Pack Tale 12
No Otter Lover: A Macconwood Pack Tale 13

**Also available in boxed sets:*
The Macconwood Pack Tales Volume 1
Shifters Furever: The Macconwood Pack Tales Volume 2
Shifters Furbidden: The Macconwood Pack Tales Volume 3
Shifters Fur Keeps: The Macconwood Pack Tales Volume 4

<u>The Falk Clan Tales:</u>
The Dragon's Valentine: A Falk Clan Novel 1
The Dragon's Christmas Gift: A Falk Clan Novel 2
The Dragon's Heart: A Falk Clan Novel 3

The Dragon's Secret: A Falk Clan Novel 4
The Dragon's Treasure: A Falk Clan Novel 5
The Dragon's Surprise: A Falk Clan Novel 6
The Dragon's Dream: A Falk Clan Novel 7
Dragon Mates: The Falk Clan Series Boxed Set Books 1-4
Dragon Mates 2: The Falk Clan Series Boxed Set Books 5-7

The Bear Claw Tales:
Bearly Breathing: A Bear Claw Tale 1
Bearly There: A Bear Claw Tale 2
Bearly Tamed: A Bear Claw Tale 3
Bearly Mated: A Bear Claw Tale 4
Also available in a boxed set:
The Complete Bear Claw Tales (Books 1-4)

The Barvale Clan Tales:
Polar Opposites: The Barvale Clan Tales 1
Polar Outbreak: The Barvale Clan Tales 2
Polar Compound: A Barvale Clan Tale 3
Polar Curve: A Barvale Clan Tale 4
Also available in a boxed set:
The Barvale Clan Tales (Books 1-4)

Barvale Holiday Tales:
A Bear For Christmas
Hers To Bear
Thank You Beary Much
Bearing Gifts
Bearly Friends
Also available in a boxed set:
The Barvale Holiday Tales (Books 1-3)

Purely Paranormal Romance Books:
Marked by the Devil: Purely Paranormal Romance Books

Mated to the Dragon King: Purely Paranormal Romance Books
Claimed by the Demon: Purely Paranormal Romance Books
Christmas with a Devil, a Dragon King, & a Demon: Purely Paranormal Romance Books
Vampire Lover: Purely Paranormal Romance Books
Grizzly Lover: Purely Paranormal Romance Books
Christmas With Her Chupacabra: Purely Paranormal Romance Books
**Purely Paranormal Romance Books Anthology Volume 1*

<u>The Wardens of Terra:</u>

Bound by Air: The Wardens of Terra Book 1
Star Kissed: A Wardens of Terra Short
Waterlocked: The Wardens of Terra Book 2
Moon Kissed: A Wardens of Terra Short
*Now in a boxed set and in audio!

<u>The Maverick Pride Tales:</u>

Purrfectly Mated
Purrfectly Kissed
Purrfectly Trapped
Purrfectly Caught
Purrfectly Naughty
Purrfectly Bound
Purrfectly Paired
Purrfectly Timed
Purrfectly F*cked

<u>Dire Wolf Mates:</u>

Shake That Sass
Breaking Sass
Pinch of Sass
Kickin' Sass
Love That Sass
Kiss My Sass

<u>Wyvern Protection Unit:</u>
Gift Wrapped Protector: WPU 1
Tempted By Her Protector: WPU 2
Alien Protector: WPU 3
Unexpected Protector: WPU4
Thrilled By Her Protector: WPU5

<u>Jersey Sure Shifters/EveL Worlds:</u>
Chinchilla and the Devil: A FUCN'A Book
Sammi and the Jersey Bull: A FUCN'A Book
Mouse and the Ball: A FUCN'A Book
Chicken and the Paparazzi: A FUCN'A Book
**Jersey Sure Shifters Books 1-3 anthology*

<u>The Guardians of Chaos:</u>
Wolf Shield: Guardians of Chaos Book1
Dragon Shield: Guardians of Chaos Book 2
Stallion Shield: Guardians of Chaos Book 3
Panther Shield: Guardians of Chaos 4
Witch Shield: Guardians of Chaos 5
Vampire Shield: Guardians of Chaos 6
**Guardians of Chaos Volume 1 Books 1-3*
**Guardians of Chaos Volume 2 Books 4-6*

<u>Twice Mated Tales</u>
Doubly Claimed
Doubly Bound
Doubly Tied
**Twice Mated Tales Omnibus*

<u>Hearts of Stone Series</u>
Shifter Mountain: Hearts of Stone 1
Shifter City: Hearts of Stone 2
Shifter Village: Hearts of Stone 3

Shifter Scrooge: Hearts of Stone 4

Moongate Island Tales

Moongate Island Mate

Moongate Island Christmas Claim

Accidentally Undead on Moongate Island

Mated in Hope Falls

Mated By Moonlight

Speed Dating with the Denizens of the Underworld

Ash: Speed Dating with the Denizens of Underworld

Arachne: Speed Dating with the Denizens of Underworld

Asterion: Speed Dating with the Denizens of Underworld

Hungry Fur Love

Hungry Like Her Wolf: Magic and Mayhem Universe

Hungry For Her Bear: Magic and Mayhem Universe

Hungry As Her Python: Magic and Mayhem Universe

Island Stripe Pride

The Tiger King's Christmas Bride

Claiming His Virgin Mate

Tiger Claimed

Tiger Denied

Tiger Rejected

*Tiger Tales Anthology Books 1-3

NYC Shifter Tales

Cuff Linked

Sealed Fate

Virtue Saved

A Howlin' Good Fairytale Retelling

Sweet As Candy

Standalones:
The Enforcer
Blood Song: A Sanguinem Council Book
Spring Fling (co-written with P. Mattern)

Witch Shifter Clan
The Hybrid Assassin

###

Coming Soon:
Fire Wolf: Witch Shifter Clan 1
Snow Fox: Witch Shifter Clan 2
River Dragon: Witch Shifter Clan 3
If The Shoe Fits: A Howlin' Good Fairytale Retelling

###

Young Adult/Urban Fantasy Books

The Grazi Kelly Novel Series
Wolf Moon: A Grazi Kelly Novel Book 1
Hunter Moon: A Grazi Kelly Novel Book 2
Rebel Moon: A Grazi Kelly Novel Book 3
Winter Moon: A Grazi Kelly Novel Book 4
Chasing The Moon: A Grazi Kelly Short 5
Blood Moon: A Grazi Kelly Novel 6
*Get all 6 books NOW AVAILABLE IN A BOXED SET:
The Complete Grazi Kelly Novel Series

The Angela Tanner Files
Casting Magic: The Angela Tanner Files 1

Keeping Magic: The Angela Tanner Files 2
**The Angela Tanner Files Paperback 2 Book omnibus*

G'Witches Magical Mysteries Series
Co-written with P. Mattern
G'Witches
G'Witches 2: The Harpy Harbinger
G'Witches 3: Summoning Secrets

Witches of Westwood Academy
with Gina Kincade
Water Witch
Air Witch
Fire Witch
Earth Witch
Blood Witch
Spirit Witch

**Be sure to check out my BUY DIRECT BUNDLES and get 30% off when you buy available only my website.*

BEWARE... HERE BE DRAGONS!

The Falk Clan Tales began as my stories surrounding four dragon Brothers and how they find their one true mates, but when a long lost brother arrives on the scene, followed by a few more Shifters...what can I say? The more the merrier!

Each Dragon's chest is marked with his rose, the magical link to his heart and his magic. They each have a matching gemstone to go with it.

She's given up on love. But he's just begun.

In The Dragon's Valentine we meet the eldest Falk brother, Callius. He is on a mission to find a Castle and his one true mate, one he can trust with his diamond rose....

His heart is frozen. Can she change his mind about love?

In The Dragon's Christmas Gift our attention shifts to Alexsander, the youngest brother of the four. He has resigned himself to a life alone, until he meets *her*.

Some wounds run deep. Can a Dragon's heart be unbroken?

The Dragon's Heart is the story of Edric Falk who has vowed never to love again, but that changes when he meets his feisty mate, Joselyn Curacao.

She just wants a little fun. He's looking for a lifetime.

We finally meet Nikolai Falk and his sexy Shifter mate in The Dragon's Secret.

She doesn't believe in fairytales, until a Dragon comes knocking on her door.

Meet Castor Falk, the long lost brother of our original four Dragons, and his sassy mate Josette. The Dragon's Treasure is full of adventure and laughs.

Nothing can surprise this six hundred-year-old Dragon, except maybe her.

Devine Graystone meets his match in Sunny Daye, an irrepressible Wolf Shifter with a heart of gold. Read their story in The Dragon's Surprise.

He's a hardcore realist until she dares him to dream.

Nicholas Gravestone doesn't know what to think when he spies Minerva Lykos on the property his Dragon covets. Can this unlikely pair come to a truce? Find out in The Dragon's Dream.

Thanks for reading.

xoxo,

C.D. Gorri

*Dragon Mates & Dragon Mates 2 boxed sets are now available in hardcover, paperback, and ebook.

EXCERPT FROM SEALED FATE

It was snowing, but that wasn't new. Konstantin huddled beneath the broken concrete and waited for the big men to leave. He'd heard the shouting from all the way down the street when he'd gone to pick up his little sister, Alina, from her ballet lessons.

Though his family was poor, Papa and Mama sacrificed much so she could learn to dance. Konstantin was proud of his sister's already budding talent at just six years old. She'd been a surprise to the older couple whose son was already a teenager, but they all doted on her.

Konstantin was almost old enough to work the docks with his father, but Mama insisted he finish school. At nearly seven feet tall and still growing, it was proving difficult to remain unnoticed by the local bratva. That was something his mother feared more than anything.

"Be a good boy, Konstantin. Stay away from the gangs, and criminals," she'd told often him.

After all, it was his dealings with the local crime bosses that had left his Papa with a permanent limp and physical disabilities from the multiple toes and fingers that were missing from his feet and hands.

Shifters could recover from many wounds and injuries, but not amputations. That was something even their enhanced healing abilities could not overcome.

The screams got louder, and Konstantin picked up Alina who'd just started to cry. The sounds were coming from the building where his family rented an apartment from Ivanovich. The head of the local bratva had many slums on the city where he took advantage of the many poor Shifter families.

His inner beast scratched and roared, but he was no match for the many members of the bratva waiting for their boss outside. Instead of facing them and risking Alina's life, he covered her mouth with his hands and hid them both in the cellar of the neighboring building.

The old man was yelling about missing rents and late payments. He was going to use Konstantin's father as an example, or worse, take it out on his mother. That was something, he could not allow.

"Alina, will you stay here? Hidden for me, yes?" he asked his baby sister.

Blue eyes clear as the sky looked up at him, swimming with tears. She nodded her head, already older than her six years and he nodded, cursing roughly under his breath. He prayed he was not too late.

By the time he reached the apartment the men were gone, and his mother was wailing over the prone body of his father. Papa was gone. Killed by the bastards who ruled over all of them.

"Konstantin!" she cried, standing up and going to him, still covered in her mate's blood. "You must run. Go to your Uncle. Je will put you on a ship---"

"What about you? Alina?"

"Where is she?"

"In the basement next door. Let me get her," he said, frantic with worry.

"Yes, get her. I will pack."

When he once again returned to the apartment, he found the neighbors gathered. They shook their heads and turned their backs on him and his family, shunning them even as his father's body grew cold on their kitchen floor. Anger surged, but his mother was there, stopping it before he could blow like a steam engine.

"Come. Now. There is no time," she said, handing him a suitcase and taking the whimpering child from his arms.

They ran through the street, ducking in alleys, and moving faster then the humans around them. Tiger Shifters had night vision and traversing through the ice slicked alleys was quick work for them. They reached his Uncle's house in no time at all.

"You've come," Uncle Petyr said, grabbing his sister in a quick hug.

The man took his niece and handed her off to his wife who cuddled the child close. All the adults were trying not to cry, but Konstantin could feel their grief. Shared it with them.

"Can you get him out of here?" Mama begged.

"Only the boy. I am sorry," Uncle Petyr said.

"It is good. he will make a good life and we will come later," she said, nodding. "Okay Konstantin? Yes?"

"I want to stay with you," he said, a boy's dream.

"No, I won't let them have you too," Mama cred, holding him tight to her breast. "I love you son, but I need you to live. Here, there is only death waiting for you. Now go. Be strong. Be the man I know you can be. We will be together one day."

"We go now," Uncle Petyr said, grabbing the suitcase and taking Konstantin's hand.

"Mama? Mama!"

"Come now, boy. Be quiet or you will bring those monsters here."

That fact shut him up faster than if his Uncle had slapped him. Konstantin looked one last time at his mother and sister, who'd returned to her side. He waved and nodded, biting back his own tears, then he left his Uncle's apartment. And Russia.

And he never looked back.

Grab the rest of the story here: https://www.cdgorri.com/books/sealed-fate

ABOUT THE AUTHOR

C.D. Gorri is a USA Today Bestselling author of steamy paranormal romance and urban fantasy. She is the creator of the Grazi Kelly Universe.

Join her mailing list here: https://www.cdgorri.com/newsletter

An avid reader with a profound love for books and literature, when she is not writing or taking care of her family, she can usually be found with a book or tablet in hand. C.D. lives in her home state of New Jersey where many of her characters or stories are based. Her tales are fast paced yet detailed with satisfying conclusions.

If you enjoy powerful heroines and loyal heroes who face relatable problems in supernatural settings, journey into the Grazi Kelly Universe today. You will find sassy, curvy heroines and sexy, love-driven heroes who find their HEAs between the pages. Werewolves, Bears, Dragons, Tigers, Witches, Romani, Lynxes, Foxes, Thunderbirds, Vampires, and many more Shifters and supernatural creatures dwell within her worlds. The most important thing is every mate in this universe is fated, loyal, and true lovers always get their happily ever afters.

Want to know how it all began? Enter the Grazi Kelly Universe with Wolf Moon: A Grazi Kelly Novel or pick up Charley's Christmas Wolf and dive into the Macconwood Pack Novel Series today.

For a complete list of C.D. Gorri's books visit her website here:

https://www.cdgorri.com/complete-book-list/

Thank you and happy reading!

del mare alla stella,
C.D. Gorri

Follow C.D. Gorri here:
http://www.cdgorri.com
https://www.facebook.com/Cdgorribooks
https://www.bookbub.com/authors/c-d-gorri
https://twitter.com/cgor22
https://instagram.com/cdgorri/
https://www.goodreads.com/cdgorri
https://www.tiktok.com/@cdgorriauthor

www.ingramcontent.com/pod-product-compliance
Lightning Source LLC
Chambersburg PA
CBHW020244030826
48979CB00030B/2577/J

* 9 7 8 1 9 6 0 2 9 4 3 4 0 *